For darling Anita.

I have shared my joys with all of you who read my books; and there are very many of you now. I have spoken of my sister, Anita, through previous dedications, and on many occasions when I have travelled the country to meet all of you. Now sadly I share a great sorrow with you. I have to tell you that our Anita is gone from us, at the tender age of thirty-six years.

Those of you who know me, will know how precious my family is to me. Anita was the baby of ten brothers and sisters. In my grief, something happened that tested my faith. Something stranger happened to strengthen it.

On the afternoon when the priest received Anita into God's house, where she remained until the morning, we drove home through a black and rainy day, the sky was dark and ominous when suddenly it split open and a shaft of sunlight pierced the blackness. As we watched, the light spread to the earth, dazzling us.

When I told my sister, Winifred, she said it was a stairway taking Anita to Heaven.

I hope that was true, because only then can some sense be made of such a tragic waste. The post-mortem revealed that there was no medical reason why our Anita died. Maybe there really is another reason we mortals don't understand?

Anita was good and kind and, like everyone who was privileged to know her, I will miss and love her to the day I die.

This book is dedicated to her, because it is the only title that reflects what she was to us. Goodbye, little sister. God keep you safe until we meet again.

Contents

Part One

1948

WHEN WE LIE

Chapter One

Rosie might have been forgiven for thinking this was the worst day of her life. Until she remembered that today was a joy compared with what was to come. The worst was still a month away. After that, all of her chances for happiness would be gone forever.

'Rosie?' The whisper of her name on his lips only made her realise what she had lost.

She didn't answer. Nor did she look at him. In her tortured mind she believed that if she ignored him it might be easier to pretend he wasn't there.

'Rosie!' This time there was a note of urgency in his voice, a rush of anger.

In the ill-lit street, the sound of their footsteps tapping against the pavement made a peculiar melody. Through tearful eyes, she stared at the ground beneath their feet; the hard shiny cobblestones stretched before them like hundreds of newly baked loaves brushed with milk. It had been a glorious June day, and now the evening was sultry, closing about them like the protective arms of a lover.

'What the hell's wrong with you?' His voice was closer now, his head bent to hers. 'You've been like this all day. If there's something on your mind, you'd best speak up now, because I'm sick and tired of this cat and mouse game.' Pressing his hand to her arm, he brought her to a halt. Swinging her round to face him, he demanded angrily, 'I mean it, Rosie. You'd best speak up, because I've had enough of your bloody moods.'

She regarded him with distaste. 'Want to know *all* my thoughts, do you?'

Realising he'd said the wrong thing, he cunningly changed tack. ''Course I don't, but you're so quiet tonight, sweetheart.' His voice was entreating. He didn't want to spoil his chances. 'Is it something I've done?' he asked. 'Something I've said?' Whenever he was close to her, the urge to make love was strong. It was strong now.

'No, it's not your fault,' she assured him. If anything, the fault was hers. He was just a man, and in all truth he had done nothing that she could reproach him for. Yet, in that moment when he tenderly propelled her backwards, leaning with her against the vicarage wall and whispering softly to her, she knew she could never love him in the way she had loved before.

Oh, he was handsome enough. Even though he was small in build, and barely taller than Rosie herself, there was something uniquely attractive about him. He possessed the most beautiful, sinister eyes: one as blue as cornflowers, the other as green as the ocean. His dark brown hair was thick and long to his ears, and he walked with a proud bearing. He could be incredibly charming, able to make a woman feel special and seduce her without her even realising it.

That was how it had begun with Rosie. She'd been swept off her feet, and only now did she realise the enormity of what she had done.

'I want you.'

'Not here, Doug.' It wasn't what she wanted to say. What she really wanted to say was: 'Don't lay a finger on me. Don't *ever* again lay a finger on me.' But she was wise enough to know that rejecting him now would not solve anything. It was too late for that.

'Why not here?' he argued. When she looked up at him like that, she stirred his every sense. In the lamplight, her brown eyes were softly beautiful. 'We won't be seen, I promise you,' he pleaded. 'There's not a soul about.'

Torn by guilt and still deeply disturbed by the letter which had arrived in the morning post, she pushed him off. 'No, Doug!'

'You didn't say that before.'

'No, I didn't, did I?' She ruefully smiled at the memory, hating herself, hating him. That was when it had all started to go wrong.

Mistaking her smile for an expression of affection, he leaned down to stroke her bare leg. 'You're so lovely,' he whispered. He felt confident enough to take her now. Sliding his hand beneath her skirt, he pushed upwards with probing fingers, quickly sliding them between the softer crevice of her thighs. 'You're ready for me now, aren't you?' he murmured breathlessly. He was so excited he could hardly wait. With his other hand he fumbled at his trouser buttons.

With her legs now pushed open, and his moist tongue lightly following the curve of her ear, Rosie couldn't deny that she *was* ready for him. When all was said and done, she was still a woman, warm-blooded, with needs much like his. Turning on him now would be tantamount to destroying herself, and what would that solve? Her mood became defiant. Why shouldn't he make love to her? As she recalled, it had been good before, so why shouldn't it be good now?

She felt herself responding. It was all the encouragement he needed. 'Open up, sweetheart,' he whispered harshly, at the same time pushing up through her knicker leg. It was when she felt him against her inner thigh that she knew she couldn't give herself to him. Not tonight. Not *any* night, if she had her way.

'Take me home,' she snapped. 'Have you no shame, Doug Selby? Are we a pair of curs, to mate in the street? Are we, eh?' A great tide of raging energy coursed through her as she thrust him off. When he stumbled backwards, with his penis jutting out like the sign over the pawn-shop window, a sense of the ridiculous made her want to laugh out loud.

'Christ Almighty! What are you trying to do to me?' he groaned, rubbing one hand over his face and making low guttural sounds as though in the throes of deepest agony. 'You want it as much as me, I know you do,' he pleaded. Reaching out, he touched her on the neck.

The feel of his damp trembling hand had a startling effect on her.

'LEAVE ME ALONE!'

Shocked and limp now, he began yanking his trousers together, anger in his voice. 'What the hell's the matter *now*?'

'I don't want you treating me like a whore, that's all,' she snapped. 'I asked you to take me home, and if you don't want to that's all right by me. I can take myself!' Quickly straightening her skirt, she brushed past him, half running to put as much distance between them as she could. She could hear him yelling, cursing her at the top of his voice. 'To hell with *you* an' all, Doug Selby,' she called back. Tears ran down her face. Tears of shame, and guilt, and frustration. She was trapped, and there was no way out.

Rosie was halfway down the street when he came chasing after her. 'Hey! It isn't me who's at fault here. It's *you*. You've been down in the dumps all day, and now, for no reason at all that I can see, you fly off the handle. What am I supposed to do, eh? Tell me that.'

By the time he'd caught up with her, she had taken off her high-heeled shoes and was sitting on the horse trough outside the railway station. The last train had long gone and the whole place was enveloped in an eerie silence.

When she saw him limping up the road, gasping and wheezing, she couldn't help but laugh. 'Look at you,' she chuckled, 'you're worse than your old grandad.' She felt in a better mood after the exhilarating run. 'I should have thought you'd have been fitter . . . what with carting them coal-bags on your shoulders every day.'

Slumping down beside her, he took time to recover his breath. 'Carting coal-bags might broaden your shoulders,' he pointed out at last, 'but it don't prepare you for a two-mile run.' Dropping forward, he buried his face in his hands. It was a moment before he spoke again, and when he did, it was to say in a harsh voice, 'I want to know what's going on? The truth, mind. Don't take me for a bloody fool.'

'Leave it, Doug. There's nothing to be gained by talking about it.' Lately her life seemed to be fraught with problems.

The look on her face told him enough. 'It's *him*, ain't it?' he demanded sharply. 'I might have known.'

Rosie nodded her head. 'We had an almighty row.'

'Hmph!' He slid his arm round her shoulders. 'About me, was it?'

'Sort of.' She felt him pulling her towards him, and though she desperately needed comfort, couldn't bring herself to lay her head on his shoulders.

Fortunately, he didn't sense her resistance to him. '"Sort of" . . . What does that mean?'

'He found my diary. He knows, Doug.'

'So what?' He gawped at her as though she had said something astonishing. 'I'm glad he knows. He would have found out sooner or later. Anyway, what does it matter?'

Shrugging his arm away, she stood up. 'It may not matter to you, Doug Selby. But it matters to *me*.'

'Don't be silly.' Reaching up, he pleaded, 'Come on, sit here. You and me were made for each other, gal. There was a time when I might have dumped you and chased something else in skirts, but, well, you've kind of got to me. I don't want any other woman, not now . . . *especially* not now.'

'Happen you'd be better off chasing "something else in skirts",' she retorted. But inside, she was more afraid than ever. Things were bad enough now, without her giving him that sort of encouragement.

'Aw, you know I wouldn't do that.' Not right now he wouldn't anyway. Maybe later, when he'd got her out of his system and boredom began to creep in. 'Come on, sweetheart. Sit aside o' me. I promise I won't try it on. We'll just have a cuddle.' He grinned stupidly. 'And happen a little feel, eh?'

She heard the childish sulkiness in his voice and despised him all the more. Ignoring his crude suggestion, she told him, 'I've got to go and face him.'

'What do you mean?'

She hung her head, all manner of emotions coursing through her. 'It was awful, Doug. Dad went mad. I tried to calm him down, but he wouldn't listen, so I just ran out.'

'He had no right looking through your diary! Who the hell does he think he is?'

'He says he knew there was something going on, and he meant to get to the bottom of it.'

'So he read your diary? Christ! He's got a bloody cheek!'

'Well, it's done now, and there are things to be mended between us.'

'Did you put it *all* in your diary . . . *everything*?'

'Everything, yes.' In the half-light her face reddened at the thought of what her father had read.

'Bloody hell! What did you do that for?' He recalled the night they had made love for the first time, and it shook him to think she had written all *that* down.

'Because that's what diaries are for.' Sometimes, like now,

she wondered what she had ever seen in Doug Selby.

'Aw, to hell with him!' He suddenly grinned. Come to think of it, he was proud of himself for that night. Happen her old man might see what kind of a man Doug Selby was after all! 'He's never liked me, you know that, don't you?' He was shouting now, growing angry. 'I say to hell with the old sod. Serves him right if he's suffering. It'll teach him not to stick his nose where it's not wanted.'

Suppressing the urge to punch him hard in the face, Rosie straightened her shoulders and turned from him. 'You can't blame him, Doug, it must have come as a shock. It's my own fault. I should have told him earlier.' In her heart she realised she should have found the courage to tell them *both* earlier, because there was still another to be told, and his heart would be broken just as hers was. 'He'll be waiting for me. I'd better go.'

'Do you want me with you?' He held his breath, waiting for her answer and hoping she would say no. There were some things that made him see red, and others that made him a coward.

'No.' She sighed noisily. 'It's best if I face this on my own.'

'Okay.' He got to his feet and draped an arm round her shoulders. When she plucked it off, he stiffened. 'Look! I'll come with you if you want me to,' he offered churlishly.

'I said no. I can manage on my own.'

'Fair enough.' Gripping her by the shoulders, he inclined his head to kiss her. When she resisted, he kissed her anyway. 'Right then. Being as you've no need of my services, I'll take myself off home.'

'You do that.'

'Don't take no nonsense from that old bugger,' he warned in a superior voice. She didn't comment, so he flicked her chin with the tip of his finger. 'We wouldn't have been seen, you know . . . back there.' His loins were still throbbing. He wanted her badly. But he consoled himself with the thought that soon he would have her any time he felt like it. 'Like I said . . . tell him to go to hell,' he suggested grandly.

'*You* go to hell!'

'You don't mean that?'

'Oh . . . go home, Doug!'

A sudden thought made him wary. 'I'd best not call round for you tomorrow, eh?'

'You're a bloody coward, Doug Selby.'

'Sensible, that's all,' he corrected. 'It would only make things worse if I turned up on the doorstep. Whether we like it or not, your dad's never taken to me.'

'I wonder why?' She couldn't keep the sarcasm from her voice.

He shrugged his shoulders. 'It don't bother me.'

'Goodnight, Doug.' She swung away, leaving him standing there.

'I'll see you at the market tomorrow, eh? Midday?' She was already at the bottom of the street. He called a little louder, 'Don't let the bugger get the better of you, sweetheart. If you need me, you know where I live.'

As he strode away in the opposite direction, he mumbled to himself, 'You'll not get me within a mile of her old man . . . not if I can help it. What! If he laid hands on me, the bugger would string me up and no messing!'

The thought quickened his feet. First he was walking, then he was stepping it out, then his boots echoed frantically against the cobbles as he took to his heels and ran.

As she approached the terraced house on Pendle Street, Rosie saw that the downstairs lights were still on. Normally, her father would have retired to his bed long before this hour. 'So you're waiting for me, are you?' she said into the warm night air. 'Mean to have it out, eh?' The thought of a violent confrontation with her father made her slow her footsteps. For one awkward minute, she wasn't certain whether to take Doug up on his offer . . . 'If you need me, you know where I live.'

Suddenly she found herself chuckling. 'A fat lot of good Doug would be,' she muttered. 'Like as not, he'd be halfway down the street even before Dad could open his mouth.' It had taken her some time, but at long last Rosie was seeing a different side to Doug. In the long run, though, she believed it couldn't really change anything.

She didn't need to use her key. The front door had been left on the latch. Inside the dimly lit passage, she took off her long white cardigan and hung it over the hook behind the door. Glancing in the hallway mirror, she patted her long brown hair, pushing it back with her hands so that it didn't tumble over her shoulders in that wanton way Doug liked. She fastened the top button of her pretty blue blouse, and straightened her skirt, blushing with colour as she remembered Doug's rough handling of her earlier.

'Who's that?' She was visibly startled as the man's harsh voice reached her from the back parlour. 'Is that you, Rosie?'

'Yes.' She was surprised at the calmness of her own voice, especially when her stomach was churning.

'Get in here!'

One last look in the mirror. 'Stand up to him, gal,' she told herself. 'You're twenty years old . . . a grown woman. Don't let him bully you.' Determination welled up in her as she went down the hallway towards the back parlour.

'Where the hell are you? I said: GET IN HERE!'

His raised voice echoed down the passageway. All her courage vanished, and the nearer to the parlour she got, the more she wished she'd taken Doug up on his offer; however reluctantly it was given. A little moral support was better than none at all, she reasoned now.

Her father made a formidable sight indeed. A retired miner, he was a big man with a mass of iron-grey hair, and pale deep-set eyes that seemed to see right through a body. 'Where've you been 'til this time?' he demanded as she appeared at the door.

He was seated in the high-backed rocking chair by the range. He didn't look round at her, nor did he make any effort to rise from the chair. Instead, he kept it rocking back and forth, back and forth, his deep-set eyes directed towards the empty fire-grate, and his long thick fingers drumming, playing out a feverish rhythm on the curved wooden arms.

'I thought it best to stay away for a while,' Rosie explained quietly, 'I thought it might give us both time to cool down.' She stepped tentatively into the room.

'Stay where you are. I don't want you any nearer.' His eyes remained focused on the empty fire-grate, and the chair continued to rock.

'What do you mean, Dad? You don't want me in the parlour?'

'I don't want you in the *house*.' The sound of the rockers against the carpet made a strange swishing noise.

'I came home to talk with you. To explain.'

'There's nothing to explain. I've sired a bad 'un, that's all.'

'I'm not a bad 'un, Dad!'

'If your mother was alive, she wouldn't walk down the street for the shame of it.'

'I'm to be wed. There will be no shame.'

'One bad 'un wed to another.'

'You shouldn't have read my diary. *That* was shameful.'

'I read the letter too.'

Rosie was furious. 'You had no right!' she said angrily, clenching her fists and wishing she was a man. 'How dare you read my private things?'

'You didn't even have the courage to tell *him*,' he accused. The rockers went faster, and the eyes never flinched. 'I always regretted never having a son, but I never thought I'd raise a bloody coward.'

It was a moment before Rosie answered. Then: 'All right, I won't deny I've been a coward, but I had my reasons.'

'Aye. *Two*! Doug Selby and his bastard.'

'The child won't be a bastard. That's why I'm getting wed.'

'I hope the other one kills him. Then you won't be getting wed, and everybody'll know you for what you are.'

'If, as you say, you've read the letter, you'll know Adam is not a murderous man. He's home on leave tomorrow. I'll tell him then.'

'Get out!'

'What?'

'I want nothing to do with you. I don't want you ever to show your face round these parts again. You'll find your things all packed . . . in the front room.'

'You're not thinking straight, Dad. Let's both get a good night's sleep, and talk about it all in the morning. I love you. I can't just leave you.'

'I don't want your kind under my roof. I'll have no part of you from now on. Get out, I said. NOW!' The rockers were suddenly still. He turned. The deep-set eyes regarded her as though she was so much dirt under his shoe.

'Dad . . .' Her ears were ringing from his harsh words, yet she knew him well enough to realise that he meant every word.

He wasn't listening. The rockers were shifting back and forth, the swishing sound all that could be heard. His eyes were turned towards the empty grate, and his big shoulders were set like stone. The time for talking was long over.

'I'll ask Peggy if I can stay there for the time being,' she offered. He didn't move a muscle. 'All right, Dad,' she murmured, 'if this is what you really want.' No reply. She was devastated.

Going into the front parlour, she collected the portmanteau.

It wasn't heavy. Four years ago her parents had been involved in a train accident. Her mother was killed, and her father partially crippled, enough to keep him out of full-time work. Her own job at the post office kept the wolf from the door, but it was never enough to buy fancy clothes and the like. Such things didn't bother her. Rosie was a simple soul, with simple needs.

The front parlour had always been reserved for special visitors. Rosie smiled at the irony of her father placing her portmanteau in here. On the oak sideboard stood a photograph of her mother; a small woman much like Rosie herself, with brown hair and browner eyes. 'Well, Mam,' she told the smiling face, 'you'll be sorry it's come to this. We could have talked it through, but he won't listen. You know what he can be like. Still, happen when he's got over the shock, he'll see reason. But *I'm* not making the first move!' She shook her head and set her mouth in a grim line. 'It's him that's thrown me out, so it's up to him to mend the breach.'

She stood there a while, tempted to take the photograph with her. But she knew her father derived great comfort from it, and so departed without it.

As she quietly opened the front door, her father's voice boomed out, 'LEAVE THE KEY!' For the sake of her mam's memory, she almost returned to reason once more with him. But she knew him too well. In the mood he was in, it was best to do as he asked.

Taking her long white cardigan from a hook on the other door, she felt in the pocket. Withdrawing the front door key, she laid it on the hallway table, then slid the cardigan over her shoulders. Taking up the portmanteau once more, she went out of the house.

The evening air had grown chilly. She shivered. It was a good walk to her friend Peggy's house. But there would be a welcome there, she knew.

Chapter Two

'Oh, Rosie! Why didn't you tell me?' At twenty-two, Peggy Lewis was almost two years older than Rosie, yet she seemed younger somehow. A scrap of a woman, with fair cropped hair, big round blue eyes and a nose that was so large it overshadowed her mouth, she looked to be in a constant state of astonishment. She was neither intelligent nor dim, beautiful nor ugly, and if you dressed her in the finest silk that money could buy, she would still look like a bundle of straw tied up in the middle. But her young heart was big and generous, and filled with love for Rosie.

'I didn't tell you because I was ashamed.'

'Ashamed?' Peggy tutted. 'And what are best friends supposed to be for?' she wanted to know. 'Since when have we ever kept secrets from each other?'

'It wasn't just that,' Rosie assured her. 'This was something I had to sort out for myself. Even if I *had* told you, there was nothing you could have done . . . except worry yourself sick.' She smiled fondly. 'And you *would* have worried yourself sick, wouldn't you? Admit it?'

Peggy twisted her mouth to one side, nervously biting her top lip, just as she always did when she was lost for words. 'I suppose so,' she reluctantly confessed.

'There you are then. So I'm glad I didn't tell you. I'm sorry I'm telling you now.'

'What? You don't trust me? You think I'll spread it all over Blackburn?'

'Don't be silly. If I thought *that*, I wouldn't have come here tonight. It's a secret between you and me, and my father, of course . . . and Doug. But they won't tell. Dad's eaten with shame, and Doug's promised me he won't let on to *anybody*. He knows I'll hate him if he tells.' She half smiled. 'No doubt he'd like to brag to the world, but I believe he'll keep his promise to me.'

Peggy shrugged her shoulders. Not for the first time, she was tempted to challenge Rosie's trust in that young man but, for the sake of friendship, she decided against it. 'You really ought to try and get some sleep,' she remarked instead.

'I can't.' Rosie glanced at the clock over the mantelpiece. 'Every time I close my eyes, I think about everything that's happened. My Dad . . . Doug . . . Adam . . . all the plans that have been spoiled. And not only *my* plans, Peggy. Dad's right. What I've done is awful, and I deserve to be thrown out.'

'Hmph! Anybody'd think you had caused the problem all by yourself. What about that rascal, Doug, eh? You've already agreed to wed him, more's the pity, so I reckon that's punishment enough.' Rolling her huge eyes upwards, she declared grimly, 'Your dad was wrong to do what he did. Cor! If anybody looked through *my* diary, I'd be hopping mad!'

Rosie was puzzled. 'I didn't know *you* kept a diary?'

'I don't. All I'm saying is, *if* I did.'

Rosie had to smile, and soon the two of them were giggling. 'You're a twerp, Peggy Lewis,' Rosie told her. 'But I don't know what I'd do without you.'

'Throw yourself in the canal, like as not.' Placing her thin hands on the parlour table, she stood up. 'It's four o'clock of a morning, and the pair of us will be fit for nothing come daylight, but now that you've woken me . . . tiptoeing down every creaky stair you could find . . . we might as well raid the pantry.'

'Your mam was angry. I shouldn't have put myself on you like that. After all, she's a widow, and there's four other children besides you in this little house. It was a bloody cheek of me to turn up like that . . . suitcase and all.'

'Take no notice. Our mam's bark is worse than her bite.' She chuckled. 'You'll feel better when I tell you she followed me upstairs to ask how much we should charge you to stop here.'

Rosie laughed. 'And what did *you* say?'

'I told her you'd pay two shilling a week, and teach her to embroider. She's always wanted to embroider . . . drives me mad, she does.'

Rosie was astounded. 'You *must* be mad! *I* can't embroider.'

'There you are then. You can teach each other.' Chuckling, she asked, 'Jam butties and cocoa . . . how does that sound?'

Shaking her head in disbelief, Rosie thought it best to ignore Peggy's little games. 'Sounds great, but won't your mam be angry if we raid the pantry?'

'Not if we don't tell her. I'll stir the jampot afterwards, so it looks full, and you'd have to be Sherlock Holmes to miss a slice off half a loaf. As for the cocoa, I bought it myself, so there'll be nowt said.' As she went into the scullery, she reminded Rosie, 'Anyway, the war's been over nearly four years. There ain't rationing like there used to be, thank God.'

Rosie could hear her bustling about in the scullery. She envied Peggy her peace of mind. 'Will you come with me tomorrow?' she called.

Peggy returned with a tray of jam butties and two steaming mugs of cocoa. 'No, I bloody well won't!' she retorted. 'There's things to be said between you and Adam that ain't for nobody else's ears.' Placing one mug and a small plate before Rosie, she added softly, 'You're made of good stuff, and you're not to worry. It'll be all right, you'll see.'

Unable to stomach the jam butty, Rosie sipped at the warming cocoa. 'I didn't mean for you to come with me into the station,' she explained. 'I thought you might sit with me in the tea rooms, just until the train arrives. Then you could go.'

'That's very big of you,' Peggy teased.

'You'll come then?'

''Course I will. Now, drink your cocoa and we'll try and get a couple of hours' sleep.'

There was little to be said for the next few minutes. Peggy was too busy polishing off the jam butties, and Rosie too steeped in thoughts of the coming ordeal.

At four-thirty, the two pals traipsed upstairs and into their respective beds. Peggy soon fell asleep, but Rosie lay awake for what seemed an age. In the soft lamplight, she read the crumpled letter time and again:

> My darling Rosie,
>
> I know it's been some time since I wrote, but, like I told you in my last letter, I had some growing up to do before settling down. I know you understand I had to get things straight in my mind, and how I needed to be out of the Army, before asking you to wed me.
>
> I'm sorry. I haven't been fair to you, and all these months of waiting to hear from me must have been sheer hell. But you knew I would write, and you knew I would never stop loving you. I've always promised we'd be wed one day. Well, sweetheart, the day's arrived! I would have written earlier, but I wanted to surprise you.
>
> I'm on my way home, and I can't wait to hold you in my arms. I've carried your picture next to my heart everywhere I've been. Now I mean to carry you over the

threshold of our home, as my wife . . . Mr and Mrs Adam Roach! Sounds great, don't it?

I've managed to put some money by, more than enough for a down payment on one of them little houses in Rosamund Street. See! I didn't forget where you said you wanted to live when we were man and wife. There won't be too much left over for a grand wedding, but we can wait a bit if you like.

Doug's dad always said he'd give me a job when I'm demobbed, and carting coal is respectable enough, I reckon, though I don't intend to do that forever because I've got big plans for you and me.

I plan to arrive at Blackburn railway station at nine forty-five on June 14th. I'll have my eyes peeled for you, sweetheart.

See you then.

All my love,

Adam xxx

'I'm ashamed to meet you.' Rosie pressed the crumpled letter to her breast. 'I don't even know if I can,' she murmured. But she could. She *must*! She owed him that much at least.

Sickened to the heart, she lay back against the pillow and closed her eyes. All she could see was the letter, every word imprinted on her mind. Her heart felt like a lead weight inside her. She loved him still, and yet she had betrayed him with his best mate. 'He's too good for the likes of you!' she told herself, bitter tears dampening the pillow. After a while, she deliberately closed her mind to it all and drifted into a restless slumber.

In her dreams she was in the eye of a raging storm, floating on a raft that was being carried swiftly out to sea. Suddenly a ship appeared with two men aboard; one was Doug, the other a handsome soldier. Both were reaching down to lift her up, and though she desperately strived to grasp the soldier's hand, it was Doug who caught hold of her. At that moment, the boat overturned and they were all flung into the waves.

The gales blew them every which way, and the waves drove them down. The nightmare worsened. And even when she awoke, it was still so real she found herself thrashing at the air with outstretched arms.

Unable to sleep now, she got out of bed and sat by the window to watch the dawn rise in a beautiful sky. 'In a little while you'll be seeing him,' she murmured. 'And God help you then.'

'Come on, Rosie!' Peggy stood by the door, hands on hips, a look of consternation on her thin face. 'Look at the time. If we don't get a move on, you'll miss the train. And listen!' She cocked an ear towards the stairway. The sounds emanating from above told their own story. 'Our mam's up and about. Any minute now, she'll be coming down them stairs with a line o' kids behind her. Then I shan't get out for *hours*. What with one thing and another, she'll keep me at it all morning.'

It was the incentive Rosie needed. 'Just coming,' she said, taking one last look in the mirror and patting her thick brown hair. In spite of everything, she so much wanted to look good for Adam.

'Bloody Nora!' Peggy hopped from one foot to the other. 'Will you get a move on?' Her anxious eyes followed Rosie's every move, and as always she was struck by her friend's simple beauty. Rosie was wearing her best frock, a pretty cream material overprinted with shadowy pink roses. Its swirling hem was a fashionable calf-length and the tiny waist was drawn in by a plain grey belt. She was wearing black slim-heeled shoes, and carrying an envelope bag of the same colour.

'I'm so nervous,' she told Peggy as they went out of the house. 'God only knows how I'm going to tell him.'

'You'll just have to take a deep breath and out with it,' Peggy declared. 'As far as I can see, there ain't no other way.' She took a sideways glance at her friend. 'You bugger! You didn't sleep after we went back to bed, did you, eh?' She had seen how pale Rosie was, and how the shadows had deepened round her lovely brown eyes.

'I couldn't,' Rosie admitted, 'I kept reading his letter.' It was in her bag now. She must have read it a dozen times, and each time she felt worse.

The tram was just drawing away as they reached the bottom of Viaduct Street. 'RUN!' Peggy yelled, and the two of them took to their heels, shouting and calling to the conductor to wait for them.

'Another minute and you'd 'ave missed it.' The red-faced fellow rolled their tickets out of his machine and gave the change to Rosie. 'Off to the market, are you?'

Before she could get her breath, Peggy chirped in, 'You're not supposed to leave 'til half-past eight, and it's still half a minute to go.' She pointed at her big round watch.

'You're not telling me that thing's right, are you? Where did you get it . . . threepence off the market?' He grinned and turned away.

'Cheeky sod! This cost me half a week's wages.'

'Well now that's a real shame, because it's running slow. If I were you I'd ask for my money back.' Before she could retaliate he'd hurried away, whistling at the top of his voice.

The market was already busy, with people jostling each other and pushing forward for the early bargains. But the tea rooms at the station end were almost empty. Rosie was glad of that. 'I've been all kinds of a fool,' she told Peggy as they collected a mug of tea and went to the table nearest the window. 'I could have been walking down the aisle with Adam, setting up home on Rosamund Street, and having his babies. Now look at me . . . three months gone and his best friend the father. Happen my dad's right. I *am* a slut.'

'No you're not. You were lonely, and when Doug Selby made a play for you, you fell for it, just like any other girl would have done. In fact, there's plenty who *have*.'

'Which only makes it worse. I should have known better. After all, he's always had a reputation.'

'He's too bloody handsome, that's what. And he can talk his way into anything.'

'Oh, Peggy, I'm so ashamed. You did warn me about him. Why in God's name didn't I listen to you?'

'Because you weren't thinking straight, and who can blame you? Adam hadn't written in a long time, and as far as you were to know, you might never have heard from him again. If you ask me, *he's* as much to blame.' She was suddenly pensive. 'Being lonely is a terrible thing.'

'Are *you* lonely, Peggy?' In that moment Rosie saw a side to her friend that she had never seen before.

'Sometimes,' Peggy admitted. 'It would be nice to have a fella, but they take one look at me and run a bleedin' mile!'

'Fella's can often cause more trouble than they're worth.' And I should know, Rosie thought bitterly.

'Aye, well . . . there ain't too much chance of being lonely in our house, what with screaming brats and my mam going off half cock when things don't suit her.' She laughed. 'Life would be dull without them, though.' She studied Rosie's sad face before asking quietly, 'How do you feel about Doug? I mean *really* feel?'

'Sometimes I hate him.'

'And other times?'

Rosie had asked herself the same question over and over, so she knew the answer by heart. 'I suppose I've grown used to having him around. But I don't love him. Not in *that* way. I never did.'

'Then don't wed him.'

Shocked at the suggestion, Rosie shook her head. 'Oh, Peggy! I don't think you're listening. I'm with child, and my dad's thrown me out. When Adam hears what I have to say, he'll wash his hands of me and the only friend I'll have in the world is you. I've put myself on your poor mam, who already has more than enough to contend with. I've a few savings put by, but that won't last too long, and in a couple of months' time I won't be able to work at all, and I'll be looking for charity.'

'You're only seeing the bad side.'

'What other side is there?'

'You could stay in our house, and let our mam bring the baby up while you go back out to work. I know she wouldn't mind.'

Rosie realised what a good friend she had in Peggy. '*I* would mind though,' she said gently. 'I couldn't put on your mam like that. I wouldn't. And anyway the whole town would know my shame then. I'd be labelled a bad 'un, just like my dad said, and the baby would be branded a bastard.' The thought horrified her. 'No. Bless you for the thought, but I can't do it.'

'There is another way.' Sipping at her tea, Peggy regarded Rosie through crafty blue eyes.

'Oh?' Intrigued, Rosie put down her mug of tea and stared at Peggy with curiosity. The faintest sense of hope stirred inside her. Though it soon fell away at Peggy's words.

'Get *Adam* to wed you.'

'What are you saying?'

'I'm saying you should keep your mouth shut about carrying Doug's child, and go along with Adam's plans. Wed him. Set up house together in Rosamund Street, just like you've always planned. You love Adam, don't you?'

'You know I do. Even though I'm promised to Doug, it's Adam I'll always want.'

'Well then?'

Rosie smiled. 'Don't think it hasn't crossed my mind, because it has, time and again. But it wouldn't work. Adam's a proud man. He wouldn't want me after what I've done. There's no way I could deceive him, and I wouldn't really want to. Besides, can you imagine Doug keeping quiet? No. He would take great pleasure in telling Adam about what went on when his back was turned. He would never let Adam forget that I was carrying his child.'

'It's worth a try. If you really must, you can tell Adam the truth, about Doug and all. *Then* tell him how you're sorry . . . that it just happened, and you still love him.'

'I intend to tell him all that,' Rosie confirmed. 'But I'm also going to tell him that Doug and I are soon to be wed.'

'Aren't you even going to *try* and win him back?'

It seemed an age before Rosie answered. How she wished everything was as simple as Peggy would have her believe. 'No. Like I said, it's all too late. I know Adam like the back of my own hand, and I know it would never work.'

'But if he loves you?'

'No. Even then. He's a fine man but he's proud and rightly so. I don't believe there's a man alive who would want to be reminded day after day that his wife and his best friend were lovers while he was away in the forces. Every time he looked at me or the baby, it would break his heart. It would break mine too. Whatever love we started out with, would soon become loathing.'

'Oh, Rosie!' Peggy's voice broke with emotion.

Moved by her friend's tears, Rosie laid her hand over Peggy's, saying softly, 'You mustn't fret, you know. I'm resigned to what has to be done. I know how concerned you are, and I know you're trying to find a way out of it for me. But I've thought it through, and marrying Doug is the only way.' She smiled wryly. 'Like my dad would say, I've made my bed and I'll have to lie on it.' Peering through the window, she turned her eyes towards the clock over the station entrance. It was almost nine-thirty. 'I'd better go,' she said brightly. 'I don't want to keep him waiting on top of everything else.' She stood up. 'Don't wait for me,' she told Peggy. 'I'll see you later, eh?'

Peggy squeezed her hand. 'Don't forget what I said,' she insisted. 'It's worth a try.'

Rosie's answer was an affectionate kiss on the cheek. Then, without a word, she turned away, left the tea rooms, and was soon lost in the milling crowd of shoppers.

'Best of luck, sweetheart. I'll be thinking of you,' Peggy said under her breath. 'Though I'd rather you than me!'

As she made her way across the market place, the train's whistle pierced the air. She paused for a minute, wondering whether she should go back. Rosie's instructions rang in her ears. Don't wait for me, she'd said. 'I expect she'll want to be on her own for a while,' Peggy thought aloud. Soon she was clambering on to the tram that would take her home, and soon after, much to the amusement of the other passengers, she was light-heartedly arguing with the same conductor who had brought them here.

Rosie paced back and forth. As the train approached, people surged forward to meet the disembarking passengers or to board the train themselves. Once or twice she was given the glad eye by certain young men who took a fancy to the slim pretty young woman, though they soon lost interest when she seemed oblivious to their bold attentions.

The train shuddered to a halt. A cloud of vapour from the engine enveloped the carriages, and Rosie stepped forward. Her anxious eyes scanned the crowds as they converged from every direction. There were men in bowler hats, harassed mothers with small crying children, soldiers and airmen on leave, old folk and young, all weary, wilting in the heat of a glorious June day, and all wanting to get home.

As they made their way along the platform, another figure caught Rosie's eye. A tall uniformed figure which intermittently disappeared and reappeared, a ghostly thing, lost in a billowing haze. 'Adam!' Instinctively she ran towards him, her heart in her mouth; a great longing surged through her as she thought of him, of the way it had been between them.

Suddenly he was there, standing only inches away yet not seeing her. He was more handsome than she remembered, upright and strong, with the same proud bearing which had first attracted her to him. She could recall it as though it was only yesterday. It was a Saturday night in February, a little over three years ago. It was Peggy's nineteenth birthday, and she and Rosie had gone to the Palais to celebrate.

Doug and Adam were best pals, and they were there that night; both in Army uniform, jointly celebrating the end of the war and Doug's imminent demob. Adam though, because he had no family ties, had decided to carve out a career in the forces. They were each handsome in their own way; Doug, with his striking, laughing eyes and tumbling brown hair, was the merry one, outgoing and fun to be with; while Adam was quiet, more serious, and incredibly handsome with his commanding height, dark eyes and black hair.

At first Doug made a beeline for Rosie, but was soon disappointed when it seemed that the only man in the room for her was Adam. Disgruntled, Doug then turned his charm on Peggy, sweeping her off her feet and starting a relationship that lasted only weeks before they began to quarrel and he eventually threw her over for the barmaid at the Swan public house. 'Bloody good shuts!' Peggy told Rosie. And the two of them went out on the town to celebrate.

Doug's best friend, though, wanted none other than Rosie. They were so right for each other, so much in love, and so excited about the future. Soon they were a couple, idyllically happy and making plans for a life together. It soon became evident, though, that there was one area where they disagreed. While Rosie begged Adam to get a civilian job, he was adamant that he would stay in the forces. 'I don't feel ready to come out yet, sweetheart,' he explained, and nothing that Rosie could say would persuade him otherwise.

For a while she went along with his wishes, telling herself that the Army had been his family, and he needed it for a while yet. But, from his letters, it soon became clear that he might *never* leave it. Then came the long empty months when he didn't write and she was left lonely and confused. The loneliness gave way to anger, and it was then that she allowed herself to be seduced by Doug. He seemed always to be near, going out of his way to be both charming and attentive. Peggy warned her against him, as did her father. In fact there were times when her father forbade her to leave the house. He became entrenched in his dislike of Doug, and blamed Rosie for the fact that she and Adam had drifted apart. Inevitably they argued, and Rosie was driven the wrong way by her father's dictatorial attitude; especially in view of the fact that the last letter she had received from Adam warned her that she may not hear from him for a while. 'Got things to think about,' he'd written. 'Not sure what to do.'

Secretly delighted, Doug seized his chance. He was quickly there at her side, to comfort and distract her, especially on the night Peggy was taken ill with the 'flu and couldn't go with Rosie to the Palais. She could remember little of that night. Yet she knew she had drunk too much, and recalled going outside to get a breath of air, and Doug kissing her. One thing followed another and on the way home they made love, right in the middle of Blackburn Rovers football grounds.

Later, when she found she was with child, she was frantic, believing he would want nothing to do with her. Astonishingly, when she told him, he proudly declared that they should be wed as soon as it could be decently arranged. Rosie was under no illusions. It took only a short time for her to see him for the shallow and vain man he was. Even so, he was hard-working, and she never doubted for a minute that he truly loved her.

Adam's letter had re-opened all the old wounds. And now here he was in person, breaking her heart all over again. His head was turned away, his dark eyes desperately searching the platform. 'Adam, I'm here,' she said, her soft voice reaching out to him.

When he turned his dark eyes to her, she trembled from limb to limb. There followed a strange silence when it seemed they were the only two people in the whole world. Then he was rushing forward and she was rooted to the spot, summoning up the courage to do what must be done. In a minute he had thrown off his rucksack and was sweeping her into his arms, laughing aloud, calling her name and crushing her so tight to his chest that she could hardly breathe. Setting her on her feet, he gazed down on those beloved features, his own face suffused with pleasure as he breathed, 'I'd almost forgotten how beautiful you are.' He kissed her then, a long hungry kiss that lit the passion inside her.

Tearing herself away, she told him, 'You look well.' She wanted to say so much more; to tell him how she had missed him, and how she still loved him with all her heart. She wanted to rant and rave, and let him know he had ruined both their lives. But how could she accuse him, when it was she who had been the impatient one?

Overjoyed to be back with her, to have finally come to a decision which would secure their future, he didn't realise there was anything wrong. 'Did you tell your dad I was on my way? He won't mind me staying with you both, will he? At least for a while. Oh, Rosie, you can't know how good it is to be home.' He was excited, and full of things to tell her. 'Tell you what,' he suggested, 'I'm starving! Do you fancy a bite to eat?'

This was Rosie's opportunity. 'I was about to suggest that myself,' she told him. 'There's the tea rooms across the way?'

'Fair enough, sweetheart.' He didn't mind where they went as long as they could be alone somewhere they could talk. Swinging his rucksack over one arm, he cradled her to him with the other. And as they walked the short distance to the tea rooms, he couldn't take his eyes off her.

'Sit yourself down,' he told Rosie, throwing his rucksack to the floor. 'What's it to be? Mug of tea and a sandwich?' He pushed his hand into his trouser pocket and began walking towards the counter. The joy at seeing her was still shining in his eyes as he glanced back.

'Tea, that's all,' she said, making herself smile.

Soon they were seated opposite each other, and he was shaking his head in disbelief. 'I can't believe I'm here with you,' he murmured. 'Miss me, did you?'

'You know I did.'

'I'm sorry I took so long to write, sweetheart.'

'You *should* have written before!'

'You're angry?'

'Yes, I'm angry.'

He cast his eyes down, his fingertips toying with the edge of the tablecloth. 'I thought about you every minute. I always meant to come back.' He looked up. Reaching out, he covered her hand with his. 'It was always on the cards that you and me would be wed. You do believe that, don't you?'

Not daring to look into those dark eyes, she kept her gaze averted. 'I don't know *what* to believe,' she answered truthfully.

'You must know I love you?'

'I suppose.'

Only then did he realise there was something not quite right. Yet he didn't immediately say anything. Instead he bit a chunk from his sandwich, then another, meticulously chewing each bite until it was gone. Taking a great gulp of his tea, he put the mug back on the table with deliberation. For a long silent moment he stared at her, his brows furrowed in thought. And all the while she avoided looking into those dark troubled eyes. At length, he asked in a subdued voice, 'We *are* going to be wed, aren't we?'

'No.' Now that the word was out, she felt stronger somehow, yet deeply ashamed.

Sitting bolt upright, he clenched his fists on the table. 'What the hell do you mean . . . no?'

'I mean, when you hear what I have to tell you, you won't *want* to wed me.' Her stricken brown eyes flickered beneath his searching gaze.

He stretched out his hand and took hold of her fingers. 'It can't be all that bad,' he said fondly.

Sliding her hand away, she faced him directly, dying a little with each word as she described how she had begun to believe that he was never coming back, that he didn't want her any more. She told him how she had betrayed him with another man, and how she was carrying that man's child. Her heart broke when he fell back in the chair as though she had felled him with an axe. 'I'm so sorry, Adam,' she murmured. 'When I got your letter, it was already too late. I'm promised to him, and that's an end to it.'

His eyes were hard as they focused on her. '*Who is he*?' His voice was curiously low, yet forceful.

She was tempted to give him another name, or not to tell him at all. But then she realised that it was only a matter of time before he found out. Once he was settled in her father's house, probably the first person he would want to see was his best friend Doug. He had to know. And it was best he should know now. 'It's . . . Doug.' There! It was said. And now she felt more ashamed than ever.

He stared at her in disbelief. '*Doug*!'

Peggy's words came back to her then, and she knew she had to try. SHE HAD TO TRY! Peggy had said it was worth it, and she was right. The thought of losing Adam and spending the rest of her days with a man she didn't love, was suddenly more than Rosie could bear. 'I don't love him,' she said desperately, 'it's always been you, Adam. It's still you. If only you could forgive me, we could still be wed. Oh, if only you could forgive me it would be all right, I know it would.' She could feel the tears streaming down her face, hot and moist against her skin. She wiped the back of her hand over her mouth, brushing the wetness away, trying so hard to choke back the emotion. But she couldn't. For months now she had bottled it all up, and now he was here, he had held her and kissed her, and her heart was breaking.

Without a word he stood up and slung the rucksack over his shoulder. One last glance from those questioning black eyes, then he was gone. As he strode from the room, she called out his name. He didn't look back. She watched him hurry across the boulevard and re-enter the station. She hoped and prayed, right up to the moment he disappeared from sight and for some time afterwards. But he didn't look back. And in her heart she couldn't blame him.

It was growing dark when Rosie returned to her friend's house. She knew at once that there was something very wrong. Peggy was waiting for her. 'You'd best sit down,' she said gently, leading Rosie into the parlour.

Peggy's face was ashen. The children were all abed and the little house was too quiet. Peggy's mam was seated by the window. She didn't speak, but her pained eyes spoke volumes.

'What is it?' Rosie was afraid. 'What's wrong?'

Peggy looked helplessly at her mam, who quickly nodded encouragement. 'The police were here. We came to the station looking for you, but you'd already gone.'

Rosie was puzzled. 'What do the police want *me* for?' When Peggy was slow in answering, it was as though a light had been switched on in her mind, and it filled her with horror. She was shaking her head, trying to push the truth away. 'It's Adam, isn't it?' she asked fearfully. Running through her confused mind was the possibility of a train crash, or even worse.

'No, it's not Adam.' Peggy held her and then Rosie knew. 'It's your dad. I'm sorry, he's gone. There was nothing anyone could do.' She didn't say how they had found him in the bath, with the razor still embedded in his wrist and the walls splattered with his own blood. Rosie would suffer that later. For now, she needed a friend. 'Shh now,' she said. 'Wait a while, then we'll go and see them, eh?' Rosie felt numb. For a moment she couldn't take it all in. Memories of her lost love filled her sore heart, she could still feel Adam's kiss burning on her lips; she remembered the awful pain in his eyes when she told him the truth. And now her father! It was too much, all too much. She started to shake, but still she couldn't grasp it all. Nothing seemed real to her. Beneath her breath Peggy murmured, 'They say it never rains but it pours.'

And she feared that, for Rosie, the storm clouds had only just begun to gather.

Chapter Three

'Are you getting up or what?' Doug's angry voice carried up the stairs. 'I'm ready for off, and my sandwiches still aren't done!'

Before Rosie could explain that she hadn't got up because she was crippled with pain, another voice intervened: his mother's. 'Leave the lazy cow where she is, son. I got your snap tin ready long before *she* came on the scene, and I can do it now.' There followed a series of loud deliberate noises when, after a few seconds, Martha Selby could be heard stamping down the stairs. 'I warned you she'd be no good, but you wouldn't listen. Oh, no! Happen you'll bloody well listen *now*!'

Inching her legs out of bed, Rosie touched the cold linoleum with the tips of her toes. The pain shot through her like a knife. 'It's started,' she gasped, running both hands over the swollen mound beneath her nightgown. The sweat was pouring from her now, and she could hardly breathe. 'DOUG!' It took all of her strength even to call his name.

Suddenly the door burst open and there he was. 'What bloody game are you playing, eh?' he demanded, striding into the room. 'Since when does my mam have to get herself out of bed at five o'clock on a winter's morning to do what *you* should be doing, eh? EH?' He poked at her with the tips of his fingers, oblivious to the fact that she was in a state of great distress.

Rosie had been sitting with her head bowed, but now she raised her eyes. In the glow from the lamp, she saw his red angry face staring down on her, and the only thought in her mind was to be rid of him. 'Get out,' she said, and he was visibly stunned.

'WHAT!' He looked at her in disbelief before raising his hand to strike her.

If he expected her to flinch, he should have known better. Defiant brown eyes stared back at him. Anger smothered the pain. 'Go on. Hit me then,' she taunted. 'What are you waiting for?'

For a minute it seemed as though he would bring his fist crashing down on her. But then he realised she was not afraid and he laughed out loud. 'Well, I'm buggered!' Sitting beside her, he slid an arm round her shoulders. All anger was gone, and in its place came a mood that was even more repugnant to her. 'You're a fiery bugger and no mistake.' One hand snaked under her nightie while with the other he fumbled at his trouser buttons. Grabbing her hand, he placed it over his exposed member. 'Feel that,' he coaxed. 'Stiff as a broom handle . . . aching for you, it is.' When she snatched her hand away, he nuzzled at her neck with the tip of his nose. 'I miss it, you know,' he moaned, frowning pathetically. 'I could have got it elsewhere, but I haven't. Not yet.'

'You'd best go or you'll be late for work.'

'We've time, if you want to.'

'Sod off!'

'Well, that's no way to talk to your old man, is it?'

A vicious pain rippled through her, taking her breath away. 'Please, Doug. Leave me be.'

'What the hell's the matter with you?' He stared harder at her, only then realising that she was deep in labour. Bent double in pain and sweating so much that her nightgown was welded to her back, she didn't have the strength to push him away. 'Christ Almighty!' Running to the door, he began yelling, 'MAM! MAM! SHE'S STARTED!' He didn't come back to the bed. Instead, he stood by the door, yelling for his mam and watching Rosie apprehensively.

Martha Selby came rushing into the room, breathless and red-faced from coming up the stairs two at a time. She was a big woman, grey-haired and scruffy; the dark stain of snuff beneath her nostrils resembled a 'tache. 'Off to work, son,' she told him, planting a kiss on the side of his face. 'Your snap tin's all ready downstairs.'

'She's started!'

'Nothing for you to worry about, son. She ain't the first woman to fetch a bairn into the world, and she won't be the last.' With the flat of her hand, she pushed him out of the door. 'Go on. I'll see to it.'

He didn't need telling twice. He was gone even before she'd finished speaking.

'Now then, young madam.' Regarding Rosie with curious eyes, Martha came across the room. 'I'll not stand for no tantrums,' she said in a hard voice. 'Giving birth ain't easy, but if you start yelling and screaming, I'm buggered if I won't tie you down. Do you understand what I'm saying?'

'I want the doctor.'

'No need for a doctor.' With her hands on her hips, she demanded, 'I asked whether you understood?'

Rosie didn't answer. Racked with pain, she merely nodded. She was in no fit state to fight. The fact was, she was alone in this room with a woman who loathed the very sight of her, and she was at her mercy.

'Good. It seems we understand each other. Now, get off the bed while I roll back the sheets. Them's my best ones and I don't want 'em soiled.' She waited while Rosie struggled to raise herself up against the bed-head, clinging to the brass rail and bearing the throes of labour without even a whimper. 'Lie down flat.' Martha Selby had removed all but the mattress cover. The bedding, even the pillow, was neatly stacked on to a nearby chair.

The bed struck cold as Rosie lay down. Her head fell back, making the pain more intensive. 'Can't I have my head raised?' she asked.

'If your head's flat, you can't see what's going on, and if you can't see what's going on, then you'll not be tempted to shout and holler. Now, let's see.' Rosie felt her legs being drawn up and stretched wide open. 'The little sod's on its way right enough. I'll away down and get things ready.' In that moment Rosie was gripped with a particularly vicious pain, which made her cry out. Her reward was a sharp slap in the face. 'I said there'll be none o' that. I won't stand for no hysterics, do you hear me?' Rosie turned away. 'I SAID, DO YOU HEAR ME?' Rosie gave a nod. 'Right. Do as you're told. Else I'll leave you to get on with it yourself, and then it'll be God help you!' With that she hurried from the room.

Rosie thought she was never coming back, but after an age the older woman reappeared. When she came through the door, Rosie was pushing against the force of the child inside her. 'Don't push, you bugger! You'll harm the child!' Dropping the bowl of hot water on to the dresser, she thrust her hands between Rosie's legs. 'Its head's nearly out,' she cried. 'It won't be long now.'

In spite of everything, Rosie was glad of this sour-natured woman. She was afraid, and lonely, and wondering how bad the pain would get before she had to yell and scream. It got bad, then worse, and still she kept her silence. Above all else, she didn't want to be left alone, and she was under no illusion where Martha Selby was concerned. The woman was hard as nails, with a vicious streak that made her more enemies than friends. If she had threatened to leave Rosie to it, then that was exactly what she would do. Even if it meant both mother and child losing their lives.

It was two agonising hours before the baby came into the world, during which time Rosie worked harder than she had ever worked before. Even then she could do no right for Martha Selby, who yelled and screamed herself as though it was *she* who was giving birth, and not Rosie. 'It's another lad!' she finally cried jubilantly, holding the child aloft. 'Just as well, 'cause I ain't got no time for split-arses.'

She took an unnaturally long time in bathing the newborn. Then she cooed and fussed and worried about what name to call it, and when Rosie asked to hold the child, tutted and moaned and thrust it into her arms with the warning, 'With your mam dead and gone, you'd best not forget I'm his only grandma.'

Wisely, Rosie made no comment, but that evening when Doug climbed the stairs to see her, she gave *him* a warning. 'You've got a month to find us a place of our own.'

'You must be mad!' He hadn't even looked at the child in his cradle, nor had he taken Rosie into his arms. 'Where the hell am I supposed to find a place, just like that? You know very well there aren't many houses for rent now, what with landlords cashing in on this new trend for *owning* property. Every house round here for miles has been sold off. There ain't a place to be rented nowhere.'

'That's rubbish and you know it. You haven't looked hard enough.'

Rosie had spoken the truth and it irked him. Punching the door with a clenched fist, he demanded. 'Bloody hell, woman! We've a roof over us head. What more do you want? My mam's been good to us, and Dad's twice upped my wages for helping him on the coal-wagon. We're living here in comfort, and it's only costing us half what we'd have to pay anywhere else, even if we *could* find a suitable place.' He swung round to face her. 'And if you've got an eye on Rosamund Street, you can bloody well forget it, because I'm not paying fifteen shillings a week for no house, in Rosamund Street or not.'

'I'm not talking about Rosamund Street.'

'Oh? And why's that, eh? There was a time not long back when Rosamund Street was all you could think about.'

'That was *then*.' A great sadness washed over her. Rosamund Street was still close to her heart. But having a house there had been a very special dream. It belonged to her and Adam, and no one else. Well, that dream might be over, but it was all she had left of him, and she didn't want it spoiled. 'I don't care *where* we live, as long as it isn't in this house.'

'Well, that's bloody right, that is!' Striding across the room, he shook his fist at her. 'My mam's had you pegged all along. You're an ungrateful little bugger. You're not asked to do any housework, are you?'

'No.'

'Washing, ironing . . . none of that?'

'No.'

'Well then?'

She looked at him with a dignity that made him feel inferior. 'You just don't understand, do you?' she asked in a quiet voice. 'Does it never occur to you that I *want* to do my own washing and ironing? That I long to clean the carpets and polish the furniture? But I'm not allowed to, because your mam doesn't want me touching her precious things.'

'She doesn't want to put on you, that's all.'

'You're either blind or you don't care. Your mam only tolerates me because she doesn't want to lose you or her grandson. That's the reason she enticed you to live here in the first place, and it's the reason she keeps us here.'

'And what's so wrong with that, eh? She's lonely. What with my dad working all hours God sends on that bloody coal-wagon of his, it's only natural she wants company.'

'Did you know she's busy choosing a name for *our* son?'

'And you object?'

'Of course I object!'

He seemed genuinely shocked by that, but made no comment. Later she would live to regret denying his mother that simple pleasure!

'I mean it, Doug. If you want me and the boy, you'll have to find us somewhere else to live.'

'And if I don't?'

'I'll take him and find lodgings.' The minute the words were out of her mouth, she realised how empty they were.

He hadn't expected a bold statement like that. Such a thing wasn't done round these parts where if a man couldn't control his family, he was not a man. Doug had no intention of being made to look a fool in front of his neighbours. Besides, he still had an uncontrollable lust for this defiant wife of his. 'Try that one and I'll break every bone in your body!'

She didn't answer. What she threatened had no real substance. How could it? Besides, she would never accept charity, so what would she live on?

Troubled by her silence, he came to her. Sitting on the edge of the bed, he said in a softer voice, 'Don't let's fight.' Running his fingers through her thick brown hair, he mistook her shudder of repugnance for delight at his touch. 'I want you so much,' he murmured. 'Yet somehow, I always feel you're never really mine.' It was a deep-down feeling that was increasingly hard to live with. 'I do love you, you know . . . you and the boy.' For the first time his eyes turned towards the cradle. 'Mam says he's just like me when I were a lad.'

For the briefest moment there was a curious tenderness in his voice, and Rosie thought she might have been a little hard on him these past weeks. 'I'm sorry, Doug. I know she's your mother, and happen she means well, but we don't hit it off. She's never liked me, you know that.'

He smiled. 'She can be a cantankerous bugger when she sets her mind to it, I'll give you that.'

'You'll find us a place then?'

He nodded. 'Aye, I expect so.' Having agreed to give her something, he expected something else in return. Kissing her on the mouth, he whispered, 'I don't suppose . . .'

'No. Not yet.'

'For Christ's sake! WHEN?'

'I don't know.'

'Tomorrow?'

'What kind of man are you, Doug Selby? Have you forgotten, I've only just given birth?'

'No, I've not bloody well forgotten. But I don't intend to wait forever, I can tell you that. I've waited long enough, and come the end of next week, I'll be after my rights, just like any self-respecting man.' Putting his hands one either side of her face he squeezed hard, until her dark eyes looked like round brown pools and she was unable to cry out. Then he kissed her so viciously on her puckered mouth that it bruised her. 'I *will* have my rights!' he said with an ugly smile. 'So think on *that* while I'm out searching for a house, eh?'

He went out of the room laughing. When the door was slammed shut behind him, Rosie stroked her sore face and cursed the day she ever set eyes on him. Then she leaned over the cradle and took the newborn into her arms. 'If it wasn't for you,' she murmured, softly crying, 'I wouldn't stay in this house another minute.' But she was trapped. And saw it as just punishment for her sins.

* * *

The days sped by. Doug swore he was looking in every direction for a house of their own; Martha Selby couldn't keep her hands off her new grandson; and Rosie spent as much time outside as she possibly could.

In the cold December mornings, she walked all the way to Corporation Park and sat beneath the willow trees by the lake. Here, she would breast feed her son in the wintry sunshine and watch the ducks at play until mid-afternoon, when she would walk all the way back to Artillery Street, where Martha Selby was invariably standing by the door, hands on hips. 'Where the hell have you been all day?' she'd demand. 'Have you no sense at all, woman? Don't you know it's too cold for my grandson to be out?' At which point she would snatch the boy from his pram and hurry inside, always with the same snide comment: 'She's a bad mammy, ain't she, eh? Lord knows what your Dad'll have to say when he gets home.' And she always made certain that Doug was riled up two minutes after he walked through the door. 'She's been wandering the streets 'til all hours again, our Doug. Have you ever heard the like? Taking a lad of his age out on such a chilly day. He's feverish, feel his forehead! I shouldn't be at all surprised if the lad doesn't go down with pneumonia,' she would crow. 'She's your wife, so it's up to you. If you ask me, you ought to take a firmer hand with her.'

Today was Friday. Rosie had spent many hours in the park, and now she turned the pram away from the lake and towards the main entrance. 'We'll go and see Peggy, shall we?' she asked the sleeping child. 'We've time enough.' A glance at the clock over the arches told her it was almost four-thirty. Normally, she would have made straight for Artillery Street, because she always made a point of being home before Doug. Today, though, she wasn't concerned, because she knew he wouldn't be home until at least six-thirty. After work on Friday, Doug usually spent an hour with his drinking pals. Rosie was glad of that, because to tell the truth, the less she saw of him the better.

It was twenty minutes past five when she got to Castle Street. As she came in at one end, Peggy got off her tram at the other. The sight of her dear friend cheered her heart. 'PEGGY!' she shouted, pushing forward at a quicker pace, yet going carefully over the cobbles so as not to shake the baby.

Peggy's face lit up. 'You're a sight for sore eyes!' she cried, coming at a run down the street. Her nose was red from the cold, but her eyes were bright at seeing Rosie. The two of them were soon hugging and laughing, and in no time at all they were hauling the pram up the steps and into the house.

Manoeuvring the cumbersome article down the narrow passage was no easy task, especially when Peggy's mam and four boisterous children decided to lend a helping hand. But they managed, and once the pram was lodged safely against the parlour wall, the children all disappeared into the back yard, and Peggy's mam took herself into the scullery where, except for the time she reappeared with a mug of tea each for the two young women, she remained throughout Rosie's visit.

'Bless her old heart, she's probably listening through the door-curtain,' Peggy whispered, her blue eyes bright with mischief. 'And what she don't overhear, she'll try and worm out of me later on.'

Rosie laughed. 'She's a good sort is your mam. And anyway, I've got nothing to say that she can't hear.'

'Hmph!' Peggy sat back in her chair. 'I don't expect Martha Selby's making life any easier, is she?'

Rosie told her everything then; how Doug's mother was interfering, trying to take charge of the boy; how Doug still hadn't found them a place of their own, and how she suspected he wasn't even looking; and, worse, how he was intent on claiming his rights this very weekend. 'Honest to God, Peggy, I can't stand the thought of it.'

'I don't know what to say,' she admitted. 'Ain't you got no feeling for him at all?'

'Well, of course I have. But I don't *love* him . . . not like a wife should.'

'Well then, to my mind, if you've got even the *slightest* feeling for him, it shouldn't be too bad.' Leaning forward, she confided, 'It has to be better than having no fella at all.'

'You're right. It's not the end of the world. I expect I'm just nervous after the baby and everything.' Rosie cast her mind back over the past year. 'Anyway, far worse things have happened.'

'As for Martha Selby, I'm surprised you ain't given her a right mouthful. Knowing you, I'm surprised you ain't put the old bag in her place by now.'

'It's not that easy. She's a cunning sort, and I have to be careful not to give her more opportunity to cause trouble between me and Doug. No, Peggy. If I'm to get a place of my own, it's best if I play her at her own game. I've been thinking long and hard, and I reckon I'll find a way. It's just a matter of time, that's all.'

The conversation took another turn when Peggy explained how she had been put on the stationery counter at Woolworths. 'We miss you, gal,' she said, 'the others are always asking after you.' Without waiting for a reply she gabbled on, curious about the christening and wondering if she was going to be a godparent. Rosie assured her she would be, and that the christening would likely be when the lad was three months old. She also explained how she'd wanted to call the boy after her own dad, but Doug was having none of it. 'Every time I come up with a name, he finds something wrong with it. As for his mam, she's intent on picking the lad's name herself.'

'You won't let her, will you?'

'Over my dead body!'

'So, what *will* you call him?'

'Doug and I have argued the point for a whole week now.' Rosie chuckled. 'We'll have to see, won't we?' She looked at the child in his pram. 'He's a grand little thing,' she said lovingly. 'It's not his fault if Martha's hellbent on using him as an excuse to cause trouble.'

'Martha won't get her own way, and Doug will want his son to have a good manly name, so I don't reckon you need worry.' Rosie tended to agree, so they talked of more general matters, like Peggy's new fashionable thick-heeled shoes, and Rosie's astonishingly slim figure after the baby and all.

They were just two old friends catching up on gossip and enjoying the experience. After a while the baby started whimpering. 'I'd best be off,' Rosie apologised. 'The lad needs feeding, and anyway I don't want Doug getting home before me, especially if he's had a drink or two and his mam's fighting fit. That would really put the cat amongst the pigeons.'

Peggy's mam emerged then. 'I couldn't help overhearing,' she confessed with a cheeky little grin. 'All men are the same. If you want a peaceful life, you have to let them be boss. As for his mam, you do right to think of playing her at her own game.' She said something then that really caught Rosie's attention. 'In spite of what your fella says, he can't have looked far for a house 'cause there's one here . . . at the bottom of our street.'

Not realising the full impact her words had on Rosie, she then went on: 'Martha Selby always did like having her own way . . . got a nasty streak in her nature, she has. And she was never popular, even at school. She used to argue and fight with everybody. But I will say one thing in her favour . . . she was never brazen like some of the lasses. What! She used to redden like a ripe tomato if a boy so much as looked at her.' She laughed out loud. 'Not that many of them ever did, because then, like now, Martha Selby was not what you'd call a pretty thing.'

Having said her piece, Peggy's mam returned to the scullery from where she instructed her daughter to: 'Set the table, lass. Tea's ready.' Hearing their mam, the four children came rushing in from the yard. 'Hey! Get in here and wash your hands, you lot.' She lined them up against the sink. 'Look at the state of you!' she remarked. Their noses were running from the cold and their little hands were chapped by the cold. 'What am I going to do with you, eh?' she chuckled. Then, amid wails of protest, she made them wash their hands and face. And: 'Don't forget behind your ears, you little buggers!'

Rosie went off down the street, still chuckling. 'God forbid that I ever have a little army like that,' she muttered with some apprehension. It wasn't that she didn't like children. It was the idea of Doug fathering them she didn't fancy. The cold air sharpened with the onset of evening, prompting her to dig out the headscarf from the pram and wrap it securely about her windblown hair. 'By! That's got chilly now, sweetheart,' she told the sleeping infant.

The nearer she got to Artillery Street, the more she thought about what Peggy's mam had said: 'Your fella can't have looked far for a house 'cause there's one empty at the bottom of our street.' That was more than enough to get Rosie's hackles up. But what she had later revealed was even more interesting to Rosie, and it had given her the germ of an idea. 'Well, well, Martha!' she said, smiling to herself. 'I just might have found a way to turn the tables on you once and for all.

'Where the hell have you been?' Doug was waiting for her as she turned the corner into Artillery Street. 'It's going on six o'clock!' He was stiff with anger as he came towards her. 'Our mam's been bloody frantic.'

Astonished to see him home, Rosie did her best not to appear alarmed. 'I can't think why,' she answered, her firm voice belying the angry knot in her stomach. 'I'm quite capable of looking after our son.' Turning round at the foot of the steps, she proceeded to pull the pram up backwards until Doug pushed her out of the way to lift the whole thing from the ground. Carting coal gave him the muscles of an ox.

'I asked where you'd been?' he insisted, taking the pram at a fierce pace into the parlour.

'I went up the park, then I went to see Peggy. It's been ages since I saw her. Anyway, I didn't think you'd be home yet.'

'Up the park?' He glared at her. 'Who in their right mind goes up the park when they can stay in a warm cosy parlour?'

The row raged all the while she fed the child. It continued while Martha Selby went about setting the table, and it went on even while Mr and Mrs Selby sat down to eat their meal. Doug was in too much of a fury to eat, and though she had been looking forward to her meal, Rosie had quickly lost her appetite.

When Doug's parents had finished their dinner, Martha slyly remained within earshot while Mr Selby did his usual vanishing trick and retired to the front parlour. Quiet and plain-faced, he was a big man with a broad back and a shrewd business brain. The complete opposite to his despicable wife, he was painfully timid, and whenever occasion allowed, escaped from the traumas of wedded life to read his beloved racing paper in the privacy of the front parlour.

'When I get home of an evening, I want you here, do you understand?' Doug ranted on. Still dressed in his work clothes, he was standing, legs astride, with his back to the fire, his fists clenched by his sides and the leather collar that protected his shoulders from the rough coalsacks hanging loosely about his neck. The round staring eyes and fine film of coaldust over his face and nose gave him a comical appearance.

'You tell her, son!' encouraged his mam who was seated at the table now, pretending to sip a cold cup of tea. 'Then get your wash and have your dinner while it's hot.'

'SHUT UP, MAM!' He could handle *one* woman, but his mam was one too many.

'Don't speak to me like that.' In a minute she was across the room and confronting him. 'I'm only saying she deserves to be told, that's all.'

'Yes, and it's me that'll do the telling. I've had more than enough of your bloody interference!'

'Well, sod you . . . and sod her . . . and the pair of you can get out if that's how you feel!'

'Aye, and we will. Don't you worry. Soon as ever we find a place, we'll be off.'

Rosie was amazed, wondering whether she was hearing things. The idea of Doug and his mam going at each other like that was unthinkable. Wisely, she remained very still, sinking deeper into the chair and hoping they would forget she was there. But it was too much to hope for.

After the heated exchange, there was a moment of shocked silence when mother and son realised how the row had escalated. 'You mustn't talk about leaving this house, son,' Martha cooed, brushing away imaginary tears. 'As long as me and your dad's alive, this will always be your home.'

He was sullen for a while, but then he answered, 'I'm sorry, Mam. You've been good to us, and I don't mean to be ungrateful. It's just that I've had a hard day.' He didn't mention that he'd lost a deal of his wages on a foolish bet.

Suddenly his mother pointed at Rosie. 'It's all *her* bloody fault!' she cried, glaring at her daughter-in-law who went across the room to gather the child into her arms. 'See how cunning she is . . . setting us at each other's throats like that?'

'Leave it, Mam.' His cold eyes studied Rosie's slim attractive figure as she bent over the pram. He hadn't forgotten. Tonight, he would hold her in his arms and make love to her. The thought made him shiver inside.

His mother opened her mouth to complain, but he silenced her with the promise, 'It won't happen again, Mam.' Smiling, he kissed her lightly on the cheek. 'Now then, can a man have a minute alone with his wife?'

Sensing his intention to paw her again, Rosie gently laid the child in his pram and began clearing away the used dishes from the table, until she felt a vicious poke in the arm from Martha. 'Get away from my table! I don't need your bloody help.'

Rosie was incensed. 'And if you *did*, you wouldn't ask, would you? Why don't you tell him the truth, Martha? You don't want me in this house, do you?'

'No, I don't. To tell you the truth, I think our Doug could have done a lot better for himself.'

Rosie laughed at that. 'It wouldn't have mattered *who* he brought home, you wouldn't have liked them, because you want to keep your precious son all to yourself. Well, you're welcome to him.' Suddenly the child began screaming. 'But you'll not get your hands on this little chap,' she warned, grabbing the child to her and rocking him back and forth. 'Much as you'd like to!'

'I wouldn't be too sure of that, my girl. Anybody can see you're not a fit mother . . . keeping a lad of that age out 'til all hours. Poor little sod, he should have been in his cot an hour since.'

'Leave it, I said, Mam.' Doug stepped between them. 'Can't you find something to do upstairs?' His meaning was clear.

One glance at her son's grim face cautioned Martha not to show too much of her loathing for his wife. There were other, more deceitful ways to oust her. 'All right, son,' she agreed sweetly. With that, she went out of the door and into the passage. Here, she went noisily up the stairs, stopping halfway and stamping her feet a few times on the step before creeping down to sit with her ear pressed to the crack in the parlour wall. From here, she could hear everything.

'Don't take too much notice of our mam,' Doug pleaded. 'She don't mean half of what she says.' He was worried that the ugly scene would mar his first night of love in a long time.

Rosie wasn't easily placated. 'She means every word, and you know it. I'm just a lodger here, and she can't wait to be rid of me.' The child was quiet now, but still fretful. Rosie lowered her voice. 'That doesn't worry me, because *I* can't wait to get out either.'

'I wish you wouldn't talk like that.'

Regarding him with hard brown eyes, she accused, 'You say you've looked everywhere for a good house to rent?'

At once he was on his guard. 'That's right.'

'You're a liar!'

'Who the hell are you to call me a liar?'

'Peggy's mam told me there's a house on the corner of Castle Street. Did you enquire about *that*?'

He looked away. 'I don't need other folks to tell me where there's property!'

'And I don't need you lying to me!'

Spinning round, he grabbed her by the arm. 'I've said I'll find us a house, and I will. But not on Castle Street.' Outside on the step, his mother grinned widely.

'And why not? It's a good house, and the rents are reasonable.' She wouldn't be put off. Not this time. 'Or is it because I'd be too close to Peggy, eh? Has it come to me not being allowed a friend. HAS IT?'

'Don't talk bloody daft.' Stroking her arm, he lowered his voice. 'I've arranged to meet somebody down at the pub. We'll talk about it later, eh?'

'We'd better.'

He stiffened. 'Hey! Watch your tongue. I've said we'll talk about it, and we will.' Tonight, he'd do anything to pacify her. But talking was one thing. Moving to Castle Street or anywhere else was another! 'All this bloody arguing's got me down. Tell my mam I'll have supper when I get back.' Another minute and he was gone from the room.

Turning at the front door, he caught sight of his mother hunched on the stairs. For a minute she looked alarmed, but when he went away chuckling, Martha believed she'd won the day.

Returning to the parlour, she told Rosie smugly, 'You'll never get him to leave his mam. Doug knows where he's best off.'

'Oh?' Taking the child into her arms, Rosie settled herself into the chair by the fire. It was time for the baby's feed. Undoing her top button, she slid out a plump firm breast. The child latched on to the nipple and began to suck. 'Don't underestimate me, Mrs Selby,' she said boldly. 'Doug and I will be leaving this house before the month's out.'

Martha Selby had been clearing the table, but now she paused to look down on Rosie's lovely face. Her gaze fell to the exposed breast. It was the first time Rosie had fed the child in full view of her. 'Cover yourself up!' she snapped, her face reddening with rage. 'Have you no dignity?' Seeing Rosie giving birth was one thing but now, suddenly reminded of Rosie's beauty, she became incensed.

Delighted, Rosie undid another button and eased the breast further out. Normally, she would never have been so shameless, but baring her breast to Martha was all part of her little plan. 'I have as much dignity as the next woman,' she declared. 'It's just that I don't seem to have as much titty.' With great deliberation, she stroked her breast towards the nipple, encouraging the milk to flow. 'We're not all blessed with big breasts, are we, Martha?' she insinuated, momentarily glancing at the bulky outline beneath Martha's pinafore. 'My milk must be strong though, because he's always satisfied.' Looking away so she wouldn't be seen to be smiling, she asked innocently, 'Was Doug always content with *your* milk?'

'I don't remember.' Martha deliberately clattered about as she put the dishes one on top of the other. 'Anyway, I don't think it's the sort of thing I should discuss with the likes of you,' she snarled. 'Save your cheap talk for your friend Peggy.' All the same, she couldn't help but glance at Rosie once more. 'Disgraceful!' she muttered, shaking her head. 'Exposing yourself like that.'

Aware that she was being watched, Rosie squeezed the nipple between finger and thumb until the milky fluid flowed over, oozing out of the baby's mouth and running down its chin. 'Doug *loves* my breasts,' she remarked with feeling. Looking up, she smiled into Martha's eyes. 'You need never worry that he's not all man,' she said meaningfully. 'Because I can tell you that he *is*.'

Martha's eyes widened in horror. 'You little slut!' she screamed, 'I rue the day he ever brought you home.' Grabbing the dishes, she almost ran into the scullery. Rosie was bursting to laugh out loud, but she dared not. Thrilled that her plan was taking effect, she finished feeding the baby in silence.

A short time later, when she went into the scullery to put the kettle on for his wash, Martha fled into the parlour. When Rosie mixed hot and cold water in the biggest saucepan and set it on the rug, Martha set about polishing the sideboard like her life depended on it. After the child was stripped and laid on a towel, Rosie leaned over him, her blouse still loosely open and showing her slight cleavage. Normally, at her grandson's bathtime, Martha would stand behind Rosie, barking out instructions and generally making a great nuisance of herself. But this time she busied herself, rushing back and forth, before disappearing into the scullery where she noisily washed the crockery in the sink.

Rosie was immensely proud of herself because this was the very first time she had been allowed to bathe her own son without a barrage of criticism from her mother-in-law. And it was deeply satisfying. 'I've got your measure now, Martha, you bugger,' she muttered as she carried the child upstairs to its cot. Recalling the look of embarrassment on her mother-in-law's red face when she saw the bare breast and flowing milk, then the horror when Rosie had hinted at how ardent a lover Doug was, she collapsed on the bed in fits of laughter. 'At last I know how to get the better of you!' she chuckled. 'And you'd best watch out, because this is only the beginning!'

It was almost midnight when Doug got home. Coming into the bedroom, he was pleasantly surprised to find Rosie ready and eager for him. For hours she'd waited for him to enter the front door, and when he did, she quickly flung open the big window, then stripped off her nightgown and got back on the bed.

In the soft glow of the bedside lamp, Rosie looked more beautiful than he had ever seen her. Stark naked, she was stretched out on top of the eiderdown, her thick brown hair fanned out on the pillow and her long legs slightly open. 'I've been waiting for you, sweetheart,' she murmured. Her dark brown eyes smiled invitingly.

'You little bitch!' he chuckled, quickly stripping off and lying over her. He had brought the cold in with him and it made her shiver. 'I'll soon warm you up,' he promised. 'You want it as much as me, and you never said.' He would have taken her then, but she wriggled away, confusing him.

'Don't be in such a hurry,' she chided. 'Play with me . . . like you used to.' Easing him on to his back, she wrapped her small hands round his huge member, gently stroking it and whispering in his ear, 'You don't want it to be over too quickly, do you?'

'Are you after driving me mad!' he gasped. He was deeply

flustered, unable to believe his luck. 'You're a wonder and no mistake,' he said, roving his hands over her nakedness. 'I really thought I'd have to fight you for what's mine tonight.'

Gently biting his lip with her teeth, she laughed softly. 'Whatever made you think that?' she asked innocently, stroking her thumb over the tip of his bursting penis.

'For God's sake, woman!' he cried, arching his back and pulling away. 'You'll have me finished before I'm even started.' She laughed out loud then, and he, anticipating the joys ahead, laughed too.

Next door, Martha lay stiff in her bed, trying not to listen, but whatever the weather, she liked to feel the breeze coming into the bedroom, and just as Rosie had intended every lewd sound carried through the open window. Slithering out of bed so as not to waken her husband, she tiptoed to the window and closed it. But still the wanton sounds filtered through the paper-thin walls. She tried putting her hands over her ears, and buried herself under the clothes, almost suffocating. And still she could hear every groan, every moan and cry. And while she detested every sound, her husband revelled in them; lying beside her and pretending to be asleep, but all the while regretting the loss of his youth, and wishing he had chosen a more warm-blooded woman.

She tossed and turned and tried to block out the sounds by pressing her hands to her ears. It was no use. Martha could hear every movement, the rusty bed springs creating telltale images and causing chaos in her mind; the ecstatic cries and frantic moans suggested they were now in the deeper throes of love-making. She felt her blood rising and her face growing redder and redder.

In spite of it all, Martha might have remained in control until it was all over. But when the by now highly aroused Mr Selby rolled over and touched her beneath her night-gown, she screamed aloud and leapt out of bed.

Too far gone to hear anything else but his own beating heart, Doug didn't hear his mother's scream. Rosie heard though, and deliberately drew Doug deeper into her, arching her back, widening her legs and moaning so loud that he was driven to greater heights.

When she flung the door open to peer in, the sight of Doug's bare rear thrashing in and out between those slim white thighs was more than Martha could stand. 'I WANT YOU OUT OF MY HOUSE!' she yelled from the doorway. Her round eyes were bulbous and she jabbed frantically at the air, as though fending off something awful.

The intrusion triggered Doug's orgasm, and he collapsed on to Rosie with a great sigh. It was all too much for Martha who fled downstairs and into the scullery where she twice dropped the tea-caddy in her haste to make herself a hot drink to soothe her frayed nerves, after which she sat hunched beside the fire-range until dawn came. When Doug came sheepishly into the parlour, she rounded on him. 'Get shut of her! I don't want her under my roof another night!'

Fulfilled and immensely satisfied, Doug called her bluff. 'Rosie is my wife. If she goes, *I* go.' At the top of the stairs, Rosie kept her fingers crossed.

'Then you can *both* bugger off.' The idea of enduring another night like that was unthinkable. 'I want the pair of you out today.' Later, she would deal with her husband, and make him sorry he'd thought to have his wicked way with her!

Rosie took the child out of its cot. 'We've done it,' she whispered, brushing her hand against his little pink face. 'It cost more than I wanted, sweetheart, but I reckon it's not too big a sacrifice if it means we'll have a home of our own.'

The winter sun was unusually warm, and the work was laborious. Doug tipped the coal through the cellar chute, then, wiping the sweat from his face, he returned to the wagon. Throwing the empty sack over the others, he turned to the big man waiting there. 'What do *you* think, Dad?' he asked. It wasn't often he asked his dad's advice because it was usually his mam who had the most to say. This time, though, he felt the need to consult another man, and his dad was nearest.

Mr Selby hitched the full sack on to his broad shoulders. He seemed astonished that anybody should ask him anything. 'Do you *really* want to know what I think?'

'I wouldn't ask if I didn't.'

'Well, I'll tell you.' He leaned his considerable weight against the side of the wagon, arms bent up above his head and the corner of the coal sack securely caught between thick strong fingers. 'I've never said this afore but I'll say it now . . . I made the worst mistake of my life when I wed your mam. It's too late for me. But you've got a good lass in that wife o' yourn, and if you let her go, then you're a bigger bloody fool than I took you for!'

Doug had never heard his father talk in such a forth-right way. In fact, he couldn't recall him ever stringing that many words together. Anger and astonishment welled up in him. 'If your marriage ain't as it should be, happen you should look at *yourself* for the reason,' he snapped. 'It can't all be our mam's fault.'

'I thought it were *you* asking *me* for advice?'

Frustrated that his comments had fallen on deaf ears, Doug stared his father out. 'And I'll thank you not to call me a fool,' he said sullenly.

'Then don't act like one.'

'If that's all you've got to say, I wish I'd never asked you.'

The big man shrugged his shoulders, hitched up the sack of coal, and turned away. He'd said his piece. Now Doug could either listen to him or be ruled by his mam.

* * *

All day Martha marched about the house doing her chores, and never a word to say to anyone. In the evening Doug came home with two pieces of news. The first was cause for celebration. The second a bitter blow to Rosie, and cruelly curtailed any joy she might have felt. 'I've got us a house,' he told her. 'It's the one you wanted, on Castle Street.'

'Oh, Doug, that's wonderful!' she cried jubilantly. 'When can we move in?'

Swinging the key before her, he said, 'I persuaded Dad to let me take the rest of the afternoon off. Get yourself ready, woman. We're off to old Tom's on Ainsworth Street.'

Rosie couldn't disguise her disappointment. Old Tom kept a second hand shop, selling all manner of paraphernalia. 'Oh, can't we afford *new* furniture?'

'No, we can't. Old Tom'll have some good strong pieces there. That'll do us. Now, are you coming or not?'

Rosie didn't need asking twice. In no time at all, she'd brushed her rich brown hair until it shone, changed into a clean jumper and skirt, put her tweed overcoat on, and got the child tucked up in its pram. 'Ready,' she said, all smiles and lighter of heart. Perhaps life wouldn't be so bad with Doug after all, she thought hopefully.

His next words not only wiped the smile from her face, but made her realise how wrong she was to assume he might be a better man. 'By the way, I've been in to register the lad,' he casually told her as they went down the street. Martha watched from the window, cursing Rosie and wondering how she could split the two of them up.

'So you've been to the registrar? That's good,' Rosie acknowledged with a bright smile. 'I was going to suggest that we do it on the way to old Tom's.' Recalling how Peggy was certain that Doug would choose 'a manly name', she asked eagerly, 'What name have you given him?'

He gazed down on her upturned face, and for one brief moment she saw the spite in his odd-coloured eyes. 'Oh, you'll like it . . . I've called him *Adam*,' he said with a grin. 'After your old lover . . . my best mate. What's more, I reckon I'll invite him to be godfather. What do you think of that?'

Rosie was shocked. 'I think you're a bastard!'

He feigned astonishment at her reaction. 'My, my! And I thought you'd be pleased. After all, you did love the fella once, didn't you, eh? In fact, if I hadn't come along, you might even have wed him.' He knew Adam Roach was a better man than he could ever be. He suspected also that Rosie still hankered after him. Naming their son Adam was a way of reminding them both that he hadn't forgotten. And he wouldn't forgive. 'We don't want you to forget a fine man like that, do we, eh?' he sniped.

Rosie continued walking in silence, keeping her distance and despairing of her life with him. Until now she hadn't realised how insanely jealous he was. To name his son after Adam was a malicious act. It told her two things; firstly, that Doug wanted to hurt her for having been Adam's love, constantly to remind her that Adam had no claim on her now, and that she and the child belonged to *him*. Furthermore, it revealed how afraid and insecure he was; although she had been careful never to mention Adam in Doug's presence, he had somehow guessed that she was still in love with his best friend.

What Doug hadn't realised in his fever to hurt her, was that he himself would be hurt. Every time he spoke his son's name, it would be like a knife through his heart.

Anger seeped through her. If he'd intended breaking her spirit, he would be very disappointed. 'On second thoughts, I think that was a lovely idea, Doug,' she lied with the sweetest smile, gazing at the child and wishing it could have been Adam's. 'Yes, *Adam*. I think it suits him.'

It was hard to pretend delight when her heart was heavy. But she must never let him know how vulnerable she was. Tomorrow, when he was out of the way, she would go to the registrar. There was time enough and hopefully there would be no problem in rectifying the mistake. For now, though, she would keep up the pretence and show her hand later, when the smile would be wiped off Doug's face.

Rosie kept her secret well. All the way to old Tom's and right up to the day of the christening.

Chapter Four

Rosie had lived on Castle Street for three months now. The little house was her pride and joy. In a row of other like dwellings, it was conspicuous by its whiter stoned front step and new brass door-knocker. Though the window frames were rotten, and there were gaps in the roof where the tiles had fallen away, and though it was cold even in summer and bone-damp in winter, it was her beloved sanctuary, her consolation for having to suffer a man she could never love.

Complaining the whole time, Doug had been persuaded to paint all the walls; cream in the front parlour, blue in the back parlour, and pale green in the scullery. Rosie had lovingly scrubbed the floorboards and helped to lay the pretty floral-patterned lino. The windows were polished until they shone, and at last the green tapestry curtains were hung.

Two days before Christmas, old Tom had delivered the furniture on his wagon: a sturdy iron-framed double bed; a walnut wardrobe and matching set of drawers for the main bedroom; an oak sideboard; a square table and four ladder-back chairs for the back parlour; and a gas cooker that furiously spat out every time it was lit. Rosie went down Blackburn market and bought a number of scatter rugs for ten shillings, and a big flowered pot on a stand with a wilting aspidistra which revived only after a great deal of tender loving care. The furniture, curtains and bric-a-brac cost a grand total of four pounds eight shillings, and though Rosie considered that to be reasonable, Doug complained it was: 'Bloody daylight robbery!'

Rosie had risen early on this Saturday morning. Last night Doug had made love to her, and as always she had pretended to enjoy it. Afterwards she couldn't sleep. She lay in her bed, listening to the rhythm of his snores and staring out of the window at the sky beyond. As the hours ticked away, the need for sleep fell from her. In the half-light of that room, alone with her most secret thoughts, she felt strangely at peace, yet somehow unfulfilled and empty inside.

After a while she gave herself up to the beauty of a new day being born. There was something especially wonderful about watching the dawn break over the land; something so immense and miraculous it made everything else insignificant in comparison.

Doug was away to his work early. 'Jack Farnham's retiring and Dad's bought the best part of his round. Canny bugger never said a word to me neither,' he said, winking at her with the air of a man who was pleased with himself. 'There still ain't enough work to take on another man, so it means we'll have to work twice as hard ourselves. I'm not complaining though because Dad reckons it'll put a few bob extra in my wage-packet.'

'A few bob?' Rosie had been feeding little Adam, but looked up at Doug's words. 'That's not much for twice the work.'

The smile slid from his face. 'Whatever I get, you needn't worry *your* head about it, my sweet, because I'll be giving you a small increase as well . . . happen enough to put a decent breakfast in front of a working man, eh?' he complained. 'I've said nothing until now because I know money's been tight, but you don't come up to Mam's standards. I'll be expecting an improvement. So, think on.'

Rosie met his sly gaze with accusing brown eyes. 'That depends on how much extra I get in *my* wage packet,' she said boldly.

'Watch your tongue,' he warned. 'Don't get clever with me.' When she merely smiled and turned her attention to the infant, he slung his work-bag over his shoulder and stormed out.

'And good shuts to you!' Rosie whispered, smiling at the child and hugging him close when he touched his tiny finger against her lips. 'I would have said he was very well looked after, wouldn't you?' she asked. 'He's never sent off to work without a full belly, and when he comes home of a night there's always a hot meal waiting for him.' Nuzzling her face against the child's pink cheek, she grumbled, 'But I can't be expected to lay a king's table with a peasant's purse.'

In no time at all, the table was cleared and the clean crockery put away; the housework was finished, and little Adam was sound asleep in his pram. The washing was done and blowing on the line outside in the yard, and Rosie was ready for her trip into Blackburn town centre. All that remained was for Peggy to show herself, and the two of them would be off.

Studying herself in the mirror over the mantelpiece, Rosie stroked at the dark shadows beneath her eyes. 'A good night's sleep wouldn't do you no harm!' she chided. 'And your hair wants cutting.' Her brown tresses were shoulder-length, falling into deep shining waves and giving her the appearance of a little girl. But she looked tired. Excitement at having her very own home wouldn't let her sleep, and lack of spare cash wouldn't allow her a visit to the hairdresser. 'Still, you don't look too bad,' she said, winking at her own image and thinking how vain she was. Suddenly she realised she had no real reason to look nice. 'What does it matter?' she asked herself. 'Who's to care *what* I look like?' The thought of Adam flickered through her mind, but she immediately shut it out.

'Where *is* she?' Glancing at the clock, Rosie realised that Peggy was already overdue. She promised to be here at nine-thirty, and already it was a quarter to ten. 'Don't let me down, Peggy gal,' Rosie muttered as she went along the passage to the front door. 'I'll go stark staring mad if I have to keep my own company for another minute!'

It seemed a lifetime since she and Peggy had enjoyed any real time together. When they first came to live in Castle Street, Peggy came round almost every day. But Doug appeared to resent her intrusion and went out of his way to make her feel uncomfortable. Now the two friends got together only when he was out of the house.

Out on the step, Rosie shivered in the keen March wind. Hopefully, she cast her gaze up the street towards Peggy's house, but there was still no sign of her.

'Morning, luv.' Mrs Best from next-door was off to the shops. A big woman with a man-size face, she kept in touch with everything that happened on Castle Street. If you wanted to know anything, you only had to ask Mrs Best. 'Settling in all right, are you?' she enquired as she went by.

'Yes, thank you.' Rosie hoped she wouldn't stop to chat, because once Mrs Best launched into conversation, there was no stopping her. Today, though, she appeared to be in a hurry.

'That's good,' she called. 'If you need anything, you've only to ask.' Hitching her basket further up her arm, and bestowing a huge smile on her new neighbour, she quickened her step and was soon gone.

Rosie smiled, her brown eyes growing wistful as she gazed after the woman. At the top of the street a group of children sat on a wall, swinging their legs and laughing aloud as the joker in the pack began doing something to entertain them. Rosie had only lived here for a very short time, but it felt so right. Castle Street was a place where good simple folk lived out their lives in full view of their neighbours. Ragged-arsed children played on the cobbles, and mangy dogs roamed the gutters in search of any titbit that might have been dropped. Old women sat on their rickety chairs outside the front door, watching life unfurl around them and dreaming of their own long lost youth. Old men leaned on the walls and sucked their pipes, chatting earnestly to a beloved neighbour and fervently putting the world to rights. Many households relied on wages earned at the mills, quarries and factories. Folks wandered in and out of other homes as though they were one big happy family, and there was a grand sense of belonging. A sense of comradeship. And now, Rosie felt part of it too.

Fifteen more minutes and still there was no sign of Peggy. 'That's it!' Returning indoors, Rosie tucked her brown jumper into the top of her long straight skirt, then put on her smart black coat and matching beret. 'If she isn't coming to us, then we must have arranged to go to *her*!' she told the sleeping child. Softly singing, she pushed the pram up the passage and down the front steps where, locking the pram-brakes, she returned to close the front door. The sound of running feet made her turn round. It was Peggy.

'Sorry I'm late,' she said breathlessly, 'I overslept.' Her hair was standing on end and her coat was haphazardly flung about her shoulders. Running her hands over her hair to flatten it, she shrugged the coat on, buttoned it up, and grinned at Rosie who hadn't the heart to chastise her. Then taking charge of little Adam, who had woken up crying, she pushed the pram along at a furious rate, chattering incessantly about nothing in particular and making baby noises all the way down the street. Rosie couldn't get a word in. But she didn't mind. Peggy was here and they were on their way out. For the moment, that was all that mattered.

The market was busy. Pushing their way through the shoppers, they made straight for the tea rooms; the very same place they had sat on the day Rosie went to meet Adam off the train. She recalled it now, and her spirits fell. In her mind's eye she could see his face, that strong handsome face, and the wonderful smile that fell away at her news.

'Would you believe it?' Peggy plonked herself on the opposite chair. 'I'm buggered if I ain't talking to myself!' She gave Rosie a gentle kick under the table. 'Hey! I might as well not be here at all.'

Rosie was startled out of her reverie. Looking up, she gave a small laugh. 'I'm sorry, Peg,' she apologised, 'I was miles away.'

'I could see that.' She eyed Rosie with concern. 'Do you want to talk about it?'

Before Rosie could answer, the waitress arrived. She was a young surly-looking creature with sharp painted nails and long tendrils of black hair floating about her neck. 'Yurs? What can I get yer?' Rosie ordered tea and Peggy asked for a strong black cup of coffee. Without a word the waitress turned away, frantically scribbling on her pad.

'Miserable sod!' Peggy stared after her.

'Happen she's got sore feet?' Rosie suggested.

'A sore bloody head more like.' Tearing her gaze from the waitress, she turned her attention to the baby. 'Who's a little beauty then?' she cooed, tweaking his fat cheek and groaning when he began to cry. 'Bugger me. *Everybody*'s miserable today,' she remarked, frantically rocking the pram. In a moment he was fast asleep. 'Never could handle kids. They always cry at me,' she confessed with a chuckle. 'Must be my ugly mug.'

'Peggy?'

'Yes?'

Rosie was about to confide in her when the waitress returned. 'One tea . . . one strong black coffee,' she said sourly, sliding the cups along the table. 'You shouldn't really bring carriages in here. The boss don't like it.' She stared disapprovingly at the pram.

'Well now, that's a bloody shame, ain't it?' retorted Peggy. ''Cause the carriage goes where we go.'

The young woman was astonished. She gawped at Peggy, then at Rosie, then shrugged her shoulders and muttered something under her breath as she walked away. After that she kept her distance, though she occasionally glanced at Peggy sourly.

'You were saying?'

Rosie sipped at her tea, wincing when it burnt her lip. Replacing her cup on the saucer, she mused for a while, acutely aware that Peggy was waiting for an answer. Presently, she summoned the courage to tell her, 'I'm pregnant again.'

'Bloody Nora!' Peggy sighed heavily. 'But you didn't want no more, did you?'

Rosie shook her head. 'I don't mind having babies,' she admitted, looking fondly at her son. 'It's the *making* I don't much care for.'

'What? You mean . . . having it with Doug?'

Rosie smiled. Peggy had never been known for her tact. 'That's exactly what I mean,' she said. 'I know I shouldn't feel that way, but every time we . . . you know . . . I can't help but wish things were different.' It was so good to have Peggy to talk to. With her Rosie didn't have to pretend. 'I still cringe every time he touches me.'

Peggy sighed. 'I ain't much help, but . . . well, I don't see what else you can do. Have you tried denying him his rights?'

Rosie laughed. 'It's easy to see you've never been wed. I've tried it once or twice, but it's difficult to justify it for too long. And anyway, it's easier to keep him happy than it is to live with the rows and long faces. The lesser of two evils, if you know what I mean.'

'Hmph!' Peggy pulled a face. 'There's you fighting it off, and there's me can't get any at all.' When she saw that her attempt to lighten the situation had little effect on Rosie who was genuinely troubled, she frowned. 'I ain't much use to you, am I, gal?'

'More use than you think. To be honest, Peggy, I don't know what I'd do without you. Just talking helps.'

'I suppose I'm a good listener if nothing else.'

The two of them lapsed into silence, Rosie's mind on the past and Peggy thinking about the future. 'When's the baby due?' she wanted to know.

'September.' Rosie had to smile then. 'It's the price I paid to get him away from his mam.'

'Not a bad swap, eh?'

'I don't regret it. Oh, I bitterly regret *other* things. But not this baby.'

'What's playing on your mind then?'

Rosie shrugged her shoulders. 'Same as before, I expect. I'm Doug's wife, and I'm having his second child. I've made mistakes and I'm not likely ever to forget that. But if I'm to live any sort of peaceful life, I'll have to accept my lot.'

'Ain't you happy at all?'

'Oh, yes.' She caressed her son's small hand. 'There's him, and there's the little one on the way. And I've got my own front door key. Isn't that what most women want?'

'But not you, eh?' Peggy reached out to cover Rosie's hand with her own. 'You still love him, don't you? Adam, I mean?'

Rosie forced herself to smile. 'Least said, soonest mended,' she said brightly. 'Now then . . . will you be godmother to this one?' she patted her stomach.

''Course I will! I'll be proud to be godmother. But it means I'll have to buy another new outfit,' she moaned, feigning weariness. 'Have you noticed how there's so much more choice now that clothes-rationing is finished? Anyway, you wouldn't want me to wear the same outfit for the christening next week, and then again for the *new* baby's christening, would you?' she asked cheekily. 'Godmothers have to set a good example.'

Her son's christening had caused more rows between Doug and Rosie than she cared to mention. 'I'm sorry, Peggy,' she said now, 'but Doug's cancelled next week's christening.'

'Cancelled!' Peggy was obviously disappointed. 'Why?'

'I wish I knew. He just told me he'd been to the church and stopped it. He wouldn't say why. And he hasn't decided on a new date.'

'You mean he just went out and put a stop to it, without talking it over with you first?' Peggy was appalled.

'You wouldn't be so shocked at that if you knew him better. Doug Selby doesn't believe in consulting *anyone*, least of all his wife.' She smiled wryly. 'But then, there's always his mother. It wouldn't surprise me if she'd had a hand in it.'

'I thought they weren't talking?'

'So far as I know they're not. But if I've learned one thing since being wed to him, it's that he can be very deceitful.'

'But why would he cancel the christening? And how do you feel about it?'

'I was furious!' Rosie recalled the night he came home to tell her. It was midnight. He was drunk, and angry, and something else that she couldn't quite put her finger on. He seemed secretive, gloating somehow. 'We had a vicious row. I told him exactly what I thought about him doing that behind my back. I even threatened to go and see the vicar myself. But he went mad.' Instinctively she put her hand to the side of her face. It still hurt. 'He's not the easiest man in the world to talk to.'

'You mean he hit you?' Peggy had seen the way Rosie subconsciously touched her face. 'The bastard!'

'Like I said . . . least said, soonest mended. The christening's off, that's all I know. When I tackled him about a new date, he mumbled something about having the two babies baptised together. I think there's more behind it than that, but he wouldn't give me an explanation.'

'Well, I suppose, if the truth be told, having the two baptised together isn't a bad idea. It would cut the expense anyway.' She laughed. 'Bugger him! There goes my excuse to buy another outfit!'

'You're right. It would make sense, I suppose.' Rosie agreed. 'But he could have avoided a row and talked to me about it first. I would have gone along with that.'

'Have you asked him? About me being godmother, I mean?'

'No. But you're my best friend, and I can't think of anyone else who would love the children more. Besides, I can't see how he could object to that.'

'Well, I'm here when you want me. Like I say, I'd be really proud.'

'Right! Now that's settled, sup up and we'll have a browse round the stalls.' Somehow, everything always seemed much easier after she'd confided in Peggy.

The morning was delightful. The sun shone and, content in her friend's company, Rosie was soon in a better mood. They wandered the market square, stopping at every stall, examining this and that and making the usual comments women do. 'What do you reckon to this?' Peggy asked, holding up a blue shawl with a long silk fringe.

'You'd look like old Ma Riley in that,' Rosie told her. The trader was so determined not to let them get away that it was a good five minutes before they arrived at the flower stall, where Rosie bought a pretty posy of lavender.

'What am I supposed to do with this bleedin' shawl?' Peggy asked, clutching the unwanted garment.

'You shouldn't have let him talk you into it,' Rosie chided good-naturedly. 'Take it back.'

'What! I daren't go back there,' she protested, eyes as big as saucers at the thought. 'The bugger'll have me buying half his stall.'

Rosie shook her head in frustration. 'You should have said no and meant it,' she said.

'Oh, aye? And what about *you*?' Peggy dipped her hand into the pram and drew out a ghastly red cloche hat with a broken feather. 'Why didn't *you* say no?' Rosie had no answer to that. Instead, she smiled, and soon the two of them were laughing like children. Almost like magic, Rosie's troubles vanished.

'Didn't you say it was your mam's birthday in a few weeks?'

'Yes.'

'And don't you think she'd look a treat in that shawl and hat?'

'So she would!' Peggy declared. 'Why didn't I think of that?' So it was settled; the shawl and hat were reverently placed into the largest bag and laid on the pram where they wouldn't get squashed. Peggy offered to repay Rosie the threepence she'd paid for the hat, but Rosie declined. 'I would have bought her a little something anyway,' she said. And that was an end to it.

At the bric-a-brac stall, Peggy purchased a blue scarf. 'Ain't it a lovely colour?' she grinned, opening wide her blue eyes. 'It'll set off the colour of my peepers.' Rosie agreed, and promptly spent fourpence on a knitted jacket for her son in the same delightful shade of blue.

They sat beside the horse trough and shared a bag of roasted chestnuts. 'Them'll warm the cockles of yer 'eart!' yelled the newspaper man. 'Fetch us one over an' I'll give you a kiss.' Peggy told him to piss off, and he turned away, roaring with laughter.

Afterwards, they wandered down Ainsworth Street and into King Street. From there they returned at a sedate pace to Castle Street. 'It's been a lovely outing,' Rosie declared. 'It's done me a world of good.'

Peggy had intended going back with Rosie for a while, but she was waylaid by her mam. 'For Gawd's sake keep an eye on these little sods while I go down the market, else we'll have nothing for us dinner!' she wailed.

Peggy argued. 'You knew I was going down the market, Mam. Why didn't you tell me what you wanted?'

'I'm capable of doing a bit of shopping!' she snapped, straightening her hat as she rushed down the street. 'And don't you take no nonsense from 'em!' she cried. With that she went at a run to catch the tram, leaving Peggy and Rosie looking at each other in bewilderment.

'If you ask me, your mam looks like a woman at the end of her tether,' Rosie remarked.

'She's a crafty old sod, that's what she is!' Peggy chuckled. 'I fetched her groceries from the corner shop last night, and I know she don't want nothing at all from the market. It's just an excuse to get away from this brood.' By now the children could be heard causing a rumpus in the passageway, 'Look at that!' Peggy cried. 'Our mam's only been gone two minutes and I'm buggered if they ain't fighting already!' As she went up the steps at a run, the children scattered in all directions. 'I'll tan your backsides when I get my hands on you, you see if I don't!'

Rosie thought that this was as good a time as any to make her way home. 'I'll see you later,' she called, going slowly past the door and peering into the passage. There was no sign of anyone, but the excited screeches emanating from the front parlour told her there was a game of hide and seek going on. 'No wonder your mam's run off,' she called. 'I might do the same if I had that lot to contend with.' Then she went down the street, chuckling to herself all the way.

The following Friday evening, two things happened to rock Rosie's world a little more.

It was almost ten o'clock and Doug wasn't yet home. 'Down

the pub again, I expect!' Rosie muttered as she laid the child in his cot. 'He'll be coming in drunk as a lord and wanting his rights.' The thought made her cringe. 'You sleep now,' she murmured, tucking the blanket over tiny limbs. 'You must have had me up and down these stairs a dozen times since I first put you to bed.' The infant was fretful, and she was bone tired. But he seemed sleepy now, and ready to give in. 'Shh now . . . mammy isn't far away.' She stroked his face and her heart melted. His skin felt like velvet beneath her fingertips.

On tiptoe, she went downstairs where she boiled some water and made herself a cup of tea. Holding the cup between her hands, she went to the window and stared out at the yard beyond. 'It's been a long day,' she murmured. In the twilight she could just make out the cumbersome shapes of the blankets hanging heavy on the line. That morning she had gone through the house like a whirlwind; changing the bed from top to bottom and spending two hours on her knees by the tin bath, scrubbing and rubbing, rinsing and dipping those blankets, until they were as clean as the day they were bought. After the arduous task of dragging them out to the yard in the tin bath, and hanging them on the line, still dripping wet, she had then set about polishing the floor. After that she'd cleaned the windows and cleared out every cupboard where the tiniest speck of dust might be lurking.

In between, the child kept her on her feet, and later, when he was sleeping and she fell exhausted into the nearest chair, she felt the tiniest fluttering in her stomach. It could have been an attack of indigestion, or it might have been the new life flickering inside her. But it raised a touchy issue, and she grew determined to have it out with Doug when he got home. This business of the christening had been playing on her mind for too long.

The tea revived her, and she decided to do a little darning. Taking her work-basket from the sideboard, she sat in the big armchair by the fire; she hadn't lit a fire today and now the room was beginning to feel cold. Wrapping her cardigan about her shoulders, she opened her basket and took out the little knitted coat. A pretty lemon thing with silk ribbons, she had bought it from an old woman who came round the houses selling bric-a-brac. One of the cuffs had come unravelled. It was a small repair, but somehow Rosie hadn't found the time to mend it, until now.

In the lamplight, hunched over her work and concentrating on the tiny stitches, Rosie let her thoughts wander. 'Is this it for the rest of my life?' she asked herself. 'One baby after another and waiting for him to come home night after night . . . never knowing what he's thinking, and forever dependent on him?' It was a depressing prospect. The more she thought of it, the more her dreams turned to her first love.

It was gone midnight. The little parlour was quiet with only the sound of the ticking clock disturbing the silence. Rosie's work had slid to the floor and she had fallen into a restless slumber. Even the sound of Doug's footsteps coming down the passage didn't wake her. In her dreams she was troubled. In life her troubles seemed tenfold.

When Adam's hand touched her face, she pressed her own fingers over his. When his warm mouth covered hers, she sighed with happiness and clung to him. It was only when he softly laughed that her joy was shattered. 'Want me, do you, you brazen little bitch?'

'DOUG!' She stared at him with shocked eyes. 'You frightened me.' Instinctively she pulled away.

'Frightened you, did I?' The stench of booze on his breath made her reel. 'Funny. You seemed to be enjoying it.' The smile froze on his face. 'Or were you dreaming of somebody else, eh? Is that it?' His face grew hard.

He was so near the truth she could hardly breathe. 'Don't be ridiculous.'

He merely smiled, a cold calculating smile. 'Ready for bed, are you?' His hand reached out to touch her breast.

'I have some darning to do. I'll be up later.' She stooped to retrieve her work-basket from the rug.

'That can wait 'til tomorrow,' he snapped, knocking it out of her hands. The contents spilled over the floor which seemed to please him. 'Didn't you hear me? I said I was ready for bed.'

Whether it was tasting freedom in her dreams, or whether it was something about the possessive manner in which he gripped her wrist, Rosie didn't know. But something deep inside her made her want to strike out at him. '*You* may be ready for your bed,' she said with surprising calm, 'but *I'm* not. I've told you . . . I'll be up when I've finished my work.' She was astonished at herself.

He too was shocked. 'You what!' he screamed. 'I'll not have no wife of mine trying to get the better of me.' Raising the back of his hand, he fetched it down hard against the side of her face. 'You'll get to bed when I tell you!'

For what seemed an age she stared at him, her small figure stiff and unyielding and her brown eyes swimming with tears. But she wouldn't cry. She told herself she must not give him the satisfaction of seeing her cry. Even when he raised his hand again, she didn't flinch. Instead, in a steady voice that belied the churning inside her, she challenged, 'Hit me again, and you may just live to regret it.'

Amused, he laughed in her face. 'Oh? Threatening me now, is it?'

But he didn't hit her again. And Rosie would never know how her words might have affected him because a knock on the front door startled them both. Slewing round, he almost lost his balance. 'Who the hell's that at this time of night?' His wide eyes and reluctance to answer the door gave Rosie the impression that he was afraid. She wondered whether he had got on the wrong side of some of the seedy characters who frequented the same pubs.

'Hadn't you better go and see who it is?' she asked with disgust. 'After all, you're supposed to be the man of the house, aren't you?'

Her jibe cut deep. 'I'll deal with you later,' he promised. Then he straightened his jacket and went down the passage on unsteady footsteps. 'Who is it?' His anxious voice carried back to the parlour.

It satisfied Rosie to see that he was a coward. 'I hope it's somebody come to knock sawdust out of you,' she muttered, hastily gathering her work from the floor.

Muffled voices filtered down the passage. Crossing to the sideboard, where she replaced the work-basket, Rosie cocked an ear. What she heard was Doug's voice, raised in surprise at first then talking low and earnestly, and a woman's voice, replying in soft affectionate tones. The voice was familiar. 'No!' Rosie couldn't believe it. But it was true, because almost immediately Martha Selby appeared at the door.

'Look who's come to see us.' Doug was grinning from ear to ear as he ushered his mother into the parlour.

Martha said nothing. Instead she remained upright and formidable as always, her grim face expressionless as she told Rosie, 'I know what you're up to. I've known for a long time, and like a fool I let you get away with it. But I'm telling you here and now, it won't work because I refuse to be parted from my son any longer.'

Rosie was not intimidated. 'I'm not sure what you're talking about,' she lied. She knew very well that Martha was alluding to the brazen manner in which she had 'persuaded' Doug away from his mother's clutches. 'It was never my intention to part you from your son.'

'Don't take me for a fool!'

'All I ever wanted was a home of my own. There's nothing wrong with that, is there?'

The big woman looked around the room. Everything was in order; the ornaments stood proud and sparkling on the mantelpiece, and the floor was clean enough to eat off. She resented that. 'You had a good home in my house.'

'And we have a good home here . . . in our *own* house.' She had seen the resentment in Martha's eyes. She had seen the loneliness too. In a different way, it echoed her own. 'It was nothing personal, Martha,' she said kindly. 'You're a woman. You know how special it is, to have your own things about you . . . to have your own front door key.' She waited for a response, but there was none. She looked to Doug for support, but the booze had fuddled his senses and he was slumped against the side-board with a foolish grin on his face.

Rosie felt very uncomfortable. Her instincts told her she had made an enemy for life in this woman. 'It's very late, Martha. What exactly did you come for?'

She turned away, ignoring Rosie and giving her answer to Doug, who clumsily stood to attention. 'Your father's been ill ever since he got home. I'm to tell you that he won't be in tomorrow. He's paying a call on the doctor. There's nothing for you to worry about, but he's anxious that the wagon's in good hands. Are you able to take care of everything? That's what he wants to know, son. I told him you were. I asked him, "What sort of idiot do you take our lad for?" But he carried on so much I thought I'd better come round and see you. Your dad says if you can't manage on your own, you're to get that lad from Taggett Street.'

Doug laughed. 'What! He's more bloody useless than a boot without laces. I can manage better on my own. You tell Dad that.'

'I already told him, son.'

His face crinkled into a smile. 'Aw, Mam! I'm glad you've

come to see us. I didn't like it when we weren't talking.' He glanced at Rosie, but addressed his mother. 'Take no notice of her. She don't mean nothing.'

Martha wasn't convinced. Returning her attention to Rosie, she asked frostily, 'How's my little grandson?'

It was Doug who answered, 'He's abed. You can go and see him if you like, Mam.' He looked at her like a little boy trying to please. 'Up the stairs, first on the left.'

Without a word, but maliciously smiling at Rosie through narrowed eyes, Martha turned and departed, going slowly up the stairs on leaden feet and striking the fear of God into Rosie's heart. She'd never thought to see Martha Selby in this house, leave alone going up the stairs and into the bairn's room. As if Doug wasn't enough to contend with, she now had his mother on her back again. God forbid!

'You make her welcome, do you understand?' Doug glared at her. 'She's my mam, and there's been enough bad feeling.' That said, he slumped into the nearest chair, laying his head against the wall and closing his eyes. 'I don't feel well,' he moaned.

'Are you saying *I* caused the trouble?'

He didn't move a muscle, but his voice was menacing. 'I'm just saying, don't get above yourself, if you know what I mean.' Rosie knew all right. He was still smarting because, far from cowering when he'd hit her just now, she had dared to challenge him.

When Martha came back down the stairs she was bristling. 'He's too thin by far,' she told Rosie. 'And there aren't enough blankets over him.' Before Rosie could answer, she told Doug, 'I expect you to do something about that.' At once sitting up, he assured her that he would.

'And what about the christening? Isn't it time you got that organised?' She looked from one to the other. 'If it's too much trouble, you'd better let *me* do it.'

Rosie was quick to point out that the date had been set for next week, and she would have let Martha know but, 'Your son cancelled it.' Just as Rosie anticipated, Martha rounded on Doug, and he took it like the coward he was.

After his mother had gone, he blamed Rosie. 'Why did you have to go and tell her that?'

'I wasn't aware it was a secret.' A thought occurred to her. 'Come to think of it, why didn't you tell her we were having another child?' He didn't answer. Unperturbed, Rosie pursued the other matter. 'And why didn't you tell her *why* you cancelled the christening?'

'I'm not answerable to her.'

Rosie was stunned. 'You used to tell your mam everything.'

'Not everything.'

'You do mean for our son to be christened, don't you?'

'Don't be bloody stupid, woman. Of course I do!'

'Then why don't you tell *me* what's behind your thinking?'

'You mean you don't know?' He grinned, crossing his legs and lying back in the chair. His odd-coloured eyes appraised her while he took his time in explaining, and when he spoke it was with a deal of cunning. 'I've written to a mutual friend, and I'm waiting for a reply.'

Something in his manner made Rosie's heart turn cold. 'What do you mean?'

'We can't have a christening without a godfather, can we? And we want the very best for our precious son, don't we?' He was enjoying the feeling of power he held over her at that moment. 'I'm sure you'd agree that the best is Adam.' The horror on her face spurred him on. 'Yes, that's right, sweetheart . . . my best friend, and yours, Adam Roach. Soldier and gentleman. Surely you can't have forgotten him? You couldn't forget a man you once promised to wed? No, of course not.' Stumbling close, he leered at her. 'I've no doubt you didn't resist when *he* wanted to make love, eh?'

Rosie was repelled. 'Are you saying you've actually written to him? I knew you mentioned it some time ago, but I thought you were just being vindictive.' She realised she should have known better.

'I've written to the regiment. No doubt he'll get the letter in good time, and when he does, I expect he'll be overjoyed. After all, if I hadn't taken you from him, you'd be wed to him now, and it might be him asking *me* to be godfather to your son.'

'You'll never let it go, will you?'

Taken aback by the hatred in her eyes, he wanted to tear out her heart. 'I'll let it go when you stop wanting him,' he hissed. Then he covered his head with his hands and bawled like a child.

Sickened, Rosie left him there. That night she slept in the chair beside her son's cot. Dear Lord, don't let Adam come anywhere near us, she pleaded. Because if you do, I can't answer for the consequences.

Doug was right. She would never stop wanting the better man. Adam Roach would always be the man for her. But Doug was the man she had settled for, and that was the ugly truth. Her whole empty future lay before her. There was no hope now. And it was *that* which was so unbearable.

'What am I supposed to do with this?' The plump and homely Mrs Jason was exasperated as she showed her husband a letter which had arrived that very morning. 'Should I send it back and say he's no longer living here, or should I try and find him? I wouldn't really know where to start though, because he didn't leave a forwarding address. All he told me was that he intended going up in the world, and that one day he meant to have his own coal-merchant's.'

'Sounds like you're talking about Adam Roach?' he remarked. 'I don't know about going up in the world. Not when he couldn't even get a job round these parts.'

'That's because there's very little work to be had in the Midlands right now. If you ask me, it's time the government put its thinking cap on. There are too many young men out of work, more's the pity.' Placing the offending article in front of him, she began to pour out the tea. 'That letter looks important, don't you think?' Sitting bolt upright in the chair, she took up a plate in one hand and a ladle in the other. Scooping out a huge helping from the large oval dish, she dropped it on to the plate. 'Steak and kidney pie. Your favourite,' she announced proudly as the aroma permeated the room. Indicating the various dishes positioned centrally on the table, she told him, 'There's peas and carrots, oh, and both lodgers are out, so there's only me and you for dinner, Ted. So eat hearty. It's a sin to waste good food.'

He was delighted. 'No lodgers, eh? It'll make a nice change to sit at my own table without strange faces watching every mouthful I take,' he grumbled. 'I never did like you taking in lodgers.'

'There, there, dear,' she coaxed. 'When your rheumatism stopped you working, it seemed a good idea to have lodgers. You must admit, they've never been a problem.' She stroked her greying hair and gazed dreamily at the unopened letter lying beside his plate. 'We've had some very nice people staying under this roof,' she said. 'You can't deny that.'

'Hmph!' he snorted. Snatching up the letter, he stared at it through angry eyes. 'I suppose you're talking about *this* fellow again, eh?'

'Adam Roach was a nice young man, and I'm sorry he's gone.'

'Are you now?' He turned the letter over in his hand. 'Well, *I'm* not! You women are all the same . . . all it takes is a good-looking fella and you can't think straight no more.'

'Don't be ridiculous, Ted. I'm old enough to be his mother.' In fact, the reason she had taken to Adam was because she had given away a son many years ago. With his dark hair and black eyes, Adam reminded her of the child.

Ted also had memories. But where *she* kept them alive, he tried desperately to bury them. 'I know, love. I'm sorry. But you can't keep torturing yourself. When you gave that infant away all those years ago, it was because I'd let you down. If I'd offered to wed you then, instead of running off like a coward, we could have kept the boy.' He bent his head and covered his pale eyes with large, surprisingly smooth hands. 'He's gone,' he murmured, 'and he's never coming back.' The look he gave her was filled with pain. 'The sooner you realise that, the better.'

She didn't answer. Instead she looked away and the gesture appeared to infuriate him. 'Let's see what we've got here,' he snapped, staring at the official stamp on the envelope. 'This is from the armed forces. I thought he was demobbed?' He remarked curiously. 'Didn't you say his papers came through to this address soon after he came here?'

'They did. And he *was* demobbed.'

'Oh, aye? A deserter more like!' Ripping open the envelope, he was surprised to find another, smaller envelope inside. Reading the accompanying letter he said aloud, 'It's a forwarded letter.' Tearing open the smaller envelope he read silently, explaining, 'It's from a mate of his . . . Doug Selby . . . wants him to be godfather to his son.' The letter was like salt being rubbed into a wound. 'I'll tell you what to do with this!' he cried. Tearing the two letters into tiny fragments, he dropped them into his saucer and lit them with a match from his waistcoat pocket. '*That's* what you do!' He watched the paper blacken and curl. 'He's gone from this house, and with the help of the Lord we'll never clap eyes on him again.' With that he went out of the room on slow tortuous footsteps. As he went upstairs his crippled legs pained him more than he could ever remember. Once inside the bedroom, he sat in the chair by the window and stared out across the rooftops.

A few moments later his wife found him hunched over and sobbing pitifully. 'I'm sorry,' she said, holding him close.

'No,' he murmured, 'it's me that should be sorry. Sorry for what I've done to you. Sorry for being the failure I am.' He turned to look at her with pitiful eyes. 'But I'm *not* sorry for destroying that letter. That young man who stayed here . . . Adam Roach . . . he wasn't your son, Doreen. I know it and you know it. And you've got to stop imagining that our lad will just turn up on the door-step one day, because he won't. Do you hear what I'm saying, love? HE WON'T!' He could feel the warmth of her tears on his face and bitterly regretted all the heartache he had caused her. 'We've got each other,' he said. 'And we should thank the good Lord for that.'

Chapter Five

Adam had worked on the sidings for almost three weeks now. Shovelling coal was a thankless task, hard and back-breaking, but it was good honest work, and in these times of unemployment, he was grateful just to be earning a living. His shoulders were broadened and honed by his labours, and his skin was tanned by the May sunshine that had spilled from a clear blue sky every day since he'd come to work at the yard.

'Put your bloody shovel down, man!' The fat fellow had come up behind him. 'Are you working right through your break or what?' Settling himself on an upturned box which groaned beneath his considerable weight, he swung the bag from his shoulder and took out a snap can. Inside the can was a pile of sandwiches, a great chunk of meat pie, and a container of cold tea to swill it down with. 'By! Me stomach thinks me throat's cut,' he chuckled. 'If it does nothing else, this work builds a man's appetite, and that's a fact.'

Adam leaned on his shovel. Stripped to the waist, he was a fine figure of a man. 'I had no idea it was that time,' he admitted, wiping the grimy sweat from his brow.

'Well, it *is*!' the other man affirmed. 'So knock off, for Chrissake. If the boss sees you working through your break, he'll make it a regular thing.' He frowned, casting a glance towards the shed where the foreman was watching. 'I don't know . . . you young 'uns seem to have too much energy for your own good.'

Propping his shovel against the heap of coal, Adam flicked the top layers of dust from his trousers. 'Not so much of the "young 'uns" if you don't mind,' he chuckled. 'I'll be twenty-seven next birthday, and that's only spitting range from being thirty.' He stretched his arms above his head and flexed every muscle in his strong lithe body. Then he went with long strides to the wagon, collected his lunch-box, and returned to sit beside his colleague. 'There aren't many wagons in today,' he observed ruefully. 'I reckon things are slackening off.' He bit into his apple and cast a wary eye along the row of wagons still waiting to be loaded. There were three. Normally there would have been six or seven.

'You're right,' the other man agreed. Blowing the coal-dust from his sandwich and sinking his large white teeth into it, he gazed dolefully at the line of wagons. 'Heard summat interesting in the pub last night,' he said confidentially.

'Oh, aye?'

'There's talk that Ben Saxon's in trouble.' He shook his large head, gulped down a mouthful of tea and wiped his mouth with the back of his hand. 'If *he* goes under, there'll be even less wagons, then we'll have to watch out for us jobs. If the merchants are having a hard time of it, they'll not be wanting the coal, and that means *we* won't be needed neither.'

'Surely it won't come to that?'

'I'm telling you! You've only to look at them there wagons.' Pointing to the three vehicles, he went on, 'And not one of 'em belonging to Saxon. It's a crying shame because he's a good man, with a good reputation. It goes without saying that if a man of his calibre can't keep his head above water, there's hard times ahead for us all.' He leaned forward as though imparting a secret. 'Truth is, I've heard he might have to sell up.'

'What? Lock, stock and barrel?'

The other man nodded, his face serious beneath the sooty mask. 'All ten wagons . . . the yard . . . house and everything.' He shook his head wisely. 'Ben Saxon's father started that business years ago. If it's sold now, it'll be a household name gone forever. What! Saxon's coal-merchant's was delivering round these parts when I were a snotty-nosed kid.'

Adam was thinking ahead. Though he was sorry for the old fellow, he was excited by a certain idea. 'How much do you reckon he'll get for it . . . if he *does* sell up, I mean?'

The fat fellow shrugged. 'Who can tell? That big old house is run down, the wagons are past their best, and as for the yard, well, there's been good yards standing empty round here since afore the war, so folk ain't likely to be queuing for it.' His white teeth tore off another chunk of the sandwich. 'In these bad times, I shouldn't think the whole lot will fetch more than a couple of thousand pounds.'

'You're forgetting the rounds, goodwill and all that. What price there?' Though two thousand pounds might as well be *ten* thousand, and every penny of it out of his reach, the germ of an idea was growing in his mind, giving him an urge to satisfy his curiosity.

Following Adam's train of thought, the fat fellow laughed aloud. 'Looking to start your own round, eh?' he teased.

'Happen.'

'You must be mad! I said you young 'uns had too much energy for your own good!'

'It was just a thought.'

'Have you got a pile of banknotes hidden away?'

'A few.'

'Not anything like enough, I'll bet,' he chuckled.

'No,' Adam confessed. 'Nowhere near. But I've saved most of my wages and I had a fair bit saved before I came here.' For one precious moment he remembered Rosie, and his heart was full. 'Saved it for a wedding that never happened,' he murmured, the memories flooding back to pain him.

His workmate was lost for words. He had seen how Adam's mood had changed. 'A wedding, eh?' he prompted, thinking he might be further enlightened. When Adam kept his own counsel, he quipped good-naturedly, 'I ain't never seen a wedding yet that would cost anything like the money you'd need to set up a coal-round.'

'Start small, grow big,' Adam said.

'It ain't as easy as that. Have you been in business afore?'

'No. But there's always a first time. Every successful businessman has to start somewhere.'

'And how do you reckon you could build up a round from scratch?'

'I'm not sure yet, but if I made my mind up, I'd give it a damn good try.'

'Capable of fighting off men who've already got a foot in the door, are you? Men who'll stop at nothing to keep their own patch?'

'I'd not be much of a man if I let myself be frightened off.' What had begun as an impossible dream, was now fixed determination. 'Yes. Given the chance, I reckon I could make it work all right,' Adam declared boldly.

The fat fellow shook with laughter. 'Talk about a dog pissing agin the wind!' he roared. When Adam remained grim-faced, he studied him with new respect. 'Tell you what,' he promised in a serious voice, 'the day you make boss, I'll be the first to take me hat off to you.'

The two men lapsed into thoughtful mood. The fat fellow regretted the passing of his youth and all that fire in his loins, and Adam couldn't let go of the idea that he should be looking to start out on his own.

'Happen there's no truth in what you heard?' he suggested.

'About Ben Saxon selling up. You know how rumours run away with themselves.'

'Oh, there's truth in it all right. No rumour starts without cause. Ben Saxon's ready to sell. That's the beginning and end of it.'

'It's a pity all the same,' Adam said honestly.

'Well, the old fella's had a good run for his money . . . been in the business nigh on forty years, has old Ben. I expect he's too long in the tooth now, and what with the young 'uns coming up and snatching the work from under his nose well, it's dog eat dog, and old Ben ain't got no teeth left to fight 'em off.'

'I would have thought there'd be room enough for healthy competition. There'll always be a demand for fuel.' Adam roved his eye over the mountainous heaps of coal. Brought from the pits in railway wagons, the coal had first been graded, then tipped into various bays. The highest grade was black and shiny, large jagged chunks that burned slowly and gave out a strong degree of heat; the lowest grade was little more than grey scrapings that congealed in the fire-grate, and turned to ashes quicker than most. The coal was taken to the merchants, who bagged it and took it round the streets to the house-holders. It was a dirty messy business, but a necessity of life. 'I'm not arguing that times aren't hard,' he admitted, 'because they are. But when they've to tighten their belts, folk will always put heat and food first,' he observed shrewdly.

'Aye. That's true enough. But coal's expensive, and Liverpool folk are canny. When needs must, they'll burn anything rather than fork out precious money for a bag of coal. Some of 'em will take the doors off the hinges, or rip up the floorboards. And who's to blame them, eh? When all's said and done, the landlord ain't to know, is he? And anyway, there's allus plenty of flotsam and timber lying about the docks. Burns well does that . . . especially if it's coated with tar.'

From the window of the shed, the foreman cast a regretful eye over the two men. 'Which one though?' he asked the gangly bespectacled fellow seated behind the desk. 'Now that it's between these two, which of 'em do we let go?'

'Last in, first out,' replied the other man without raising his eyes from his paperwork. 'That's the proper way.'

'Not always the best though. The fat fellow must be knocking on forty.'

'I've known Ted Laing a good many year, and I've always found him to be worth two men.' The boss looked up then, his thin flat face expressionless. 'Has he slacked off or caused any trouble?'

'No. But Adam Roach works like a horse, and he's years younger. That must count for something?'

'In my experience young men become ambitious, and sooner or later they'll be looking to move on. Ted Laing has a family. He can't afford to move anywhere.' His small eyes drilled into the other man's face. 'We've four men working these sidings. With work dropping off, we can manage with three. Get rid of Roach.'

The foreman shrugged his shoulders. 'You're the boss.'

'And don't forget that. You can tell Roach that once work picks up . . . and it always has . . . he's welcome to his job back.' That said, he returned his attention to the paperwork, leaving the foreman wondering how he might tell Adam that he was to pick up his cards and be on his way.

Three days later, on Friday afternoon, the men queued for their wages. As always, Adam was the last to finish work. By the time he came to the window, the other men were sauntering off, counting the notes in their wage packets and putting aside the price of a jar of ale before they delivered the money to their wives.

'Cheer up, mate,' Adam told the grim-faced foreman, 'it's a Friday. You've a whole weekend before you.'

'I'm sorry.' The foreman regarded him with serious eyes, 'I've been told to let you go.'

'What do you mean, "let me go"?' He knew exactly what that meant, but was reluctant to believe it.

The foreman handed him a fat wage-packet. 'You'll find your week-in-hand, together with a good bonus in there. You've earned it. But the boss says we've to cut down on manpower, and you're it.' He threw out his arms. 'If it had been up to me, I'd have kept you on. I'm sorry, mate.'

Adam was momentarily lost for words. Presently he told the other man, 'As long as it wasn't my work that was unsatisfactory.'

'Good God, no!' The foreman's relief was obvious. He'd seen some men turn nasty when they were handed their cards. And this particular fellow could no doubt flatten him with one blow if he took a mind. 'You're one of the best workers we've had here,' he explained. 'What's more, the boss says when trade picks up, you can gladly have your job back.'

'*If* I want it.' Adam had other things on his mind; like a coal-round of his very own. 'First time in my life I've ever been given my cards. But who knows? It might be a blessing in disguise.'

The foreman was intrigued, smiling with him. 'Oh? Got something up your sleeve, have you?' he queried.

Adam touched his nose with the tip of his finger. 'Who knows?' he hinted. 'I just might come back as a customer.' With that he stuffed the wage packet in his pocket and went away whistling. At the gate he turned back and surveyed the blackened heaps. 'See you,' he called to the foreman, who had followed his progress across the yard.

'Aye. Best of luck, mate,' he returned. Then he went inside to tell the boss, 'In my opinion you've let the best man go.'

'You're not paid to have opinions,' snarled the thin-faced

misery, rising from his seat. Going to the coat stand, he grabbed the black bowler hat and rammed it on his head. 'I suppose I can leave you to lock up, can I?' he said sarcastically. Without waiting for an answer, he went outside and cranked his little black car until it spluttered into life. Clambering inside, he fussed and fidgeted, before being carried away in a series of jerks and spurts as the vehicle negotiated the many hollows and mounds that littered the unmade road. They got as far as the gate before the car coughed and died, reviving only when its ungrateful owner got out and gave it another cranking, swearing and moaning the whole time.

'Serves you right!' The foreman kept out of sight in case he should be called on to exert himself. 'It'd do you good to catch a tram . . . or even *walk* home like the men who sweat for you.' He was still rankled about having to give a good man his cards. Still and all, he felt in his bones that: 'We ain't seen the last of Adam Roach. Not by a long chalk.'

Chapter Six

Dell Place was a miserable little dead end near the Liverpool docks. The houses were terraced and the landlords, greedy to cash in on the shortage of living accommodation in this area, had divided the houses into rooms and the rooms into cubicles, where often a whole family would reside in poverty.

Here, the stench of fish from the docks permeated the air, and the many sounds kept a body from sleeping: drunken sailors released from months at sea and let loose to fill their bellies with booze; street women making love against the walls with men hungry after being deprived for too long. Vicious dogs roamed the neighbourhood, and men fought each other with knives and fists. There were robbers and scoundrels and people who would steal the shirt from your back. But, amid all this, the ordinary law-abiding folk eked out a living where they could; good God-fearing neighbours who helped each other when times were hard.

Adam lived at number two, in a dingy room at the top of two flights of stairs. From his window he could see the cobbled streets below, and if he raised his eyes he could make out ships anchored in the docks, their tall masts and chimneys creating a unique skyline. In this neighbourhood life went on twenty-four hours a day, a throbbing pulsing ebb that flowed from the docks and swamped everything around. He didn't mind it here. He would mind it even less if he lived on Albert Street. That was where Ben Saxon lived.

'Happen he'll sell the furniture with the house,' Adam mused aloud. He stared round the room, a tiny place with a single iron bed up in one corner, a sink in the other, a small table and two chairs, a crotchety old settee with the stuffing hanging out, and a faded rug covering the floorboards in the centre of the room. 'Anything would be an improvement on this lot!'

Since coming in from work, he had sat by the table with a mug of strong tea, his wages spilled out before him, and his heart filled with regret. 'What made you do it, Rosie?' he murmured, gazing at the one picture he had of her.

Held with great tenderness, the picture lay in his palm. So many times he had meant to throw it away, but couldn't bring himself to do it; not even when he reminded himself that she now belonged to someone else. 'I love you so much, sweetheart . . . always will. We could have been so happy, you and me.' Big brown eyes smiled back at him, and it was more than he could bear.

Going to the wash-basin, he began to shave. With the lather thick and rich on his face, he studied himself in the discoloured mirror. 'Don't kid yourself, Roach,' he chided softly. 'Rosie made her choice, and it wasn't you. So you might as well get on with your life. There's no future in being head over heels in love with a woman when she prefers your best mate.'

But he *was* head over heels in love, and for too long all his thoughts, all his plans, had revolved around Rosie. He couldn't altogether blame her. He hadn't written, so what was she to think? Even then she might have come to him, but his pride got in the way. He deeply regretted that. Some time ago he had even gone back to Blackburn, only to learn that Rosie and Doug were wed. It had taken him a long time to come to terms with that. Yet every day was like a new penance, and in spite of everything, it was hard to see a future without her.

He shaved, stripped and washed all over. In no time at all he was ready for out. In his blue cord trousers and open-necked dark shirt, he was incredibly handsome. His thick black hair shone like new coal, and his dark eyes sparkled with the confidence of a man with a plan. A plan to set him on a new path.

He gathered up his money. With the back week and the bonus it amounted to forty-one pounds. Together with the rest of his money, which was in the bank – representing the major part of his wages while he was in the forces, and the main bulk of his earnings since – the grand total came to two hundred and twenty pounds. 'It might have been enough to pay for a wedding and a down payment on a house in Rosamund Street.' He hadn't forgotten how Rosie had always wanted a house on Rosamund Street. 'But I can't see it putting me in with the big boys.' His strong features broke into a smile. 'Still, it's a nice little pile all the same. With a bit of luck, it might be enough to get me started.'

After taking out eight shillings for the rent and five for a night out, he carefully replaced his wages behind the loose brick in the chimney-breast. First thing Monday morning, with the exception of a few shillings to feed himself, the money would go into the bank with the rest of his savings.

Winding his way round a warring couple and pausing to play hopscotch with a group of giggling children, Adam came out of Dell Place and into Fish Street. From there he went along Merseyside and down towards Albert Street. He had an idea in mind, and wouldn't enjoy a pint until he'd put the idea to a certain Mr Saxon. The nearer he came to Albert Street, the better he felt and the more merrily he whistled. 'Steady as you go, Roach,' he warned himself as he approached the house. 'You're still not certain the old fella means to sell up. What's more, you're a stranger to him and may not be welcome.'

Albert Street was a long winding row of narrow terraced houses. Like every other street of its kind, it had a life of its own. From one house could be heard the voices of a man and his woman having a raging argument; four doors away, a middle-aged mother sat on a chair, her withered breast hanging over a stark white blouse and a tiny infant sucking contentedly at the nipple. Some way off two dogs were fighting over a bone, while nearby a group of children played five-stones on the cobbles.

Ben Saxon's house straddled the corner. It was a big old Victorian building with a multitude of windows and a wonderful carving over the porch. But it was past its prime; the window-frames were rotting and the whole place appeared to be sagging in the middle. Through the wooden gates at the side, Adam could see the yard with its many bays, still half-filled with coal. At the far end, an old grey gelding peered out from his stables, sad-eyed and lonely.

Having come along the length of Albert Street and now standing before Ben Saxon's house, Adam thought of all kinds of reasons why he should turn tail and head for the pub. 'Happen it *is* all a rumour,' he told himself. 'Happen he'll run me up the road with a shovel . . . and so he should, you cheeky bugger!' His courage almost deserted him when a white head appeared at the window, narrowed eyes regarding him with hostility. But, no. He had come this far, and he might as well see it through.

Adam had his arm raised ready to knock on the door when it was flung open and a little wizened figure thrust itself at him. 'What do you want here?' it demanded, small dark eyes staring him up and down.

Being on the bottom step, with the little man peering down on him, Adam felt at a disadvantage. More than that, he was aware that a group of youths had gathered at the sight of a stranger down their street. One of them was standing nearby with one foot on the kerb. 'Anything wrong, old man?' he asked, addressing Ben Saxon.

The old fellow shook his fist. 'Bugger off,' he snapped.

The young man laughed. 'Threatening me, are you, Grandad?' He leered at the others who sensed a rumpus brewing. 'Hear that, did you?' the scruffy youth asked. 'The miserable old sod don't like me taking an interest.'

The other youths grinned and began to close ranks. 'I'd call that real ungrateful,' said a large red-faced lad. 'Especially when there's a *stranger* standing on his step. I mean . . . how are we to know he ain't here to cause trouble?' He stared at Adam whose expression hardened when the lout asked, 'What have you to say to that, Mister?'

Turning to face him, Adam smiled. 'What would you *like* me to say?' Bracing himself, he remained ready and confident.

The lout laughed aloud. 'See what I mean? This bugger's a troublemaker if ever I saw one!' he told the others. Glaring at the old man, he warned, 'You should know better than hobnobbing with troublemakers. Round here, we like to keep ourselves to ourselves.' Returning his attention to Adam, he suggested slyly, 'I reckon you'd best be on your way.'

'I'll be on my way when I've finished my business here, and not before.'

Loud hoots greeted his words. 'Oh, and what "business" would that be then?'

'Not *yours*.'

'My, my! Looks like we'll have to teach you a lesson, big fella.' The youth stepped forward, his eyes round and staring as he dipped into his pocket and drew out a chain. Wrapping it round his knuckles, he told the others, 'This one's mine!'

Whipping off his jacket, Adam tied it round his arm. He didn't speak. But there was a look in his dark eyes that momentarily halted the youth, who glanced back to make certain the others were not far away. The only one to move was the old man who quickly shuffled back into the house, muttering and swearing beneath his breath.

'Come on then, big fella!' goaded the youth, giggling nervously when Adam stood his ground, shoulders broad and straight, and grim determination shaping his features. 'I'm gonna have to give you a hiding.' He tightened the chain round his wrist and turned to laugh at his friends.

None of them saw the old man return, and when the broom-head caught the youth in the nape of the neck, sending him sprawling across the pavement, everyone was stunned with shock.

Adam glanced up to see the old man jabbing at the air with his brush and warning the open-mouthed youths to: 'Bugger off, the lot of you! I ain't so old that I've forgotten how to look after myself!'

Suddenly, the one who had first accosted Adam started chuckling. 'You silly arse, Bernard,' he cried, pointing at the lad on the ground. 'Ain't I always told you to watch out for your back!' Soon they were all laughing aloud and the tension was eased.

Even the big lad sprawled on the ground could see the funny side of it. 'I ain't never gonna live this down,' he giggled; in truth he was immensely relieved that he didn't have to test the stranger after all. 'Floored by an old fella with a broom-head!' Gripping the back of his neck, he winced. Which only made the others laugh all the more.

Scrambling to his feet, he glanced first at the old man and then at Adam. 'You're lucky I'm in a good mood,' he bragged. Then he threw his arm round the other lad, and the pack of them went away down the street, their laughter lingering even after they had turned the corner.

'They're all right,' the old man said, 'They're Liverpudlians . . . high-spirited that's all.' Propping the broom against the wall, he invited, 'You'd best come in and state your business.'

As they went down the passageway, he turned his head to glance at his visitor. 'What name do you go by?'

'Adam.'

'Adam what?'

'Roach . . . Adam Roach.' They turned into the parlour. The stench of damp made Adam wrinkle his nose. He lost no time in putting on his jacket. Outside the May sunshine warmed the air, but in here the cold had bitten right through his shirt.

The inside of the house was surprisingly tidy. There was little furniture in the parlour; only a chest of drawers, two horsehair armchairs by the fireplace – one a rocker and one a tall-backed uncomfortable-looking article, and a square oak table surrounded by four high-backed chairs.

'Sit yourself down. I'll make us a brew.'

Adam did as he was bid. The old fellow ambled into the adjoining scullery, and soon returned with two mugs of steaming tea, one of which he placed on the table in front of Adam. 'I can't recall the name Roach, and I know most of the families about here.' Seating himself, he regarded Adam with some curiosity. 'But then, you don't *sound* as though you're from these parts?'

'I've no family. I went into the forces when I was seventeen, and I'm recently demobbed.' He felt as though he was being interrogated, but the quicker he satisfied the old man's curiosity, he thought, the sooner they could get down to business. 'And you're right, I'm not from these parts. I was born and bred in Blackburn.'

'Hmm. Blackburn, eh? Town of pubs, church spires and cotton-mill chimneys. I should have thought you'd have been able to find work there?' He blew on the hot liquid and carefully sipped while waiting for a reply.

When Adam remained silent, he said knowingly, 'Ah! Don't want to talk about it, eh? No doubt there's a woman involved.' He scanned Adam's handsome face, that coal-black tumbling hair and those dark brooding eyes. And he was convinced that some woman somewhere had caused him grief.

'I'm sorry about that little argument out there.' Deliberately drawing the conversation away from himself, Adam recalled the confrontation on the steps. 'They won't give you any trouble when I'm gone, will they?'

Ignoring Adam's question, the old man remarked, 'You could have wiped the floor with the lot of 'em. I'd put money on it. Matter of fact, happen I should have let you get on with it. It's been a long time since I enjoyed a bloody good set-to.'

Adam laughed. 'And what makes you think I could have wiped the floor with them? That red-faced bloke was built like a Churchill tank.' He took a great gulp of his tea. It warmed him through.

'You've worked on the sidings, that's why.'

'How do you know that?'

'I've only to look at you.' He eyed Adam's physique with pride. 'I've been a coal-merchant all my life . . . and my faither afore me. Working on the sidings . . . shovelling the stuff from morning 'til night . . . that sorts the men from the boys, I can tell you.'

'I *did* work on the sidings.'

'Oh?'

'Been given my cards.'

'Can't say I'm surprised. There isn't much money about. Every day it gets harder to earn a living.' He glanced at the picture on the wall. 'That's Arnold Saxon, my father.' Waiting for Adam to turn and look, he went on, 'In all the years we've been coal-merchants, I can't recall a time as bad as this.' He gazed at the picture for a while, lost in the past and despairing of the future.

Glancing round that spartan room, Adam thought it strange there appeared to be no picture of Ben Saxon's mother. He wasn't to know Ben's father burned every reminder of her after she ran off with a tailor from Manchester. The old man was remembering though, and his eyes welled with tears. After a while, he remarked, 'I suppose you know I'm selling up?'

'That's what I heard.'

'And that's why you're here?'

Adam felt uncomfortable. 'I feel a bit like a jackal after blood,' he apologised, 'but you know the way it is . . . if you don't get in quick, you might live to regret it.'

'Go on.'

'I had a mind to set up on my own.'

'What? As a coal-merchant?' The old man's eyes widened in disbelief. 'I've only just told you what hard times we're living through. Besides, shovelling on the sidings is a lot different from being a coal-merchant.'

'I know that.'

'Oh?'

'Before I went into the forces, I worked for a coal-merchant in Blackburn. The hours were long and the work was back-breaking, but it taught me a lot. I reckon I could put all that to good use.'

'What were the name of this 'ere coal-merchant?'

'Selby. He was a good man . . . quiet and hard-working.'

Ben Saxon shook his head. 'Selby, eh? Never heard of him.'

'He had just the one wagon . . . he worked it with me and his son, Doug. Doug and I went to school together . . . grew up like brothers we did.' While he talked he remembered.

Like brothers we were, and while I was still in the forces, he was busy stealing the girl I loved. In his mind's eye, he could see old man Selby, and with that image came the image of Doug and Rosie, and the pain was deep as ever.

'So! You know a bit about coal-merchanting. But you've little chance of making it work here. Go home and think about it, that's my advice to you.'

Adam was undeterred. 'I've got no job, and little prospect of one. As you say, times are hard and there's not much about. What have I got to lose?'

'How much money have you?'

'A little over two hundred pounds.'

The old man roared with laughter. 'You're wasting your time,' he said at length. 'When this lot goes under the hammer, I'm looking for upwards of *three thousand*! Can you raise that sort of money?'

Adam gave no reply. Instead, he sipped at his tea and thought long and hard.

'You can't, can you?' The old man grew angry. 'You're a dreamer, just like the bloody rest.'

Adam looked up. 'The rest?'

'Aye! You didn't think you were the only one that's knocked on that door with an idea to buy me out afore I got to auction?'

''Course not,' Adam lied, 'but I'm not looking to buy you out altogether,' he explained hopefully. 'I never thought I'd have anywhere near enough money to do that.'

'What is it you're after then? Out with it.'

'A wagon. One sound wagon to get me started . . . two dozen sacks of best coal, and a good round. That's all.'

'You've got a nerve, I'll give you that.'

'So we can talk business?'

'No, we bloody *can't*!' The old man leaned back in his chair and looked at Adam through new eyes. 'I've had some cheeky buggers here, but you take the biscuit,' he declared without malice. 'You come to my house with two hundred pounds in your pocket and expect to get started up in business? Have you any idea how much blood and sweat went into building them rounds? Have you the slightest inkling of how much a good wagon costs new?' Before Adam could answer, he went on, 'Well, I'll tell you! The best part of four hundred quid, that's what. And I've kept my wagons good. They'll fetch a handsome price or my name's not Saxon.'

'You just finished telling me how times are bad,' Adam reminded him. 'The wagons may not fetch as much as you hope.'

The old man studied him for a while before he spoke again. 'Finish your tea and get out.' Standing up, he leaned forward, fists resting on the table. 'You're full of fresh ideas and brimming with energy . . . eager to get started on someone else's back. Well, it won't be *mine*.' He saw himself in Adam, and it only reminded him how old and frail he had become. Once he too had been young and virile, filled with energy and raring to go. Where had it all gone? What happened to his youth? What price the dreams of wife and family? He envied Adam, and it showed. 'Go on! Be off with you.' He snatched the mug of tea from Adam's hands, spilling a dark trail across the tablecloth. 'Your business here is finished.'

'I'm sorry you feel that way,' Adam said, rising. 'But we don't have to part like enemies.' Extending his hand he waited in vain for the other man to shake it. 'All right, if that's the way you want it,' he conceded, dropping his hand to his side and turning away.

The old man followed him to the door. 'You've got a bloody cheek coming here! I should have known better than to let you in. You're all the same. Something for nothing, that's what you're after.'

Before the door was closed on him, Adam apologised. 'You can't blame a man for trying. But you have my word, I didn't come here to get something for nothing. I might not have enough to buy one of your good wagons, but I'll get started somehow, even if I have to build up a round from scratch. You say your father did it, so why not me? As for my two hundred pounds, I agree it isn't all that much, but it's hard-earned and better than nothing.'

'As good as nothing!'

'Thank you for your time, Mr Saxon.' With a friendly smile he bade Ben Saxon good day and went down the street, somewhat disappointed but not dejected. He meant what he said. Somehow, he'd make his savings work for him, and he *would* find a way to get started.

Ben Saxon remained at the door, his unhappy eyes following Adam's upright figure. 'Good luck to you,' he said sullenly. Until now he hadn't fully realised what the coming events would mean to him . . . no more work, no planning of schedules or passing the time of day with old customers. Nothing to look forward to but a narrow terraced house alongside the docks. It was hard being an old man with nothing else to give when once he had meant something round these parts.

Suddenly it didn't bear thinking about. Unwittingly, Adam had made him see what lay ahead, and it crushed his old spirit. Returning to the back room, he sat on the chair which Adam had vacated only minutes before. 'Ben Saxon, you're an old fool!' he said. 'All right! Happen you *couldn't* afford to sell him a wagon and round for two hundred pounds . . . but you didn't have to pour scorn on his ambitions. Instead, you could have given him a deal of advice.' Thumping a gnarled fist on the table, he chided himself; 'You're a selfish, jealous old bugger! It isn't *his* fault if the custom's not there. It isn't *his* fault you're having to sell up. And if you were half a decent man, you'd have set him on the right path.'

He paced the floor and thought awhile. And for the first time in months, the glimmer of a smile crossed his aged face. 'So he reckons he can get started on a lousy two hundred pounds, does he? You can't help but admire him, and that's a fact.' Reaching up to take his pipe from the mantelpiece, he chuckled. 'If you can pull it off, you'll be a better man than I gave you credit for, Adam Roach. But we'll see.' Settling in the fireside chair, he rocked it back and forth, seemingly content. 'We'll see!'

Chapter Seven

As soon as he opened the door to his room, Adam knew the money was gone. The mattress was turned over and everything was in disarray. The few articles from the mantelpiece were littered across the floor and the brick from the chimney breast was flung in the hearth. 'Jesus Christ!' He rushed across the room and thrust his hand into the void where the brick had been. It was empty. All his precious bank-notes gone.

At first he was filled with rage. Then he wanted revenge. Then, after realising that he had no hope of ever finding out who had stolen the money, he sank into a chair, head forward in his hands and his dark eyes staring at the carpet. In his shocked mind he began to work out how the loss had reduced his chances of buying a wagon. 'You're right, Saxon,' he said, laughing cynically, 'I'm just a dreamer, no different than the rest.'

He remained immobile for what seemed an age, despondent and frustrated, angry with himself for having been so stupid as to leave his precious wages where they must easily have been found. 'I should have kept them in my pocket,' he muttered. 'They'd have been safer there!' He wondered how he could possibly start a business on what little money he had left. And the more he thought on it, the more ludicrous it began to seem.

After a while, he collected the few coins scattered on the rug, kicked his way through the debris and went out into the growing darkness. 'Might as well enjoy what's left!' he decided grimly, making his way to the nearest pub. In that moment it seemed all his plans were shattered. 'Whatever bastard took that money, I hope he realises it was hard earned and meant for better things!'

When he came into the pub, his dark handsome looks turned heads. One particular young woman seated at a nearby table could hardly keep her eyes off him. Connie Wilson was lonely, and far from home. Tall, slim and blessed with china doll looks, she had a warm heart and generous nature. Sipping slowly at her drink, she watched as Adam gave his order. As though quenching a fire within him, he gulped down the first drink and promptly ordered another.

Taking her own drink, she crossed the room and climbed on to the stool beside him. Close to, he was even more handsome than she'd first thought. With one hand thrust deep into his pocket and his long legs straddling the rail at the foot of the bar, he sat on the edge of his stool, dark eyes staring into his drink and a deeply thoughtful expression on his face. He was totally oblivious to her attentions.

'Need some company?' Her soft voice infiltrated his thoughts. When he turned to look at her, she smiled warmly. Shifting nearer, she murmured, 'I'm a good listener.' She made no attempt to touch him. Instinct warned her he was not the sort of man you got too friendly with too quickly. 'We could go somewhere?' she suggested tentatively.

His dark eyes appraised her. How different she was from his Rosie, he thought. 'Thanks all the same,' he answered with a devastating smile, 'but I don't think so.'

'Okay. Suit yourself.' Returning to her table, she watched him for a while. Not once did he turn to look at her. Obviously not interested, she told herself. Pity. He looks a decent sort.

She switched her attention to the two men seated at a table at the far end of the room; one was a thin white-faced creature with bulbous eyes, but the other brown-haired fellow was reasonably attractive, dressed in a pin-stripe suit and smoking a fat cigar. 'Could try your luck there, Connie girl,' she muttered to herself.

When she sauntered up, the two men were deep in conversation. 'Got time for a chat with me?' she asked the man in the pin-stripe suit. When he merely glanced up and looked away again, she seated herself on the chair beside him. 'If you can tear yourself away from your business here, I don't think you'll regret it,' she said, crossing her legs and shifting her skirt in a suggestive manner.

The man didn't speak. Instead, without warning, he clenched his fist and viciously lashed out, catching her on the side of the face and sending her crashing into a group of chairs. While she lay, shocked and bleeding on the floor, he merely grinned and spat over her before calmly resuming his conversation.

He had only spoken two words when he was lifted right out of his chair and knocked to the ground. Stroking his knuckles, Adam stood over him as he lay crumpled on the floor. 'I think you forgot your manners,' he remarked casually.

Dazed, the man stared up at Adam, then, without another word, he scrambled to his feet and staggered towards the door. Alarmed, the thin man followed, and by the time Adam had helped Connie back to her chair, the two were long gone.

'You'll have to watch they don't wait for you outside,' she warned.

'I shouldn't think there's any danger of that,' he assured her. 'Their kind take great pleasure in knocking women about . . . but they've no stomach when it comes to trading fists with other men.' Examining the tear on her chin, he thought it wasn't too bad considering. But she was shocked and bruised.

'What's your address? I'd best see you home before you get into any more trouble.'

'No address. Sorry.'

'What do you mean? You've got a home, haven't you?'

'Nope.' The bruise on her face was beginning to swell. Beneath those wonderful dark eyes, she grew embarrassed. 'It's not your problem, and I'm sorry you were caught up in mine.' She made an effort to stand but almost fell over. 'Don't worry. I can look after myself.'

'Hmph! Looks like it.' Cupping her elbow with his hand, he helped her across the room. Outside, he told her, 'Wait there. I'll get us a taxi.' Stepping off the kerb, he peered up and down the street. It was only minutes before he'd hailed a cab and they were on their way to Dell Place.

As he helped her up the stairs to his room, she wondered what a man like this was doing in such a run-down place. 'How long have you lived here?' she wanted to know.

'Too long. And I know what you're thinking.' Recalling how the thief had turned the place upside down, he half smiled. 'When you see inside, you might wish I'd left you in the street.'

When the door was opened to reveal the mess the thief had made, she was open-mouthed. 'God Almighty! It's a bloody pig-sty!'

Depositing her in the nearest chair, he confessed, 'I should have cleaned the place up. Truth is, I was burgled, and I was so bloody mad, I couldn't think straight.'

'So you thought you'd go out and get drunk?'

'Something like that.' Going to the sink, he swilled a corner of the towel with water from the tap. 'The bastard took two weeks' hard-earned wages and a handsome bonus. On top of that I've lost my job.' He dabbed so hard at her face that she cried out.

'Hey! It weren't *me* that robbed you.'

Shamefaced, he apologised. Dabbing more gently at her face with the cloth, he explained, 'It's just that the money was for starting up my own business.'

'I'm sorry.'

'So am I.' Lifting her fair hair, he examined the side of her temple. 'You're lucky he didn't split your skull open.'

'Serves me right. I thought it would be easy. I was wrong.'

'You mean you haven't . . . done it . . . before?'

'Solicited, you mean?' She smiled and he was astonished at her beauty. 'No, I've never done it before. I only arrived in Liverpool this morning . . . it's taken me years to summon the courage to leave my old man . . . *another* coward who likes to knock women about.' She stood up then. 'I've taken enough of your time and you've got your own troubles. I'll be on my way.'

'Oh, and where will you go?' He had taken a liking to her.

'I'll find somewhere.'

'You could stay here.'

Feigning shock, she teased, 'And here was I thinking you couldn't get me out of the door fast enough, when all the time you can't wait to get me in bed!'

'I should *throw* you out the door,' he said with a grin, 'but you're welcome to stay, at least for tonight. Tomorrow you'll feel better able to find yourself a place.' Pointing to the settee, he explained, 'As for getting you into bed, that's where I'll be sleeping.'

Without a word she got out of her chair and began clearing the mess up. 'You don't have to do that,' he protested. Going to the sink, he washed her blood from the corner of the towel and hung it over the rail. Then he flung his coat off, hung it on the hook behind the door and set about tidying up with her. 'I'd like to get my hands on the bastard who did this,' he muttered.

Replacing a drawer, she paused to look at him. 'Judging by the leathering you gave the man in the bar, I reckon the burglar can count his lucky stars you *didn't* get your hands on him.'

He smiled wryly, but remained silent all the while they were clearing up. Later, when the room was ship-shape, Adam insisted she sat down while he made her a cup of tea. 'Nothing stronger, I'm afraid,' he apologised. 'As a rule I'm not a drinking man . . . one with my mates on a Friday night and that suits me fine.' Handing her a mug of tea, he stretched himself out in the chair beside her, wondering how he would ever get started in business now, with no job and a good chunk of his money gone.

Connie had been secretly watching him. It occurred to her that such a man ought to have a woman sharing his life. 'Do you have a family?'

'No.'

'Parents? Wife? You must have *somebody*!'

'No.'

'But that's terrible!'

'There are worse things.' His smile was cynical.

'I can't think of any.'

'Oh, I can.'

'Such as?'

'Never knowing where you are. Being brought up in a succession of children's homes. Going into the forces and being afraid to come out in case you're lost again. Coming home early to be told your sweetheart is expecting your best friend's child and they're to be wed. Working yourself to the bone with the dream of someday being your own boss. And then having your hard-earned wages pinched by some lazy bugger who's probably never done a hard day's work in his life, and never intends to!'

Sensing the frustration in him, she simply said, 'I see what you mean.'

There followed an uncomfortable silence until she asked, 'What will you do now? I mean, what with all your money stolen and no job. Fresh air won't pay the rent.'

Collecting her cup he went to the sink where he swilled the crockery under the tap. 'I'm not broke,' he answered, at once wondering why he should confide in a complete stranger. 'I have money put by . . . money I've been saving for a business venture.'

'What kind of business venture?' She came to stand beside him. Taking up the kitchen cloth, she wiped the cups and placed them on the drainer.

'I had visions of being a coal-merchant.' Seeing the surprise in her face, he added with a chuckle, 'Oh, it's not glamorous, and happen it won't make me a millionaire, but it's all I know, apart from army life. And it's good honest work. What's more, there *is* money in it, if you think on a big enough scale.'

'And you meant to do that?'

'The *thinking*'s already done. I meant to have a fleet of my own coal-wagons.' He chuckled. 'They'd all be sign-written in big bold letters: ADAM ROACH, COAL-MERCHANT. In time I would have bought out every small merchant for miles around.'

'And now?'

The smile fell from his face and was replaced with a resolute expression. 'I haven't altogether given up. Not yet.'

She half smiled. 'Somehow I can't see you as a loser.'

Laughing, he pinched his finger and thumb together. 'I'm that close,' he admitted. But, after talking it through, he knew he could never give up his ambitions. 'You're right,' he said finally, recalling what she had told him in the bar.

'Oh?'

'You are a good listener.'

She gazed up at him, her face suddenly serious. 'I'm a good lover too,' she whispered boldly.

To Connie he was just a man, though not quite like any other she had met, and she needed a man. Men were like a magnet to her, but there could be no in between; they were either friends or lovers. She didn't want a full relationship, and the thought of being committed to one man frightened her like nothing else. Now that she had won her freedom, she meant to keep it. All the same, in this instance she was sorely tempted. 'What I said in the bar,' she reminded him softly. 'The offer's still open.'

For a long moment he continued to gaze at her. There was no denying he was attracted to her and God alone knew how much he needed someone, but not *anyone*, he reminded himself. His heart was too full of Rosie. Just as he had not altogether given up on his ambitions, neither had he given up on her; though for the life of him he couldn't see a happy ending to it all. 'It's nothing personal, Connie, but the answer's still the same. No thanks.'

She didn't answer. Instead, she nodded her head wisely and returned to the settee where she spread herself out. Taking a box of matches and a pack of cigarettes from her pocket, she lit one up and all the while her pretty blue eyes followed his every move. When he went to the window, she saw how he stared out, as though expecting someone to walk up the street towards him. 'Want a cigarette?' she asked, holding out the pack of Woodbines. He shook his head but didn't look round. 'Okay. Suit yourself,' she said, thrusting them back into her pocket.

Adam was shocked to see how the night had closed in. He and Connie had talked for so long that the time had flown by without his realising. 'It's late,' he said abruptly. Striding into the bedroom area, he could be heard moving about until a few minutes later he returned, carrying crumpled sheets. 'I'm allowed only one set of clean sheets a week,' he explained. 'I've stripped the bed.' Indicating the laundry in his arms, he went on, 'These will do me. You'll find clean ones at the foot of the bed.'

'Won't you need a blanket?' She was on her feet now, stubbing out the cigarette in the ashtray.

'I'll be fine. Don't worry.'

'We could cuddle up together? Or we could talk, if you'd rather. I'm not ready to go to bed yet.'

'Goodnight, Connie,' he said firmly. To tell the truth he wouldn't have minded sitting up a while and talking. She was easy company, and he hadn't talked to a woman in that way for so long. But he felt he had disclosed enough of his life to her. Somehow she had managed to get under his skin. That troubled him.

'Okay,' she said, peeking through the curtains. 'It's just that where I come from, one good turn deserves another, and if it hadn't been for you, I'd probably be dossing out there on the streets.'

He turned to smile on her and she felt cheated. He was so handsome. 'I'll bear that in mind,' he promised.

'Well, you know where I am if you want me.' When he didn't answer, she closed the curtains and undressed. The act of sliding off her clothes felt sensuous. Sighing, she roved her hands over her warm firm breasts. 'You're sure you won't share the bed with me?' she asked hopefully. 'I promise not to pinch all the blankets.' When he laughed, she was encouraged to open the curtains and look out, making certain that one of her breasts was exposed. He was stripped to the waist, his broad chest tanned and muscular. His beauty took her breath away. 'We could keep each other warm,' she said invitingly.

'Goodnight, Connie,' he told her determinedly, quietly chuckling when she sighed longingly and closed the curtains.

Taking off his trousers, he lay on the settee and covered himself with the sheets. Connie was right, he thought, shivering, it did get chilly of a night. All the same it wasn't long before he was deep in sleep. The booze still lay heavy on him. Since ploughing all his wages into the bank, he wasn't used to upending the number of pints he'd sunk tonight.

He dreamed of Rosie, but she was always out of reach. Yet tonight in his deepest dreams, he felt her touch him. She was warm and soft, and his passions were roused. Half-asleep, he got off the settee and into the bed. 'I thought you'd never find your way in here,' Connie told him. Seeing him now in all his glory, she knew the wait had been worth it.

Hungry for the love of a woman, he played with her awhile, enjoying the velvet texture of her flesh and exploring her until she gasped with pleasure. When, thrilled and impatient, she cried out for him, he pushed himself into her. Their mating was fiery, almost angry. When it was over they fell away from each other, exhausted and immensely satisfied.

In the morning, he could hardly look at her. 'It won't happen again,' he said grimly. The muscles in his face were like chiselled stone.

She too realised it had been a mistake. Not because she hadn't enjoyed it, because she had. Making love with Adam was something beautiful. But she knew he was not making love to *her*. Even in the throes of ecstasy, she sensed that he was somewhere else. His mind was on the sweetheart he had lost to his best friend. 'I'm sorry,' she told him now, 'I'll get out.'

He stopped her then. 'The fault was mine.' He was at the sink shaving. When he turned, the blade nicked his chin and a trickle of blood ran down his chest, but he appeared not to notice. 'You don't have to go.'

She smiled. 'Oh, I see. I'm welcome in your room, but not in your bed?'

Returning her smile, he agreed. 'That's about the size of it, but you *can* stay until you find somewhere else. I don't want to be responsible for you walking the streets.'

'But we can't be lovers?'

'Not wise.'

'Because you still love your sweetheart?'

He looked away, and for a moment she thought she had gone too far. But then he said softly, 'You're a very perceptive woman, Connie Wilson.'

'Friends then?'

'I think so, yes . . . friends.' Giving her a quizzical look, he asked, 'Have you given any thought to what I said before? About giving up the idea of soliciting?'

'Yeah. I've thought about it. But to be honest, I can't see myself washing up dishes in some hotel kitchen, and believe me, there isn't much else.'

'Perhaps you haven't tried hard enough?'

'Look. I won't try and run your life, if you don't try and run mine.'

Laying the razor on the edge of the sink, he splashed his face with cold tapwater and towelled it dry. 'Two conditions then. You don't bring your "clients" back here, and I'll expect you to pay a full share of the rent.'

Laughing, she stretched out her arms. 'A deal!' With that she waited her turn at the sink. A few minutes later, she threw on her jacket and went jauntily out of the room. 'See you later,' she called. And he couldn't help but wonder whether he'd made a rod for his own back.

During the following week, while Adam trudged miles looking for work, Connie proved her worth. She kept to their agreement, and though she soon became popular with the many men she canvassed, she never brought them home. When Adam returned, footsore and weary, she would have a meal waiting for him, and a big smile that lightened his heart. 'You don't have to cook for me,' he told her, but she insisted, and so it became a regular pattern. They dined together, and laughed together; they discussed their fears and hopes, and soon became firm friends. She paid her way and even bought odd items of furniture for the flat.

One Friday night she proudly showed him the new floral curtains that decorated the windows. 'What do you think?' she asked, beaming from ear to ear.

'You know what I think,' he remarked, 'I object to you spending your money on this place.'

'But it's our home, and I want it to look nice.'

'Aw, Connie! If it belonged to us it would be a different matter. But it doesn't, so as far as I'm concerned, it's as good as money down the drain.' An unpleasant thought crossed his mind. Glancing furtively at the door, he warned her, 'For God's sake don't let the landlord see how you're tarting this place up, or he'll want extra rent.'

She laughed at him. 'Don't you worry about him,' she said winking knowingly. 'He and I have an understanding.'

Groaning, Adam told her that was the worst thing she could have done. 'Never on your own doorstep, isn't that what they say?'

'Oh, it's all right. I've got him eating out of my hand. In fact, I'm tempted to ask for a reduction in the rent.'

'No! The rent is *my* department. Look, Connie, are you sure you know what you're doing?'

'Of course I'm sure. You don't think I'd do anything to cause you trouble, do you?' She began to explain her relationship with the landlord, saying how he was "a good soul at heart".

Groaning, he pleaded, 'That's enough, Connie. I don't want to know any more. Our landlord isn't the angel you make him out to be, and if you'd been around this neighbourhood longer, you'd realise he's a bad lot. To be honest, I think you're making a grave mistake getting involved with him, but it's your life, and I've never pretended to be your keeper.'

'Quite right,' she answered cheekily, 'I'm done with having keepers. And my life *is* my own.' Her mood had changed. 'I'll get your meal,' she said sharply, beginning to make her way to the oven. 'And don't tell me I shouldn't cook for you because I like to!' she snapped. 'So you'd better bloody well enjoy it!'

Taking a steaming meat pie from the oven, she placed it on

top. The gravy ran down the sides as she sliced a huge chunk off and placed it on a large white plate; to this she added a helping of cabbage and a scoop of roasted potatoes from the tin. That done, she enacted the same procedure for herself, with a smaller slice of pie and fewer vegetables. 'I'm a good cook if nothing else,' she declared, carefully setting the plates on the table. 'It's your favourite.' That was something she had soon discovered. She also knew he had a large birthmark on his thigh, and he was ticklish just under his right rib. 'Aw, look, I'm sorry,' she said. 'We're good mates. I don't want to have bad feelings between us.'

'Neither do I,' he confessed. 'And, like I say, you do what you like. It's no business of mine . . . unless it threatens the very roof over our heads.'

'Surely you don't think that?'

'I don't know *what* to think. All I know is, you're playing a dangerous game.'

Smiling, she told him, 'Ain't that what makes life interesting?'

He couldn't help but return her smile. She was like a child. 'I worry about you,' he confessed.

'Well, don't! I can take care of myself.' During the meal she admitted, 'Perhaps you're right and I shouldn't have struck up a relationship with the landlord. But, honest to God, he's not as bad as people make him out to be.'

Adam had warned her to be careful. Beyond that he wouldn't go.

Later, he scanned the local newspaper, looking for work. As usual, there was nothing worthwhile. But something else caught his eye. 'It's tomorrow!' he cried excitedly. 'They're auctioning Saxon's goods . . . wagons, coal stocks . . . the whole shebang!'

Connie was mending a pair of her sheerest stockings, and almost ruined them when he leaped out of the chair. 'A coal-merchant!' she said with immense patience. 'I might have known.' But he wouldn't be put off. His dream was alight again, and he couldn't wait for the morrow.

Suddenly he recalled what Ben Saxon had said, about his not having enough money – and that was *before* he was robbed. 'I don't know what the hell I'm getting excited about,' he told Connie. 'There'll be men there with money in their pockets to make my little bankroll look sick.'

'Do you reckon there'll be much interest then?'

'Enough. When times are hard, you can always rely on two things that folk will spend on. Food and heat. Always a priority.'

'Come to think of it, you might be right.'

'I *know* I am!'

'You've forgotten a *third* priority.'

'What's that?' He was intrigued.

'Love. A man will spend his last shilling for a cuddle and a grope in the dark. Business has been going well, Adam, so if you're short, I can lend you some money.' She wasn't surprised when he graciously declined. 'Suit yourself. But the offer's there if you want it.' He didn't. If she had learned anything else about Adam, it was that he had high principles. That was another of the reasons why she admired him.

Adam arrived at the yard early, but already there were men milling all over the place; eager-eyed merchants looking to increase their own fleet of wagons, and maybe buy up a month's stock of prime coal at half the price. Many of the would-be buyers were strangers to Adam, but he recognised two of the town's most prominent coal-merchants, and his spirits fell. His chance of buying a wagon seemed more remote than ever.

He bought a catalogue for a shilling and found a pencil in his jacket pocket. Might as well take a note of how much it all goes for, he told himself. Soon the auctioneers were set up and everyone gathered round. The air was filled with a sense of excitement, and the first item was put up for offer.

'A fine wagon,' a bald-headed man announced, 'bought last year and only done three hundred miles. The tyres are good as new, and you all know its worth. Right then . . . who'll start me at five hundred guineas?' The atmosphere was electric. Silence reigned, and he grew impatient. 'Come on now! Let's get underway. Five hundred to start?' Again, nobody moved. Everyone was playing the game. Sighing, he scratched his shiny pate. 'All right . . . *three* hundred, and I must be mad!'

Straightaway someone's catalogue was raised. Adam recognised the man as being Arnie Burton, one of the big merchants. If he was up against people of that calibre, he might as well go home. But he didn't. He stayed, and later had reason to be thankful.

The wagon went for four hundred and twenty guineas. Adam wrote the figure against the item in the catalogue. The sale continued; first the wagons, then the coal.

Dejected, Adam would have walked away then, but he was held, mesmerised by the auction, curious as to what price the coal would fetch, and who might buy it. All around him the serious-faced men made their various moves, indicating to the auctioneer that they were prepared to pay a little more. Suddenly the bidding was less hectic and folk began drifting away to pay for their bargains. Now there only remained the ones who had come for the coal. The auctioneer tapped the hammer once, twice, and a new voice came into the proceedings. Adam's attention was caught. The voice was strangely familiar.

Turning round, he stretched his neck, dark quizzical eyes scanning the faces. Astonishment crossed his face when he saw the big man himself. Ned Selby! At first Adam was shocked, but then he reminded himself that Blackburn wasn't all that far away, and after all, why shouldn't Doug's dad bid for that prime coal, along with any other merchant? In fact, judging by the strangers here today, it was plain that a number of them had travelled in from further afield than Liverpool.

Adam's first instinct was to push his way through the crowd and make his presence known to Ned. But a deeper instinct made him look about, searching the faces for another, wondering whether Doug had come here with his dad. He didn't care to see Doug. It was still too soon. Doug was a married man now . . . married to Rosie. Adam could not easily forgive that.

When he was sure Doug was nowhere to be seen, Adam made his way to the big man's side. He owed a lot to Ned Selby. It would do his heart good to talk with him now.

The big man was just as surprised to see Adam. 'Good God above!' he exclaimed. 'I never thought to see *you* here.' Having secured some coal, he was about to make his way into the house where he would pay for it. Now he led the way towards the temporary bar. 'You'll take a drink with me?' he asked. 'I want to know how you've been doing.'

Adam insisted on buying two pints, and when they were seated at the table it was he who spoke first. His question came as no surprise to the big man. 'How is she . . . Rosie?'

'She's fine.' Sipping his ale, Ned Selby took stock of the younger man, and he knew without a shadow of doubt that Adam still ached for his first sweetheart. 'You know she and Doug got wed?' When Adam nodded, he went on, 'Aye. They've a son too . . . and another bairn on the way.' He felt it necessary to tell Adam how Rosie was both a wife and mother now. She was part of a family, and though his son didn't deserve her, Rosie was his wife. Sadly, Ned felt it his duty to remind Adam of that.

'I knew they were to be wed, and that she was with child.' Adam bowed his head. 'I didn't know there was another on the way.' Somehow she seemed further from him than ever. Yet, deep inside, he still couldn't accept that he would never again hold her in his arms.

'Doug wanted you to be godfather to his son, did you know that?'

'I had no idea.'

'Oh, aye. He tried to track you down. When he couldn't find you, he was bitterly disappointed. So much so that he still hasn't had the boy christened.' No sooner were the words out of his mouth than he regretted them. He anticipated Adam's reaction.

'Not christened!' Adam knew Rosie, and he realised with a shock that she would desperately want her son christened. 'What does Rosie think to that?'

'I'm afraid it's caused friction between her and Doug.' There was no point in lying. 'And Doug's mam makes it worse by constantly interfering.' Afraid that Adam would say or do something he might regret, Ned hastily added, 'No matter. It's all a storm in a teacup. Doug and Rosie have a good life together, and it'll take more than a little upset to come between them.'

Adam reflected on Ned's words, and felt instinctively that something was horribly wrong between Doug and Rosie. *He wouldn't rest until he'd seen her.* 'If the lad can't get christened unless I turn up to be godfather, then I'd best buy myself a new suit, eh?' He sounded light-hearted, but in fact his heart was heavy. He knew Doug of old, and also knew that he had a sullen and nasty side to his nature.

'You mean you're willing to do it?' Ned had hoped Adam would want no part of it, although it broke his old heart to know his grandson was still not baptised. 'Aren't you too busy?' He glanced around the yard. 'I mean, you must have a business going if you're on the lookout to buy coal and wagons?'

Adam had to laugh at that. 'Chance would be a fine thing,' he said.

'You mean you *haven't* got a business?' He wouldn't have

been surprised to learn that Adam was a high-flyer, because, like Doug, Adam was always a hard worker. He also had the ambition and brains to make it on his own.

'Haven't even got a *job* at the minute.' Before Ned Selby could comment, Adam went on, 'I do have aspirations, though, and a decent sum of money put by. So it's only a matter of time before I get something going.' He didn't want to seem like a charity case. Certainly not in front of Doug's father.

Ned nodded his head thoughtfully. 'You don't have to explain anything to *me*, son. Times are hard right now for all of us, but I've no doubt you'll pull yourself up by the bootstraps and make something of yourself. You were always the one with the drive to be a rich man. Like you say, it's only a matter of time.'

Adam was ashamed. 'It's not as easy as I imagined. Just when you think you've got it made, something happens to knock you down.' His jaw set hard. 'All the same, I'm not finished yet.'

'I'm sure you're not.'

The two men talked a while longer. Ned explained he was here for the day only, having travelled over on the train, he was now in a rush to catch the next one home. 'I'd best go and pay for that coal before they think I've changed my mind,' he said, glancing at his pocket-watch. 'It's a good buy, and every little helps. Lord knows it's a bit of a struggle at the minute.'

As he walked towards the house, Adam accompanied him. When the coal was paid for, they shook hands and parted; but not before Adam had written down his address, and Ned had put the paper safely in his pocket. 'Tell Doug I'll be honoured to be godfather,' he said. And meant it. Though it would be hard being godfather to Rosie's son when he would prefer to be its natural daddy.

Reflecting on their conversation, he remained on the step of the Saxon's house. There was a sadness about him as he watched Ned Selby's familiar figure walk away. 'So Rosie has a son, and another bairn on the way?' he mused aloud. Somehow he couldn't really believe it. Or didn't want to!

He was so engrossed in his thoughts that he was visibly startled when a voice sounded in his ear. 'You turned up, then? I wondered if you might.' Ben Saxon had not forgotten the young man who had come to see him.

Stepping aside to let another man pass, Adam reluctantly confessed, 'I couldn't stay away.'

'Like them, you mean?' The yard wasn't so busy now, and the auction was almost over. One or two bargain hunters could still be seen pawing over Saxon's possessions. 'I should have stayed away myself,' he mumbled. His eyes were bright with tears. He was an old man, and old men had the right to show their emotions. 'Down there in that yard is everything that made life worthwhile. And now it's all gone.'

'I'm sorry.' Adam was in the right frame of mind to understand how Ben felt.

'Oh? Sorry are you? Sorry for me, or sorry because you didn't get *your* pound of o' flesh?'

'I'm no vulture. All I want is the right to start up on my own, just as you did years ago. Is that too much to ask?' There was an anger in him then.

Ben peered at him with interest. He had spoken harshly and now regretted it. 'I don't reckon it is,' he agreed. 'To tell you the truth, I'm in no position to criticise because it was easier for me. You see, I took over this business from my father so it was all there . . . the wagons and rounds, and all the contacts. Oh, he'd told me tales of how he got started, and by all accounts, that was hard.'

He saw the straight-cut line of Adam's strong jaw and the way he returned his gaze, with clear honest eyes. There was something about his lithe physique and broad shoulders that struck a chord with Ben. 'I'm buggered if you don't put me in mind of my father,' he chuckled. Suddenly he felt a whole lot better for having met this determined young man. Slowly, the tiniest germ of an idea was growing in his mind.

'Come with me. You might be interested to see something.' Without waiting for an answer, he went down the steps into the yard. Bemused, Adam followed him to the big barn at the far end. It was locked. Reaching behind a loose plank, Ben fumbled about until he found the big rusty key. 'I always keep it locked,' he explained. 'Especially today, with all these nosy louts poking about!'

Turning the key in the lock, he swung the door open just wide enough for the two of them to squeeze through. When a man in a flat cap and boiler suit approached, Ben told him, 'Bugger off, mate. This is private property!' With a sour look and a muttered curse, the man turned his attention to a nearby pile of railway sleepers.

Adam stood in the gloom, wondering what this was all about, when the lamp was lit and his astonished eyes beheld a wagon. One of the earliest types, it was propped up on wooden boxes, without wheels or engine. There were no seats in the cab, and two of the boards were missing from the flat carrier at the back, but the paintwork was polished and the chrome gleamed; as he drew nearer he could see his face in it. 'It's beautiful!' he breathed, running his hand over the smooth paintwork.

'It was the very first wagon my father bought.' Laughing, Ben explained how it had been a rogue right from the start. 'We took her out four times, and each time she let us down. One time she lost a wheel and we tipped the entire load of coal in the middle of Albert Street. Before we could rebag it, there were women everywhere. In minutes they'd scooped the bloody lot up and disappeared back inside their houses! Another time we were going up Arnham Hill when the brakes failed. We started rolling backwards and I thought we were goners. Luckily, she veered into a lamp-post and we escaped with a few cuts and bruises. Mind you, the Council charged us for a new lamp-post.' The memory made him laugh. He hadn't laughed in a long time, and it felt good. Slapping Adam on the back, he said in a low voice, 'She's yours if you want it . . . what's left of it.'

Adam couldn't believe his ears. 'You mean it's for sale?'

'I mean what I said. She's yours if you want it.'

'What . . . you mean for *nothing*?'

'That's exactly what I mean.'

Never having been given anything for nothing, Adam was suspicious. 'I don't understand. When I came to you the other day, offering you good money for a wagon, you all but threw me out.'

'That was then.'

'And now?'

'Now, I can see how we can help each other.'

Understanding dawned. 'Ah! I knew there had to be a catch. Before I accept, I think you'd best tell me what you have in mind.'

'Nothing sinister, believe me. All I want is for you to promise me you'll look after this old wagon the same as I've looked after it.' His eyes clouded over. 'When you're old, all you have left are your memories. This wagon is a special part of my life, and I couldn't bear to put it in the sale. Since I won't be keeping this house on, I've been wondering what to do with this 'ere wagon. You seem like an honest fellow. If you tell me you'll look after it, I'll believe you.' Going to the wagon, he took a while to climb on to the cab; his old bones were not what they used to be. Sitting on the wheel arch, he asked, 'Well? Will you give her a good home?'

Adam could only nod, and wonder if he was dreaming. He could hear Ben talking, but he was too stunned to listen. 'Of course you'll have to find an engine for it . . . and a set of wheels, but you reckon you've a bit of money put by, so you should be able to manage that. Once you've got her ship-shape again, you'll have to concentrate on getting a round. You've worked in the coalyards so you know the business there. Getting folks in the street to buy your coal is a different kettle of fish. You'll find it hard, but you're young and eager. All the advice I can give is: don't undercut the opposition by too much or you'll go broke . . . and treat your customers fair so they'll always come back to you.' He was standing by Adam's side now. 'Do you hear what I'm saying?'

He dragged his gaze from the wagon. 'How in God's name can I thank you?'

Ben laughed aloud. 'You haven't heard a bloody word I've said!' he spluttered. But it didn't matter. There wasn't much time left now, but there would be time enough to go through it all again.

In that moment, all that mattered was what he saw in Adam's face. It told him that here was a man he could trust. Here was a man who deserved a chance, and who would willingly work his fingers to the bone for it. Today had been a heartache. But now at least he could rest assured that something good had come of it all. And he could go to his maker with a clear conscience.

The month that followed was a busy and exciting one during which Adam worked long arduous hours restoring the cherished wagon. The cost of the spare parts took most of his hard-earned cash, but because he carried out almost all the labour himself, he made a great saving. The only time he called in expert help was when the engine was ready for fitting.

In the week that followed the auction, Ben and Adam talked for hours. Ben explained what made a good coal-merchant, and Adam listened intently. They were good friends, growing closer by the day. But, much to Adam's dismay, all that ended when he started work on the wagon.

Ben took an interest, but only from a distance. Adam thought it strange that he never came to the barn until the end of the day, when he knew Adam would be preparing to leave. At seven o'clock sharp he would stand by the door, hands in his pockets and a faraway look in his eye. He never spoke. One minute he was there, and the next time Adam looked round, he was gone. The first time this happened, he had gone to the house and tapped on the door. 'Ben, was there something you wanted?' he called.

Ben didn't answer then, nor did he answer when, on arriving the next morning, Adam saw him coming out of the barn. He called out, but Ben appeared not to have heard. Without a backward glance he scurried into the house and only came out for that peculiar vigil just as Adam was finishing work. It was plain that he didn't want to talk with Adam, and so Adam accepted his need for privacy.

Something even stranger happened on the day when Adam climbed into the cab and drove the wagon into the yard. He was thrilled and excited, and most of all he wanted to share this moment with Ben. When he saw the older man watching from an upstairs window, he scrambled out of the cab and shouted up to him. 'Ben! Come and see,' he invited eagerly. 'She's purring like a kitten.'

Ben's answering smile was proud. There was a fleeting moment when he gazed on the wagon. Then he was gone. Adam waited, expecting him to show at any time. But the door remained firmly closed, and Adam grew impatient. This was Ben's moment as well as his, and he so much wanted him to drive down the street in this wagon which had been retired since the old Mr Saxon had passed on.

Determined, Adam went to the house and knocked on the door. There was no answer, so he boldly pushed open the door and called out Ben's name. All that greeted him was a chilling silence. Anxious, yet not knowing why, he climbed the stairs. 'Ben! Are you there?' he called. Still no answer. With his heart beating fast he inched open the bedroom doors one after the other. Ben's room was at the front of the house. He had gone to bed. His face was still and white, and there was a wonderful expression of peace in his features.

The doctor said he had suffered a heart attack. Adam believed his suffering was over, and that Ben Saxon had waited until the wagon was working once more. Now he could go to his father with a sense of pride instead of shame. 'I made you a promise,' Adam told him at the funeral. 'Rest in peace, Ben, I won't go back on my word.'

Two days after Ben was laid to rest, Adam received a letter from Doug telling him that his son was to be christened on 2 July, and saying that both he and Rosie would be delighted if Adam could be there as godfather.

Against his better instincts, but longing to see Rosie again, Adam lost no time in writing back graciously accepting the kind offer. Connie told him it was a mistake, but Adam wasn't listening. This time, his heart was ruling his head.

Chapter Eight

Rosie shivered as she got out of bed. Though it was June and the sun was already shining outside, the air inside the house struck cold. Like all the other dwellings along this street, it was damp and old, and never properly warmed up until the sun had been high in the heavens for at least two hours.

Creeping about so as not to disturb Doug, Rosie threw her robe on and reached into the cot. 'Come on, sweetheart,' she told the sleeping child. 'You'd best come with your mammy because if you start crying for your breakfast and get him out of his bed, we'll not hear the end of it, will we, eh?' Doug had a nasty temper if he was woken before ten o'clock on his Saturday off.

Wrapping the infant in his shawl, she pressed him close and went out of the door. These days, with Rosie nearly seven months pregnant and with a child in arms, it was increasingly difficult to negotiate the narrow stairs so she took her time, inching her way along and being especially careful where the steps curved dangerously halfway down. Behind her she could hear Doug loudly snoring, 'Sounds like a train in full steam,' she chuckled.

Downstairs, she wedged the child between cushions in the corner of the settee. 'You'll be fine while I treat myself to a cup of tea, won't you, darling?' she cooed. But the infant had other ideas. In answer to her question, he opened his big eyes and began sucking on his fist. 'Hungry are you?' she asked, settling herself on the settee beside him. She had hoped he might allow her a few quiet minutes when she could gather her thoughts, but babies were unpredictable as she well knew. 'All right, I'll see to you first,' she conceded. 'Then I'll make myself a cup of tea before getting your daddy's breakfast ready.'

Undoing the front of her nightie, she lifted the child to her breast, laughing when he instantly clamped his mouth round her nipple and began frantically sucking. 'Where are your manners?' she teased. 'Going at your poor mammy like a sink plunger!' But she was never happier than when the child was feeding. Somehow she felt closer to him. While he fed, she allowed her mind to wander, and as always it wandered to the time before Doug, to the time when she and Adam had been together.

The infant was soon fed, washed and changed into his day clothes. Rosie glanced at the clock. It was already half-past eight. There was the dusting to be done, the mats to be taken out and beaten, and a pile of washing a mile high sitting in the dolly-tub. 'No good looking at it,' she said aloud, 'the work won't do itself.'

It was quarter to ten when she came in from the yard where she had been hanging out the washing. 'That's it for now,' she told herself in the parlour mirror. 'You look like something the cat dragged in. Best wash and dress. You know His Majesty moans if you're still in your nightie by the time he gets up.' Going to the stairs cupboard she dragged the ironing basket out and found a clean blue blouse, a straight grey skirt and clean underwear. Taking the garments into the scullery, she heated the iron and ran it over them. In no time at all she was washed, dressed, and feeling good. By the time she had finished washing herself, the water in the bowl had gone cold, and she soon discovered that there was nothing more revitalising than a rush of cold water on your skin.

The aroma of sizzling sausages and frying eggs began to fill the little house. Going into the parlour, she laid the table and checked that the baby was all right. He was fast asleep. 'You're a little beauty,' she told him, tenderly stroking his face. These past few weeks he had changed. His eyes were colouring to a soft hazel hue, and his hair was deepening to a rich brown colour like his mammy's. 'It's been weeks since he mentioned about you being christened,' she said. 'But if he thinks I've forgotten, he's very much mistaken. I intend having another go at him this morning. I mean to get you christened, and I'll fight him tooth and nail until he gives in!'

Returning to the scullery, she glanced at the calendar on the wall. 'June the twenty-fourth,' she said aloud. 'Half the year nearly gone and the bugger's *still* playing games!' She was angry, frustrated, and determined that, one way or another, the christening would take place before the year was out.

She was turning the eggs when suddenly she froze. 'Good God!' A smile spread over her face as she perused the calendar. 'Look at that, gal,' she chuckled. 'June the twenty-fourth 1949. It's my birthday, and I'm twenty-one!' Going into the parlour she leaned over her son to whisper in his ear, 'Shame on you! Fancy sleeping on your mammy's *twenty-first birthday*!'

She had completely forgotten that this was a special day and, for just a brief moment, there was joy in her heart. But it was soon curtailed when Doug appeared at the parlour door, dishevelled and irritable. 'Ain't my breakfast ready yet, woman?'

His irritation transferred itself to her. She wasn't surprised to realise that he too had forgotten her birthday. 'I've only got one pair of hands!' she snapped. 'Your breakfast will be on the table in a minute.' With that she went smartly into the scullery while he seated himself at the table.

Rosie picked at her toast. After all the work she had done in the past two hours, she was famished. Now, though, her appetite had vanished at the sight of his sullen face. Her instinct told her not to broach the subject of the christening just yet. There would be time enough later, after he'd been to the betting shop, when he might come home in a better frame of mind.

'I don't need to ask what *you'll* be up to today,' he grumbled. 'I expect you'll be gadding about with that bloody Peggy.' Viciously stabbing at his food with the prongs of his fork, he rammed it into his mouth, all the while staring at her with those odd-coloured eyes.

'We'll be going to the market together, yes,' she said defiantly.

Jabbing the fork at her, he said, 'I don't like you going about with that one.'

'She's my best friend. My *only* friend, as it happens.'

'That's beside the point. You're a married woman, and she's not. To my mind that spells trouble.'

'Oh? And are you forbidding me to see her?' There was a note of warning in her voice that cautioned him. 'And who says it spells trouble? Your mother, I suppose?'

'Watch your bloody tongue when you speak about my mother. She's been a better friend to you than ever your precious Peggy could be . . . let you move in when we had nowhere to go, didn't she? Gives you advice on the lad here, doesn't she?' He jabbed his fork again, this time towards the sleeping child. 'And all you've ever done is throw it all back in her face.'

Wisely ignoring his attempt to draw her into an argument concerning his mother, she asked in a calm voice, 'So, does all this mean you're forbidding me to see Peggy?'

He looked at her then, at her strong brown eyes and the determined set of her pretty jaw, and he knew he was on dangerous ground. 'I didn't say that,' he snarled. Picking up his mug of tea, he swilled the hot liquid down his throat. 'Just think on,' he warned, slamming the mug down. 'There's folk watching you, that's all I'm saying.' Pushing his chair away, he left the table and went into the scullery where he quickly washed. Coming back to the parlour, he took his jacket from the nail behind the door. 'I'm off out,' he said, slinging his jacket over his shoulder. As he did so, a white envelope fell out of his pocket. Before Rosie could see what it was, he scraped it up and thrust it out of sight.

'What time will you be back?'

'When I think fit.' Flinging open the parlour door, he went down the passage and out of the house, leaving the front door open and a chill whipping down the passage and into the parlour.

Hurrying up the passage, Rosie closed the door. 'HEATHEN!' she called after him.

Suddenly a smile lit her face. 'Why, Rosie darling,' she mimicked his voice perfectly, 'isn't it your twenty-first birthday today?' Pursing her lips she feigned a kiss. 'Now then, sweetheart, where would you like to go? We can get the old battleaxe to babysit if you like? How about an evening at the Palais? Or we could go to that nice little restaurant on the corner of Dewhurst Street. I'll buy you a nice big box of chocolates afterwards . . . or a bunch of flowers. Or would you prefer a pretty silk scarf? No? What then? Oh! I know. Of course, why didn't I think of it before . . . a diamond ring! That's what I'll get you, sweetheart . . . a beautiful diamond ring. And a new dress! After all, you deserve the very best.'

She smiled and she cooed and she pranced up and down the passageway, fancying herself in this and that, holding out her work-worn fingers to admire the diamond ring. 'My! See how it glints and sparkles!' she exclaimed with big surprised eyes. Sweeping into the parlour, she fell into the nearest chair and laughed until she cried.

The stain of tears was still under her soft brown eyes when the knock came on the door. 'Who the devil's that?' she muttered, going up the passage and hoping it wasn't Doug come back.

It wasn't Doug, nor was it the devil. It was Peggy. 'Took your time opening the door, didn't you?' she remarked, following Rosie into the parlour. 'Anybody would think I were the rentman.' The two often laughed at how Peggy's mam had occasion to hide from the rentman some years back, and one of her indignant brood told the visitor through the letterbox, 'If you're the rentman, our mam says she ain't here!' To which he promptly yelled back, 'You tell your mam who "ain't here" that I've been called some things in my time, but never a rentman. You tell her I'm from the Widows' and Orphans' Charity, and I've brought her a free sack of firewood. But if she "ain't here" I'd best take it to some other deserving case.'

Before he'd even finished speaking, Peggy's mam flung open the door. 'Get inside, you!' She clipped the foolish boy's ear and sent him scurrying to the back room. 'And as for you,' she addressed the young man, 'you'll not find a more deserving cause than me in the whole of Blackburn, so kindly drop the sack of firewood on the step and bugger off!' Instructing the driver to offload one sack of firewood from the wagon, he doffed his flat cap and bade her good morning, and was still laughing as he climbed back into the cab. The incident had been a source of amusement ever since. After that, whenever she found the need to hide from the rentman, Peggy's mam bundled the children behind the settee with her.

Remembering the occasion, Rosie chuckled. 'I'm sorry if I kept you waiting,' she apologised. 'I thought it might be Doug coming back for something, that's all.' Realising Peggy was intently studying her face, she said hastily, 'I'll make us a brew, eh?'

Peggy shook her head. 'No, thank you all the same. I've just had my breakfast. But you *can* tell me why you've been crying.'

Seating herself opposite her observant friend, Rosie feigned surprise. 'What makes you think I've been crying?'

'Oh, nothing much . . . just the time it took you to open the door, and your eyes, all red and swollen.' Peggy would not be put off. 'Then there's your frantic hurry to get into the scullery and make a brew, when you know very well I always make *you* one since you've got big with child.'

'You're too clever for your own good, my girl,' Rosie said light-heartedly. She knew there was no use trying to hide anything from Peggy. 'Anyway, I might be "big with child", but I'm not an invalid.'

'Come on. Out with it.'

Rosie sighed wearily. 'It's nothing. Honest.'

'Liar!'

'I had a set to with Doug, that's all.'

'Oh? What about?'

'This and that . . . his mother mostly.' Rosie thought it might sound childish to say she was peeved because he'd forgotten her birthday.

'Has the old cow been interfering again?'

'She thinks our friendship is bound to cause trouble, what with me being married and you being single.'

'I've a bloody good mind to go and have it out with her!'

'Not a good idea.' All the same, the thought of Doug's mam and Peggy going at it hammer and tongs on the street tickled Rosie's imagination.

'Well then, tell her to piss off and mind her own business!'

'Oh, don't you worry. Soon as ever I get the chance, that's exactly what I'll do.'

'Good for you!' Getting out of the chair, Peggy asked coyly, 'Aren't you going to ask me why I'm not at work this morning?'

Going along with her, Rosie put the question. 'All right then. Why aren't you at work this morning?'

'Because our mam's thinking of decorating the parlour and she wants the furniture moved. I told her we could do it tomorrow, but she said not on the Sabbath. Anyway, you know what our mam's like. Once she's made up her mind there's no changing it. I was due a Saturday off, so I thought I might as well get the agony over with. As it is, there's not much hope of that trip to the market this afternoon. I'm sorry.'

'Do you need any help? Though I won't be any good at shifting the heavier stuff.'

'You're a mind-reader.'

It took fifteen minutes for the two of them to clear away and wash the breakfast things. After which Rosie put the child in its pram and the three of them made their way to Peggy's home.

Peggy's mam was waiting, and so were the children, all standing round the table which was laid with a white cloth, a mountain of home-made goodies, and a round cake in the centre, with icing that spelled out her name. Rosie was completely taken by surprise.

'Well? Ain't you got nothing to say?' Peggy laughed. 'Surely you didn't think I'd forget me best mate's twenty-first?' Taking the child from Rosie's arms, she sat him in the deep armchair and grabbed Rosie in a great big hug. 'Happy Birthday, sunshine,' she said, and the tears ran down Rosie's face.

'I don't know what to say,' she whispered through her tears. 'I was sure nobody would remember.'

'Well, you were wrong, weren't you?' Peggy chided. And without further ado, she fetched a box of matches for Rosie to light the candles on her cake. 'You ain't getting any younger, gal,' she teased. 'There's all twenty-one there, so you'd best take a deep breath and blow them all out together.'

Most of them went out in one blow, but it took two more little tries to extinguish them all; at which point a loud cheer went up and the party began. Twenty-one balloons, blown up the night before by Peggy and the children, were set loose across the room, with the young ones scrambling to pop them before they stuck to the ceiling. The children squealed and laughed and filled their bellies with jelly, cakes, cheese butties, and finally a large wedge of birthday cake, which Rosie vowed was, 'The most delicious I've ever tasted.'

'I've allus been known for my cakes,' Peggy's mam boasted, and Peggy laughingly told her not to get a big head. Rosie gave the kindly woman a heartfelt kiss, and she blushed a warm shade of pink. 'Why's our mam gone all red?' piped up a little voice, and Peggy's mam playfully clipped him round the ear.

By midday, the food was gone and so were the children. 'Gone out to terrorise the neighbourhood,' Peggy joked. The three women set to and tidied up, but when Rosie offered to help wash the dishes, Peggy's mam told her, 'You're a good lass, Rosie Selby, and you've been a good friend to my lass. I'm ashamed to say there have been times when I've been a sour-faced old sod, and I'm sorry about that. I didn't need no asking twice when our Peggy said she was planning a party and needed my help. I've been glad to do it, and now I'll be glad to wash up.'

'Come on, gal,' Peggy said. 'You look worn out. Put your feet up, and I'll do your hair for you . . . a special birthday treat, you might say.'

Rosie *was* tired and couldn't deny it. Her feet ached, her face was flushed and the unborn child inside her felt like a ton weight. Easing herself into the standchair by the table, she watched as Peggy went to the sideboard and took out a shoe-box. 'What are you up to?' she asked suspiciously when Peggy put the box on the table; she was visibly startled when her mam charged in from the scullery, crying, 'It's bad luck to put a shoebox on the table!'

'You mean *shoes*!' Peggy corrected.

'You keep shoes in that box, don't you?' her mam argued. 'So do as you're told and get it off the table.'

Placing the box on a nearby chair, Peggy took out a bowl and another small box. Inside the box was a sachet of dark liquid, a wad of cotton wool, and a small comb. 'I'm going to turn you into a raving redhead,' she told Rosie.

Rosie was horrified. 'You're not, you know!'

'Well, happen I'll just bring out the pretty highlights in your hair then?'

'What's wrong with my hair as it is?' In spite of her fears, Rosie was intrigued.

'There's nothing at all wrong with it,' Peggy assured her. 'It's very pretty. But I can make it glint like gold if you'll let me.' She laid the things out on the table. 'I got it at discount. We've just started this new line in cosmetics, you see, and like I said, it's a special birthday present for you.' She saw how hesitant Rosie was. 'Go on, gal,' she entreated, 'I promise you'll look great.'

Rosie thought of how she never did anything exciting, and how every day ran one into the other without anything to distinguish them. Lately she had been feeling like an old woman, instead of someone only twenty-one. She remembered how Doug had forgotten her birthday and she thought how good it would be to shock him. 'Do what you like,' she told Peggy. 'If I go bald, happen Doug won't want me in bed.'

Peggy's mam could be heard laughing in the kitchen. 'You're a pair o' buggers!' she said, and she was right.

It was ten o'clock at night when Doug came home. He wasn't drunk, but he was in a foul mood. 'What money have you got in your purse?' he asked, glaring at her from the doorway.

'A few shillings,' she answered. 'Enough to see us through 'til payday.'

'Give it here.'

'What for?'

'Never mind what for. I said . . . give it here.' Striding into the room he stretched out his hand and waited for her to empty her purse into it. 'I ain't got time to argue.'

Rosie didn't argue either. She knew it wouldn't make the slightest difference if she did. Besides, she wanted to humour him so she could ask about the date for the christening. With this in mind, she gave him half of what she had. It was enough to placate him. When he turned sharply and went out of the house again, she ran into the front room and peeped through the window. There were two other men waiting on the doorstep. They hurried away once Doug had paid his dues. Rosie suspected they were gambling partners. 'You're a fool, Doug Selby,' she whispered, hurrying back to the parlour. 'One of these days you'll get in over your head.'

When he came back he was smiling. 'I could drink the sea dry,' he said, throwing himself into the armchair. 'Put the kettle on, sweetheart,' he coaxed.

Rosie hated him when he turned on the charm like that. She was about to say she was tired and off to bed, when she stopped herself. Until he set the date for the christening, she would have to humour him. Without a word she went into the scullery, returning with his tea a few minutes later. 'Have you been to see the vicar?' she asked, giving the hot mug into his outstretched hands.

For a moment he stared at her. 'There's something different about you,' he commented, sitting up in his chair.

Knowing how he would react when he saw the red highlights in her brown hair, Rosie had deliberately kept in the shadows. 'What do you mean?' she asked innocently.

He shook his head. 'I'm not sure . . . something.' He stared a moment longer, but he had drunk a pint or two and his vision wasn't perfect at the minute. Puzzled, he sank back in the chair, sipping at his tea and infuriating her.

Just as she opened her mouth to remind him of her question, he astonished her by saying with a smug little smile, 'Not only have I been to see the vicar, but I've set the date for Sunday next.'

Rosie was thrilled. 'Oh, Doug! You can't know what a weight you've lifted off my mind.' If only he hadn't put her through so much, she might have embraced him. But he was too cunning, too arrogant. And her memory was too vivid.

Besides, she thought with amusement, she'd better stay in the shadows. If he was to see the carrot-coloured streaks in her hair, there would be an unholy row. She could handle that all right, but the little one had been fretful with his teething, and she didn't want him woken again. 'I began to think we'd be getting the two children baptised together,' she remarked coolly. 'What made you change your mind?'

'I got what I wanted, that's why.'

'In what way?'

He stared at her again, trying to distinguish what was different about her. 'What have you been up to?' he asked, getting out of the chair and starting towards her. It was then that his eyes caught sight of Peggy's birthday card, which Rosie had stood proudly on the mantelpiece. 'What the hell's this?' Snatching it up, he ran his eyes over it. A look of surprise came over his features, and for a moment it seemed as though he was about to make a comment but he replaced it without saying a word. Instead, he came to where she sat and proceeded to look her up and down. 'It's your bloody hair!' he gasped. 'You've had it dyed ginger.'

Summoning every ounce of courage, Rosie bestowed her loveliest smile on him. 'Don't you like it then?' she asked coyly. She didn't like it either, but she wasn't about to admit that.

He ran his fingers over the top of her head, ruffling the thick strands of hair before viciously grabbing a fistful and demanding: 'Do *you* like it?'

'Yes,' she lied, 'I do.' Standing up to face him, she waited for the outburst but was unprepared for what happened next.

'Your hair's pretty enough the way the good Lord made it, but yes, I think it suits you,' he replied, astounding her.

Before she could answer, he took out the envelope from his pocket and thrust it into her hand. 'After all, I do want you to look your best for the christening. We wouldn't want *him* to think the goods had become soiled, would we, eh?'

'What game are you playing, Doug?' She had known him long enough to realise that he was up to something.

'No game, sweetheart. It's just that things have turned out exactly how I wanted them to.' With that he went up the stairs, chuckling all the way.

Opening the envelope, she read the letter from Adam. It was short and polite, not at all like that of a friend. But it confirmed that Adam had graciously accepted the invitation to be godfather to Doug and Rosie's son. 'Oh, Adam, I thought you of all people might see through him,' Rosie sighed. 'He's using you, just like he uses me.' Now she saw what Doug had meant when he said things had turned out exactly like he wanted them to.

Pacing the room with the letter clutched in her hand, Rosie was tempted to sit down and write to Adam, warning him how Doug had intended to name his son after him only to antagonise her – though he was in for a real surprise when they got to the church. All the same, she wanted Adam to know that he had been asked to be godfather for the very same reason . . . to punish the two of them for having dared to love each other.

But then she realised she would only be hurting herself more by persuading Adam to stay away, because then Doug would never allow their son to be christened. 'And in spite of everything, I do so much want to see you, Adam,' she murmured, putting the letter against her face. She was both excited and afraid. Excited at the prospect of being in the same room as Adam again, and afraid because, though he was forever out of her reach, she would never stop loving him.

Carefully, she laid the letter on the sideboard where Doug would find it. 'A week,' she whispered, going up the stairs to bed.

'Only one week, and then he'll be here, in this house.' She shivered with delight. When she entered the bedroom and saw Doug waiting for her, the delight turned to dread.

Monday morning brought a wonderful surprise, but not before Doug had alarmed her with the news, 'Dad's losing work hand over fist. There are more folk out of work, and consequently they're counting their pennies. Last month we only sold a hundred and fifty bags of coal, when we normally sell upwards of four hundred.'

As always, Rosie was optimistic. 'Happen it's just a bad month. After all, it is June, and there are only a few people who light a fire in summer . . . old folk and them with small bairns.'

Scraping back his chair, he got up from the breakfast table. 'Don't talk daft, woman!' he snapped, glaring at her as though she was a total imbecile. 'The summer's always been a good time for selling coal. Folks have allus stocked up their cellars while it's cheap, and you bloody well know that.'

Rosie made no comment. Instead, she concentrated on clearing away the breakfast things. Only when she heard him slamming down the passage and out of the front door did she straighten herself from the task, and that was to roll her eyes to the ceiling and say, 'Dear Lord, you made a miserable soul when you made that one!'

The postman was late, but Rosie wasn't worried. He never brought anything exciting, just bills and circulars. When she heard the familiar plop of letters on the carpet, she went down the passage to collect them, absent-mindedly sifting through them as she returned to the parlour. 'Same as usual,' she muttered; there was a gas bill, a reminder about the instalment on the new gramophone, and a leaflet from the chimney-sweep, saying how he could 'Sweep a chimney so clean you could hang your Sunday-best coat in it'.

Rosie was still chuckling at that when she came into the parlour. But as her smiling brown eyes saw the writing on the last envelope, her heart almost stopped. The letter was addressed to her, and she had seen enough of his letters to know without a doubt that this one was from Adam.

Seating herself at the table, she opened the envelope and took out the contents. What she saw made her gasp. It was the most beautiful birthday card; in the cream-coloured background, little robins and kittens could be seen nuzzling up to each other, and there were clusters of exquisite red roses in all four corners. Inside there was a simple message that tore at her heart and filled her eyes with tears. It read:

To Rosie,
Did you think I would forget your birthday?

It was signed 'Adam'. There was no other message, nothing about the christening or Doug. At first she was puzzled, but then she understood. Adam had effectively shut out everyone but the two of them, and because of that, she would cherish the card all the more.

Her first instinct was to hide it. In fact, she even went so far as to turn back the lace-cover on the sideboard, 'No!' she declared. 'I *won't* hide it. Why should I? It can't hurt Doug to know there are people who think enough of me to remember my birthday.' Having decided to display it, she put it on the mantelpiece alongside Peggy's. 'There you are, Rosie gal,' she said, hands on hips as she stared at the two pretty cards. 'Don't ever say nobody loves you.' She daren't wonder whether Adam might love her still. It would only be wishful thinking, and anyway, even if it were true, all it could ever bring was heartache.

All day long, Rosie went about her work with a song in her heart. That song was cruelly ended when Doug walked in and saw the card there. 'Who's that from?' he wanted to know, striding across the room and snatching it up. He opened the inside and read the message. 'Bastard!' he roared. 'What gives him the sodding right?' Taking the card between his fingers, he began tearing it apart.

Seeing that precious card torn in front of her eyes was like a red rag to a bull. Darting forward, Rosie grabbed at it. There was a fury inside her, an insane rage that had built up over many months and now was let loose like a burst dam. 'He's got *every* right!' she cried, her nails scoring his arm as she struggled to take the card from him. 'Just because I married you instead of him, doesn't mean he can't still be a friend.'

Holding her at arm's length, he peered at her through red, dirt-rimmed eyes. 'Why, you little whore! You want him, don't you?' His voice was low, unsure. Then, when her gaze fell from him, he shook her, his voice rising in a fury. 'Admit it, or I swear I'll take your bloody head off at the shoulders!'

'Oh, aren't you the big man?' she demanded, her brown eyes mocking him. 'If you think there's something going on between me and Adam, why don't you ask *him*? After all, he'll be here on Sunday.'

'You little cow!' With one backward swipe of his hand he sent her crashing against the table. 'If I ever thought you and he . . .' Stretching himself to his full height, he glared down on her. 'So help me, I'll swing for the pair of you!' He made a low guttural sound in the base of his throat, then he was gone: unwashed, unfed, back on to the streets and into the pub, where he could drown his terrible thoughts in a jug of ale.

Covered in the fine coal-dust that had fallen from his clothes, Rosie remained bent across the table, using it to hold her steady. '*You're* the bastard!' she said softly. Any affection she had felt for him had grown cold long since. To tell the truth, she wouldn't care if she never saw him again.

Long after she had washed and changed and all the work was done, she was so churned up inside, she could hardly keep a limb still. Only when the child cooed on her lap and smiled up at her did she begin to melt, and love again. 'I've still got you, ain't I?' she said, holding the child closer. She glanced up at the crumpled card on the table. 'What shall I do with it?' she mused aloud. 'I ought to put it right back on the mantelpiece!' Shaking her head, she gave an odd little smile. 'Better not, eh?' She had been darkly angry, then indignant, and now she was filled with a terrible fear. Fear for Adam, fear that once the two of them came face to face again, so many feelings would be unleashed. 'It would be better if you stayed away, Adam,' she whispered. 'For all our sakes.'

Later, when the child was asleep in its pram, she took the card, held it close for the briefest moment when she could feel him near. Then, with a firm and final gesture, she threw it in the midden. 'Sorry, Adam,' she said with a wry little laugh. 'The time for pretty things is long gone.'

During the following two days, Rosie remained inside the house, venturing out only to collect the milk from the doorstep; even then she made sure no one saw her. 'Don't want the world and its neighbour to know he's been belting me,' she said, glancing in the mirror at the dark bruise that coloured her eye and cheek bone. 'Best keep myself to myself for a while.'

She reckoned without Peggy's determination though. Twice she had been round to see her friend, and each time she had been sent away by Doug. 'She's not well,' he told her. 'She's taken to her bed.'

Now, when the knock came on the door, Rosie wasn't certain whether to answer it or stay quiet until whoever it was had gone away. She decided to remain quiet, holding her breath and hoping the child wouldn't wake and start crying.

The sound of the letter box being opened almost turned her

heart over. 'Rosie!' Peggy's voice sailed down the passage. 'I know you're in there. Open this bloody door or I'll scream blue murder up and down the street.'

Half laughing, half crying, Rosie ran down the passage and flung open the door. 'It's *you*!' she said, ushering her friend in and closing the door before any nosy neighbour might look in.

''Course it's me!' Peggy replied, making her way before Rosie. 'Who the sodding hell did you think it was?' Once inside the parlour she turned to examine Rosie's face. 'I thought so!' Her voice hardened with anger. 'I had an idea you two had been fighting. By! He's a worse coward than I imagined.' Going into the scullery, she put the kettle on. Peering at Rosie through the doorway, she insisted, 'Any man who'd do that to a woman ain't worth spit!'

When she came back into the parlour, carrying two mugs of piping hot tea, she asked, 'Tell me to mind my own business if you like, but they do say a trouble shared is a trouble halved.' Giving one of the mugs to Rosie, Peggy waited for her to sit down on the chair opposite. Through the scullery window she had seen the sheets and bedding hanging out on the line; the flagstoned floor had been scrubbed until it shone; the mats had been beaten and relaid in the parlour; even the fire-grate was black-leaded, and one glance told her that the child was washed and now fast asleep in its pram. 'Good Lord, you must have been up at the crack of dawn,' she remarked.

'Four o'clock,' Rosie informed her. 'I couldn't sleep. I haven't slept properly these past two days.' After all that had happened, she had been at sixes and sevens. 'Doug wrote asking Adam to be godfather, and he's accepted.'

Peggy's face said it all. 'So *that's* what you've been fighting about?'

'Sort of.'

'What's that supposed to mean?'

'Why aren't you at work?'

'You may well ask. I've been round here twice and that bloody husband of yours has sent me away each time. I began to think the only way I'd find out what was going on was to take an hour off work, so here I am.'

'Oh, Peggy! You'll get the sack.'

She chuckled at that. 'Give over. Didn't you know they've got their eye on me as the next manager?' The smile fell from her face. 'You don't want to tell me then?'

'He saw the birthday card you gave me.' She decided she might as well tell it all. 'Then he saw the one Adam sent.'

Peggy looked surprised. '*Adam* sent you a birthday card?'

'It was innocent enough . . . a simple card, with a simple message.'

'But your old man didn't see it that way, eh?'

Rosie had to laugh. 'He went berserk.'

'That were his lousy conscience, I expect. I don't suppose you had a card from *him*, did you, eh?' When Rosie shook her head, Peggy asked, 'How did he come to see Adam's card?'

'I displayed it next to yours on the mantelpiece.'

Punching the air with her fist, Peggy said, 'Good for you, gal!'

'Now I've got this to show for it.' Rosie pointed to the bruise on her face.

'But you stood up to him, that's all that matters.'

'I sometimes wonder whether it's worth it though.' She smiled a sad smile. 'Oh, Peggy, you should have seen Adam's card. It was so pretty, with roses and everything.'

'I suppose he tore it up, did he?'

'No. It were me who tore it up.' Seeing the look on Peggy's face, she explained, 'I had to, don't you see? I made my mistake way back, and now there's no point spending my days dreaming and wishing. What's done is done, and that's an end to it.'

'Are you sure?' Peggy saw how desperately unhappy Rosie was, and couldn't help but wonder if there was a way out of it.

'Oh, Peggy! Of course I'm sure. What's to be gained by clinging to the past? Adam must have a life of his own now . . . I'm wed to Doug.' She pointed to the pram. 'There's the lad to consider, and I'm nearly seven months with another. Ask yourself, what chance could there be for a woman like me on my own?' When Peggy seemed lost for words, she went on in a softer tone, 'If Adam were to knock on that door right now and ask me to come away with him . . . which I'm sure would never happen . . . I would still have to think twice. Doug Selby is a vindictive and possessive man. You can depend on one thing. He would fight for the children and leave no stone unturned to make my life a misery.' She made an odd little sound that might have been a sob. 'You can depend on something else too. His mother would be right behind him, spurring him on with her hatred.'

'I suppose you're right, gal,' Peggy was loth to admit it, but she could see the awful truth in Rosie's words. 'But I swear if he hits you again . . .'

Rosie interrupted. 'Don't worry,' she promised in a serious voice, 'this is the last time he raises a bruise on me.'

'By! You sound as though you might kill the bugger.'

'Don't think it hasn't crossed my mind.'

A strange silence fell over the little parlour while each young woman considered the implications of what had been said. 'I'm surprised Adam agreed to be godfather,' Peggy commented finally.

'So am I.'

'Are you glad?'

'It means my son can be baptised at last.'

'Oh? And you're not pleased because you'll see Adam again?' Peggy teased with a knowing little smile.

Rosie returned her smile. 'All right then, yes,' she admitted.

'But one look at me and he'll thank his lucky stars he went when he did.'

'Whatever do you mean?' Peggy looked at her. Though Rosie's face was bruised, she was still the loveliest creature on two legs. 'The bruise will be cleared up in time.'

'Maybe. But I wasn't just talking about that.' Stretching her arms out, she invited Peggy to take a closer look. 'I'm big as a barge, my hair needs cutting, and there are bags under my eyes where the baby's kept me awake night after night.' It was a hot and humid June afternoon, and she felt completely drained of energy.

'You're too hard on yourself, gal!' Peggy reprimanded. 'Anyway, you've forgotten about my considerable talents. I haven't been put on the cosmetics counter for no reason, you know.'

'You're not dyeing my hair again!'

'Why not? The dye washed out, didn't it?'

'Yes, and so did handfuls of my hair.'

'All right then, we'll forget that.'

'And anything else you've got in mind,' Rosie said good-naturedly, 'I'm past being a guinea-pig.'

The child woke then. 'It was early when I fed him, so I expect he's bawling for his titty.' In a minute Rosie had collected him and was preparing to feed him.

Lately, Peggy's career had overtaken her desire for husband and children. But now she watched how tenderly Rosie held the boy, and how lovingly she let him suck the milk from her. There was something uniquely special about the relationship that deeply moved her. Oh, she had seen her own mother feed the young ones, but with Rosie it always seemed different. Peggy wondered if it was because her friend was younger than her, yet here Rosie was with an infant son and another bairn due soon. There was no denying that she was not only beautiful in appearance but that she had a warm and giving soul. 'You're so lovely, Rosie,' Peggy told her, 'Adam will rue the day he let you go.'

She smiled. 'I don't think so.'

'That's the trouble with you, my girl!' Peggy's hackles were up. 'You've too low an opinion of yourself. You'll see! I'll have you looking like a million dollars on Sunday.'

Rosie laughed. 'That'll take some doing,' she said, cuddling the boy on her lap. 'I'm a wreck.'

As Peggy cast a gaze over her friend, she experienced a fleeting pang of envy. With her rich brown hair, sparkling hazel eyes and those classic features, Rosie was very special. And even though she had been through the mill with Doug and his hateful mother, her strength of mind had carried her above it all with a dignity that was impressive. 'Trust me,' she said now. 'When Adam claps eyes on you, he'll want you all over again.'

'I'm not sure that would be a good thing.'

'If it makes that bloody husband of yours value you more, then it *will* be a good thing.' Peggy chuckled. 'In fact, I wouldn't be surprised if on Sunday we don't see the cat among the pigeons.'

'I've been thinking that myself.'

'And are you worried?'

Rosie's eyes sparkled with mischief. 'I was. But now I'm really looking forward to it.'

The two friends laughed and talked, and the hours ticked away. When Peggy was gone, Rosie thought about the christening, and how she had told her friend she was looking forward to it. Now, though, in her solitude, she wondered what Sunday would really bring, and a feeling of mounting trepidation rose within her.

Chapter Nine

Connie was in tears. Yet again she had been battered by her husband, and now here she was looking to Adam for comfort. As he sat her in the chair, Adam warned, 'If you go back to him, you deserve everything you get.'

Through her tears Connie smiled up at him. 'Thanks for not saying, "I told you so".' It was obvious from her red eyes that she had cried all night. Wincing from the pain in her shoulder, she bit her bottom lip. 'I think he's broken it.'

Tenderly roving his fingers along the line of her shoulder, he was satisfied when she showed how she could raise her arm and bend it at the elbow. 'No. It's not broken . . . badly sprained though.' His mouth drew into a thin angry line. 'How did it happen?'

As always, Connie defended her lover. 'It was my fault,' she insisted. 'I shouldn't have put my shoulder against the door.'

'Ah!' He realised now. 'So, he's thrown you out again?'

Grinning, she admitted sheepishly, 'Looks like it.'

'For Christ's sake, Connie! Why can't you see him for what he is? The fellow's no use to you.' Anger was welling up inside him, forcing him to pace the floor. 'Everyone knows what a womaniser he is. What! There must have been umpteen young women in and out of these premises over the years, and he's used them all . . . he lets them have a room, and for that he takes their rent money *and* expects to bed them.'

'He didn't take any of them into his own house though, did he?'

'Not that I know. But a man like that always has his own devious reasons for doing what he does.' Adam hated raising this particular issue, but felt he had to make Connie see what she was letting herself in for. 'I hope you haven't forgotten how he brought men to the house and expected you to sleep with them?'

'I wish I hadn't told you that.'

'Yes, well, so do I! Because in spite of everything I say, you still think the sun shines out of his arse!'

'I know all the arguments, Adam, so you might as well save your breath.' Very carefully, she flexed her arm muscles. 'I think you're right, it isn't broken.' She sighed with relief.

'But it might have been. That bastard deserves a bloody good thrashing!' Grabbing his coat from the chair-back, he flung it on. 'Matter of fact, I'm in the mood to see to it.' In two strides he was at the door.

Scrambling to her feet, Connie stopped him. 'He's not there.'

'You would say that.'

'No. Honest to God, he's cleared off. Business, he said. But to tell the truth, I reckon he's trying to shake me off altogether.'

Realising she was telling the truth, he took off his coat. 'You'd be better off if he never came back.'

'No, I wouldn't.' Looking pleased with herself, she said, 'I'm pregnant.'

Adam groaned and shook his head in despair. 'And I don't suppose he wants to know?'

'That's why he's took to his heels and buggered off.' She chuckled. 'But he won't get away that easily, because now I've got him where I want him. He can't ignore me, can he, eh?' For the first time her voice wavered and she seemed unsure of herself.

'Can he, Adam? Not even he could desert a woman who's carrying a child.' Tears welled up in her eyes. Now, when Adam opened his arms to her, she clung to him. 'I know I've been a fool,' she confessed, 'but I love him.'

Holding her tight, he reassured her, 'I know. And if he had any eyes in his head, he would see that. Happen he will. Happen he'll change his ways.' He laughed wryly. 'Even a snake can shed his skin.'

'I shouldn't bring my troubles to you, Adam.'

'Isn't that what friends are for?'

Moving away, she asked, 'Can I stay here tonight? I'm not short of money, and I could go to a hotel, but I don't want to be on my own.'

'Of course you can, but only for the one night. I'll be checking out myself tomorrow.'

Her eyes lit up. 'Does that mean you've got Ben Saxon's house . . . the one with the yard and everything?'

'It does.' A look of immense satisfaction came over his handsome features, but it faded when he thought of Ben. 'They say one man's misfortune is another man's opportunity, but I can't help feeling sad for Ben.'

'From what you told me about him, I reckon he would have been pleased to know you had come into good times. I mean, he was the one who gave you the chance of a wagon, and he took a liking to you straight away.'

'God knows why!'

'Because you're a good man, that's why. And Ben Saxon saw that.'

'It's early days yet,' Adam reminded her. 'I've only just really got going, and the rent on Ben's place will be crippling at first. Besides, the house is in bad repair and I won't be able to renovate it for some time yet.' But even though he had a daunting task ahead of him, Adam couldn't suppress his excitement. 'Oh,

Connie! At long last I'm seeing it all happen . . . first the wagon, and then the best round in Liverpool, and now the house and yard! Sometimes I still have to pinch myself to make sure I'm not dreaming.'

'You're not the kind of man to waste time dreaming,' she said. 'Whatever you've achieved it's no more than you deserve, because you've worked bloody hard for it.'

'Aye! And I'll go on working hard until every fireplace in Liverpool burns the coal I fetch to the door.' Every day brought a new opportunity, and ambition burned so fiercely in him that he worked with a frenzy. A frenzy that was meant to shut Rosie from his thoughts. It didn't though. And he was a fool to think it ever would.

'I'll find somewhere tomorrow,' she promised. 'It's just that I don't want to be on my own tonight.'

He smiled. 'Reminds me of that first night I brought you here.'

'One of the better things in my life.'

'Where's your suitcase?'

'Outside the door.' He went to get it, and on his return she asked impishly, 'I don't suppose . . . ?'

Anticipating her question, he shook his head from side to side, his dark eyes smiling. 'No. I'll sleep on the couch as always.'

'Pig!'

Teasing, he asked, 'Anyway, I thought you were head over heels in love with the landlord?'

'That don't mean to say I can't snuggle up to someone else when he's not around.'

'Bed and breakfast, that's all I'm providing. Do you still want to stay?'

'Okay.'

He laughed aloud. 'I never know what to think of you.'

'I wouldn't mind going out for a drink later . . . cheer me up, it would.'

'I've no objection to that.' Taking her case to the bedroom, he reminded her sternly, 'Then it's you to your bed, and me to mine.'

'All right. I'm grateful for small mercies.' Being in Adam's company always cheered her up. 'In return, I'll help you move out tomorrow.'

'Nothing to move, except myself.' He saw how downcast she looked. 'I tell you what, though. You know I'm travelling to Blackburn tomorrow afternoon?'

'Oh, yes, I'd forgotten. You're going to a christening. After my bad behaviour am I still allowed to go along?'

'You don't deserve to, but I'm sure Rosie and Doug wouldn't mind.'

She was thrilled. 'If you're sure?'

'I know you'll be miserable if I leave you behind,' he said. And so it was settled.

That night, while Adam slept on the settee, Connie came through the room to get a glass of water. On her way back, she glanced at his tousled hair and sleeping face. Women like me don't fall for decent blokes like you, she thought. It's a pity, but we always end up with someone as bad as ourselves. As she clambered back into bed, she stared at the door and whispered in a sad voice, 'I know he's a bastard, but I'd give anything to keep him.' She was momentarily filled with shame. 'Goodnight, Adam. And thanks for being a friend.'

Chapter Ten

The family had gathered in Rosie's tiny parlour. Ned Selby looked stiff and uncomfortable in a light grey suit with a striped shirt that was done up so tight round his neck he looked choked. 'I'll have to go home and change into something looser,' he complained to his wife. His neck was red raw where he had constantly run his fingers beneath the shirt collar.

'You'll do no such thing!' While she spoke, Martha glared at him through narrowed eyes. 'I'm not having you in church looking like a rag-bag.' She was dressed in a sober green two-piece that stretched over her ample figure like a net over a bag of peas; every awful curve and wrinkle was exposed for all to see.

Rosie looked unusually lovely in a flowing dark dress that wonderfully camouflaged the round bulge beneath. Her brown shining hair was left loose to her shoulders, and there was a wonderful radiance about her.

For two days now she and Peggy had worked hard getting the little house ready for visitors, finally this very morning laying out the table with all the food which had been made by their own hands, apart from the scones which Peggy's mam had eagerly contributed. Only two hours ago, Rosie was bone-tired and it showed. Now, after bathing and resting awhile, and with the event in sight, she appeared to be more relaxed; though in truth her heart was beating tenfold at the thought of seeing Adam again.

Doug was running back and forth to the door, impatient for Adam to arrive. 'Where the hell is he?' he raged. 'If he don't soon turn up, you can forget the whole bloody thing!' His remarks were aimed at Rosie.

With a calmness that surprised everyone, she walked across the room to confront him. 'Whether Adam arrives or not, our son *will* be baptised,' she assured him in a quiet voice. 'No more delays, Doug. I won't stand for it.'

He laughed aloud, pointing a finger at her as he addressed the other three. 'Will you listen to that, eh? The little woman's getting too big for her boots, don't you think?'

Ned Selby stared hard at his son, and felt ashamed. Martha, however, stepped forward to tell Rosie, 'It's the *man* who decides these things, my girl, and don't you forget it!'

'And don't *you* forget, we're not in your parlour now, Mrs Selby.' Rosie had long ago ceased to be afraid of this woman, though she was always wary of the influence Martha held over Doug.

Looking smart in a navy-blue two-piece and white frilly blouse, Peggy had remained near the pram, occasionally glancing out of the window and watching for the arrival of Adam Roach. Now, she was relieved to see a black vehicle draw up by the kerbside. 'He's here!' she cried, and when Doug rushed out, everyone else turned their eyes towards the door. A strange atmosphere settled over the tiny parlour. Ned Selby mentally recalled his meeting with Adam and wondered whether he had made headway with his ambitious plans; Martha's thoughts were more vindictive because she remembered how Rosie and Adam had once been sweethearts. Peggy too remembered and was quietly anxious, while Rosie herself was lost in a multitude of emotions, trembling with excitement one minute and filled with dread the next. What would he look like? Would he think she was still attractive? Would he be put off by her swollen stomach and puffy ankles? And what about Doug? She had no doubt he had insisted on having Adam here out of sheer jealousy, and knew he harboured a deal of loathing towards both her and his former friend; her for choosing Adam before him, and Adam for being more handsome, more intelligent, and in Ned Selby's words, 'A decent bloke'.

All manner of thoughts raced through her mind as she heard Doug go to greet Adam. Even the sound of Adam's voice touched her deep inside. 'Here he is!' Doug came through the door first, a look of triumph on his face and his odd-coloured eyes lost in a broad smile. 'The man himself,' he said, stepping aside to let Adam enter. And all the while Doug kept his sharp gaze on Rosie. She felt his animosity and, not for the first time, was afraid of the awful consequences this day might bring.

Adam came into the room, and at once the little parlour was full of his presence. He was everything Rosie remembered: tall and incredibly handsome, his dark eyes smiling, and his thick mop of black hair spilling over ears and forehead as though it had a life of its own. As he paused, his gaze seeking her out, his broad shoulders seemed to fill the doorway and the parlour was cast into shadow. 'Good to see you, Rosie,' he said, and the sound of his voice turned her heart over.

'I'm glad you're here,' she replied truthfully. She knew Doug's eyes were on her, but couldn't tear her gaze from Adam. For the two of them, time seemed to stand still. It was almost as though they had gone back to that fateful day when he went into the forces. Nothing had happened between . . . no long periods when he didn't write and she was devastated, no Doug, no deceit, no wedding. There was just Adam and her, and a love so powerful it almost breathed.

It was Peggy who wisely broke the spell. 'You ain't changed

much,' she remarked. 'But then, I don't suppose any of us has.'

'You certainly haven't,' he said. 'You're still as bright as ever.' He kissed her on the cheek, and would have done the same for Martha if she hadn't glowered at him and stepped away.

'There's no time for all that,' she said sullenly when he shook hands with Ned. Turning to Doug, she suggested, 'We'd best go, son, or we'll be late.'

'Wait, there's someone I want you all to meet.' Adam looked behind him and ushered in Connie who was pretty as a picture in a bright pink outfit and black high-heeled shoes. 'This is Connie,' he explained. Addressing Doug he said, 'I hope you don't mind, only I didn't want to leave her behind.'

Doug's face lit up. 'Mind? Whyever should I mind?' He stared her up and down and was pleased with what he saw. Then he turned to Rosie. 'Come along, sweetheart. Like Mam says, we don't want to be late now, do we?'

In the church, Rosie's son was quiet as a lamb. Instead it was Doug who exploded when the priest declared the little chap's name to be 'Danny'.

'You're wrong,' Doug interrupted, and was embarrassed when all eyes turned to him.

'Oh?' asked the priest, looking puzzled, 'What shall I christen him then?'

Rosie spoke out. 'Danny,' she said calmly. 'His name is to be Danny. That's the name he's registered by, and that's the name he'll be christened.' Fortunately, the registrar was an old man with an understanding nature. Changing the child's name had not been the arduous task she had feared. She smiled at Doug and his eyes bored through her. Some time back she had called on this very priest and she gambled that Doug wouldn't cause a scene here in church in front of everyone. Thankfully, she had been right.

The ceremony continued, and throughout it Rosie could feel Doug's hostility towards her. But she didn't care. Her son had been given the name she had chosen, and if she had to pay the price later, then so be it. For now, the moment was hers, and she was revelling in it.

The child slept when the priest poured water over his head, and snoozed through the heartfelt rendering of 'The Old Rugged Cross'. He slept on while Adam cuddled him, and was still deep in dreams when they arrived back at the house. 'I've never known an infant so good,' Connie remarked, and everyone had to agree.

'I'm proud you asked me to be godfather,' Adam told Doug, who had stopped off at a mate's to collect a crate of ale and was now busy working his way through it.

'Who else would I ask but my best mate?' Doug said sulkily. The more he drank, the surlier he became.

Aware that Doug was deliberately being offensive, Adam guessed the reason and made a great effort to stay away from Rosie. Leaving Connie chatting to Doug, he spent a few minutes making small talk with Martha, who seemed hell-bent on making him feel unwelcome. He was relieved to talk with Ned, who discussed various current affairs, including the recently retired world heavyweight, Joe Lewis, and the lifting by the Soviets of the Berlin blockade. The talk soon came round to home, and industry, and inevitably came the question, 'Are you making your fortune then, Adam?'

'Not yet, but I'm heading in the right direction.' Occasionally he would glance at Rosie, and everything he had achieved so far meant nothing to him. 'I've got one wagon and just recently took on the lease of a yard and premises . . . the very same premises where we met at the sale.' Ned Selby seemed impressed so he went on, 'Ben Saxon did me a favour I'll never forget.' He explained how it had all come about, and added, 'It was the kick-start I needed. There'll be no holding me now!'

Especially not now, he mused bitterly, sneaking a glance at the heavily pregnant Rosie and thinking how lovely she was. In fact, he said the very same thing to her when Doug fell asleep on the settee and the two of them were able to sneak a moment together. 'I don't think I've ever seen you look more beautiful,' he said, smiling into her brown eyes.

'Away with you,' she said softly, feeling suddenly shy beneath the intensity of his gaze. 'I'm seven months pregnant and looking like the side of a house.'

'Not from where I'm standing.'

'Thank you for that.'

'Rosie?'

'Yes?'

'Tell me, are you happy? *Really* happy?'

She couldn't bring herself to answer. Instead she looked to where Connie and Martha were talking. 'Your girlfriend . . . she's very pretty.' She was grateful that Connie had innocently drawn Martha's attention from her, because ever since Adam had crossed the room to talk with her, Rosie had been acutely aware of her mother-in-law's eyes boring into them.

'Rosie, you didn't answer my question.' Adam was insistent. 'Are you happy?'

'Of course. You can see for yourself.' It was more than she dared do to let him think otherwise. Besides, her pride wouldn't allow him to believe she was less than happy. Not when he obviously had a woman of his own who he 'didn't want to leave behind'.

'You've changed.'

'Oh?'

'You're quieter, more subdued . . . as if the spirit has gone out of you.'

'What nonsense!' She forced herself to laugh. 'How like a man. Here I am, with a bairn in arms and seven months carrying, and I'm expected to leap about like a two year old.' It wasn't his fault but she felt angry, sad even. Perhaps because he was right. She had changed.

'I didn't mean that, and you know it.' He glanced at Doug who had woken up and after talking briefly to his father was now glowering at them from the other side of the room. '*He* hasn't changed at all. He's still fond of the ale, and his temper hasn't improved.' When she didn't answer, he voiced the suspicion that had played on his mind ever since he had arrived here. 'I don't have to ask why he wanted me as godfather?'

'Are you sorry?'

'If he expected me to be that, then he's the one who should be sorry.' He gazed down on her lovely face, and sensed the sadness there. 'Doug should thank his lucky stars that he has a woman like you for his wife,' he murmured. 'Walking out on you was something I can never forgive myself for.' Leaning towards her, he lowered his voice. It was now heavy with emotion. 'If there should come a day when you need me, I'll be there. Always remember that.'

'Thank you, but I honestly don't see how I'll ever have need of you,' she lied. 'Doug has his faults, I know, but he takes good care of us.' Her gaze went first to the sleeping child, and then to her husband. He was beginning to drink heavily and she feared he might cause trouble. 'It seems such a long time since we were all footloose and fancy free,' she mused aloud, 'but that's all water under the bridge.' She wondered how she could sound so matter-of-fact when inside she was crying out for him. 'The past is gone, and it's only the future that counts. We all have our own roads to travel.' In her own way she was trying to tell him that even if she should ever need his help, she could never ask for it.

Her words were like a slap in the face to Adam. 'I'm sorry,' he said, 'I didn't mean anything. It's just that, well, I hope we can remain friends, you and I? But of course you're right. It's no good dwelling on the past. Nothing ever comes of that.' So they talked about the child and how bonny he was. They talked about how Adam was working his way up in the world, and how Ben was a good man who had advised him well. They had a little laugh about how Martha was still an old warhorse, and Rosie told him what a good friend Peggy was. They chatted about everything in general and nothing in particular, and not once after Rosie's timely warning did they talk about themselves. In her heart, though, Rosie cherished these precious moments together, and he was tortured by her nearness.

It was Doug's slurred and bad-tempered voice that broke the spell between them. 'What the bloody hell's this then?' he asked, flinging his arm round Rosie's shoulders and almost knocking her over. 'A secret meeting, is it? Or can anybody join?'

Adam's face broke into a wide smile. 'I was just telling Rosie how well she looked . . . considering.'

'Oh, aye?' Pushing Rosie aside, he thrust his face forward, glaring up at Adam with bloodshot eyes. 'And what's that supposed to mean, eh? Considering?'

Adam knew Doug of old. He had seen him the worse for drink before and, though he could have shaken him by the scruff of the neck, simply smiled and told him, 'Considering the wonderful do she's put on here, the food and everything. It's a credit to her. It can't have been easy.'

Doug laughed. 'Rubbish! This sort of thing is what women are best at.' Turning his attention to Rosie he asked, 'Enjoyed every minute of it, didn't you, sweetheart?'

'If you say so.' Her brown eyes deepened with anger. She didn't like being made to look a fool, especially in front of Adam.

Sensing her animosity, he tightened his grip on her shoulders, making her wince. 'Oh, I *do* say so!' he murmured, kissing her on the mouth and laughing aloud when she pulled away. 'No need to be shy in front of old friends,' he argued.

To make his point he would have kissed her again, but lost his balance. It was Adam who saved Rosie from being squashed against the sideboard. 'Don't you think you've had enough of that?' he asked grimly, pointing to the jar of ale in Doug's fist; most of the frothy brown liquid had splashed over Rosie, but she chose not to make a fuss in front of everyone. Instead she quietly dabbed at the stain with her hankie, realising with dismay that her one best skirt was possibly ruined.

'Stop that!' Doug knocked her hand away. 'Bugger the skirt,' he yelled, 'I'll buy you a new one. Or would you rather *he* bought you one, eh? Then happen he'd have a right to take it off when he felt like it!' With every word he jabbed at her arm until it was red raw.

Something snapped in Rosie then. Whether it was the sight of Martha's smug and satisfied face gawping at them from across the room, or whether it was Adam's grim features that told her he was about to wipe the floor with Doug, or even her own humiliation at being shown up in front of everyone, she would never know. But in a minute she was facing Doug, telling him in a calm and dignified voice, 'Please keep your hands to yourself and lower your voice. Have you forgotten this is our son's christening, and that we have guests here?' Forcing a nervous smile while he stared at her open-mouthed, she went on, 'If you can't behave in a civilised manner, I think it might be a good idea for you to go upstairs and sleep it off.' Nothing in her manner betrayed the fact that she was inwardly seething.

But Doug's fury was written on his face for all to see. 'You little bitch!' Grabbing her by the arms he shook her hard. 'Who the hell are you to talk to me like that, eh? I ought to take the skin off your back!'

'Not if I have anything to say.' Adam had seen enough. Stepping forward, he gripped the neck of Doug's shirt. 'I reckon Rosie's right. I'll even give you a hand up the stairs if you like.'

There was a threat in his voice and Doug turned a sick shade of grey.

'Take your bloody mitts off me!' Squirming and kicking, he still couldn't shake himself free from Adam's vice-like grip. 'And get out of my house, you bugger, afore I have you thrown out.' He looked to his father, but Ned was thoroughly enjoying seeing his son being taken down a peg or two. Martha had taken a few steps forward to intervene, but was forced to a standstill when her husband caught hold of her arm. It seemed she was more shocked by his action than by the heated argument between Adam and Doug.

Out of the ensuing awkward silence, it was Rosie who spoke. 'I think you'd better go,' she told Adam. 'And it might be wisest if you never came back.' He couldn't have known what an immense effort it took for her to say that. 'I'm sorry,' she whispered. Those last two words were only for the two of them, and he knew that.

'I understand,' he told her, 'and I wouldn't want to outstay my welcome.' For a seemingly endless minute his grip on Doug remained fierce, before he released him with such force that the smaller man staggered backwards. 'I wish I could turn the clock back, but I can't. Rosie's your woman now, though God knows you don't deserve her.' His warning was unmistakable. 'You'd best look after her, Selby.'

Doug didn't answer but watched him go, calling Rosie back when she would have gone with him. 'He can find his own way out!' he snarled. When Martha rushed to his side to comfort him, Doug pushed her away. Peggy winked at Rosie who, in spite of her husband's warning, hurried after Adam and Connie; at the same time acknowledging Peggy's wink with a knowing smile.

As she came to the door, Rosie's smile froze on her face when she saw Connie with Adam at the car. Connie was on tiptoe with her arms round Adam's neck. She was kissing him.

Quickly, before they saw her, Rosie returned to the parlour, the image of what she had just seen burned on her mind. Yet she chided herself for feeling hurt. She had no right. Adam was his own man, and she had only just finished telling him in her own way that they must not dwell on the past. Yet, she did hurt, and she envied Connie with all her heart.

'Are you all right?' Peggy met her at the door.

'I'm fine, thanks, Peggy.'

''Course she's all right!' Martha had found her voice and was fighting fit. 'Why shouldn't she be? If anybody should be upset, it's our Doug here. That bloody Adam Roach has a thing or two to answer for!'

'Shut up, Mam!' Swaying on his feet, Doug came across the room to stare at Rosie. She had never seen him so enraged.

'I *won't* shut up,' Martha cried, coming between him and Rosie. 'I'm your mother, and I don't take kindly to folk like Adam treating a son of mine like that.' She pushed at Doug's chest with the flat of her hands. 'You ought to have leathered him. Why didn't you leather him?'

'GET OUT!' He saw her words as an accusation that he was either a coward or a lesser man than Adam. On top of everything else it was more than he could bear. With one great sweep of his arm he lifted her clean off her feet and sent her flying against the heavy oak table. There was a grinding thud, one awful minute when she stared at him with wide open eyes, then she fell to the floor with her back strangely twisted and her arms trapped beneath her own weight.

'God Almighty!' Ned fell to his knees beside her, cradling his wife and afraid to move her. 'She's hurt bad.' Looking up at Doug with accusing eyes, he ordered, 'Get out of my sight, you!' When he spoke to Peggy it was to ask, 'Get the ambulance, lass . . . quick as you can.'

As Peggy fled from the house, Rosie urged her to run as fast as she could. With a surge of compassion she stared down on Martha's unconscious form, and, rightly or wrongly, blamed herself for all that had happened here.

Rosie wasn't to know that Martha's back was broken, and that she would never walk again. In her worst nightmare she could not realise how the events of this day would make her already unhappy life even more unbearable. For the moment all she could think was that Martha had been hurt, and needed help.

Ned and Doug went with Martha to the Infirmary. Before they left, Doug made Rosie a promise. 'I'll teach you to interfere with my plans!' he told her, and she knew he was referring to her having secretly changed the child's name. He then blamed her for his mother's injury. Ned, however, was quick to reassure her.

'It was an accident,' he said softly. 'I don't want you getting yourself in a state.' Glancing at her swollen stomach, he said, 'You've got enough to worry about. Anyway, Martha's a tough old bird. She'll be all right.'

Peggy offered to stay, but Rosie would have none of it.

'You look awful,' Peggy argued. 'Are you sure you're all right?' She wasn't exaggerating when she said Rosie looked awful. Her face was drawn and pale, and she looked desperately tired. Feeling the need to be left alone with her troubled thoughts, however, Rosie assured her she was fine, and Peggy reluctantly went home to tell her mam what had happened, and to explain how she wouldn't have Rosie's life 'for all the tea in China'.

No sooner had Peggy gone than Rosie felt the first pangs of early labour. Two hours later the pains were intensifying and she could hardly breathe.

In the early hours, doubled up in agony and alone except for little Danny, Rosie made her slow tortuous way down the street. When Peggy opened the door she found her friend crumpled in a heap on the step.

When those brown eyes looked up at her, Peggy's heart turned over. 'Help me, Peggy,' she pleaded. 'I don't want to lose my baby.'

Yet she knew. In her heart Rosie felt the child's life ebbing away inside her. It seemed like a penance, a shocking punishment for secretly wanting Adam's love.

In that moment she prayed she would never set eyes on him again.

Chapter Eleven

'The end of another week, thank God.' Kindly-faced, with the shoulders of a bull elephant and hands the size of shovels, the man's eyes were stark white in his sooty face, and when he walked across the office little pockets of coal-dust fell from his clothes, leaving a dark trail across the floor. 'Have you ever known such a stifling day?' he groaned. 'Hottest July I can ever remember.' Wiping his brow, he left a smear of white skin exposed beneath.

Adam was busy putting the wages together, his head bowed and his lips silently counting. Undaunted, the fellow continued, 'It's a miracle the way you've picked up more work when other merchants are losing hand over fist.'

'That's because I have a good eye for an opportunity,' Adam teased. It was Friday night, and like his men he felt lighter of heart with a good week's work behind him.

Taking up the envelope, the fellow laughed. 'Hopefully the missus won't miss the price of a pint out o' me wages.' He said something then that struck Adam to the quick. 'What would you know about being wed, eh? You've been too bloody clever to get yourself lumbered with a wife and family.' He meant it as a compliment, not realising how he had touched on Adam's deepest longing.

Tipping the money into his large palm, the fellow counted his wages. 'But you do pay yer men well, I'll not deny that.' Standing up and stretching his back with a groan, he wet his lips with the tip of a pink tongue. 'I reckon a pint of ale would do me nicely. By! I can taste it slithering down me throat . . . dry as a bone I am. Matter o' fact, being as I've done a deal of overtime this week, I reckon I might treat meself to a *couple* o' pints.'

Adam met the other man's gaze, his dark eyes brooding now. 'Off you go then, before the ale gets warm.'

'I can wait, if you want to join me?'

'You'll wait a long time. There's four wagons to clock in yet, and a mountain of work to be done before I can lock up.' He waved a hand over the pile of papers and documents strewn across his desk. 'I'll be honest, Tom. There are times when I wish I was back on the rounds with the rest of you lads. In fact, now that the business is thriving and I can afford it, I've been thinking about getting somebody in to take all this paperwork off my hands. I'd much rather be shifting coal any day of the week.' He stretched himself in the chair and thought of Rosie. When a man's back was heavy with his work, his heart was somehow quieter.

'Don't be daft, man!' At fifty years of age, Tom Lockwood was the oldest man there. He felt it his duty to look after the others, and to this end he spoke his mind now. 'You could get a clerk to do the paperwork, but who could you trust to go after the contracts, eh? Who would grade the coal and haggle about price? What about the buying and selling of wagons? You said yourself we need to keep a good fleet. Get somebody to do the paperwork, aye! No doubt you can offload the financial side of it too. But there ain't nobody who can run this business like you, and it's you we rely on to keep our wages coming in. No. There's more to running a business than doing paperwork and making up the wages. This is your own business. You've worked bloody hard to get where you are in a tough world. And, as far as I'm concerned, there ain't nobody who can look after your own interests better than yourself.'

Adam had to laugh. 'Sounds like I should set *you* on?'

Tom pursed his mouth and winked an eye while he considered that. 'No,' he said at length, vigorously shaking his head. 'You've got the best man doing the job now. Like the rest of 'em, I know what's needed, but there ain't a man here who could do what you've done, and that's the God's honest truth. There's them that lead, and there's them that's content to follow. Besides, think on what you've achieved here. Hand it over for somebody else to take care of, and you could end up with nothing.'

Adam leaned back in his chair. He knew that what had been said made sense. All the same, in spite of everything he had gained, he felt as though he had lost a great deal more. 'Sometimes I don't feel as though I've achieved *anything*.'

'Away with you! To take on a rundown outfit and build it up to a flourishing concern, and all in less than two years. Well, I'd say *that* were some achievement.'

'I was in the right place at the right time, that's all.'

The other man shook his head. 'There's more to it than that. You're a grafter like the rest of us, but you've got brains too. That's what makes the difference between us. And you ain't afraid to take a chance when you see it.' He chuckled. 'To tell you the truth, none of us ever thought you'd do as well as you have . . . but you've proved us wrong, and I'm glad of that.'

'So am I.' Holding out his hand, Adam suggested, 'You'd best let me have this week's work-sheet . . . unless you don't want any wages next week?' In that minute two other men walked in, eager to collect their wages and make for home or the ale-house.

Producing the work-sheet from his overall pocket, Tom leaned forward. Lowering his voice he said. 'I hope you don't mind me speaking my mind?' When Adam assured him that he didn't mind in the least, he visibly relaxed. 'Right then. I'll be off for that pint.'

Once outside, Tom strode off in the direction of the Liverpool Arms. It wasn't long before one of the other men caught up with him. 'Heard you say you were going for a pint,' he confessed, 'I've a thirst of my own. Mind if I walk along with you?'

The two men talked over what had been said in the office, and they were agreed that they would never find a better boss than Adam Roach. 'Still an' all, it's a crying shame,' the second man said, 'a young fella like that . . . living on his own in Ben Saxon's big old house. He ought to have a pretty wife to come home to, and a dozen kids running round his arse.'

'It wouldn't do no harm if he were to tell that brassy blonde where to get off. Old friend or not, she fetches more trouble to his door than any dozen kids. What! It's a wonder there ain't been bloody murder between that landlord fella and our man. If you ask me, there's trouble brewing, and I wouldn't like to make a bet on which one of 'em will come off worse.' From the look on his face when he glanced at the other man, it was plain he was thinking of Adam.

Thankful that the last man had gone, Adam finished his paperwork and locked up for the night. It had been an especially busy week. For months now he had battled to secure the lucrative contract to supply all the coal for the local Infirmary. The competition was fierce, and all the sealed tenders had been submitted last Tuesday. Adam had learned only yesterday that he was the successful candidate, and even now could hardly believe it. He was in no doubt that he had made many enemies over that particular contract, and because of the extra work was forced to consider increasing his manpower and consequently reappraising his whole operation. He was into big business now, and such were the implications that he still had not told the men.

The office was situated in the ground floor of the old house. When Ben Saxon was alive, the room had been a junk-hole, cluttered from top to bottom with rubbish. Since Adam had taken over the house some two years back, the room had been transformed; there was a desk and two filing cabinets, and the walls were painted a quiet green.

The window of this particular room still overlooked the street, but Adam had commissioned builders to knock through a door leading straight to the yard. It had proved to be a real asset because now there was easy access in and out of the office and the men could come straight in on pay-day instead of going all the way round to enter the house from the scullery door.

In fact, the entire house had been subject to a great deal of change. The large room at the back was now a comfortable place where Adam could relax at the end of a long day. The freshly painted walls reflected the light, and were now hung with pictures; landscapes mostly, though there was also a seascape whose quiet mood and sun-kissed waves never failed to soothe his troubled heart. The big black fire-range had been restored to its original beauty, and the new light oak furniture was both attractive and serviceable. Where the floors had been covered in tattered old carpet, the boards were now exposed. Adam had spent many back-breaking hours sanding and polishing the boards, until now the beautiful grain in the wood made a splendid sight.

When Adam took over the tenancy on this house, every room was neglected and dingy. Now, they were bright and easy to live in. The kitchen had been remodelled the most with Adam ripping out everything that could move and refitting it with a new sink, a shiny gas cooker, and a large pine dresser that was six feet wide and reached almost to the ceiling. Right along the wall nearest the sink, he had fitted a deep shelf that served as both table and a working surface.

The bedrooms were all painted in soft colours and, like the downstairs living room, every floorboard was exposed and polished, with soft scatter-rugs spread to give a homely feel. The main bedroom, which overlooked the street, had a huge four-poster bed which he had acquired from the rag-man after a long and enjoyable haggle. Built of dark oak and draped with a patchwork eiderdown which Connie had bought in a curio shop, it was a wonderful, comfortable thing. Together with the dark oak dresser and wardrobe and two armchairs which he'd rescued from the tatter's wagon for a pound and recovered with his own hands, the room reflected his own strong personality. It was undoubtedly a man's room. Yet, every time he entered it, Adam saw how it lacked a woman's touch, and couldn't help but think about Rosie, and wonder what other touches she would bring to the whole house.

Now he wandered from room to room, feeling incredibly lonely, and wondering, not for the first time, where his life was leading. He felt empty, unfulfilled and immensely sad. Suddenly he could feel her in his arms, soft and warm, loving him as he loved her. 'You bloody fool, Roach!' he snapped angrily. 'When will you learn, she's done with you for good?' The truth seemed finally to overwhelm him, and suddenly all the trappings of success meant nothing.

The mantelpiece clock struck eight-thirty. After a long soak in the bath-tub, and afterwards an enjoyable meal of crusty bread and cheese, Adam was seated in the living room. The *Evening Telegraph* was set out before him on the table. He kept a close eye on local adverts, for you never knew when a bargain might crop up, or who was undercutting who in the coal war.

The sound of a knock on the door startled him. He wasn't expecting anyone, but his thoughts flew straight to Connie. 'Surely to God she's not been fighting with him again, has she?'

he asked himself as he went quickly to the front door. When he opened it, he was astonished to see not Connie but Ned Selby. 'Good Lord! You're the last person I expected to see,' gasped Adam.

'I'm sorry to disturb you.' Doug's father looked haggard, and his shoulders were stooped as though he was carrying a heavy load. In these two years since Adam had last seen him, he had aged more than ten. 'I've been meaning to come and see you for weeks now,' he explained as Adam led him into the living room. 'Only it's taken some courage, and lately I don't have too much of that, I'm afraid.' A look of embarrassment crossed his downcast features. 'I shouldn't have come so late. I can always come back tomorrow.'

'You'll do no such thing!' Adam told him. 'I'm delighted to see you, Ned, and now that you're here, I won't let you go that easily.' He ushered him into the most comfortable armchair. 'What'll it be . . . a jug of ale down at the pub, or a mug of tea?' His smile was designed to relax the older man, and it did.

'I don't feel like going to no pub, lad.' Even though Adam was now a mature man of thirty, Ned still saw him as the boy who'd grown up with his own son. 'If it's all the same to you, I'd rather stop here. What I have to say isn't for any other ears.'

'Fair enough.' Adam was both intrigued and bothered by Ned's comment. 'A mug of tea then, eh?'

Ned shook his head. 'Not for me,' he declined. 'Like I said, it's taken a lot of courage to come here, and if I don't speak my mind now, that courage will be gone.'

At once Adam sat down, his dark-eyed gaze settling on the older man's face. 'Go on, Ned,' he encouraged kindly, 'I'm listening.'

Ned couldn't speak for a minute. He wiped his hands over his face, then sighed and looked up through work-worn fingers. His eyes were those of an old, old man, and when he spoke the words were barely audible. 'I've come to the end of the road, lad,' he murmured, and his voice broke with emotion.

Adam was loth to reply. He felt instinctively that to do so would be an intrusion. The eyes that stared at him now were tear-filled in the folds of that aged face, reflecting the tortured soul inside. When it seemed as though Ned was lost for words, he said softly, 'You're safe enough speaking your mind here. Whatever you have to say won't go no further, I can promise you that.'

Taking his hands from his face and leaning back in the chair, Ned sighed deeply, his gaze never leaving Adam's concerned face. 'I don't know how to start,' he confessed. 'So much has happened that you don't know about.'

'Is it Rosie? Is she in some kind of trouble?' Sitting bolt upright now, Adam was ready to leap from the chair.

'No. I didn't come to talk about Rosie . . . at least not directly.' When Adam relaxed into the chair, Ned went on, 'It's not one thing in particular. I wish to God it was, because then I might be able to cope.'

'Whatever it is, Ned, I'm sure you're man enough to deal with it. And if I'm able to help in any way, you know I will.' This man had been like a father to him.

'I know. And I'm ashamed that I didn't reply to your letters.'

'I thought you must have your reasons.'

'Oh, it was all to do with our Doug and misplaced loyalty, I suppose. And, to be honest, I'm a bloody coward. In spite of what you might think, I've *allus* been a coward at heart. But I've kept them all, though, and I've read them time and again.' He smiled for the first time since entering Adam's house. 'I'm proud of you, lad. You've done well for yourself.' He glanced around the room. 'Your own business, and a grand place like this to come home to. By, you have! You've done well.'

'It was you who taught me everything I know. The master and

the boy.' Memories came flooding back as Adam looked at Ned with affection. 'I owe you a lot.'

'Aye, maybe, lad. But now the master's gone down in the world while the boy has gone up. And rightly so, because I couldn't see what was happening under my own nose.' No sooner were the words out than Ned clamped his lips together for fear he might let slip more than he'd intended. *The last thing he wanted was for Adam to suspect how Doug had been robbing his own father blind.*

'You're not making too much sense, Ned. What exactly do you mean about not seeing what was happening under your own nose?'

Thinking swiftly, Ned sought to allay any suspicion. 'What I mean is, I should have seen it coming . . . the market failing the way it did . . . customers going elsewhere to save a penny or two.' He slammed one gnarled fist into his palm. 'Damn and bugger it, Adam! I should have seen it. But I didn't, and now I'm in a spot o' bother.' He laughed, a low ugly sound. 'In fact, I'm about to lose it all.'

Adam sat up. 'Not if I have my way! How much, Ned? How much to keep you on top?'

Ned smiled again, and this time it was filled with warmth and regret. Oh, if only his own son was made of the same stalwart goodness. 'Bless you for that,' he said, 'but I've not come here looking for a loan.'

'What then?'

'I want you to buy me out.'

Adam couldn't believe his ears. 'Give over, Ned! You've *years* before you need to think of retiring.'

'Oh, I don't mean to retire, lad.' Now that the subject had been broached, he was more at ease. 'Whatever would I do with myself, eh? No, what I'm asking is this . . . buy me out at market value, then let me carry on as though it were my own business?

That way, I'd have the capital to get myself out of debt, and the only people who'd know that the business was yours and not mine, would be the solicitor and the two of us. Then, when the time *does* come for me to retire, it'll be yours to do with as you like.'

Adam didn't care for the proposition. 'You built that business up with your own sweat and blood, and believe me, Ned, I know now just what that entails. Besides, it was always there as your security for when you grew old. If I buy you out, where will that security be then, eh?'

'Look at me, son,' Ned entreated. 'I *am* old.' Following Adam's thoughts and afraid that he would turn him down, he went on, 'If I don't sell to you, I'll sell to somebody else, and they'll not give me a fair price the way things are. There are jackals out there, lad, and if they smell blood, they'll move in for the kill. As it is, I've still got two good rounds . . . not as lucrative as they once were, I'll admit, but they're good rounds all the same. If I could get a fair price, an outright sale should fetch enough to get me out of trouble, and happen leave a little to put by for a rainy day.'

'You really mean to sell, don't you? Whether it's to me or to somebody else?'

'That's right. I've already made discreet enquiries . . . sounding out one or two possible buyers. Honest to God, son, you wouldn't believe the measly offers I've had. Daylight robbery, that's what it is.'

'And you'd want to stay on, you say?'

'I'll run it well for you, you know that. Besides, to tell the truth, I need the wages.'

'What about Doug?' Always, his thoughts came back to Rosie.

'He doesn't work for me any more.' Quickly now, before Adam could voice the questions forming in his mind, Ned added, 'We went through a real lean time last year. I told him to keep his eyes open for a more secure job. He found it with Leyland's.'

'I see.' Adam pictured Doug leaving his own father floundering, and hated him for it.

'No, you *don't* see!' Ned had been worried that Adam's instincts would tell him a story. Afraid it might be the right one, he said, 'It were *my* decision that Doug should go, not his.' That at least was the truth, though he was careful not to reveal that he had sacked Doug after a bitter argument. 'There are other things too,' he went on. 'Things that have taken their toll on both me and the business. Martha had a bad fall . . . her back was broken and she's paralysed from the waist down. She's confined to her bed, and there are times when I have to neglect my work to look after her.'

Adam was shocked. 'I'm sorry to hear that.' He had always been in awe of Martha, and knew what a taskmaster she could be. All the same, it was a terrible thing. 'Is there anything at all that I can do?'

'There's nothing anyone can do. The thing is, she's become harder, more difficult to handle. Earlier on, I paid for a nurse to look after her . . . most of the money I earned went on medical expenses and the like. But I didn't mind that, because it meant I could work all day same as usual, and at night I tended her best I could. That went on for about a year, until she became hostile to the nurse, and every blessed other that came after.' He smiled, but there was sadness in his face. 'At least I knew she was feeling better, because she was getting more like her old self.'

'So you had to stay with her all day?'

'I couldn't very well leave her on her own, though I'd be a liar if I didn't say she wore me to a frazzle. Like the little trooper she is, our Rosie offered to go round each day, but Martha went mad at the idea.' When he saw the surprise on Adam's face, he quickly explained, 'There's always been resentment there. Martha's never really forgiven Rosie for taking Doug away. Anyway, the fact of the matter is this . . . she wouldn't let nobody but me take care of her. Consequently, the business was badly neglected at a time when I should have been concentrating all my efforts on keeping it afloat.'

'Let me lend you the money you want, Ned. Take as much time as you like in paying it back. I would never press you, you know that.'

Ned was adamant. 'You should know I'm not a man to borrow,' he said firmly. 'I've made up my mind. The business has to go. There's nobody else who'll buy it at the right price, and pay me a wage to stay on. If you're not interested, I'll be on my way. If I've caused you any embarrassment, I'm truly sorry.' He made to rise from the chair, but sat down when Adam began to speak.

'What price had you in mind?'

'I'm open to offers.'

For the next half hour they talked earnestly, and a deal was done. Adam would pay Ned a generous lump sum for the goodwill and all equipment, and in return, for an exceptionally handsome wage, Ned would stay on to run it as he had always done. The transaction was to remain a secret between the two of them; with the exception of the solicitor named by Ned.

'I wouldn't be in this dire position if I'd had the guts to stand up to Martha when she insisted I look after her. But all that will change now, and you can be sure I'll look after your interests. First thing on the morrow, I intend to find a nurse to stay at the house while I'm out at work.' Ned smiled wryly. 'I'm certain that if Martha is made to realise how much money we owe, she'll come to her senses right enough. Of course I shan't tell her how, thanks to you, we're now able to rid ourselves of debt. I'm not denying she's been ill, and my heart goes out to her for the predicament she's in. For a woman like Martha, paralysis must be the worst punishment of all. But she's made of hard stuff, and to be honest I reckon it's time she was made to realise the world doesn't revolve round her all the time.'

'It's a sorry situation, and I don't envy you, Ned.'

'I've been too bloody soft! What's happened has made me see that.' His face hardened. 'Like I say, things will change from now on.'

'I hope it all works out for you.' Adam could never remember the big man being so furious. But then he recalled everything Ned had told him, and it seemed that, though Martha had suffered a sad and terrible affliction, Ned had gone out of his way to protect her from undue hardship or discomfort. Like the man he was, he had shouldered all the responsibility and allowed himself to be dominated. It seemed that Martha's unfortunate accident had not only ruined her life, but everything Ned cherished along with it. And, seeing him now, Adam could only imagine the state of affairs that existed between him and his wife.

'Don't forget what I said . . . if there comes a time when you want to buy back the business, you've only to ask.'

Ned stood up then, his hand outstretched. 'I'll never be able to thank you enough,' he said, taking Adam's hand in a firm grip. 'As for buying the business back, it's all too late for that. No, I'll be satisfied just to earn a wage and let someone else do the worrying.'

'Ned?'

The big fellow smiled. 'I might be an old fool in some ways, but I know what's been on your mind ever since I stepped through that door. You want to know about Rosie?'

'How is she . . . really?'

'She's well. They all are.' He was careful not to mention how Rosie had lost the child she was carrying.

Adam eyed him curiously. 'I've written many times and sent presents for my godson, but as yet I've had only one reply, and that was a very polite letter from Rosie. Doug has never written.'

He thought on that for a minute. 'I've been tempted to go and see them, but wondered if I'd be welcome after what happened at the christening?'

Knowing in his heart that Adam was the right man for Rosie, Ned wondered whether he should tell him everything . . . how Rosie was suffering too. Time and again Ned had threatened Doug himself after discovering he had beaten Rosie for no good reason. And though she could give as good as she got, the constant rows and unhappiness were beginning to tell on her. Yet, for all that, he had to deter Adam from ever visiting. 'I'm afraid what happened on that day has turned Doug against you. And you're right, I don't think he would welcome another visit from you, more's the pity.'

'That's what I thought.' Adam had long suspected that, but to hear Ned say it now was upsetting.

'Still, you never know,' Ned remarked in a brighter voice. 'He's bearing a grudge now, but happen there'll come a day when he'll value the friendship you once had.' Like any father would, he lived in hope that Doug would come to his senses and that he and Rosie would resolve their differences. Even though he could not in all honesty see that happening, he still couldn't put the final nail in the coffin by telling Adam what was really going on. Ned was in no doubt that if he knew of Rosie's miserable life, Adam would move heaven and earth to get her back. He couldn't risk that. He had to cling to the smallest hope. 'Rosie and Doug have never been happier,' he lied, and felt the shameful flush creep up his neck. 'I'd best be off,' he said, wanting to get away. 'Thanks to you I've got a new lease of life, and there's a lot to be done.'

They shook hands on the doorstep. Adam went back inside and Ned went on his way to the railway station.

'Well, look who's here!' Connie's voice came at him out of the darkness. 'It's me, Connie!' she laughed, holding on to the lamp-post for support. 'You remember . . . Adam brought me to your grandson's christening.' Swaying and laughing, she was obviously the worst for drink.

Ned recognised her at once. 'Of course.' He recalled how Connie and he had talked, and he had thought her a delightful creature. 'How could I forget?' In the halo of light she looked like a child. 'I've been to see Adam,' he explained. 'A matter of business.'

'Business, eh? Well, you couldn't find nobody better than my lovely Adam. He's becoming a wealthy man now, did he tell you that? I love him to bits, but it ain't for his money, oh no! Between you and me, I don't know what I'd ever do without him. What! I'd have been in the gutter before now. But he's always watched out for me. And no matter what some people think, he always will.' Stepping towards him, she rubbed her hand up and down his shirt collar. 'He's a good man. One of the best.' Holding out her hand, she said, 'Look . . . a wedding ring. You're talking to a married woman now. Bet he didn't tell you that, did he, eh?' In the lamplight the ring flashed like so many stars.

'No, he never mentioned it.' Ned felt elated and dismayed at the same time; dismayed because he had been so bent on talking about himself and his troubles that he hadn't even asked Adam about his own life. And yet he felt elated because now it was clear that Adam had finally put his love for Rosie aside and taken a wife. The news couldn't have been better. 'Congratulations,' said Ned, putting out his hands to steady her. 'You're right. Adam is a good man.'

She giggled at that. 'And you should know. Adam tells me you were like a father to him.' Lurching sideways, she would have fallen had he not caught her.

'I think I'd best get you to your door,' he offered, gently propelling her up the street towards Adam's house. 'Been out celebrating, have you?' He couldn't help but wonder whether she and Adam had rowed. Sadly, he thought, it seemed to be the way with married folk these days.

'I've been enjoying a women's night out,' she said with a twinkle in her eye. 'And I've had a little too much to drink. Oh, but don't you worry about me,' she chuckled, 'Adam will put me to bed as usual.' Realising he was holding her upright, she told him haughtily, 'It's very kind of you to help me, but I *can* manage, thank you.' Shaking herself free, she toddled off.

He watched her go up the steps, and waited for the door to open. He saw her fall into Adam's arms and went on his way with a smile on his face. 'Looks like you've got your hands full with that wife of yours, lad,' he said. With Adam agreeing to help him, and now, seeing how Adam had taken himself a wife, Ned felt as though a lead weight had been lifted from him. All in all, his visit here had been more worthwhile than he could ever have hoped.

'What in God's name have you been up to now?' Adam was exasperated. 'You shouldn't be wandering the streets at this time of night . . . and drunk into the bargain!' He almost had to carry her into the living room.

'Now now, don't scold me.'

'I ought to tan your backside.' He tumbled her into a chair. 'Go on then. What's it about this time?'

'He's a pig!'

'I told you that before you married him.'

'I know, and I should have listened.' She giggled again. 'Oh, but I do love him.' She sat up at the sound of someone knocking on the front door. 'If that's him, tell him you haven't seen me.'

'I'm not lying for you again, Connie.'

'Don't tell him I'm here!' she pleaded. 'Please, Adam.'

Tutting, he shook his head. 'I should feel sorry for him. I don't know who's the worst, you or him.'

'It's *him*!' she retaliated, 'And I'm teaching him a lesson, that's all. It'll do him bloody good to worry about me.'

He had to smile. 'I know the feeling,' he chuckled, going to the door. 'It's the last time though, Connie.'

'Okay.' Her pretty blue eyes grew wide.

'Stay quiet then.'

'Okay.' Her eyes grew wider still. 'I know what to do.'

He knew from experience there was no use trying to reason with her, so he hurried down the passage to open the front door. 'Oh, it's you!' He hoped he sounded suitably surprised.

His previous landlord was a greasy little man with a pencil thin moustache and a weaselly smile. 'Is Connie with you?' he wanted to know. From the doorstep he peered down the passage. 'When we have an argument, she always comes to you.' He sounded peeved.

'Not this time.' Adam had no intention of letting him in. He had never liked the fellow. 'I haven't seen her for a fortnight.' Under his breath, he asked the good Lord to forgive him.

'I don't know where to look next. One minute she was putting April to bed, and the next she'd disappeared.'

Adam was alarmed. 'If Connie's gone missing and you're here, who's with the little girl, now?'

'Oh, don't concern yourself. We've got a friend staying, and *she's* keeping an eye on April.' Connie's daughter was now a delightful toddler. On the many occasions when Connie had fled to Adam for comfort, he and the infant had become fast friends.

'You should know Connie by now. I dare say she'll come back when she's good and ready.'

'If she comes here, you'll tell her to come straight home, won't you?'

'Depends.'

'On what?'

'On whether you've been hitting her again.'

The little man grinned. 'These days it's more likely to be *her* hitting *me*!'

'I hope you're not looking for sympathy?'

Bestowing a sour expression on him, the man turned away to go at a fast and furious pace down the street.

From behind him Adam could hear Connie shouting, 'Good shuts to the old bugger! It'll serve him right to think I've done a bunk!'

Coming into the living room, he wasn't surprised to see her lounging in the chair with her bare legs hanging over the side. She looked as though she'd been in the wars; her yellow hair was unkempt, the top two buttons of her low-cut blouse were undone, and her tight skirt had ridden up her thighs. 'He'll be sorry,' she muttered, and for the first time that night a note of bitterness crept into her voice.

Patiently, he looked at her pretty face, which was made up like a clown's. 'All right, what have you been up to?'

'Teaching the bugger a lesson, that's what.'

'You heard what he said?'

'About you sending me home? Ah, but you wouldn't turn an old friend away, would you, eh?'

He chuckled. 'I must have been a fool to tell you where I'd moved to.'

'At least I don't have to sleep on the settee these days.'

'I should make you sleep out in the yard.'

'But you won't.'

'Fool that I am.' He rolled his eyes and sighed. But something about her cheeky manner ensured that he could never stay angry with her for long.

'Same bedroom?'

'You know where it is,' he answered wearily. After saying goodnight, he went to his own room while she made herself a hot toddy. Some time later, his bedroom door opened and Connie peeped in. 'Want some company, big boy?' she whispered.

'Goodnight, Connie!' The tone of his voice brooked no argument.

'Goodnight then.' He heard her singing as she went along the landing. Then the slam of her bedroom door. And he knew that, like so many times before, when he woke, she would be gone.

The house grew quiet and the night became darker. Soon the darkness lifted with the promise of a new day, and still he couldn't sleep.

Ned had set him off thinking about the past, and Rosie. Though he carried her lovely image deep in his heart, it had been an age since last he saw her. But now he felt so close to her that he could hardly breathe.

Chapter Twelve

Peggy's mam was goggle-eyed. 'Oh, you should have seen it!' she gabbled excitedly. 'There we were, all crammed into the grocer's front parlour . . .' She glanced at Peggy and Rosie to make certain they were still listening, then, with a proud little smile she went on, 'Of course he invited only his very best customers, and Lord knows I spend enough money to have *bought* him that blessed television set, so it's only right that I should watch the Coronation on it. Mind you, it were stifling hot in that little room. Twenty-two of us there were . . . packed in like sardines.'

'Well, you wanted to see it, our mam, and now you have, so stop moaning.' Peggy winked at Rosie and as always, Rosie enjoyed their light-hearted banter.

'Too right I wanted to see it!' Peggy's mam exploded. 'And so did you two buggers, but you couldn't, 'cause you ain't customers.' Recalling the physical discomfort of being pressed between Mrs Armitage and that big woman from Leyton Street, she blew out her cheeks and flapped the top of her blouse. 'Good job an' all if you ask me, 'cause two more bodies in that parlour and we'd have all fainted right out.'

'You shouldn't have been too uncomfortable, our mam,' Peggy argued. 'It were a miserable day . . . cold and raining.'

'Oh, aye! And wouldn't you know it would be the coldest wettest June *outside*, but inside that parlour it were like a bloody hothouse.' She smiled then and said dreamily, 'Oh, but you should have seen it. I'm telling you, it were a sight to last me a lifetime. Did you know there were two million people waiting outside in the rain?' Without waiting for an answer, she went on: 'It were wonderful! Our Elizabeth looked so tiny and fragile, a princess made Queen . . . Oh, and the pageantry! June the second 1953 . . . a red letter day I'll never forget.'

'No, and I don't suppose you'll ever let *us* forget it either.' Getting up from the table, Peggy took out the cups and washed them at the scullery sink. 'Anyway, I thought you and the kids were going to the flicks?' she called out. 'They've been waiting out there for ages.'

'My God! I forgot about them.' In a minute she was gone, leaving the instruction: 'Mind this place is tidy when I get back, or I'll want to know the reason why!'

'Honest to God, she gets worse as she gets older.' Peggy laughed as she flopped into an armchair. 'Come and sit here,' she told Rosie, who was still seated at the table where the three women had enjoyed a light tea, along with the exciting report on the new Queen's Coronation.

'I'll help wash up the tea things while little Danny's still fast asleep,' Rosie offered. Her brown eyes glanced to where her young son lay fast asleep on the settee. Now four years old, he was making a fine young lad. His mop of thick hair was the same dark brown colour as Doug's, but his eyes were warm and brown like Rosie's. She had always been thankful for that because one set of odd-coloured eyes staring at her was more than enough.

'Hey!' Peggy's commanding voice stopped her in her tracks. 'I didn't ask you over so you could wash up the tea things. Come and sit down. It ain't often these days we can have a natter, and it'll not be long before our mam's back. It's the first time she's taken the kids to an early evening matinee, and it means she'll have to let them stay up late.' Laughing aloud she promised, 'I wouldn't mind betting she'll be back within the hour on some excuse or another.'

Rosie was glad to sit and talk. In her heart she was deeply unsettled. Yet, even when she was seated in her armchair, she couldn't bring herself to talk about certain matters. Instead she said, 'I would have loved to have seen the Coronation on television.'

'You heard it on the radio, didn't you?'

'Well, yes. But it's not the same, is it?' She didn't reveal how Doug had thrown the radio across the room, and now it was broken beyond repair.

'I suppose not.' During the brief silence that followed, Rosie seemed a million miles away, unaware that Peggy was regarding her with concern. It was only when Peggy spoke, asking whether she had something on her mind, that Rosie looked up with surprise. 'What do you mean?' She had been thinking of Adam, and of what Ned had told her some time back. The news that Adam was married had raised all manner of emotions in her, and even now, after all this time, she couldn't stop thinking about him.

'I know you.' Peggy half guessed the truth. 'Whatever's on your mind, the best thing is to talk about it. A trouble shared is a trouble halved, they say.'

'Do you think he's completely forgotten about me?' Her brown eyes were soulful.

'Ah! Adam, you mean?'

'You knew I was thinking of him, didn't you?'

'I've known you for too long, gal. And no, even though he's married and should have, I don't expect for one minute he's forgotten you. After all, *you're* wed, and you ain't forgot him, have you, eh? You love him just as much as you've ever done.

And what good will it do, tell me that, for God's sake?' She thought about Rosie's hard life and that miserable husband of hers, and wished with all her heart that it could have been different. But it wasn't, and now perhaps it never would be. Shaking her head in frustration, she pleaded softly, 'Oh, Rosie, will you *never* stop tormenting yourself?'

'When Ned told me he'd married that young woman who came to the christening, well, I don't mind admitting, I was surprised. Oh, it's not that I didn't think she was nice, because she was. But somehow she just didn't seem to be the type I imagined he'd settle down with.'

'I thought the same, and yes, she did seem nice enough in her own way . . . chatty and friendly. But, like you, I never saw Adam as going for the brassy hair and deep cleavage type.'

'Happen we're being unkind?'

'Happen.'

'I *hope* he's content. It would be nice to think he had a family of his own . . . children . . . a son maybe.' She smiled, but it was an unhappy expression.

'It's just as well he got wed because now you know he's out of reach.' Peggy believed the only way to be kind was to be cruel.

'You know he's done well for himself?' There was pride in Rosie's voice.

'I should know, gal. You've told me a million times.' Like Doug and Martha, they believed what Ned had told them about bumping into Adam at another sale two years back. They weren't to know he had sold his business to Adam.

Deliberately thrusting Adam from her mind, Rosie was genuinely delighted to report, 'Ned goes from strength to strength. Lately, he's a different man. It's as though somehow he's shed a deal of worry. Certainly his business is picking up, and what's more, he's just taken delivery of a new wagon.' Rosie had a great deal of affection for her father-in-law, and had never blamed him for sacking Doug. The only regret she had was that Doug could not be the man his father was.

Thankful that Rosie had wisely changed the subject, Peggy answered, 'I've always liked Ned Selby, and I'm glad he's doing better these days. Do you think he'll take Doug on again?'

Rosie's eyes darkened with anger. 'Why should he? Doug's unreliable, lazy, and half the time he's drunk. I'm not surprised Ned's turned his back on him. Besides, he's got his hands full with Martha.' Every day she grew more and more vindictive, making that poor man's life an absolute misery. And though she did feel sorry that Martha must be suffering too, Rosie couldn't help but wonder at Ned's immense patience.

'What? You mean she's playing up again? I thought she'd got to like this new nurse.'

'You know her. She can't like anyone for more than five minutes at a time. Yesterday when I went round to see if I could be of help in any way, Martha was throwing a terrible tantrum. Ned was sitting at the kitchen table with his hands over his ears, and the nurse was close to tears.' She sighed. 'If you ask me it's only a matter of time before that one follows the others out of the house. Soon Ned won't be able to get anybody to look after her.'

'By! She's a wicked old sod. If I was Ned, I'd bugger off and leave her to it!'

Rosie shook her head. 'Never. Ned's a good man. He'd have to be at his wit's end to do a thing like that.'

'Oh, aye? And how long will it be before he is at his wit's end? The man isn't a saint, when all's said and done.'

Noises from the front hallway made Rosie look round. 'Sounds like your mam's back,' she said with a chuckle.

Peggy listened too. 'Well, I'm buggered!' she exclaimed. 'So she is. What did I say, eh? I knew it. She must have ants in her pants because she can't sit still for two minutes at a time.'

After a lot of shouting and pushing and cries of, 'I wanted to see the end of the picture!' the little tribe came bundling into the parlour. 'These two wouldn't keep quiet,' Peggy's mam moaned. 'Three times the usherette threatened to throw us out.' She cuffed the three eldest round the ears. 'Get washed and off to your beds.'

'We wanted to watch the end,' they argued in unison. But when she glared at them, they soon scooted into the scullery.

'An' this little sod wet himself!' she explained, pushing the young one before her.

'I ain't!' he wailed, tears in his eyes as he appealed to Peggy. '*I* wanted to watch the end an' all.'

'Why didn't you wait for the end, our mam?' Peggy wanted to know. 'There's nothing worse than seeing a picture nearly all the way through, and not knowing what the end is.'

All she got for an answer was the suggestion that she: 'Mind your own bloody business!' It was obvious that taking all the children to the pictures had turned out to be more of an 'adventure' than Peggy's mam could cope with. She looked harassed and weary. 'I'd best make you a brew,' Peggy offered.

'That's nice, dear,' sighed her mam. Then she fell into the nearest chair as though her legs had given out.

When little Danny woke with a start and began screaming at the top of his lungs, Rosie thought it was a good time to leave. She said goodbye to Peggy's mam, who smiled wanly from the depths of the chair. 'See you later,' she called out to Peggy who was in the scullery overseeing the younger ones. But Peggy was being bombarded with complaints and didn't hear.

Outside, Rosie sighed and glanced at her son, who was now contentedly walking along beside her, his hand securely tucked into hers as they made their way home. 'It's a madhouse,' she said, ruffling his brown hair. 'But it's a happier house than ours, and that's a fact.'

* * *

That night, Doug came home late. He was in a foul mood. 'Old Leyland's going senile,' he complained. 'He says I came back to work drunk after the break. He's a bloody liar. I was sober as a judge.' His face twitched as he spoke. It was obvious to Rosie that he *had* been drinking and that he badly needed a drink now. 'What money have you got?' he asked, pushing his tea aside. The meat pie had been light and fluffy, oozing with gravy and crispy at the edges when Rosie baked it earlier. Now, after being kept warm for two hours, it was dry and shrivelled.

'None for booze, I can tell you that.' Taking up the poker she jabbed at the coals with it. All day she had felt a chill, and now she feared she was coming down with 'flu.

In two strides he was across the room. Snatching the poker out of her hand, he flung it into the grate. 'What the hell have you got a fire lit for?' he snapped. 'It's the middle of summer for Christ's sake. We ain't got money to waste!'

'No, and if you get sacked from Leyland's, for being drunk at work, we won't have money to feed us neither.' Her eyes were hard and bright as buttons.

Incensed when she dared to defy him – and that was too often lately – he insisted, 'You've got money all right. I know you keep a few shilling tucked away.' When she said nothing but continued to challenge him with those forthright brown eyes, he reached out to touch her mouth. 'You're a handsome-looking woman, Rosie,' he murmured. 'To be honest, I don't know which I want most . . . a pint of ale at the pub, or an hour on the floor with you.'

She hated it when he talked like that, as though she was little better than a jar in his fist. 'There's two shilling under the clock.' In that moment, giving him the few coins she had put by was the lesser of two evils. 'Take it, and to hell with you!'

For a long unbearable moment he stared at her with avaricious eyes and she felt herself cringing. Taking her by the shoulders he leaned forward to cover her mouth with his. 'Later,' he promised, reluctantly pushing away. He laughed in her face before taking the money from the clock and making a hasty exit. 'Right! I'm off for a pint or two, okay?' he said brightly. She didn't answer. She was astonished that he should expect her to.

After he had gone, she went upstairs to check her son. Sound asleep and contented, he had obviously not stirred since she took him up some two hours before. 'You're such a little innocent,' she murmured. 'But you're growing so fast, and I'm afraid he might pass his bad ways on to you.' When Danny was a baby, the fear wasn't so great. But now that he was a little man in his own right, talking and listening and looking up to his dad with the loving eyes of a son, she was desperately afraid. 'I won't let him ruin you,' she vowed.

But that night, when Doug stumbled into the bedroom, blind drunk and hardly able to stand, she wondered whether in the end he would ruin them all.

Over the next few days, Rosie kept out of Doug's way as much as possible. When he came to bed she pretended to be asleep, and when he woke in the morning she was already downstairs preparing his sandwiches for work. Two out of three nights he managed to arrive home sober, and though he badgered her for money, she was determined that he would not have the money which she had hidden in the rent book.

The days came and went and each was the same as the one before. As though in defiance of her mundane existence, Rosie sang at her work, keeping the little house clean, taking advantage of the fine weather to dip the blankets and scrub the mats. Every grubby garment in the house was washed, ironed and neatly stacked into the laundry cupboard at the top of the stairs, and the windows were cleaned until they sparkled. Even grumpy Ada from the bottom house had to admit, 'By! Them windows look a right treat, lass. Happen you should come and do mine?' If Ada had been badly or old, or if her legs were swelled up with varicose veins, Rosie might well have offered, but the woman wasn't much older than Rosie herself. She was also known to be bone idle so Rosie just smiled and thanked her, and quickly retreated into the house.

On Thursday night Doug went out on money borrowed from 'an old mate'. Peggy popped round and told Rosie she just had to get out of the house. 'I've had a bad day at work and the kids are making that much noise I'm tempted to suffocate the little sods,' she groaned. They talked until nearly midnight and Doug still wasn't home. 'Happen he's found another woman and run off with her?' Peggy suggested.

'I should be so lucky!' Rosie laughed.

Realising how the time had run away with them, and that her mam would have put the children to bed by now, Peggy rose to leave. 'Keep sane, kid,' she told Rosie, and Rosie promised she would.

After letting Peggy out, she locked the door and went to bed. A quick peep into the smaller bedroom told her that little Danny was still sleeping. *She* couldn't sleep though. Her mind was too alive. She thought on what Peggy had said just now, about Doug running off with some woman. 'There's no other woman would have you!' she muttered, her gaze following the antics of a spider on the ceiling while she reflected on her own life.

After a while she slid down between the sheets and closed her eyes. She felt strangely afraid, as though waiting for something to happen. It was an odd and eerie feeling, so strong that she had to get out of bed and go downstairs again. 'You must be losing your mind, Rosie gal,' she chuckled. Making herself a cup of cocoa, she curled up in the big armchair, thoughtfully sipping at the hot drink and warming her hands on the mug at the same time. 'It's freezing in here!' she moaned, taking Doug's overcoat from the back of the door to fling over her legs. Once the night had settled, the cold chilly air from outside seeped in and the temperature dropped.

She finished the cocoa and put the cup in the hearth. She felt tired, yet not tired enough for sleep. She dozed and woke, and thought awhile. The clock ticked the minutes away, chiming the hours between, and soon the night was almost gone and the sky infused with the colours of morning. And still Doug wasn't home.

'Why should I care if you choose to stay out all night?' she asked aloud. 'God only knows, I should be pleased to see the back of you.'

All the same she couldn't help but worry. When all was said and done he was her husband and, even though she was eaten up with regret for having committed herself to him, she was essentially a woman who took her marriage vows very seriously. This was the first time he hadn't come home, and she began to wonder whether he really did have a woman who served him better. That made her smile. If there was a woman out there who wanted him, she only had to ask.

Having sat in the chair for so long, she began to ache all over. The mantel clock struck four, and above the chimes came the sound of a child crying. Hurrying up the stairs, she found the boy on his feet and rubbing his eyes. 'Shh, sweetheart. It's all right.' He felt cold to the touch as she helped him back to his bed. Tenderly she settled him beneath the blankets. 'Mammy's here,' she coaxed. Lying down beside him, she folded him in her arms and there she fell asleep.

It was the rattle of the milk cart that woke her. Sitting up with a start, she was momentarily confused. With sleepy brown eyes she glanced round the room and finally her gaze fell on the lad sleeping beside her. Realisation dawned and she got carefully from the bed.

It was only a few steps along the landing, but even before she had opened the bedroom door, she sensed that Doug was still not home. When he was here there was a brooding atmosphere in this house she loved. Whenever he was out, it was as though the sun shone in every room.

Dropping on to the bed, she drew her hands over her face as though to wipe away the sleep that was still on her. 'Where in God's name is he?' she murmured. Going to the window she looked out. Apart from the milk cart that was already turning the bottom of the street, there wasn't a soul to be seen. A quick glance at the bedside clock told her it was still only five. Soon the street would be filled with the sound of people wending their way to work, but for now the men were still snoozing, although the women were no doubt busy in their kitchens, packing sandwiches and making flasks of tea.

Wide awake now, Rosie went downstairs and boiled a kettle full of water. That done she tipped most of it into the bowl, tempered it with a rush of cold water from the tap, and stripped off her nightgown; a thorough strip-wash, and then to work. She cleaned out the ashes from the fire-grate, washed the hearth and brought the tiles to a high polish, then she pushed the sweeper over the carpet and dusted the furniture. By that time it was nearing six-thirty.

Just as she was straightening her back from her labours, a small voice called out from the parlour doorway, 'I'm hungry.' The little fellow looked tousled and tired as he came into the room.

'You're as bad as your mam,' Rosie softly chided when he put his small hand in hers. 'I reckon we both look the worse for wear.'

Fastening his pyjama top, she sat him up at the table. 'What do you fancy, little man?' she asked, tickling him under the chin with the tip of her finger.

'Chuckie egg,' he said, his drooping eyes growing round with anticipation. 'And soldiers.'

'Well now, that's just what your mammy fancies too,' Rosie told him. 'But we don't have our breakfast before we've washed, do we?' He shook his head. 'Right then. I've had my wash, so now it's your turn.' Lifting him from the chair, she took him by the hand and together they went into the kitchen. Using the remaining water in the kettle she soon had him washed, dried and dressed in clean grey trousers and pale blue jumper. 'There!' Running the comb through his bouncy brown locks, she regarded him with pride. 'You're a handsome fellow, I'll not deny it,' she told him. But he wasn't listening. Instead, he was reaching into the cupboard where Rosie kept his toy box. 'Play trains,' he said proudly. Falling to his knees, he tipped the entire contents on to the carpet.

'All right,' Rosie said. 'But only until I've got breakfast. Because then we're going out. I want to catch Grandad Selby before he goes to work.' She would need to be quick, as these days he always left home sharp at eight o'clock. 'Happen *he* might know where your daddy got to last night . . . and where he is now!' she muttered beneath her breath.

The breakfast was soon got ready, and though Rosie's appetite vanished once the soft-boiled egg was in front of her, little Danny eagerly devoured his, together with Rosie's toasted soldiers as well as his own.

'Come on then. Let's be off.' She wiped his face with the flannel and soon the two of them were ready for the chilly morning air, the boy looking smart in his short grey jacket and cap, and Rosie wearing her best tweed coat and the new red scarf which Peggy had bought her last Christmas. 'If we hurry, we'll just catch the early tram,' she said, gripping Danny's hand and running him down the street.

The tram was about to leave, but the driver saw them and waited. When the conductor swung the boy on to the platform, Danny thought it was all a wonderful game and, much to the annoyance of a fat woman with a snappy pooch, insisted on pulling faces at it all the way to the next stop where he and Rosie disembarked.

Ned Selby's house was only a short walk from the tram stop at the bottom of Artillery Street. As they approached, Rosie saw the wagon parked on the common opposite. It was Ned's. 'Good. Your grandad hasn't left yet,' she said, hurrying the rest of the way. Excited at the prospect of seeing his grandad, the boy ran ahead.

By the time Rosie got to the house, Ned had already answered the door. 'By! I thought you were gonna knock the blessed thing down,' he chuckled, stooping to swing the child into his arms. Smiling at Rosie, he added, 'It's a mercy he didn't wake Martha or I'd have got the length of her tongue and no mistake!' It was obvious she had been difficult again.

As he led the way into the back parlour, Rosie sensed there was something very wrong. Usually proud of his appearance, Ned was wearing a grubby shirt which was haphazardly rolled up at the sleeves and hung open to the waist. He was unshaven and red-eyed, looking much like Doug when he'd been on one of his drinking binges. 'Is everything all right?' she asked, taking off her coat and eyeing him with concern.

He didn't answer straightaway, obviously aware that the boy was paying attention to all that was being said. 'Let's get your coat off, young 'un,' he said, undoing the buttons on little Danny's jacket. 'Then, if you're quiet, you can play with your grandad's lead soldiers.' No sooner were the words out of his mouth than the boy was off. He knew the soldiers were kept in a tin box beneath the sideboard, and would play contentedly for hours if let be.

'What's brought you and the young 'un here so early?' Conscious that he must look a sight, Ned hastily rolled down his sleeves and did up the top buttons of his shirt. His self-conscious action only heightened his unkempt appearance.

Standing by the table, Rosie leaned forward, her hands supporting her weight, and her dark eyes worried as she remarked pointedly, 'Ned! You didn't answer my question.'

'What was that?'

'I asked if anything was wrong?' When he hesitated to answer, she came round the table and looked fondly up at him. 'There is something, Ned. I could tell the minute I walked in. For a start you're not shaved or dressed properly, and normally you'd be ready to leave for work.'

'I'm not going to work today, lass.'

'That's not like you, Ned.' A thought struck her then. 'It's Doug, isn't it?' If so, it wouldn't be the first time he had caused trouble in this household. Many was the time he had taken his mother's side, even when he knew his father to be in the right.

Ned was surprised she should ask such a question. 'You must know I haven't clapped eyes on Doug for weeks. He's never forgiven me for sacking him, and only visits when I'm out. Even then he manages to upset his mother so she's difficult to handle for days after.' He raised his eyes to heaven. 'Though, God knows, it wasn't him this time.'

Rosie had her answer as far as Doug was concerned. He hadn't been here last night, and he wasn't here now. But Ned was upset, and for the minute her concern over Doug took a back seat. 'Is Martha being difficult? Is that why you're not going to work?'

He sighed and closed his eyes. 'You could say that. She's been impossible these past few days. Last night when I got home the nurse met me at the door. Her face was bleeding where Martha had thrown a cup at her. So now she's gone and she's not coming back.' He dropped his head and stared at the floor. 'I've failed her, but as God's my judge, I can't think where I'm going wrong.'

'Oh, Ned!' This new nurse had been with Martha for even less time than the last one. 'You've done more than any man could be expected to do, and still she won't help herself. Why can't she see what she's doing to you?'

Seeming not to have heard, he went on, 'I can't blame the nurse. Poor thing, she were only a young lass, and Martha's enough to try the patience of a saint. Honest to God, I don't know what to do next.' He sounded desperate. 'Sometimes, I'm tempted to take off and leave her to her own devices, then she'd be put in a place where they'd know how to deal with her.' His eyes were moist with threatened tears as he looked up for reassurance. 'I know it sounds heartless, lass, but what am I to do, eh? Tell me that.'

'You say she's in a sulk?' To tell the truth, Rosie was tempted to go up there and give her a piece of her mind. But she knew from past experience that it would go in one ear and straight out the other.

'She's sleeping now, and she bloody well ought to be 'cause she's kept me awake all night with her bawling and shouting. When the lad knocked on the door just now, I half expected it to be the neighbours come to complain.'

'They're good folk, Ned. I'm sure they understand.'

'Mebbe, but I'd like to bet they'll not put up with it for much longer.' He glanced up at the ceiling. 'She can be a wicked bugger when she sets her mind to it. I've told her I can't afford to lose my work . . . that we have to have someone in to take care of her, but she won't listen.'

Sad to see him like this, she made up her mind. 'Don't worry, Ned. I'll stay with her.' Though she had always disliked Martha, Rosie had never been afraid of her. 'You get yourself off to work.'

He was astonished. 'I can't let you do that. What! She'd take a deal of pleasure in making your life a misery.'

Rosie smiled craftily. 'She's been trying to do that for years, but so far I've survived. She won't get the better of me, I can promise you that.'

His eyes lit up and a smile crept over his tired old face. 'Are you sure, lass?'

'I'm sure. Now be off before I change my mind.'

He gazed at her and for a minute he was too choked to speak. But then he grabbed her by the shoulders. 'You're a good lass,' he muttered. 'And though I say it as shouldn't, our Doug doesn't deserve you.'

She laughed wryly. 'I'm always telling him that.'

He rushed around, getting a wash and telling Rosie how he'd already got everything prepared for Martha's breakfast. 'She normally wakes with the appetite of a bull elephant,' he said. In a surprisingly few minutes he was ready for off. 'I'll try and be done early so you can get home,' he promised. 'I don't want you getting in trouble 'cause Doug's tea's not ready when he gets in.'

Rosie had had no intention of telling him about Doug, but somehow it slipped out. 'That's *if* he comes home.'

'Are you saying he's taken to staying out?'

'Something like that.' When she realised it was only another worry for Ned, she quickly assured him, 'I'm not too worried so you mustn't be. No doubt he'll turn up with his tail between his legs and a fine excuse to tell.'

Ned paused, ready to take off his coat again. 'But it's not like him to stay out, is it? It hasn't happened before, has it?'

'Many times,' she lied. 'Now get off to work. I saw a gang of big lads hanging round your wagon. If you don't hurry, they'll be off up the street in it.' That did the trick. There was nothing more precious to Ned than his lovely coal-wagon. In a minute he was out of the door and away. When Rosie went into the front parlour and looked out of the window, it was to see him driving past the house, looking far more contented than when she'd arrived. 'Now for the old battle-axe!' she said through gritted teeth. 'Like mother like son, and that's a fact.'

* * *

'I want Ned. Where's Ned?' Martha was shocked to open her eyes and see Rosie standing there with her breakfast tray. 'Get out of my house. Bugger off, damn you!' She was a terrible sight to see. Her eyes were sticking out like hatpins and her hair was a spiky mess because she had flatly refused to let the nurse comb it. Stretching her neck, she yelled at the top of her voice, 'NED! NED, GET HER AWAY FROM ME!'

'You can shout 'til the cows come home.' Rosie calmly placed the tray on the bedside table. 'But he won't hear you because he's gone to work.' With her hands on her hips she stared at the other woman, a quiet test of strength going on between them.

'You're a bloody liar!'

'No, I'm not.' Rosie smiled sweetly. 'It's your own fault. After what you did, the nurse won't show her face again. Ned's gone to work, so I've come to look after you for the day.'

Martha's eyes were bulbous and her face turned a deep shade of red. 'You'll get out of my house now, or I swear to God I'll raise holy hell.'

'Hmh! Sounds like you've already been doing that. If you hadn't attacked the nurse, she would still be here now. As it is, Ned's running out of capable people to take care of you.'

'None of your business what goes on in this house.'

Rosie's face was grim. 'I'm very fond of Ned and I don't like to see you hurting him the way you do . . .' Martha was about to interrupt, but Rosie shouted her down. 'No, you're going to listen to me. It's about time somebody told you what a tiresome and selfish creature you are. All right, so you've had a tragic accident and I'm truly sorry that it happened to you. But there's nothing I can do to change that, and neither can Ned. Though no man could have done more to make you comfortable.'

'NED, YOU BASTARD . . . I KNOW YOU'RE HIDING DOWN THERE.' Martha had her hands over her ears and a murderous look on her face.

'He's gone to work, I tell you.' In a softer voice, she appealed to Martha's better instincts. 'Don't you realise how worried he is, Martha? If he doesn't go to work, he can't pay the rent and you'll be evicted.'

'Don't talk bloody stupid! Ned will provide for me. He always has.' There was just the faintest note of concern in her voice.

'He's always provided for you because he's always worked. Take away his work, and the money dries up. You know what I'm saying is the truth. Ned might have had a bit of money put by for a rainy day, but the rainy day's come and it won't go away. Think about it, Martha. Where do you suppose the money came from for the nurses you keep frightening off? And what about the special aids he's got for you?' Pointing to the strap above the bed, she explained, 'This useful contraption for instance . . . the special bath, and the wheelchair . . . it all cost money. You know yourself the coal industry has been going through a bad patch and it's dog eat dog. But, as you say, Ned's always provided, and he will go on providing – if you treat him like the human being he is, and not something to be whipped and tortured, as though what happened to you was his fault.'

'It *was* his fault! And yours too. I blame the lot of you.' Turning away, she grabbed the pillow and pressed it to her ears, at the same time yelling and screaming for Ned to come and: 'GET THIS BITCH OUT OF MY HOUSE, DAMN AND BUGGER YOU!'

Rosie sighed and shook her head. She could only imagine what Ned had been going through and her heart went out to him. As always, Martha had no intention of listening to reason. 'All right, Martha. I've had my say, and I'll leave you alone now. After you've had your breakfast, I'll give you a wash.'

'You come anywhere near me and I'll wring your bloody neck!' She glared at Rosie and her eyes were dark with loathing. 'I might have lost the use of my legs, but the Devil compensates.

The strength has all gone to my arms. I mean what I say, so you'd best stay away from me.'

Rosie shook her head, considering what to do. The mood she was in, Martha might work herself up to a fit. Then Rosie would never forgive herself. 'I see. There's no getting through to you, is there? All right then. I won't come upstairs again, unless you want me to. But you have to eat, and you'll need to go to the toilet.'

'I'll eat nothing, and Ned can take me to the toilet.'

'You'll be waiting a long time, Martha, because he won't be home until this afternoon.'

'Piss off.'

Undeterred, Rosie lifted the tea cosy from the teapot and pushed the tray closer so it was within easy reach. 'If you need me, tap on the floor with your stick.' Ned had given Martha a cane and with it she had driven him almost beyond endurance, banging on the floor to summon him up the stairs so he could suffer tirades of abuse. When Rosie told him he was too quick in responding, he said he was afraid to keep her waiting in case she was really in trouble. But she never was.

With as much dignity as she could muster, Rosie departed from the room, to the tune of Martha swearing and threatening. 'You'll be sorry, Ned Selby,' she told the bedroom door. 'I don't know what game you're playing, but you'll be sorry!'

Closing the door, Rosie leaned against the wall outside, her eyes closed and her face raised to the ceiling. 'God give me strength,' she murmured. And, as the day wore on, she certainly needed it.

'What's the matter with Gran'ma?' Frightened by all the noise, Danny was waiting at the foot of the stairs.

'It's all right, sweetheart.' Rosie ushered him into the front room. 'She's in a bad mood, that's all.'

'She's *always* in a bad mood.' There had been a time when

Martha doted on her grandson, but these days she was only interested in her son, Doug. Even though he had crippled her, he was the light in her life, and he could do no wrong.

'I'll tell you what, sweetheart.' Rosie sat on the rug beside the upturned cardboard box. 'I reckon Grandad would be thrilled if you could give all these soldiers a really good clean.' Plucking one up between finger and thumb, she said, 'If I give you a rag and some polish, do you think you could have them all ready for inspection?' Her smile was bright, but she was subdued after the scene with Martha. She was also riddled with guilt. The woman was disabled after all. So had she gone too far . . . or been too cruel in her frankness? Should she have merely humoured her? But then the answer came back . . . a resounding no! Martha had punished Ned for too long, and it was time she was told a few home truths.

'Can I wash their faces too?'

Deep in her own thoughts, Rosie's attention had wandered. 'What? Oh, yes, 'course you can,' she laughed, giving him a cuddle. 'I think that's a marvellous idea.'

For the next few hours Rosie busied herself about the house, and her son washed and polished the lead soldiers. In between making a meat dumpling and scraping the potatoes ready for Ned's evening meal, Rosie willed her mother-in-law to knock on the ceiling. But the silence was unnerving. Compelled to go up and check that everything was all right, she climbed halfway up the stairs but restrained herself from entering the room, especially when she could hear Martha still chunnering madly to herself. 'I'm here if you want me,' she called in a soft voice. 'You've only to knock on the floor.'

The chunnering stopped and Martha's voice fell quiet. 'All right, I'll play your little game,' Rosie told her, going down the stairs. If that was the way Martha wanted it, there was little she could do. And anyway, it wouldn't be too long before Ned was home. With a bit of luck, he might have managed to find someone who was prepared to look after the cantankerous old bugger.

What with the baking and clearing up after, and the games between with little Danny, Rosie was surprised at how quickly the morning sped by. But the next two hours crept along, and still Martha remained sullen and uncooperative.

At five minutes to four Ned returned. 'Finished early,' he told her with a bright smile. 'By! That does me good to get out of the house.' His smile faded as he remembered what lay waiting for him upstairs. 'How is she?'

'Same as usual. She hasn't thrown anything at me, but that's because I was ordered out of her room and threatened with certain death if I returned.' Rosie had to chuckle but her sympathy was with him. 'I'm sorry, Ned. I did try but she's been calling for you.'

His whole countenance changed. Where there had been a light in his eyes when he came in, there was now only despair. 'It can't go on like this,' he murmured, sinking into the fireside chair. 'You'd think there'd be somebody who could help, but it seems when you're in this situation, you're expected to cope best you can. Oh, the authorities do their bit, but it never seems to be enough. By rights she should be in a hospital of sorts.'

Before Rosie could answer, another voice intervened. 'You'll put her away over my dead body!' Doug strode into the room. 'What the hell's going on here, eh?' he demanded. 'It seems I've arrived just in time. By the sound of things you're all set to put my mam in a home.' He stared from one to the other, condemning them with his expression.

'Oh? So you've decided to show your face then?' Rosie was astonished that he wasn't rolling drunk.

'I'll deal with you later,' he snapped. 'Right now I'm having words with my dad here.' Addressing Ned, he went on, 'Well? I reckon you've got some explaining to do.'

At once Ned was on his feet, eyes blazing. 'Don't question what you don't understand!' He hadn't forgotten how this man, his own son, had robbed him blind when every penny was needed for Martha. 'You of all people should know I do my level best by your mother,' he said, controlling his anger. 'As for an explanation, I'd say I don't owe you *anything*.' The look on his face conveyed his meaning, and Doug was momentarily conscience-stricken. 'Now, if you don't mind, I think your mother needs me.'

When Ned had gone, Rosie was compelled to ask, 'What did your father mean . . . "you of all people"?' Something in Ned's manner told her there was something very wrong between these two, something she had not seen before.

'I think you might be forgetting your place, woman.' Doug sauntered over to the fireplace and stood with his back to it, his odd-coloured eyes regarding her with contempt. 'You'd do well to keep your mouth shut.'

'Forgetting my place, eh?' Rosie mimicked. 'And where exactly do you think my "place" is?'

'You should be at home. I'll want my tea on the table when I've finished here.'

'Oh? And what about you? Shouldn't *you* be at home?' Stepping closer she remarked in a low voice, 'I don't suppose you'll tell me where you were last night?'

'What's been going on here?' Deliberately evasive, he answered a question with a question. It wouldn't do to let her know how he'd been subbing from work, and had spent an entire week's wages. On top of that, he'd been late there today after spending the night with a whore. The boss had given him a final warning, and now he was in the right frame of mind to cause a heap of trouble here. 'If he thinks he's putting my mam in a home, he's got another think coming.' He would have gone on, but Martha's call cut across his words. 'You get home!' he told Rosie. 'There's things to sort out here.'

As he went from the room she shouted after him, 'It's not for *you* to sort out.' When he ignored her and ran up the stairs, she sensed trouble brewing and wanted the boy out of the way. Taking his coat, she went to the front room and quickly dressed him for outdoors. 'Come on, Danny, let's be off, eh?'

'Why's Daddy shouting?'

What she said was, 'He was just calling up to his mam.' What she *thought* was: because he's a bloody bully.

'Can I put grandad's soldiers away?'

Having always taught him to tidy up behind himself, Rosie could hardly argue now. ''Course you can, but hurry up, there's a good fella.'

There was an unholy row building in Martha's bedroom. First she could be heard yelling, then came the murmur of Ned's controlled voice, then the sound of Doug's above it all. 'Don't listen to him, Mam. I caught them talking about it . . . THE BUGGERS WANT TO PUT YOU IN A HOME!'

One minute Rosie was tempted to intervene, and the next minute she couldn't get away from that house quickly enough. Dropping to her knees she helped the boy put away the soldiers, and soon the two of them were outside and going down the street at a run. 'If we hurry, we'll just catch the five o'clock tram,' Rosie said breathlessly.

The boy giggled and she was relieved that he thought it was all a game.

On the tram he fell asleep, and she lapsed into thought. She imagined the row still to be raging, and wondered whether she had done a cowardly thing in running away. But then she had the boy to think about and it was unhealthy for him to witness the scene that she believed was now taking place in that sad house.

Moreover, even if she *had* stayed, she knew from experience it would have made no difference. Martha would still shout, and Ned would still try to reason with her. Doug would still come between them like he had always done, and in the end the outcome would be the same. *And she dared not think too much about that!*

She cared for neither Doug or his mother, but she felt deeply concerned for Ned. When she had first arrived that morning, it was plain to Rosie that here was a man in the depths of despair. She hoped he would stand his ground against his wife and son. She believed he would. 'Ned's made of strong stuff,' she told herself in a whisper. 'He'll manage.'

But he was only flesh and blood, a man who, after giving his all and being scorned for it, had come to the end of his tether. Even while Rosie thought of him, he was losing ground between these two selfish creatures who cared only for themselves. 'Doug heard wrong,' he argued, red in the face from trying to explain. 'As God's my judge, I wasn't planning to put you away. All I said to Rosie was that you really ought to be in a hospital where they could look after you properly.'

Martha would have none of it. 'You're a liar!' she told him, 'Do you think I'd believe you before my own son?'

Ned sighed. 'No, Martha,' he admitted, 'I don't believe that for one minute.' He glanced sideways at Doug, who was standing at the head of his mother's bed, one arm draped round her shoulders and a look of cunning on his face. 'You've always believed him before me, so why should it be any different now?' He was beaten and knew it. It showed on his face, and in the stoop of his broad shoulders. 'I think Doug should go now. It's better if you and I talk this thing through, Martha. There's only the two of us can find a solution.'

She stiffened. Clinging to Doug's hand, she declared in a resounding voice, 'He's not going anywhere.'

Ned stared from one to the other. His heart was weary, and he had no more stomach for these awful set-tos. But he was still master of his own domain and felt the need to remind them of that. 'This is *my* house, and I don't want him here. In fact, it wouldn't bother me if I never saw him again after what he's done.' He saw Doug's face and knew the taunt had hit home. 'I reckon it might be a good idea if he goes before I say too much I might regret.' He was alluding to the money which Doug had robbed from him.

Martha caught the look that passed between them, and her curiosity was aroused. Looking first at Doug she saw that he had turned a shade paler, and she was instinctively suspicious. All the same she refused to accept that he could have done anything really wrong, so when she addressed Ned, it was angrily. 'Stop bloody well insinuating, you old fool! If you've summat to say to our Doug, get on with it.'

Tired of always being the one in the wrong, Ned answered, 'When will you come to see that you've a liar for a son? I'm telling you the truth, Martha. I wasn't planning to put you away, like he says. Your precious son is out to cause trouble, and he doesn't care if you get hurt in the process.'

'Why would he want to cause trouble?'

'Because he's never forgiven me for sacking him.' There! It was said. That would give her something to think about.

Martha couldn't believe her ears. 'What! You sacked your own son?' If she could have got from the bed, she would have thrown herself at him. 'You've gone bloody mad!'

'I was mad to trust him in the first place.'

'What are you getting at? Why did you sack him? I want to know.'

Doug was frantic. 'Whatever he tells you, Mam, don't believe him. He had it in for me because I turned up late once or twice. Honest to God, I didn't do nothing to deserve the sack!'

'You can believe him if you like, Martha, but it's time you

knew what kind of man your son is.' Now that it was all coming out, Ned had no intention of keeping anything back. If he could get her to see the truth, it might be just the shock she needed to make her mend her ways. 'While I've been breaking my back to earn the money needed to keep you comfortable, *he's* been robbing me behind my back . . . collecting money and short-changing me. Money that should have gone on you, but went instead on booze and women.'

'Lying bastard!' Doug launched himself through the air, sending Ned backwards when his fist crunched against his jaw.

Horrified to see them fighting like two wild dogs, Martha screamed for them to: 'STOP IT!' But it was too late for that. There was too much anger, too many years of suppressed emotion.

Doug fought with the brute strength that comes from a kind of madness, and Ned, though fit and able, was no longer a young man. When Martha saw her husband falter, she whipped Doug into such a frenzy that he soon over-powered the older man.

When it was over, Doug kicked at the figure lying on the floor. 'Get up,' he snarled. 'You ain't half the big man now, are you?'

Ned gave no answer. Instead he got to his feet and stood up as straight as his painful bones would let him. Staring at Doug through bruised eyes, he said in a wonderfully calm voice, 'No. It seems *you're* the big man now.' He wasn't angry any more, nor was he filled with a lust for revenge. Instead, he was strangely elated, as though he had been released from his burden.

Doug burst out laughing, giggling insanely as he snatched a glance at his mother's smiling face. 'I gave him a bloody good beating, didn't I, Mam?' He was like a child hoping for a reward.

It was Ned who answered. 'I'm only sorry I didn't give *you* a similar beating when you were younger. Happen then you might have turned out to be a son I could have been proud of.'

'That's enough,' Martha ordered. 'I want you to take him back. It's only right that father and son should work together.

And if he did help himself to a bit of money, it doesn't really matter. There'll come a day when he'll inherit the business anyway.' She smiled encouragingly at Doug and he smiled back, but their smiles fell away when Ned spoke in his new dignified voice.

'He can't inherit what isn't mine.' Delighted by their astonishment he went on, 'I sold the business some while back, soon after I discovered there was money missing. What with all the expenses and business being quiet, I had no choice. So you see, there's nothing to inherit.'

Doug stared at him with disbelief, and Martha was trembling. 'Who did you sell it to?' she hissed.

There was a world of regret in Ned's voice, but strangely enough he was smiling as he went to the door. 'Adam Roach,' he said, and heard them gasp aloud. Before they could recover, he made a further statement. 'I won't be coming back again,' he told them. Nothing else. Just that. And their shocked silence was immensely satisfying to him.

Chapter Thirteen

'God Almighty! Why didn't you put a stop to it?' Peggy was horrified to learn that Doug had moved his mother in with him and Rosie.

'What could I do, Peggy?' As they hurried across the road towards the park. Rosie held hard to the boy beside her. Daniel was a sturdy little fellow, with a ready smile but a quiet disposition. 'Hurry up, sweetheart,' she urged, always wary of crossing the road with him, though there was not much traffic because it was Sunday and most people were either in their beds or talking to the Lord in church. 'My hands are tied and they both know it,' she told Peggy now.

'Is there nothing at all you can do, gal?' Coming to the bench just inside the park, Peggy fell heavily on to a seat, her blue eyes watching Rosie's every move as she took off the boy's jacket and folded it over her arm. The July sun was beating down and his face was growing redder by the minute. When he asked if he could play in the sand, Rosie let him go, but warned him not to stray. After he'd toddled off to make sandcastles, Peggy resumed her questioning. 'Have you talked to Doug about it . . . having his old woman there, I mean?'

''Course I have.' Day and night, whenever he was sober enough to listen, she had gone over the same arguments that

Peggy was raising now. 'I've told him time and time again that it's impossible for the four of us to live under the same roof.'

'And?'

'He doesn't want to know. He just says I'm selfish, and that I should be glad it's not *me* lying in bed and having to rely on other folks.' Rosie had come to the end of her tether, but she couldn't help wondering about what Doug had said. 'The trouble is, he does manage to make me feel guilty because it's true, isn't it? Evil as she is, Martha must feel every bit as bad as me. After all, she can't really want to live with me, hating me like she does.'

Peggy sat bolt upright, her blue eyes blazing. 'What! She's probably enjoying every minute of it . . . knowing how unhappy she's making you. You're just too kind-hearted, that's the problem, and the pair of 'em are taking advantage.'

Rosie knew it. She also knew that the situation was an impossible one, and that there was no easy solution. Leaning back on the hard bench, she let her eyes rove over the colourful flower-beds. At home there was an atmosphere you could cut with a knife, while here in this lovely place there was a sense of peace and her heart felt at ease. 'I've thought and thought about what to do, but I can't see a way out and that's the truth.' Her sad brown eyes gazed at Peggy, and not for the first time she envied her friend's independence.

'You could leave.' Peggy voiced the same possibility that had lately crossed Rosie's mind. 'If you like, I'll help you to find a place of your own?'

She answered with a sigh, 'I've already been looking at rooms to let, and I can tell you, it's a thankless task. These past weeks I've lived on the tram, going in every direction. Last week it was Darwen, the week before that it was Accrington, and the day before yesterday I walked the streets of Bolton.'

Peggy sat forward, an expression of surprise on her face. 'You little sod! You never told me that.'

Rosie winked cheekily. 'Makes a change for me to be one step ahead of you.'

'So when are you moving out?'

'I'm not.'

'*Why* not?'

'It's the same old story, Peggy . . . no money to speak of, and a young child. I'd be struggling worse than I am now, and on top of that Doug's already threatened that if I should try "taking my hook" as he puts it, he'd have Danny away from me.'

'Happen he'd *try*! Knowing you, though, you'd fight him tooth and nail.'

'Oh, I'd do that all right, but it's a risk I'm not prepared to take.' Rosie's whole life revolved round her son. 'Besides, I've thought the whole thing through, and I've decided I'm staying put. Not because of his threats to take the boy, and not because of his mam's wickedness.'

'I think you're mad. If it was me, I'd be off in a minute.'

'No, you wouldn't, Peggy,' Rosie answered softly. 'Not if you think about it. At first I felt exactly the same. I was afraid and unhappy about the situation. I still am. But why *should* I leave? That little house is my home. I've loved it since the first day I walked through the door.' Rosie's brown eyes shone defiantly. 'No, Peggy. I'm on to Martha's nasty little plan. She thinks she can get me out, but she'll be sadly disappointed because I'm staying!'

Peggy's smile said it all. 'I should have known. If Martha wants a fight, she's met her match in you, I reckon.' In a softer voice, she went on, 'Be careful though, gal. She's a wicked old biddy and she'd stop at nothing to see you out on the street.'

'Happen she's forgotten I'm a fighter.' When she'd got up that morning, Rosie had felt as though she was carrying the world on her shoulders. But now, in Peggy's company, relaxing in this lovely old park, she felt stronger of heart. 'So you reckon I'm right to stay put then?'

Peggy nodded. 'If it were me, I'd have cut and run the minute she came through that bloody door, gal. But I ain't made o' the same strong stuff as you, and yes, thinking about it, I reckon you're right to stay. If you cleared off, the artful old sod would have won the day.' She laughed out loud then. 'Who knows? When she sees the other side of you, happen she'll bugger off herself.'

'Do you know what *would* be nice?' Without waiting for an answer, Rosie went on, 'If we really *could* live together. I mean, without all the rows and her dreadful temper. After all, she is my son's grandmother.'

'I thought you said she doesn't have much to do with him now?'

'Not since the accident.' Rosie had always wondered about that. 'Do you know, Peggy, she's so deranged I sometimes think she suspects the boy to be Adam's.' The words came out without her meaning them to, and now she blushed to the roots of her hair. 'I know it's impossible, but why else would she turn on her only grandson?' she finished lamely.

Peggy was quick to notice Rosie's frustration, and equally quick to put her at her ease again. 'She's turned on the lad because she's an old cow, that's why. And for no other reason.' Following Rosie's gaze to where Danny was playing, she suggested, 'It's such a glorious day, why don't we walk back by way of Blakewater?'

Rosie didn't need asking twice. Having mentioned what had been in her heart these past weeks, she now wished the earth would open and swallow her up. Time and again, she had been tempted to contact Adam, but each time she cursed herself for such weakness. There was nothing to be gained from contacting him, and besides, there were other reasons why she hated herself for even having entertained the idea. She had cut him out of her life, and rightly so. The Adam she had known was not the same as the one who had snatched an old man's living from under him. Ever since Doug had told her how Adam had schemed to price his father out of the market, she had felt like a traitor. It was obvious he wasn't the same man she had known.

But then, so much had happened. So many years had passed. He had changed, and so had she. Unwilling at first to accept Doug's version of the story, she had spoken to some of Ned's old cronies. But they had only borne out what Doug told her: how Adam Roach had bought him out, and it had broken his heart. The story was that Adam wanted Ned out altogether, but the older man had made it a term of the contract that he stay as an employee. Even now Rosie found it hard to believe that Adam could have done such a callous thing. Yet it was true, and like poor old Ned, she had to accept it. But in spite of all that, and even more to her shame, she still held a deal of affection for Adam. Strangely enough, Peggy touched on that very issue now.

'It would have made it so much easier.'

'What do you mean?'

'If the boy had been Adam's son.'

'He's not, and you know that.'

'I know. All the same, it's a pity, because then Doug couldn't really threaten to take him from you.'

'As long as I live and breathe, Doug will *never* take Danny from me.' The dark and forbidding look in Rosie's eyes momentarily subdued her companion.

'Have you forgiven him?' Peggy's thoughts were running along the same lines as Rosie's.

'Who?'

'You know who. *Adam*, that's who. Have you forgiven him for taking away. Doug's inheritance?'

'Doug lost the right to that a long time ago. Ned's business was his own . . . built up over many years. I don't believe he had any intention of leaving it to Doug. Oh, it might have been different years ago when Doug was a boy. But, thanks to Martha, whatever respect there once was between father and son long ago turned to indifference.' There was bitterness in Rosie's voice. 'I've never heard Doug say one kind word about his father.'

'It shocked me, I can tell you, when I heard about Adam Roach buying Ned out. I never believed he would part with his beloved wagon and trade. You know, gal, I reckon there's more to all this than meets the eye. Ned wouldn't have sold easily, I'm certain.'

'I don't suppose we'll ever know what actually happened to make Ned sell. Apparently he was in financial trouble, and I'm not surprised at that. Happen he had no choice but to sell, and happen it was forced on him, I don't know. But I do know this much. Ned taught Adam everything he knows, and all the thanks he got was to become Adam's next takeover. It's common knowledge how Adam Roach is fast becoming one of the county's biggest coal-merchants.'

'I suppose we should be proud of him. When all's said and done, you don't achieve that unless you work damned hard.'

'Or *cheat* damned hard.'

'Aren't you being a bit hard on Adam?'

Rosie's lovely face set. 'I don't think so. There's something else. According to Doug, his dad borrowed money from Adam in the lean times, and Adam used that to drive him under.'

'Doug doesn't always tell the true story.'

'I know that. But the fact of the matter is this . . . Ned lost his business, and now he's gone. Adam Roach has painted his own name on the wagon, added another two routes and expanded Ned's old ones. *That* tells me the truth. He isn't the man I knew and loved. As far as I'm concerned, Adam has beaten a good man in Ned, and I'll never forgive him.'

'Have you heard from Ned?'

'Just that brief letter soon after he left, telling me he was all right and asking me to take care of his grandson.' She recalled how there had been no mention of either Doug or his mam, and that night Doug had gone out on one of his worst drinking binges yet. 'We knew Ned was having a job to make ends meet. It stood to reason, with Martha needing a nurse and everything. But I didn't know how troubled he must have been, and I never imagined he would turn to Adam.' She had tried so hard not to believe it, but she knew now that Adam really had taken advantage of the situation. 'Ned lost everything he'd worked for. I can't forgive Adam for that.'

'Come on, gal.' Peggy rose from the bench and stretched her limbs. Afterwards she surprised Rosie by saying softly, 'One way or another, we're *all* carrying a cross of sorts.' When Rosie tried to draw her on the remark, she would have none of it. But it left Rosie unsettled, wondering whether she had misjudged Peggy's cavalier attitude. Happen she was not so happy to be footloose and fancy free after all?

While Rosie was gathering the boy's coat, Peggy made her way to the sand-pit. 'Come on, young 'un,' she said in a brighter voice. 'We're off home now.'

It was nearing midday when they passed St Peter's church. The congregation spilled out of the great doors, keeping Rosie and Peggy to one side of the pavement. When the path was clear again, they went away at a slower pace. 'I keep promising myself to go to Mass,' Rosie murmured, ashamed. 'Next Sunday, I will.' And, come what may, she would, because lately she had a desperate need for the Lord's guidance.

'You know, I'm not sure we should believe everything we hear, gal,' Peggy remarked. 'Why don't you contact Adam? Get his version of the truth?'

'I *know* the truth, Peggy.' Rosie had asked many questions after Ned's disappearance. 'There's a pattern to it all. Adam Roach is eaten up with ambition. He buys out the smaller merchants to eliminate competition. It's common knowledge. You've said so yourself.' Soon after Ned went, she had been tempted to get in touch with Adam. But common sense prevailed, and now she was glad she had resisted the temptation. 'I never want to set eyes on him again!' she said firmly.

'Are you saying you don't have any affection for him at all?' Peggy sensed Rosie's despair, and could only imagine what her friend was suffering.

'I suppose if I'm honest I do still love the Adam I remember,' Rosie reluctantly admitted. 'No woman can easily forget her first love. But I loathe what he's become. Doug has his failings and they're many, but he's weak more than wicked.'

'You and Doug . . . how are things between you now?'

'The same. He hates me when he's sober, and wants me when he's drunk.' A wry little smile appeared at the corners of her mouth. 'Fortunately for me, when he's drunk he falls asleep before he can get his pants off.'

Peggy laughed out loud. 'Poor sod!' she cried. 'What happens then?'

'I throw a blanket over him and he sleeps where he drops,' Rosie answered merrily.

'It must be rotten when *he* wants it to stand up, and all *it* wants to do is lie down.' Peggy's laughter was infectious, and the two of them were still laughing when they turned into Castle Street.

The laughter was short-lived. At Peggy's house they parted company and Rosie made her way along the street with a heavier heart. The thought of Martha sitting up there in the bedroom, waiting to spoil what little pleasure Rosie and her son had got from the morning's outing, was more than enough to take the smile from her face. Little Danny said it all now when he whispered, 'I don't have to go and see Gran'ma, do I?'

'Not if you don't want to, sweetheart,' she answered, giving him a hug. Fumbling in her purse she took out the key and unlocked the door. 'If you like, you can play in the back yard while I get some food on the table. No doubt your daddy will be home soon, starving hungry as usual.' She smiled, but there was no smile in return.

As soon as they were inside, the boy lost no time in making his way to the back yard. 'Wish I could do the same,' Rosie muttered, watching him through the window. No sooner had she spoken than Martha's voice called down, 'Rosie, you bugger! Is that you?'

Going to the foot of the stairs, she called back, 'Can you wait a minute? I'm just about to get the food ready.'

'No, I bloody well can't. Get up here now.'

Rosie shook her head. Every day she hoped Martha's mean mood would improve, and every day it seemed to get worse. 'On my way,' she replied, reluctantly climbing the stairs. As she went, she mimicked Martha's voice, muttering beneath her breath, 'Where've you been all this time? You're a heartless bugger, Rosie Selby, leaving a poor defenceless woman to fend for herself. One o' these days you'll come back and find me lyin' here dead! But I expect that's what you want, ain't it, eh? Clap your bloody hands if I should pop off, wouldn't you, eh?'

At the top of the stairs, Rosie took a deep breath. 'Do your worst, you old sod!' she said, glaring at Martha's bedroom door and imagining the hostile face behind it. Going the remaining few steps along the landing, she pushed open the door. Straightway Martha's voice took up where Rosie's had left off, repeating word for word what she had said while climbing the stairs. And all the while, Rosie stood by the door, waiting for the tirade to end. But when it did, it was on a note of such malice that it made Rosie shiver. 'You've been with a fella, ain't you?' Martha sniggered. 'Look at you, you dirty little bitch, breathless and red-faced, still panting from what you've been up to.'

Tempted to cross the room and ram the pillow down that

wicked throat, Rosie forced herself to remain calm. 'If I'm red-faced and panting it's because no sooner am I back from a long walk in the warm sun, than you're yelling for me to run straight up the stairs. You don't even give a body time to get her breath!'

'Been for a walk, eh? More like you've been rolling in the grass with a fella. What! You've only to look at your face to know you're guilty as hell. And I'll tell you this – our Doug will know the minute he gets home, because I'll make it my business to tell him.'

'Well, now you've got all that off your chest, Martha, what can I do for you?' Rosie's voice was deliberately kind and soft, and there was even a smile on her face.

'I've shit the bed!'

The smile fell from Rosie's face. 'I don't believe you.'

'What? Same as I don't believe *you*?' She chuckled and clapped her hands at the horrified expression on Rosie's face. 'Don't smell too sweet, do it, eh?' she pointed out with glee.

'If you *have* messed the bed, you've done it on purpose.' Rosie made no move. Instead she remained by the door, letting her disapproval be known.

'So say you.' The ugliness of Martha's soul showed in her countenance. Her eyes had grown smaller from years of being narrowed with hatred. Her brow was furrowed in a permanent deep frown, and her greying hair stood up round her large head, as though she'd been caught in a high wind. There was shocking satisfaction in her smile. 'You'd best clean me up, hadn't you? Miss High and bloody Mighty.'

Rosie stood her ground. 'You've never messed yourself before.' She had always admired Martha for her ability to do most things in spite of her disability. 'How come you can manage to use the pan yourself whenever Doug's home, but when I'm out, you find it impossible? You *did* do it on purpose, and I've a good mind to let you swill in it.'

Martha was pleased. 'Be very careful, lady,' she warned gruffly. 'My Doug would be upset to hear you threatening me like that.'

'Happen "your Doug" should clean you up then.'

Rosie turned as though to leave, but swung round when Martha screamed out, 'Don't you dare turn your back on me!'

Rosie was suitably wide-eyed and innocent. 'I'm so sorry, Martha, was there something else?' she asked in a dignified voice.

'All right, you bitch! I *did* do it on purpose, but I ain't sorry.'

'Well, you should be. Your grandson hardly ever moves out of this house, and today was the first time he's been to the park in weeks. I don't often leave you, but when I do I always make sure you've everything to make you comfortable. And I always ask Ma Rushden next-door to keep an eye on you. You know perfectly well you've only to knock on the wall and she'll be here in a minute.'

'Sod Ma Rushden!' Martha began thumping her fists against the covers. 'You'd best clean me up or I'll yell blue murder!'

Seeing that she was fighting a losing battle, Rosie conceded. 'All right. Give me a minute to boil the kettle, and I'll be straight back.'

'And fetch the boy.'

Rosie glared at her. 'We'll see.'

'I need to see him now! Or shall I tell Doug that on top of everything else, you're trying to keep my own grandson from me.'

'You know that's not true, Martha. I've never refused to let you see him.' Not that she wouldn't *like* to because the boy was obviously frightened of his grandmother. 'It's just that I'd rather you were in a better mood, that's all.'

'You bloody well fetch him, do you hear?'

'All right, I'll fetch him. But not until after you're washed.' Martha's smile widened and Rosie hurried from the room.

Downstairs, Rosie was shocked, when she glanced at the clock over the firebreast. It was almost two o'clock. 'God Almighty! He'll be in any minute, and no food on the table.' Before she went out that morning, she had cleaned the fish, prepared the vegetables and set the table, so all that remained was for her to place the fish in the oven and put a light beneath the pans. She did that now, then checked that her son was all right, and finally boiled a kettle full of water and got the bowl ready for Martha. And, above it all, she could hear her mother-in-law shouting for her to: 'Get up here, damn and bugger you!' To which Rosie replied under her breath, 'Your language doesn't change, Martha. It's still colourful as ever.'

A short time later, after the vegetables were nicely simmering and the aroma of baking fish was gently issuing from the oven, Rosie tested the water in the bowl, making sure it was neither too hot nor too cold. She dropped a flannel and soap into it, draped a large towel over her arm, and went back upstairs, being careful not to slop the water over her own legs.

'About time too,' Martha complained. She complained when Rosie turned back the covers and she complained when her clothes were stripped away. She swore that the water was: 'Hot enough to scald the skin from me back,' and she grumbled the whole time she was being washed, dried and dusted with powder.

Finally the task was done, and Rosie prepared to leave. 'Your dinner won't be long,' she said. Her every bone ached. Martha was no easy handful, and had gone out of her way to make the job more difficult.

'You can fetch the young 'un now.' Sitting up in bed, Martha finally looked presentable, with her freshly laundered nightgown and pretty pink bed-jacket, and her hair combed to a semblance of order. 'I'm waiting, so get a move on.'

Rosie's answer was a forlorn shake of the head. She had hoped Martha would change her mind about wanting to see the boy.

Instead she was adamant, and Rosie was obliged to comply. But she would watch her! Like a hawk, she would watch Martha's every move.

'I don't want to go up.' Danny tugged at Rosie's skirt and pleaded with big frightened eyes. 'She's been shouting again. She'll shout at *me*.' Martha's room overlooked the yard where he had been playing, and her voice had carried to its every corner.

Rosie's heart went out to him, but she knew it would be wrong to encourage the bad feeling that was beginning to develop between her son and Martha. 'Your grandma's not well, sweetheart,' she explained. 'She didn't mean to shout.'

He blinked away the tears, dropped his head to his chest and cast his gaze to the floor. 'If I go, will you come too?'

''Course I will.' She took hold of his hand. Slowly, the two of them went up the stairs, he in front and Rosie behind, and it was hard to tell whose heart was sorrier for that short journey.

Martha's smile was terrifying. 'Come to see your gran'ma, eh?' she asked, grinning through yellowing teeth. 'Come on then, right up to the bed.' She beckoned him closer and, on hesitant footsteps, Danny went to her. Anxious as ever, Rosie stayed close behind.

At first, it seemed as though the boy would turn tail and run. But then Martha became surprisingly charming, asking him about the park and the sandpit where he played. 'And did you build any castles?' she asked, affectionately ruffling his hair. Her warm smile was totally disarming. Slowly but surely the child warmed to her, and Rosie began to think she had judged Martha a little too harshly after all.

Danny told her about this and that, and Martha kept on with her questions. When they discussed his grandad's soldiers, and Martha asked whether he would like to keep them, Danny nodded excitedly. Chuckling, she produced the soldiers from the bedside cupboard, and he was enthralled. He even laughed a little and seemed to forget his past unease with her. Watching from nearby, Rosie was delighted that they were getting on so well. It was all she had ever wanted. If Martha was bound to remain in this house, and it seemed as though she was, then it would certainly be wonderful if they could all live peacefully together. For whatever reasons, her son had already lost his grandfather. It would be some compensation if he should gain a grandmother who came genuinely to care for him. After all, she did once love him dearly. Surely that feeling was still alive deep down in Martha's heart?

When Doug's voice called from downstairs, Rosie had few qualms about leaving the two of them together. 'I'll be back in a minute,' she promised, and they hardly glanced up as she departed. However, Martha did bestow a smile on her, and Rosie hoped that at long last everything might be coming right between them.

Doug wasn't drunk, but he was merry. 'I've been at a mate's house,' he explained. 'Had a game of cards, and look at this!' He produced a wad of notes from his pockets and grabbed her into his arms. 'Your old fella's a canny bugger when it comes to cards.' His open smile took her back to when she first fell for his charms. Even now, after all that had happened between them, he could still raise a smile from her.

'It's nice to see you're not drunk on your winnings,' she said simply. 'Happen you can fork out for some new clothes for your son.' When he pushed a couple of notes into her hand, she could hardly believe it. 'What are you after?' she asked light-heartedly. When he was like this, she could forgive him at least some of his behaviour.

He tickled her under the chin and clicked his tongue at her. 'You're a real beauty, do you know that, Rosie Selby?' His lascivious gaze travelled over her classic features, the small heart-shaped face and the straight proud nose, her rich brown hair that looked the colour of ripe chestnuts against her pale skin, and those pretty brown eyes with their long lashes and perfectly shaped eyebrows above. Pushing closer, he put his arm round her, his eyes boring into hers. 'Where's the boy?' he asked in a voice hoarse with passion.

'Upstairs with your mam.'

'We've time then?' His fingertips crept over her throat, then down to the neck of her blouse. Sliding his hand in, he stroked the small taut breast, expertly rolling the hard nipple between finger and thumb. Bending his head, he opened his mouth over hers, at the same time gruffly whispering, 'I've wanted you all day.' Pushing her backwards against the sideboard, he began undoing his trousers. 'We've time,' he kept saying. 'We've time.' In a minute his member was thrust out, large and erect in his hand.

'What the devil's the matter with you?' Rosie was mortified in case the boy should see. 'Have you no sense of decency?'

'Aw, come on, we'll be over and done before they know it.' He was frantic by now, and in no mood to be refused.

Before Rosie could push him off, he was all over her. But then he was startled by the sound of Danny's voice calling out for his mammy. 'Ignore the little brat,' he gasped, his whole body forcing her down.

When Rosie heard the boy running down the stairs and loudly sobbing, she gathered every ounce of her strength to push Doug's weight off her. 'You're like an animal,' she accused. 'If you ask me, you wouldn't even *care* if the boy saw us at it.'

His face was flushed with anger. 'To hell with him,' he snapped. 'To hell with *both* of 'em!'

Astonished to hear him cursing his mother, Rosie pushed him aside and ran to meet the child. He was deeply distressed. When she opened her arms to him, he collapsed into them. 'Gran'ma hurt me,' he cried, lifting his face to show the red weal that went from one side of his forehead to the other.

He was still crying bitterly when Rosie brought him into the living room. 'You'd best have a word with her,' she told the disgruntled Doug. 'Because if you don't, I will. And I can promise you, I won't be so particular in what I have to say!'

Incensed at being cheated out of his lovemaking, the anger was still on Doug when he stormed towards the door. 'Is there no peace for a man in his own house?' he demanded. When he ran up the stairs two at a time, Rosie took the child into the kitchen and set about washing the wound on his forehead. Thankfully the skin was unbroken, but he had been badly frightened. Little by little, Rosie discovered what had taken place up there in Martha's room. First she had quizzed Danny about whether his mammy had met a man in the park. Then, when they were playing cowboys and Indians, she took a knife to his head and threatened to 'scalp' him if he didn't tell her 'the truth'. Rosie was made to wonder whether the old lady had finally lost her mind.

Upstairs, Doug vented his frustration on his mother. 'This is *my* house, and don't you forget it,' he told her. 'No wonder Dad buggered off. But I'm not as soft as the old man, and I'll not stand for your peevish little games so you'd best be warned. If you can't behave under my roof, you can bloody well find somewhere else to make mischief.'

At first, Martha turned on the tears, fantasising to herself that Rosie's old meat knife had been under her pillow for protection. But when she realised her cunning wiles were getting her nowhere, she flew at him in a rage, 'It shouldn't be *me* you're yelling at,' she snarled. 'It's that wife o'yourn. *She's* the one who needs throwing out, the little baggage.'

All the while she was speaking she dabbed at her eyes with a hankie, making small sad noises in the back of her throat. 'I may have been a bad 'un to your dad, but I never cheated him, not once all the years we were wed.' Through her fingers she spied

Doug's face, satisfied when it turned a pale shade of grey. 'It's *her* you should be turning on, not your poor old mam.'

He was bending over the bed, one hand on the brass headrail and the other clenched into a fist not far from her face. But now he straightened his back and stared down at her, his odd-coloured eyes like round glittering marbles. 'You'd best tell me what you're getting at,' he instructed in a strangely quiet voice.

Leaving him to brood on the suspicions she had planted in his mind, Martha sighed and groaned and muttered her discontent. She plumped up her pillows, then tidied the neck of her nightgown, and now, much to his frustration, was patting at her dishevelled hair.

When he made a small grunting noise and bent over her again, she looked up and saw she had punished him long enough. 'Don't you think you'd better ask *her*?' she suggested. All trace of her distress was now gone and in its place was a bristling authority. After being belittled by Rosie, it felt wonderful to relive the power she'd had over her husband, now over her son. 'You can ask her, but I doubt if she'll tell you the truth.'

'I'm asking *you*!' His face was twisted with rage.

'All I'm saying is, you should keep your eyes open. It wouldn't be the first time a woman strayed when she thought her husband wasn't looking.'

'You're a bloody liar!'

'You think so, do you?'

'If she was carrying on with another bloke, I'd know, I can promise you that.'

'Then there's no need to worry, is there?' The damage was done. The seed was planted and she could leave it to grow. 'Go away and let me sleep,' she grumbled. 'I'm tired. First *she* upsets me, then the brat, and now you.' She flung herself to the far side of the bed and began softly crying. 'I've always done my best by you, and now none of you want me. Shame on you!'

She buried her face in the pillow and waited for him to go. Once the door was closed, she raised her head and chuckled to herself. 'Talk down to your betters, will you Miss High and Mighty? Well, now you'll see who comes off worse, won't you, eh? Happen you'll remember in future . . . make trouble for Martha Selby and you'll get more than you've bargained for.'

Rosie was curious as to what had gone on between mother and son. But when Doug came downstairs, he had nothing to say. He remained quiet throughout the meal, and afterwards sat sullen and moody in the fireside chair. Occasionally he would glance at her as though on the verge of saying something, but then he would look away, eyes downcast and his fingers playing on the arm of his chair.

'Your mam's fast and hard asleep,' she told him, returning to the living room with Martha's tray. 'I thought to wake her, but then I decided to let her sleep a while longer. I'll steam the meal up later. It won't spoil.' What she had really wanted to do when she stood over Martha just now was to tackle her over what she had done to the boy. But she reasoned that, if Doug had dealt with it, she ought to let it rest, although hell would fuse with heaven before she ever again left her son alone with Martha.

'I'm tired, Mammy.' Danny was heavy-eyed and still upset from his ordeal at Martha's hands. He had barely touched his meal, and was now clambering down from the table.

'All right, sweetheart.' Rosie led him into the kitchen. Normally he would have been given a thorough strip-wash before being allowed up to his bed. But on this occasion, Rosie gave his hands and face a quick lick-over with a damp cloth, before returning him to the living room.

'Say goodnight to your daddy,' she said, and was astonished when Doug opened his arms to hug the child. As a rule it was a quick 'Goodnight, son', and the boy was sent straight off to his bed.

Tonight, however, Doug held on to the boy for a full minute before thrusting him away. He hadn't spoken one word since his confrontation with Martha, and Rosie was deeply perturbed by his strange mood. She felt guilty without knowing why.

Upstairs, she helped Danny to change into his pyjamas. She reassured him when he looked fearfully at the door and remarked in a small voice, 'I don't like Gran'ma any more.'

'If you want me, I won't be far away, you know that,' Rosie told him.

He didn't want to let her leave. 'Sing to me, Mammy,' he begged, and she did.

The nursery rhyme was an old favourite of hers. The words calmed her fears and lifted her spirit, and soon her soft lilting voice was lulling Danny to slumber. 'Go to sleep my baby, close your big brown eyes . . . Angels watch above you, peeping at you from the skies.' Even before she had finished the verse, he was sound asleep, a look of contentment on his face and his arms stretched out above his head. 'Sleep well, little one,' she whispered, tucking the blanket over him. She kissed him gently on the forehead and tiptoed from the room, softly closing the door behind her. Outside she paused a moment, listening. All was quiet. A smile wreathed her face as she murmured, 'If I never have anything else in this life, I'll always thank the good Lord for you.' More and more, her son had come to mean the world to her.

Before going down again, she took a look in Martha's room. Her heart turned over when her mother-in-law sat bolt upright in bed and grinned at her. 'Got the brat to sleep, have you?' Her voice was low and grating, her eyes glittered with malice, and Rosie's dislike of her intensified.

She had promised herself she would leave it to Doug to deal with Martha. But, at that moment, it was obvious to her that he had made little or no impact on his mother. There was something very wrong about Martha. Something sinister. 'I ought to see you through that front door for what you did to my son . . .' Rosie started.

'Don't threaten me,' Martha interrupted. 'You can't do anything to harm me, and you know it. This is my son's house, and I'll answer to *him*, not you.' She smiled, sending shivers down Rosie's spine. 'You can leave now,' she said.

Rosie was convinced. '*You're completely mad*,' she murmured.

'I don't want no dinner either. How do I know you ain't trying to poison me?'

'We're not all painted with the same brush,' Rosie said sharply. 'But if you don't want your meal, that's fine by me. I'll leave it steaming until you do.' She knew from old that Martha would soon be demanding her food. 'But before I go, I want you to know that if you ever hurt my son again, you'll answer to me.'

'Is that so?'

'You can depend on it,' Rosie insisted angrily. When Martha merely smiled, she thought it best to leave. If she stayed she might be tempted to do something she would regret.

'Must you go out?' Doug was putting on his coat when Rosie came into the living room. 'I really wouldn't mind some company tonight.' Martha's oddness had unnerved her. But then she recalled how Doug himself had been in a strange mood since talking to her. Between the two of them, Rosie was made to feel insecure.

He stared at her for a minute, his mouth set in a grim line. He shrugged and fastened his coat, and as he was leaving, asked cynically, 'Are you sure it's *my* company you're after?' Before she could question his remark, he was gone, slamming out of the house and leaving her in a quandary.

She went about her work with a vengeance. When everything was done, she got out her sewing basket and replaced all the loose buttons on her best frock. She stitched the tear in little Danny's play trousers, and darned the sleeves of Doug's jumpers. When that was done, she turned on the radio and tried to get interested in the mystery story. It was already halfway through. Unsettled, she turned it off and went to the bottom of the stairs where she listened a while. Silence. Not a sound came from upstairs. 'You ought to sleep, you old bugger!' she murmured. 'But it's a wonder your conscience will let you.'

In the kitchen Martha's meal was slowly steaming but the water in the pan was almost gone. Filling the jug from the tap, Rosie poured the contents into the pan until it was nearly full. After taking a look at the food, she set the plate on top once more; the meal was nicely kept and would remain so until Martha started shouting for it. 'I ought to chuck it in the bin!' Rosie grumbled.

For the next two hours she looked for things to do, and the more she thought about what Doug had said, the more she was ready to have it out with him. She felt angry, confused by his parting remark, yet convinced Martha was behind it all.

It was midnight when he came home. Rosie was in bed fast asleep. She had tried to stay awake, but it had been a long and arduous day and the minute after her head touched the pillow she was in a deep, if restless, slumber.

It was a sense of horror that woke her. At first when she opened her eyes, she couldn't see him. The room was steeped in darkness, the only relief being the slit of moonlight that cut through the narrow opening between the curtains. With a gasp she sat up, clutching the bed-clothes to her breast. 'Who's there? Doug, is that you?' Fear was betrayed in her voice.

His reply was low and angry, his voice slurred with drink. 'Expecting somebody else, were you?' Narrowing her eyes, she could just make him out, slumped against the dresser, his face like a pale mask in the gloom.

In a minute she was out of the bed and reaching for the light-switch. A ripple of fear went through her when his fingers quickly locked over her wrist. 'I'm sorry if I've disappointed you,' he hissed, tightening his grip on her arm. 'But then, I'm only your husband when all's said an' done.'

Anger bubbled up in her. Wrenching herself away, she demanded, 'It's your mother, isn't it? Something she said to you before you went out has got you all riled up.' Snapping on the light, she stared into his face, her brown eyes alive with anger. 'For God's sake, Doug, can't you see what she's trying to do?'

The sudden influx of light made him blink. Impatient, he switched off the light. 'It's got nothing to do with her,' he lied. 'But I'll tell you this . . . if I find out you're seeing another man, I'll kill the pair of you.'

Rosie should not have been surprised, but she was. 'So, she *has* told you I've got another man? Are there no depths to her wickedness?' Martha's spitefulness had always been foreign to Rosie's more generous nature. 'I take her in, run up and down the stairs at her beck and call, wash her, feed her, wait on her hand and foot, and *still* she's bent on making trouble between us.' Something inside her snapped. 'If you're fool enough to believe the lies she tells you about me, then happen I should take the boy and clear off.'

'It's lies then?'

'Of *course* it's bloody lies!' Stiffening with rage, she swung away. Throwing herself on to the bed, she sat upright and grim-faced, her troubled eyes staring out of the chink between the curtains. The sky was dark as black velvet. Out there was another world, one she had never really explored. 'I can't take much more of her,' she confessed. 'I do what I can, but it's never enough. Happen it really would be better if I found somewhere of my own.' At this minute in time, it seemed so simple. 'Besides, after what happened with Danny today, I'm afraid. She hates him, you know that, don't you?'

'Don't talk daft! He's her grandson. Why would she hate him?' There was something in his voice that told Rosie he also had been deeply shocked by what had taken place here today.

'I don't *know* why. But she's turned on him, and you can't deny it.'

'You swear on Danny's life . . . you're not seeing another man?'

'I'll do no such thing!' Rosie rose from the bed and crossed the room. 'You can believe what *she* tells you, or you can believe *me*. I am NOT seeing another man.' She actually laughed out loud. 'God Almighty! Don't you think I've learned my lesson with *you*? One man is more than enough.'

He let out a great heaving sigh. 'I know I'm not the best husband in the world, Rosie, but I do love you.'

Hating the dark, she again flicked on the light and was astonished to see him crying. Huge teardrops rolled down his face. With his hands thrust deep into his trouser pockets and his head inclined to one side, he looked a pathetic sight. Yet her heart remained hardened against him. He was ready to believe anything of her. She could not easily forgive him for that.

'She's been a good mother to me, but lately she's changed. Or I've only just begun to see her as she really is,' he confessed. 'She's a wicked old biddy, and I'll have to take a firmer hand with her,' he promised. 'Only please don't leave me. I'd be nothing without you.'

Rosie was torn in so many directions. There was no longer any love in her heart for this man. The only real thing that tied them together was the fact that he was the father of her child. In many ways he was too much like his mother. There were times when she loathed the very touch of him, and there were times when he was more of a child than Danny. She looked at him now, and felt ashamed. She also felt more trapped than ever. Why couldn't she have seen all of this years ago? Before it was all too late? But she hadn't, and there was only herself to blame. She could never love him again, never as long as she lived. Hers was a life without love. Only her son touched her heart, yet he was only half hers. She felt instinctively that if she left, Martha would side with Doug, and between them they would move heaven and earth to take the boy from her. No. She had made her own decision in life and, rightly or wrongly, would have to live it through; for the boy's sake if not her own.

'I'll never let another man come between us.' There was murder in his words, and it startled her.

She gave no answer. His remark needed none.

When he laid her on the bed, she made no resistance. She didn't want him, but neither did she want the upheaval of turning him away. Quietly, she submitted. The sooner it was over with, the better, she thought bitterly.

The smell of booze on his breath was nauseating, though he was not so intoxicated as not to have his way with her. 'Take your nightgown off,' he said. Before she had time to refuse, he was pulling it up round her waist. She could feel his hard member against the warmth of her skin and, for one regretful minute, she was roused. Sensing it, he coarsely laughed as he began probing into her. He had been interrupted before, and his appetite was all the more ravenous because of it.

This time he was deep in the throes of ecstasy when the cries of his son cut through his passion. He would have ignored the cries and carried on to fulfilment, but Rosie wriggled away and ran from the room, leaving him bitterly frustrated and in a dark rage at having been deprived yet again.

When Rosie opened her son's bedroom door, what she saw would live with her for the rest of her days. The light from the hallway flooded in. Martha was lying on the floor, twisted and wild-eyed. The child was caught up in her arms and she was holding a knife to his throat. His brown eyes were huge with fear, and his little hands were pulling on his grandmother's arms in a futile attempt to loosen her deadly grip. Tiny droplets of blood trickled over his fingers, and Rosie's heart turned somersaults.

'Let him go, Martha. *Please* . . . let him go.' Her voice was astonishingly calm, belying the terror she felt inside.

'Didn't hear me, did you?' Martha's laugh was terrible to hear. 'Didn't hear me crawling along on my belly, did you, eh?' she asked again. 'Oh, but I heard you . . . and him. I heard you going at each other in there.' The smile slid from her face. 'I told him about you, but you talked him round, didn't you, eh? You managed to convince him you ain't got another fella, when you and I know you bloody well have!'

'Please, Martha . . . let Danny go now.' Rosie had a mind to dart forward, take her unawares, but instinct warned her not to.

As though reading her thoughts, Martha warned in a sinister voice, 'Be very careful, dearie. He means nothing to me.' Her gaze went beyond Rosie to the doorway. Doug had come upon the scene and was momentarily struck dumb, his odd-coloured eyes going from his mam to the boy and then to Rosie.

At the sight of Doug, Martha's face broke into a wide smile. 'Send her away, son,' she pleaded. 'We don't need her. We don't need *either* of them.' Digging the blade into the boy's tender skin, she chuckled when he began sobbing again.

Hastily dressed in pyjamas, and slightly swaying from the effects of booze, Doug ventured further into the room. 'That's enough, Mam. Let him be,' he instructed. His voice was quick and angry. 'Whatever you think of Rosie, it has nothing whatsoever to do with the boy.'

Martha met his gaze with bold eyes. 'That's where you're wrong, son,' she declared knowingly. ''Cause this boy is right at the heart of it all.'

'Do as I ask you, Mam. Let Danny go.'

'You don't believe anything I say, do you? You and me, son, we were fooled all along. I believed the child to be my grandson, and you imagined him to be your own flesh and blood. Well, he ain't! He don't belong to neither of us, 'cause it were another man as fathered him.'

'You'd best stop, Mam. You're letting your tongue run away with you, and I don't want to hear no more of your mischief-making.' He took a step into the room but paused when she jerked the knife up against the boy's chin.

Behind Doug, Rosie was frantic, warning him in a hoarse whisper, 'For God's sake, be careful!'

He glanced round as though listening more intently to what she had to say, and even later, when she recalled the awful thing that happened, Rosie could never pinpoint the exact second when Doug bounded forward and launched himself at Martha. She heard an ear-splitting scream, and the dull thud as the two of them fell backwards together.

She saw Martha's surprised face, the wide open eyes and lolling mouth. Suddenly there was blood everywhere. It spurted up on the bedspread and spilled over the carpet, and the sound of Doug's cries rose above her own. She saw and heard all that, yet she could not say how it happened exactly. In that same split second, she darted forward and grabbed her son from beneath Martha's crumpled body. He was bleeding badly and limp as a rag doll in her arms. But he was breathing. Thank God, he was still breathing!

'She's dead!' Doug's voice was like a dull rhythm in her head. 'Mam's dead!' He kept repeating it. 'She's dead. Mam's dead!'

Beneath his weight, the knife had somehow embedded itself in Martha's neck. Now the handle was in his fist, and Martha was staring at him through flat glazed eyes. He began screaming. He was still screaming when Rosie summoned help from next-door, and was quietly sobbing when the police took him away. Like a child, he wanted his mam. They had to tear him from her, and as they walked him across the bedroom he turned his head to look on that familiar face, now shockingly quiet. In repose it seemed too normal, too devoid of expression.

He was still looking at her as they took him out of the door. Never once did he glance towards Rosie or the boy. He didn't show any interest when the ambulance-man gently took Danny from his wife's arms. Nor did he care.

All the way down the stairs he could be heard crying, 'I've killed her!' Over and over, 'I've killed my own mam. *May God have mercy on my soul.*'

Chapter Fourteen

It was the last day of July 1953, and the first time since Doug had been taken into custody that Rosie was able to visit him. Since that dreadful day, she had been torn between her love for her son – who was still not fully recovered from his ordeal – and her loyalty as a wife.

Last Friday the postman had brought the visiting voucher which she was to present at the gate on arrival at Strangeways Prison in Manchester. The voucher was for Tuesday. That was tomorrow, and already Rosie's stomach was turning somersaults at the thought of seeing Doug again. She was ashamed to admit it, but since he had been locked up, she hadn't missed him for one minute; though there were times when the house seemed strangely silent and empty with only her and Danny here. In fact, Rosie loved it with just the two of them.

After a restless night, she awoke feeling troubled. Leaving Danny sleeping, she hurried downstairs to find a letter on the mat by the front door. As soon as she picked it up, she recognised the handwriting. It was from Ned. Switching on the passage light, she read it where she stood. Ned was never known for his letter-writing, and she was surprised to find that it was long and soul-searching:

Dear Rosie,

You must think me all kinds of a coward for not coming to Martha's funeral. The truth is, I believe she would not have wanted me there. But you must know that.

Like I said in my earlier letter, I was deeply shocked by what happened. When I read the newspaper reports of what Doug had done, my first thoughts were for you. But even then, I could not bring myself to come back. I couldn't explain it in my first letter, and I can't explain it now; except maybe I really am the worst coward.

There is no love in me for Doug, but I do miss you and my grandson. One day, when I miss you both enough, you'll find me on your doorstep.

Forgive me, Rosie. Please don't tell Doug you've heard from me. We've been like strangers for too long now. I know he would only reject anything I have to say.

Please accept this five-pound note. Give Danny a big hug for me. Tell him my work keeps me away, but I will not forget him.

Keep well.

Yours affectionately,

Ned

'Shame on you!' Neatly folding the letter, Rosie replaced it in the envelope, and this she put in the pocket of her dressing-gown. Switching out the passage light, she made her way to the living-room. Once there, she took out the letter and opened the sideboard drawer. 'I won't hug your grandson for you, Ned,' she said bitterly. 'When he needed you, you weren't here. We've both done our crying for you, and now I'd rather he forgot you ever existed.'

Opening the drawer, she was about to put the letter inside when the other envelopes caught her eye. There were four of them, an earlier letter from Ned, and three from Adam. She didn't need to read them for she knew every word; especially the ones from Adam. After Doug was arrested, Adam had offered his help. She didn't answer that one so he wrote again, this time threatening to come and see her. She replied then, a cursory note to say that she wanted nothing more to do with him. She told him how she believed she was partly to blame for what had happened, and asked him never to write again, or try and contact her in any way. Taking out the last letter, she read it once more:

Dearest Rosie,

I was sad to receive your note, but not wanting to add to your distress, of course I'll do as you ask though it goes against my natural instincts.

You must know I still love you.

If you want me, I'll be here. You have my address.

Yours always,

Adam

Incensed that any man could write such a letter when he was married to another woman, she had thrust it in the drawer with the others, and there it had remained. Now, before she could ever be tempted to read it again, she tore it into little shreds, before throwing it in the bin along with all the others. But it was engrained on her mind. I love you. 'Damn you, Adam Roach!' Because she loved him too, and she always would.

Busying herself in readiness for the day ahead, Rosie quickly put the letter out of her mind. The idea that soon she would be sitting in the same room as Doug was more than enough to occupy her every thought.

Peggy was on her annual fortnight's holiday, and had agreed

to stay in Rosie's house with Danny. 'With school out, that lot indoors would drive him crazy,' she laughed. She laughed a lot lately, and Rosie knew it was for *her* benefit. Like Rosie, Peggy had been stunned by the whole ordeal, and neither of them had yet talked about what the future might hold for her and her son. It was a subject that dogged Rosie day and night, and she could see nothing ahead but trouble and heartache.

'You look real smart,' Peggy told her on this Tuesday morning. In her brown two-piece and white blouse with the frill at the neck, Rosie did look smart. She had on her best black patent shoes and wore a deep-brimmed cream hat that suited her shoulder-length brown hair. But her eyes were shadowed with tiredness, and her face was pale and gaunt. She had lost a deal of weight and her jacket looked too big across her frail shoulders. There was a haunted expression about her that persisted even when she smiled, and when she spoke it seemed as though her mind was elsewhere.

'You're not listening, are you?' Rising from her chair, Peggy crossed the room to where Rosie was looking in the sideboard mirror and fiddling with the neck of her blouse. Putting her two hands on Rosie's shoulders, Peggy gently turned her round until they were facing each other. 'You don't really want to go, do you?' she asked softly.

Suddenly Rosie was opening the drawer and her hand was on the letter. 'This was lying on the mat when I came down,' she explained, handing it to Peggy. 'It's from Ned.'

She read the letter. She had also read the first one so the contents didn't surprise her. 'Don't blame him,' she said. 'Nobody knows what he went through with Martha.'

'He should be here, Peggy, and you know it.' Rosie didn't find it so easy to forgive. 'Whatever happened between Ned and his wife and son is no fault of Danny's. To a child, everything is black and white. How can he understand why his entire family have been taken from him? How in God's name can I ever hope to explain such a thing?' She choked on the words. 'Ned should have been here. Now we don't need him.'

'I know how you must feel, Rosie,' Peggy entreated. 'But you can't really know what he's thinking right now. What happened has affected all of you . . . not just Danny.'

'It's Danny who's suffering the most because he doesn't understand. If Ned had been here, we could have helped each other.' Rosie was not convinced that he should be cleared of all blame. 'What kind of man can stay away when his wife is murdered and his son is imprisoned? What kind of a man is it who won't come to his grandson when he needs him?' She shook her head. 'No, Peggy. Until Ned has the guts to face me, I can't altogether forgive him.'

Momentarily silenced by Rosie's outburst, Peggy was lost for words. Presently she said, 'I don't think I've ever heard you speak so harshly. Don't shut Ned out, Rosie. Everyone has their own way of dealing with tragedy.'

There had been a terrible anger in Rosie until that moment when she looked into Peggy's dear face. Suddenly the anger softened and tears welled up to choke her. 'Oh, Peggy, I don't know what to think. Sometimes I believe it was all *my* fault, and I can't bear it.' Her lovely brown eyes were hauntingly sad. 'If it hadn't been for me taunting Martha, maybe none of this would have happened.' The tears had been held back, but now they spilled over and, throwing herself into Peggy's arms, Rosie sobbed like a child, words tumbling over one another. 'Oh, Peggy, I wish to God I could turn the clock back.'

Peggy let her cry. Rosie had comforted her so many times, and now it was *her* turn. She held on to that dear soul, horrified by how thin Rosie had become, and wondering where it would all end.

Ashamed, Rosie drew away. 'I'm sorry,' she murmured,

'I shouldn't heap my troubles on you.' She felt better for crying, but there was a great hard lump in her heart still, and nothing she could do would break it down. Suddenly weary, she sank into the fireside chair. 'I don't know how I can face him,' she murmured. 'I won't know what to say.'

'You can't think *he* blames you?' Collecting Rosie's hat from the floor where it had fallen, Peggy came and sat opposite. 'You mustn't think that.'

Rosie opened her mouth to speak, but her throat was tight and her heart too full. Eventually she whispered, 'He killed his own mother, Peggy, and it was me who called out for him.'

'Well o' course you called out for him!' she retaliated. 'So would any other woman. Martha was holding a knife against your son's throat. What else could you do?'

'Happen I could have talked her out of it?'

Peggy shook her head. 'Didn't you try that? Before Doug came into the room, didn't you try and talk her out of it?' She was desperately concerned for Rosie. Day by day she had seen her going downhill until now she hardly ate and it was obvious from the dark circles beneath her eyes that she was not sleeping either.

'I did try! Honest to God, I did try.' In her heart, though, she was convinced that there must have been something more she could have done . . . been a better person perhaps? . . . kinder to Martha? . . . kept a lock on little Danny's door? She hadn't even realised that Martha was becoming a much more dangerous enemy. Now she was cold in the churchyard, and Doug was locked up for her murder.

The funeral had been a strange affair, with curious crowds lining the way, but only herself and Peggy at the church. Even the service had been short and to the point. When Martha was laid into the ground, the earth was quickly shovelled over and she was lost to sight as though she had never been.

'Look, Rosie, I know we mustn't speak ill of the dead, but the woman was completely mad,' Peggy remarked now. 'Folks round here heard her screaming and yelling at the top of her voice at all hours of the day and night. Like I said, it were a tragedy waiting to happen. And if you didn't realise it, that's because you've a kind heart and see only the good in people.'

Rosie gave a wry little laugh. 'You're wrong, Peggy. I saw the evil in her all right. But I mistook it for wicked mischief.' Clasping her hands together, she stood up, driven by the awful memories. 'When she hurt Danny that first time . . . made a mark on his forehead, I should have known. I should have been more on my guard.' She breathed in, a long slow breath, and then let it out on a great sigh. She pushed Martha from her thoughts. 'I'd better be going or I'll be late, and like as not they won't let me in.'

Realising that Rosie had deliberately changed the subject, Peggy also stood up, to remark in a lighter voice, 'As long as they let you *out*, gal, that's all as matters.'

The typical remark made Rosie smile. Reaching out she took Peggy in her arms and the two of them hugged each other tightly. 'You're a good friend,' Rosie acknowledged. 'I don't know what I'd do without you.'

'You'd go to ruin, I expect,' Peggy said in a mock serious voice. They laughed then, and the tension was broken.

Surreptitiously brushing away a tear, Rosie went to the mirror and put on her hat. Then she patted the creases from her skirt and picked up her bag from the chair. Peggy watched her every move. 'Thanks for looking after Danny,' Rosie said simply. 'I checked him just before you came in, and he was sound asleep. Let him be. He's had little enough rest lately.' Not a night passed without her being woken by his cries. The nightmares never seemed to end.

Peggy walked her to the door. 'I know somebody else who

hasn't had much sleep either,' she chided. 'And I've come to a decision.'

'What?'

'There'll be time enough to talk about that when you get back. Now be off with you!' Giving Rosie a little push, she nudged her out of the front door. 'And don't worry about the lad, I won't disturb him. I'll be too busy doing your ironing.'

Before Rosie could protest, the door was closed and Peggy was inside, leaving Rosie standing on the pavement, a little smile lifting the corners of her mouth. Gazing at the house, she shook her head and fondly imagined Peggy inside. 'God bless you,' she murmured. Then, before she might change her mind, set off at a brisk pace towards the tram-stop.

Having missed the ten o'clock tram, she had a fifteen-minute wait for the next one. The minutes seemed like hours, and she grew more and more nervous. It was bad enough going to prison in the first place, without being late. The queue began to swell, and many of the women knew her by sight. Normally they would have passed the time of day, but this morning they turned to talk to each other, ignoring her as if she wasn't there. They all blame me for what happened, Rosie thought bitterly. Suddenly the sun went in and the skies darkened over. It turned chilly and she wished she had put on her mackintosh.

'They don't mean any harm, luv.' Mrs Norman from two doors down had never liked Martha Selby, and was quick to state her support for Rosie. 'Folks is funny,' she added with a smile. 'They're embarrassed, d'you see? They don't rightly know how to behave in matters such as these. Some are quick to point the finger, others reckon it's none o' their business, and them like me want to help but don't know how.' Her round face beamed a smile that lit up Rosie's sorry heart.

'I know,' she declared gratefully. 'On the whole, people have been kind.' She was thinking about the grocer who had sent a basket filled with food; the postman who expressed his sympathy at what had taken place; neighbours who had carried out the old tradition of going round the houses for a small contribution which was then given to the bereaved. When Mr Pope knocked on her door a week back, Rosie had been tempted to refuse the gift. But to do so would have been an insult, so she had thanked him kindly and spent the whole two pounds on a wreath for Martha. Though she knew there would come a time when that money might be sorely needed, Rosie couldn't bear the thought of spending it on anything else. The large floral tribute was the only one on Martha's coffin, and had made a lonely sight.

'And how's your little lad, me dear?' The entire episode had been reported in the newspapers, down to the smallest detail, together with a description of how the boy had been used.

'Mending well,' Rosie told her. There was no need to say any different.

'Aye, that's the way.' The older woman nodded and beamed, and turning to the queue, declared in a loud voice, 'It's a pity folks don't realise at times like these, it's just a bit o' kindness that's needed!' She was particularly alluding to a fat brassy-faced lady in a blue hat and carrying an umbrella. 'Isn't that right, Dora Lockley?' Widow Lockley had a vicious tongue and the declaration was more of a warning than retribution, because, with regard to the Martha Selby affair, she had so far managed to keep her opinions to herself.

Silence ensued, during which Rosie didn't know which way to turn. But then the woman in question came and stood before her. 'I know I'm an old gossip,' she apologised, red-faced, 'but I swear I've never said one bad word against you. In fact, I can only imagine what you went through with that dreadful woman. Believe me, Mrs Selby, you do have my sympathy.'

'Bless you for that,' Rosie said. And at once there was a

chorus of cheering and laughter, and light-hearted shouts for Dora Lockley: ''Ere, you old bugger, get yerself back to the end of the queue!' The tram arrived. Rosie sat in the first seat and, as they each passed her, the passengers tapped her affectionately on the shoulder. 'Keep your chin up, lass,' they said. And Rosie arrived at her destination with a lighter heart.

The forbidding sight of Strangeways Prison wasn't enough to dishearten her. Neither was the long wait and the curious stares of the warders, nor the miserable room into which she was eventually shown; though she did feel highly apprehensive while seated at one side of a table, with a prison warder behind her and a vacant seat for Doug opposite.

Rosie believed she had prepared herself for anything. But when Doug came through the door, she gasped aloud. He was a shadow of his former self. In his drab prison garb and with his hair cut within an inch of his head, he was almost a stranger. Yet there was something horribly familiar about him, a kind of intimacy that shook her to the core. For one unnerving moment, when Rosie looked into these wild odd-coloured eyes, it was Martha who stared back at her. And it was Martha's voice that addressed her in clipped tones. 'You're late!' Grabbing the back of the chair, Doug drew it out and sat down. 'Couldn't face the thought of seeing me, eh?' he demanded sharply.

'I missed the tram.' It seemed such a lame thing to say, but it was the truth. 'I'm sorry.' She half smiled, but it died on her lips when he sat before her, his peculiar eyes boring into her face.

'I suppose when it came right down to it, you couldn't stay away. Curiosity got the better of you, did it? Wanted to see the kind of place you'd put me in, did you?' When she hesitated, he raised his voice. 'ANSWER ME, BITCH!'

At once the officer stepped forward. 'All right, officer,' Doug acknowledged humbly. The officer stepped back, and Doug returned his gaze to Rosie. It wasn't humble now. It was hard and penetrating. 'I've had time to think in here.' Though he spoke in a quieter tone, his voice was sharp and cutting. 'Oh, yes, I've had plenty of time to think.' His hands were clenched together on the table, and while he spoke he rubbed the palms one against the other. They made an odd rasping sound, like two dry pieces of wood.

'I've done some thinking too,' she told him softly. There was an air of dignity about her that momentarily silenced him. Her eyes regarded his ashen face. 'There's been a great deal on my mind of late.'

'Hmh! Not about me, that's for sure.'

'Yes. About you, and Martha, and how desperately sorry I am for what happened.'

'Sorry!' he sneered. 'Won't bring her back, will it, eh? Won't save me from the gallows either.' He watched her reel back at his words and was glad to have shocked her.

'Surely to God it won't come to that? I mean, they can't hang you for defending your own son.' The idea that he could be hanged had never seriously entered her head. 'She would have killed him, Doug. I *know* she would have killed him.'

'Happen I should have let her.' His lips curled wolfishly. There was so much loathing in his eyes that Rosie could almost feel it.

'Why would you even think such a terrible thing?'

'Because he ain't mine, that's why.' His fingers shot out and gripped her hand. 'That's what she said, weren't it, eh? The little bastard ain't mine.' His fingers closed tighter until she winced with pain.

'You *know* he's yours.' Shocked and enraged, Rosie wondered how in God's name Doug could think otherwise.

'Mine, eh! And how would I know that? You were always yearning for Adam. Even after we were wed, you still wanted him. Oh, don't deny it. Every time I looked at you, I could see it. I could feel it whenever I took you, and as far as I know you *still* want him! How can I be sure you and that bugger didn't copulate behind my back, eh? Come to think of it, the boy don't even look like me.' All these things had been churning over in his mind since he'd been put away. Now it was all he could think of. Eating, waking and sleeping, his mother's vicious accusation burned in him until he was almost crazy. 'If you ask me, it were all a set-up!' His finger-nails dug so hard into Rosie's skin that they drew blood. 'You deliberately antagonised my mother. That night, you could have handled her, but you called out for me. Why? I'll tell you why! Because it were all part of your plan. You wanted me locked up, so you and Adam Roach could have it all your own way.' Kicking away his chair, he dragged her up by the hair. 'My mam knew what you were up to, and you *wanted* her dead, didn't you, eh? You wanted me out of the way and her dead! That's right, ain't it?' In his madness he had lost all reason.

The pain was so bad, Rosie couldn't even scream. It was as though her scalp was being torn off. Suddenly the officer was grappling with Doug, and she was caught in the middle. A whistle sounded, and the door was flung open. It took four burly men to tear him from her, and when he was led away, she was left bleeding and deeply shocked. 'It's all right, luv.' The officer gently showed her to an office. From a distance she could hear Doug yelling: 'He can have you . . . you *and* the little bastard! But I'll find you. I swear to God, if I get out of here, I'll hunt you down wherever you are!'

'Not the nicest fella that ever walked, is he?' The officer stayed with her while she received first aid. Handfuls of hair came out with the bathing, and there were deep scratches all over her forehead. 'You can press charges, you know.'

She shook her head. 'I don't want that.' Even now, Rosie was reluctant to make things worse for Doug. But, as far as she was concerned, they were even. If she had ever blamed herself for what happened to Martha, her guilt had now turned to contempt. How could he have believed his mother's vindictive lies about Danny being Adam's son? God! If that had been true, she would have gone with Adam right from the first. Marrying Doug was the biggest sacrifice she had ever made. And the reason was because she was carrying *his* child. When Danny was conceived, Adam was serving in the forces. Doug knew that. And still he was taking Martha's word against hers. If only she'd been given the chance, Rosie would have argued this with him.

The kindly officer escorted her to the front gates. As he let her through, he eyed her up and down. 'You don't deserve a man like that,' he declared. 'But when he's allowed visitors again, you'll be safe. I can promise you that.'

Glancing beyond him to the barred windows and the open yard, she replied simply, 'I won't be visiting again.'

His lined face softened slightly. 'I understand,' he said, closing the gates.

The sound of the huge bolts being thrust home sent a shiver down Rosie's spine. For a long poignant moment she remained perfectly still. In her mind's eye she recalled the awful scene in that tiny room. When Doug accused her of bearing Adam's son there was such loathing in his voice it had made her blood run cold. When he'd dragged her up by the hair, there was murder in his eyes.

There in the street, with the smell of the prison still on her, Rosie made a heartfelt vow. 'Doug Selby, even if you were to be set free tomorrow, it's all over between us. As long as I live, I can never forgive you for renouncing Danny.' Danny *was* Doug's son. Now, he was an outcast without a father. 'But he'll have *me*,' she murmured, making her way to the tram-stop. 'With the help of the Lord, I can be mother and father to him.'

* * *

Peggy knew as soon as she opened the door that there was something wrong. She saw the way Rosie's hair was pulled over her forehead, saw the determined expression on that lovely face, and sensed there had been trouble of a kind. But the only comment she made was to assure Rosie, 'Danny's been as good as gold. He ate all his breakfast and now he's playing in the yard.'

'Thanks, Peggy.'

'I'll put the kettle on, shall I?' Peggy suggested. When Rosie gave no answer, but instead closed her eyes, Peggy went to her. 'Was it such a dreadful ordeal?' she asked kindly.

Turning, Rosie smiled, but it was a sad little smile. 'I shan't be going to see him again.' Coming away from the door, she sat herself at the table. 'Doug and I have nothing more to say to each other.'

Astonished, Peggy followed and sat in the chair opposite. The tea could wait. This couldn't. 'I can't say I'm sorry,' she confessed. Leaning forward on the table, she put her chin in her hands. 'I knew there was something the minute I saw you. What happened in that place?'

Rosie described everything. About how Doug believed Danny was not his, and how he'd viciously attacked her and had to be dragged away screaming. 'There's no future for us, not now,' she explained decisively. 'For Danny's sake more than mine, I've turned a blind eye to many things. Now that he's rejected his son, there's no need for me to go on pretending.' Though her heart was breaking for Danny, the fact that she would never live with Doug again was a great relief.

'You could go to Adam?'

'I could no more go to him than I could love Doug! You know how I feel about Adam taking Ned's business. Besides, one way or another, Adam is at the bottom of everything that's gone wrong in my life.' She could hear herself saying these things, but she was not entirely convinced. She might hate herself for loving him, but she couldn't stop that same love from growing more intense over the years. Adam was her first love. He was her *only* love. Now, though, it was all too late. 'Please, Peggy. Don't ever speak of him again.'

'If that's what you want?'

'Haven't I said?'

'Okay. But there's something *I* want to say, and the sooner I get it off my chest, the better.'

For the first time since she came through the door, Rosie smiled, a one-sided, knowing little smile. 'Go on then,' she suggested. 'You've been itching to tell me something since this morning, so you'd best let it out before you burst.'

'I want to come and live with you. I've been thinking about it for ages, gal. You and me, in this little house with Danny. It'll be really cosy. I can pay you a proper board, so you won't be too strapped for cash. I'll help with the cooking and washing, and I'll even mind Danny if you want to go out once in a while of an evening . . .'

'Whoah!' Rosie laughed. 'What brought all this on?'

'Well, it makes sense, don't it?'

Rosie shook her head. 'Thank you, sweetheart, but no,' she said. 'I know why you want to do this, and I'm deeply grateful.'

Looking Rosie in the face, Peggy blushed, 'I never could hide the truth from you, could I?'

'Not that I can remember.' She met Peggy's contrite gaze and her heart was warmed. 'Like I said, Peggy, no one could have a better friend. But your place is with your mam, and you know it. Danny and me, we'll manage well enough.'

'I'm really worried about you, Rosie, especially now, when you say you and Doug are finished for good an' all. You're on your own, and it's a cruel place out there for a woman on her own.' There was genuine concern in her voice. 'It's going to be real hard.'

'I know.' In fact, Rosie was acutely aware of her desperate situation. A short time ago she was a married woman with a regular, if small income. Now, suddenly, she was on her own, with a child to care for and no man in her life. What with her meagre savings all gone, and the authorities dragging their feet to help out, the time had come to make serious decisions. The last thing she wanted was to receive her friend's charity. Such a thing didn't bear thinking about! 'I intend getting a job,' she announced proudly.

'What about Danny? He can't start school until next year, can he?'

'I've thought about that.' Rosie hesitated, not certain how Peggy would react. 'And I'm going to ask your mam if she'll mind him. I know he'll be well taken care of, and I'll pay her good money.'

Peggy was thrilled. 'She'll like that. She keeps on about how we'll all be leaving home afore too long and nobody will want her then.' She laughed aloud. 'Honestly, the way she carries on at times, anybody would think she were headed for the rubbish tip.'

'So, you really don't think she'd mind me asking?' Rosie was visibly relieved. 'Only I wasn't sure.'

'What! She'll bite your hand off!'

'I'll ask her first thing in the morning.' Rosie felt as though she was once again in charge of her own destiny. 'Then all I need to do is find a job.' That would be the hardest thing because well-paid jobs without Saturday work were still hard to come by.

Sitting back in her chair, Peggy quietly regarded her. 'Are you any good at figures?' she asked.

'All right, I suppose.' Rosie was curious. 'I managed to feed and clothe us all on what little I got from Doug. And I was never more than two weeks behind with the rent.' She sat up, frowning. 'Why?'

At first Peggy was coy. Rosie didn't realise how lovely-looking she was. Once she was let out, men would fall over themselves to court her. Someone like Rosie could bring trouble on her own head without even realising it. 'There's a job going in the offices,' she said reluctantly. As soon as the words were out, she regretted them. It would be ironic if Robert, the office manager, took a liking to Rosie.

Rosie's brown eyes danced. 'Oh, Peggy, do you honestly think I stand a chance?' The idea of making her own way in the world was both daunting and exciting. 'Won't they want someone with experience? After all, it's been a long time since I went out to work. And anyway, I've *never* worked in an office.'

'You're right. They may not want you. But then again, the job's been vacant for a couple of weeks and, as I understand it, they haven't found anyone suitable yet. I even considered going after it myself, but I'm hopeless at figures and wouldn't know one end of a ledger from the other.' She giggled. 'Give me twenty-four hours and I'd have the whole place in chaos. The orders would be all wrong, and I'd be bound to get the sack.' She looked at Rosie and saw a different kind of trouble ahead, but knew that nothing she could say would stop her friend now. 'It's up to you,' she said. 'If your mind's made up, give it a try. What have you got to lose?'

While Peggy was talking, Rosie was thinking and now could hardly contain her excitement. 'I've got nothing at all to lose,' she said, suddenly pacing the floor and thinking aloud. 'I do have a bit of experience because a couple of times I prepared Ned's ledgers for the accountant. It was easy. All I did was copy some invoices into the book, and tot up the total at the end. But in a big store like Woolworths, there must be mountains of paperwork.' Her courage began to waver. 'Oh, Peggy! I'm so afraid something will go wrong . . . either I won't land a job, or your mam won't agree to have Danny.'

'She'll have him all right.'

'If I don't see her right now, I won't sleep tonight.' For the first time in years, Rosie was beginning to think of herself. It was a good feeling. 'If she says yes, that will be the biggest obstacle overcome, because I wouldn't dream of leaving Danny with anyone else.'

'By God! You don't let the grass grow under your feet, I'll give you that.'

'Will you mind Danny for a few minutes?' Rosie didn't want to take him with her. 'I know he wouldn't object to staying with your mam because he likes her a lot. But I won't mention it to him until it's all settled.'

'Go on then.' No sooner had she said it, than Rosie was out of the door and away down the street. 'Me and my big mouth!' Peggy chuckled. 'If Robert takes a fancy to her, I've only myself to blame.'

Peggy's mam was delighted. ''Course I'll have the lad,' she agreed. 'And if you're still at your job when he starts school, I'll take him and fetch him home. It won't be no trouble, luv.' Her face beamed from ear to ear. 'By! And here were I thinking me useful days were nearly over.' A shadow crossed her face when Rosie reminded her that she hadn't yet got a job.

'Oh, but I will!' she promised. 'I'll have work before the week's out, you see if I don't.' Suddenly the whole world was opening up and nothing would stop her now.

Peggy wasn't surprised to learn her mam had agreed to have Danny. 'I told you she'd bite your hand off.' Strangely subdued, she made her excuses and left soon after. Rosie noticed the change in her mood, but put it down to tiredness. After all, Danny could be a handful when he put his mind to it.

After Peggy had gone, Rosie couldn't settle. The idea of being responsible for her own life again, made her nervous. At the same time she was looking forward to it immensely. Strange how unforeseen circumstances can change a woman's life overnight, she thought. When Doug was here, the idea of going out to work and leaving Danny with someone else was unnecessary and unthinkable. Then, when Martha came to live with them, Rosie became a prisoner. Now, because of a series of tragedies – Ned losing his business and deserting his wife, Martha's death and Doug's imprisonment – she was set free. Everything was changed forever.

Thinking of all that had happened, Rosie's joy faded. Going to the back window, she watched her son at play. He was a fine boy, and yes, Doug had been right because, except for the colouring of his hair, Danny bore little resemblance to his father.

When emotion threatened to overwhelm her, Rosie launched into a fever of cleaning. She cleaned the cooker and washed the curtains. She scrubbed the kitchen floor, then, when Danny came in tired and hungry, set about making the evening meal.

When at last she sat down with him, weariness washed over her like a tide, seeming to take the last vestige of her energy. Watching the boy tuck into his fish-dabs and scallops, she envied him his appetite. For days now she had been unable to eat. She couldn't recall the last time she had slept soundly, and though she knew the damage she was doing to herself, had seemed powerless to reverse the downward spiral. Now, though, when she began toying with the food on her plate, she was surprised and delighted to find that she was really hungry. She took one mouthful of fish, then another, and before she knew it, had finished the meal, leaving her plate as clean as Danny's.

Rubbing his eyes, he climbed down from the table. 'I think it's time you were in your bed,' Rosie told him. And he didn't argue.

When he was washed and in his pyjamas, she took him by the hand and led him upstairs. Normally he would talk all the way, but tonight he was unusually quiet. 'Where's my little chatterbox then?' she asked, tucking him into bed. She felt his forehead. There was no fever. 'It's all that fresh air made you tired, I expect,' she surmised. 'Peggy told me you played out all the time I was gone.' Reaching out, she took his favourite teddy from the bedside cabinet and laid it beside him.

In a move that took her by surprise, he grabbed her hand. His big eyes looked up, moist with tears, as he asked in a whisper, 'When's Daddy coming home?'

For one awful minute she was uncertain how to answer. Danny had asked the same question many times since Doug had been put away, and each time her heart was torn in two. 'Not yet, sweetheart,' she told him. He had suffered enough since that night, and she had to protect him from the truth for as long as possible.

'Is he with Gran'ma?' A tremor of fear touched his voice, and he visibly shivered. 'Has Gran'ma taken him away?'

'Don't you remember, I told you how Gran'ma went to heaven?' The boy nodded so she went on, 'And no, he isn't with your gran'ma. He's just gone away for a while.'

'Is he coming home?' That same question, over and over.

And always the same answer: 'I don't know for sure.' But now she *did* know for sure, because 'home' was her and Danny, and Doug had forfeited the right to both. As far as the house itself was concerned, if the day ever came when Doug walked in through the front door, she and Danny would pass him on the way out. But Danny was too young to be caught in the middle of the bad feeling between them. 'I'm sure Daddy will come home as soon as he can.' She hated herself for misleading him, but what else could she do? If she told him the truth, the nightmares would start all over again, and he might never mend. Later, when there was no option, there would be time enough for the truth. Right now Danny desperately needed reassurance.

'Is he a long way away?'

'Not too far, sweetheart.'

'Does he still love me?'

Rosie's heart almost stopped. 'I thought you already knew that?'

He considered her reply before raising his arms and wrapping them round her neck. Placing a sloppy kiss on her mouth, he said sleepily, 'Night, God bless.' He fell back into the pillow and closed his eyes.

'Night. God bless, sweetheart.' It was a long time before Rosie could tear herself away. She sat on the edge of the bed, gazing down at that small sleeping face and silently offering a prayer. 'You ain't given me much in life, Lord,' she whispered, 'but this little fella makes up for it all.'

After a while she returned to the living room. From the door, she let her gaze roam round the room, from the few stalwart items of furniture to the threadbare carpet and yellowing net curtains. She recalled the very first time she had set foot in this house. After living with Doug's folks, it was like a dream come true; her very own place, a sanctuary from Martha and her vile ways. Now, Martha had tainted this place too, and it would never be the same again. 'You're still here,' she said aloud. 'You and him. You'll always be here.' Their presence was like a tangible thing, pressing down on her. But she wouldn't let it! In her heart Rosie had a new dream. A dream that didn't include Doug. It was just her and Danny, living in a different place, a place where they would be safe from the past, a place where nobody knew them. A safe and quiet place where they could start afresh. Not much to ask, but for now it was an impossible dream.

Rosie actually laughed aloud. 'Stop fooling yourself, gal,' she chided. 'First things first. Get yourself a job. Come next year

Danny will be starting school, and wanting all kinds o' things. Meanwhile, there's two mouths to feed, the rent to be paid, and decent clothes for your backs.' Tomorrow, she would put on her best bib and tucker and present herself at the Woolworths offices.

Coming into the room, she began clearing the table, all the while wondering what to wear. She had a nice two-piece, two pretty frocks, one best blouse and two well-worn skirts. She also had a very smart jacket hanging upstairs in the wardrobe. Yes, she might wear that. 'Best try it on before you decide,' she told herself. 'You've lost that much weight, it might resemble a blanket on a scarecrow.'

Her thoughts flew in another direction. Wonder what he's like this Robert Fellows? Until now, she had felt confident. Suddenly, with the office manager to confront, she was apprehensive. 'Don't get above yourself, my gal,' she warned. 'Happen he'll take one look at you, and show you the door.'

With that sobering thought, she washed the dinner things, locked up and went to bed. But she couldn't sleep. Instead, she conjured up all manner of appearances for Robert Fellows. She regretted not asking Peggy about him. Was he tall, short, thin or fat? Dark-haired or fair? Did he have a kindly manner, or was he sharp-tongued? But, whatever he was, she was determined to make a good impression. 'You can be sure of this, Mr Robert Fellows,' she muttered, 'if there's a job going, and I can do it, you'll find I'm not easily put off.' With that she drifted off to sleep. But it wasn't Robert Fellows she dreamed of. It was Doug. And beside him stood Adam, and it was like looking through a mirror at everything that had ever happened in her life. Soon, Doug's image faded and she was left alone with Adam. In her dreams, she let herself love him. When he took her in his arms the tears of joy ran down her face, and all her fears were gone.

When she awoke in the light of a new day, the tears lay stale against the coldness of her skin. There was a pain in her heart that wouldn't go away, and even when she threw back the curtains to let the sunshine flood in, it didn't lighten her spirit. Instead, she recalled how she had felt in Adam's strong warm arms, and was filled with the deepest regret. At that moment, she felt she was the loneliest creature in the world. 'Come on, Rosie gal!' she told herself. 'Feeling sorry for yourself won't pay the rent.'

Going to the wardrobe, she sifted through the meagre items until her hand came to the jacket. Drawing it out on the hanger, she took it to the mirror and held it against herself. It was a fitted style, slate grey in colour, with a dark velvet collar and velvet pocket flaps. 'That'll do,' she decided. 'It looks smart enough, and I reckon it will still fit a treat.' If not, she could always move the big bone buttons to make it fit better.

At nine o'clock on the dot Rosie went down the street hand in hand with Danny. He was excited about staying with Peggy's mam and chatted non-stop all the way there. 'My! You look very posh.' Peggy's mam regarded her with a critical eye. 'If you don't get the job, I'll eat me best Sunday hat!' she exclaimed. Rosie looked very elegant in her straight navy skirt and grey velvet-trimmed jacket. The hardest thing to decide was which blouse to wear beneath, but eventually she'd settled for the white one with the frilly collar; though the frill hid most of the velvet collar, it lent a touch of efficiency to her appearance, which she thought might appeal.

'Why, thank you,' Rosie said, flushing with pleasure. 'You don't think I've overdone the make-up?' Normally she wouldn't wear such a strong shade of lipstick, but Peggy assured her it suited her.

'You look grand, lass.' Peggy's mam beamed her approval.

'And the shoes?' Rosie raised her foot to show the black

patent shoes. 'You don't think the heel is too high?' They were a heady three inches and already they were killing her.

'I reckon you look a real treat,' Peggy's mam told her firmly. 'Now be off about your business.' She smiled at the boy who was still clinging on to Rosie's hand. 'Me and Danny have got things to do.' Stooping to whisper, she told him, 'I thought we might go into town and have a sticky bun in that little café near the railway station. What do you say to that, eh?'

'Can I, Mam?' Looking up at Rosie, Danny's eyes were shining at the prospect.

''Course you can, sweetheart.' She took him in her arms and they clung together for the briefest minute, before he was running up the steps. 'You be good now,' Rosie warned.

It was Peggy's mam who answered. 'He'll come to no harm,' she said. 'Now be off with you.'

Going down the street, Rosie recalled where Peggy's mam was taking the boy, and her heart was heavy. It was the very same café where she had told Adam she was marrying his best mate.

The memory stayed with her on the tram, and it was with her when she stopped off the tram outside Woolworths. 'It's now or never, gal,' she told herself. 'So put your best foot forward.' She did, and it hurt. In fact, she would be surprised if the wretched shoes hadn't crippled her by the time she got home!

Taking a deep breath, she went into the main store. Peggy was the first to see her, and came rushing forward. 'Shouldn't leave me counter,' she said, furtively glancing round, 'but I saw you come in and wanted to wish you luck.'

'Where's the office?' Rosie felt completely out of place, and already her confidence was vanishing.

The woman came out of nowhere. 'Back to your counter, Miss Lewis,' she said in a frosty voice. And, with a little grimace at Rosie, Peggy hurried away. 'Is there some problem, madam?' Tall and sharp-featured, with her fair hair rolled into a sausage shape, the young woman was immaculately dressed in a black two-piece, with just a touch of white at the throat and a silver bar across her breast-pocket. The bar was etched with the words 'Miss B. Emmanuel, Floor Manager'. The woman looked Rosie up and down as though she was tasting something nasty. 'Perhaps I can help?' Her smile was stiff and her hands were constantly agitating against her skirt. She made Rosie feel nervous.

'I've come about the vacancy in the office.' When the woman closely scrutinised her, Rosie was tempted to turn tail and run.

'I wasn't aware they were interviewing anyone today.' Holding out her hand, she asked, 'May I see the letter?'

'I haven't got a letter,' Rosie explained, shifting from one foot to the other and wondering why she had been so vain as to wear such uncomfortable shoes. 'I heard there was a vacancy, and called in on the off-chance.'

The woman's face lit up and her smile broadened. 'Oh, I see!' she exclaimed. 'In that case, you've made a wasted journey, Miss . . . ?'

'It's *Mrs*.' More's the pity, Rosie thought. 'Are you sure I couldn't have a word with someone? Perhaps the office manager, Mr Fellows, might see me?'

She knew at once she had said the wrong thing because the smile slid from Miss Emmanuel's face and in its place came a look of horror. 'Good heavens! Mr Fellows is far too busy to waste time on someone who just walks in off the streets. No, I'm sorry. You must write in with all your particulars, and, if you're lucky, you may be called for interview. Good day, Mrs . . . ?' She paused, her mouth open, waiting for Rosie to provide the necessary information.

She bristled. She had taken an instant dislike to this arrogant woman. 'The name is Mrs Selby, and I would appreciate it if you could go and ask the gentleman himself. After all, it would be *his* time I'm wasting, not yours.'

The woman was adamant. 'We follow a procedure here, Mrs Selby.' Her voice was controlled, but her attitude was hostile. 'And I can assure you, there would be no point whatsoever in my going to Mr Fellows because his answer would be exactly the same.' Her handsome grey eyes were enhanced by thick mascara and a heavy pencilled line. Now, when they opened wide and stared at her, Rosie was put in mind of a panda. They opened even wider when a man's voice intervened.

'I heard my name mentioned, Miss Emmanuel?'

Both Rosie and the woman were startled. But it was the woman who became flustered at the sound of Robert Fellows' voice. 'Oh, Mr Fellows!' She swung round and almost fell over. 'It's this young woman.' Casting a cursory glance at Rosie, she went on, 'I *have* tried to explain that we can't just interview anyone who walks in off the street. I have also suggested she should follow regular procedure. But I'm afraid Mrs Selby is being rather rude and aggressive.' She sulked a little and her crimson lipstick stuck to the corners of her mouth. Rosie tried not to look, because it was one of those things that would irritate her all day.

Robert Fellows had a nice face. Not as handsome as Adam's, Rosie thought, but pleasant to look on. He was much the same build as Adam too, with strong broad shoulders and an easy manner that put her at ease. His eyes were softly brown, not dark like Adam's, and when he smiled, like now, she smiled with him. 'I think I can spare a moment for a little chat,' he told Miss Emmanuel in a charming voice. 'After all; we've already interviewed several people for the post, and as yet we've not been able to find one suitable candidate.'

'But we do have a proper procedure, Mr Fellows,' she protested haughtily. 'And I don't think we should make any exception.' She was aware that certain members of staff, including Peggy Lewis, were watching, willing her to lose the argument. 'It would set a bad example, if you see what I mean?' What she really meant was that she might lose face if he went against her advice.

Stepping between her and Rosie, he smiled. 'Oh, I think we can be forgiven in this instance.' Turning to Rosie, he said, 'All the same, I do hope you're not wasting my time.'

'So do I.' Rosie calculated him to be about thirty years old, yet he had a boyish charm that made her want to giggle. Strange, she thought, how she was constantly comparing him to Adam.

'To the office then.' He set off towards the bottom of the store and she followed, finding it difficult to keep up with his long strides, especially when the shoes on her feet were gripping her toes like a vice.

They passed Peggy's cosmetics counter. She gave Rosie the thumbs up sign. For her trouble, Peggy got a severe glare from Miss Emmanuel who was fuming by the front doors and blocking the shoppers' access. Then past haberdashery and on to the confectionery counter. At the point where the fabric racks met houseware, Robert Fellows took a left turn. For a frantic moment he was lost to Rosie's sight, but then she caught a glimpse of him hurrying up the stairs. Breathless, she ran after him. When she got to the top, she paused for breath. 'You ain't as fit as you thought, Rosie gal,' she chuckled. When she raised her head, Robert Fellows was looking at her, and she blushed to the roots of her hair.

A long, meandering room with large windows all round, the office was surprisingly welcoming. There were three desks with members of staff sitting at them. One man was aged and grey, the other fat and balding. At the third was seated a kindly-looking woman aged about fifty. She put Rosie in mind of Peggy's mam. Each desk had a large black telephone, and they all started ringing at once. 'We're a team,' Robert Fellows explained. Seating himself in a big leather chair behind his desk, he gestured for Rosie to occupy the upright chair immediately in front. 'Some people object to working in one big office, you know. They prefer to be shut away in a little room on their own. How do you feel about that?' His question was abrupt, taking her by surprise.

'I like the idea of working as a team,' she answered truthfully. 'And I would imagine it to be more efficient.'

His eyes gleamed. 'My sentiments exactly, Mrs . . . ?'

'Selby.' She wished it could have been any other name, because no sooner was the word out of her mouth than the three clerks swung round to stare at her, three pairs of eyes all looking her up and down as though she was a curiosity. Robert Fellows appeared not to have noticed so she went on, 'I'd best tell you straight off, I don't know the workings of a big office. The only ledger I've ever tended was my father-in-law's, and that was just to tot up the coal invoices.' That information appeared to have confirmed the three clerks' suspicions because they turned to stare at her again, although the woman did give her an encouraging smile.

Robert Fellows quietly regarded her. He liked what he saw. She was smart and presentable. She was not coarse or loud, like many of the applicants he had seen. And from what he could gather downstairs, she had stood her ground with the formidable Betty Emmanuel. As far as he was concerned, that alone spoke volumes for her character. On top of all that, she was exceptionally lovely; a little thin perhaps, but that was by the way. 'Write your name and address for me,' he suggested, pushing a fountain pen and a sheet of paper towards her.

As she wrote, he watched her closely, noting the rich brown hair that tumbled to one side of her face when she inclined her head, the long thick lashes and that perfectly formed face. It was one he would never tire of looking at.

'I'm sorry.' Pushing the paper back across the desk, she

apologised, 'My handwriting isn't all that wonderful.' The truth was, she hadn't had much practice, and all the while she was writing she had been aware of his gaze on her. It had made her tremble a little. Consequently, the writing was unsteady.

He studied it. 'You have a fine hand,' he told her truthfully. 'You say you know how to keep ledgers?'

'Well, it was only my father-in-law's, and just the one. I entered invoices and totted them all up at the end.'

'One . . . ten, it's all the same.' He smiled encouragingly. 'Are you good at sums?'

'Good enough, I think.' In fact arithmetic had always been her strong point.

'And the telephone?' When she frowned, he added, 'You'd be amazed at how many people are frightened to use a telephone.'

'I don't have occasion to use a telephone all that much. I don't have one at home.'

'What? You mean your husband hasn't had one installed?'

Rosie felt all eyes on her again, and thought the time had come to put her cards on the table. 'My husband is in prison.' Since the others knew, there was no point in pretending otherwise.

In fact, he had already sensed the atmosphere when she mentioned her name, and knew of the case. He doubted whether there was one person in the whole of Lancashire who hadn't read about Doug Selby and the tragedy that had led to his mother's death. He hadn't mentioned it because he wanted the truth to come from her. 'I know,' he said. And once again his smile put her at ease.

Rosie stood up then. Now that the truth was out, there was no point in continuing. She cursed herself for even thinking she could get a job. No one in their right mind would employ a woman with her background. She had intended lying, but the clerks had known instantly. While she carried the name Selby, she also carried its stigma. 'I'm sorry,' she apologised, preparing to leave. 'It seems I have wasted your time after all.'

'What are you like at making tea?'

'Nobody makes it better.'

'When can you start?'

'Tomorrow, if you like.'

'See Meg Benton.' He gestured to the kindly-faced lady, who readily beckoned. 'Give her your details, and I'll expect you to report for duty at nine o'clock in the morning.' With that, he pushed the chair back and strode out of the office, leaving Rosie too stunned to take it all in.

'You're one of us now, dear,' Meg told her.

Rosie couldn't believe her ears.

Chapter Fifteen

Rosie had been employed at Woolworths for five weeks. With Danny being well taken care of, and not seeming to miss her too much, she was happy in her work, and learning more by the day. Soon after she started, Robert Fellows went away on a course and one of the clerks fell ill, so it was left to the others to carry the extra workload. Rosie didn't mind; in fact, she liked to be kept busy, because it made the day go quicker before she went home to Danny. Now though, all the office staff were present, and Rosie had learned a great deal about the running of the place.

'Open that window, there's a dear.' Meg Benton loosened the collar of her blouse. 'I've never known it so hot in here.' She peered at Rosie from over her tiny rimless spectacles; teetering on the bony precipice of her nose, it seemed that any minute they would slip over the narrow edge, but they never did. 'Thank you, dear,' she said, when Rosie threw open the window and resumed her seat.

'Would you like me to fetch you a cup of tea from the canteen?' Rosie too was feeling uncomfortably warm. The August sun blazed in through the window, warming everything in its path; including the clerks bent to their work. 'It's almost lunchtime anyway.' She had arranged to meet Peggy in the canteen and, as always, was looking forward to their daily chat.

'That would be nice, dear.' Like the other two, Meg always ate her sandwiches at her desk. During this time there would be a smattering of small talk and gossip; the most recent discussion being the hanging of John Christie, found guilty of 'the most horrifying murders'. Beside this was the recent Commons debate on whether to suspend all death penalties for five years. Meg Benton agreed. Horace Sykes declared: 'Hang them all', and Mr Mortimer had little opinion either way. As for Rosie, she still wasn't altogether convinced that innocent people would not be hanged.

'If you're going to the canteen, you might fetch me a glass of water?' That was old Mr Mortimer. He had worked in this office for many years now, and, as Meg Benton whispered to Rosie on her first day here, he was 'almost part of the furniture'. With his grey hair and starched white collar, he resembled a vicar. Old-fashioned and blessed with a sharp mind, he kept himself to himself, usually only making his presence known by loudly blowing his enormous nose.

Addressing Horace Sykes, Rosie asked, 'Can I get you something while I'm down there?' He was a sullen little man, balding on top but with a wild tuft of ginger hair sticking out over each ear. In fact, old Mr Mortimer had more hair than Horace.

Without looking up, he merely grunted. Rosie took that to mean no. 'I'll just finish this,' she said, feeding the invoice figures into the adding machine. 'If I leave it halfway done, I'll forget where I've got to.' Quickly now, she wrote down the sum total and ticked off the spent invoices.

'Oh, I'm sure you wouldn't do that, dear.' Meg Benton regarded Rosie through her tiny specs. 'You know, it really is remarkable how quickly you've picked up the routine here. If you continue to make progress the way you have these last few weeks, I shouldn't be at all surprised if you were next in line for a wage rise.' Broadly smiling at one and all, though neither men noticed, she pointed out, 'Mr Fellows always rewards the good workers, you know, and before long, you'll be quite indispensable.'

Mr Mortimer blew his nose. 'Nobody's indispensable!' he muttered, glaring at Meg Benton.

Horace Sykes had his say too. 'I really don't see how you can call Mrs Selby a good worker. What with Mr Fellows away on a course I'm amazed she could ask for tomorrow off. Selfish, I call it. It will only make more work for the rest of us.' Since Rosie had made it known that she would not be reporting for work tomorrow, it had been a bone of contention with him.

Meg wagged a finger at him. 'Now then, Horace Sykes! You know very well why Rosie can't come in tomorrow.' In fact, the whole of Blackburn knew that Doug Selby was being brought to court to answer the charge of murder. Smiling encouragingly, she turned to Rosie. 'Besides, I'm quite certain our newest recruit will bring all her accounts and figures up to date before she leaves today.' Regardless of what she might say, she didn't like the idea of having her own workload increased either.

'My desk will be cleared, I promise,' Rosie assured them. 'Even if I have to work through most of my lunch-break.' As she spoke, the big clock over the door chimed twelve. 'I'll come straight back with your drinks,' she said, rushing from the office.

Outside, she paused, leaning against the wall, with her gaze turned towards the ceiling and her mind in chaos. 'Bugger you, Horace Sykes!' she muttered. 'You make it sound like I'm going on a picnic.'

She was still fuming when she joined the queue for the drinks, 'One glass of water and a cup of milky tea, please,' she said. Within minutes the burly woman had put them on a tray, taken her money, and was already asking for the next order before Rosie turned away. 'Hmph! *She's* in a bad mood!' remarked Liz Rothman from houseware. 'I expect her old man refused her again last night!' Rosie left her giggling with her friends. If she didn't get a move on, she wouldn't even have time to eat her meat and potato pie.

Though the window was open and allowing a breeze through, the office was stifling after the coolness of the canteen. Mr Mortimer thanked her kindly for the water, taking it quickly from the tray and swilling it down his throat at an alarming rate. The glass had a magnifying effect on his nose and from where Rosie was standing, it appeared to fill the tumbler.

'If you like, I'll bring you another glass when I come back.' Collecting her lunch-box from the top drawer of her desk, Rosie waited for his answer. When none came, she said aloud, in a voice very much like Mr Mortimer's. 'Why, no thank you, Rosie, but it's very kind of you to ask.' He didn't even look up, but as she hurried away he blew his nose and said in an odd squeaky voice, 'All the same, nice of you to offer.' He ain't such a bad old geezer, she told herself as she went down the stairs two at a time.

Peggy was seated by the table nearest the door. 'I've got your mug o' tea,' she said. Shifting along the bench, she made room for Rosie. 'How's it going then, gal?'

Rosie took a refreshing gulp from her tea. 'By! That's good,' she said. Running her fingers through her hair, she pushed it from her face. 'Apart from it being like a steam bath up there, it's going all right,' she answered. Undoing her lunch-box she took out a paper bag. Curling the top back, she inched the pie forward until half was showing. 'I can't stop long,' she declared between bites, 'I've got a stack of work to do. Horace and Old Mortimer are already making sly remarks about me having tomorrow off.' She was quiet then, recalling how nasty Horace had been.

'You ain't taking notice o' them two, are you?' Peggy tapped her consolingly on the hand. 'Come on, cheer up. Tomorrow will be here and gone before you know it.'

'I wish the others would see it that way.' She sighed. 'Honestly, Peggy . . . why do some folk get so much pleasure out of being miserable?' Miss Emmanuel walked by just then, giving them each a fiery glance. 'Her and Horace should swap notes,' Rosie said with a giggle. 'They'd have a great time being miserable together.' She didn't feel like laughing, but it was either laugh or cry, and she had done enough crying to last a lifetime.

'Bugger her, and bugger Horace!' Peggy exclaimed. 'It ain't *them* who's got to face the judge tomorrow.' Lowering her voice, she added softly, 'I've said I'll come with you if you like?'

Rosie shook her head. 'No. Can you imagine if you were to ask for time off an' all? Likely we'd both lose our jobs.'

'You love your job, don't you?' She had seen a remarkable change in Rosie during these last weeks. Her brown eyes shone like chestnuts and there was a certain sparkle about her that made people stare when she walked by.

'I feel useful again, if that's what you mean.' But it was much more than that, and Rosie knew it. For the first time in years she had a real purpose, getting up in the morning with somewhere to go and knowing that come Friday she would have a wage, enough to pay the bills and even the occasional shilling or two to put by. She alone was responsible for herself and Danny, and she liked that. For too long, she'd felt as though she had shrivelled and died, and now something inside her was beginning to blossom. It was a good feeling. 'The best thing of all is that Danny really loves staying with your mam.'

Peggy laughed. 'The feeling is mutual, I can assure you. What! It's Danny this and Danny that. But he's a smashing kid. You've done a good job with him, Rosie, gal.' In a more serious voice, she asked, 'Do you reckon his grandad will turn up tomorrow?'

'Who knows? He might, but to tell the truth, Peggy, I've given up on him.' Her troubled brown eyes belied her flippancy. 'All the same, it would be nice if he did, for Doug's sake at least.'

'Happen Doug doesn't want him there?'

'Happen not.'

'Do *you* want him there?'

'I'm not bothered either way,' she lied.

'And Adam?'

Rosie was shocked. Peggy couldn't have known how, in that very moment, she had been thinking of Adam. 'Anybody can turn up. As far as I can tell, it's open to the general public.'

'I didn't ask that,' Peggy insisted. 'I asked whether you wanted Adam there.'

Rosie thought long and hard. Did she want him there? Yes! Did she love him? Yes! Was she ready to admit it? No! He was married, and so was she. Taking a deep breath she answered truthfully, 'It would be better for everyone if he stayed away.' She took another gulp of her tea, then absent-mindedly twiddled her hair between her finger and thumb. Now she was looking at Peggy with fire in her eyes. 'Why do men always take us for fools?'

Peggy laughed. 'Robert Fellows could take me for a fool anytime.' She pursed her lips in a kissing gesture and made clicking sounds with her tongue. 'Nice bit of all right, he is.'

The mood was lightened, and the minutes ticked away agreeably. 'I'd best get back. See you later.' Before Peggy could answer, Rosie had replaced her empty cup on the rack and was soon gone from sight. 'Like a flaming will-o-the-wisp!' Peggy chuckled. Rosie's half-eaten pie was lying on the plate. 'Waste not, want not,' said Peggy, tucking in.

At half-past five, Rosie had finished the bought ledger. 'Good girl,' Meg Benton said as she put on her coat and left. Half an hour later, Mr Mortimer departed, grumbling at how 'some people have no consideration for others'. When Rosie asked him what he meant, he blew his nose twice and made a hasty exit.

'Ah, good!' exclaimed Horace Sykes as he passed Rosie's desk on the way out. 'I see you've started entering the stock orders for tomorrow.' He peered at the pile of sheets before her and, smiling to himself, went on his way. 'I hope your wife's burnt your tea!' Rosie mumbled after him.

When Peggy tapped on the door soon after six o'clock, Rosie was only halfway through. 'You'll have to go without me, Peggy,' she apologised. 'I've got to finish this or my name will be mud round here tomorrow.' She didn't want to give either of the men an excuse to complain about her. 'I did warn your mam I might be late, but she said not to worry . . . that she'd give Danny his tea.'

''Course she will,' Peggy confirmed. 'Do you want me to wait for you?'

'No, thanks. You get off home. Tell Danny I'll be as quick as I can.'

'All right, but I think you should have left it for them to do. *I* would have!' Making ghostly noises, she went down the stairs. 'Mind the bogey man don't get you!' she called out, and her echoing voice sent shivers down Rosie's spine. Soon everyone but the night watchman would be gone, and most of the place would be in darkness. Frantic, she sent her pen across the pages at a faster pace. 'If anybody puts a hand on me, they'll be sorry!' she warned Mr Mortimer's creaky old desk. And for the next half hour, even the smallest sound had her peering into every corner.

The office clock loudly ticked away the minutes; tick-tock, tick-tock, the rhythmic sound reverberating from the walls. It was half-past six, then quarter to seven, and still she seemed to be making little impact on the stock sheets.

At five minutes past seven, she turned over the last page and gave a sigh of relief. 'If I hurry, I might just catch the seven-fifteen tram!' When a man's voice answered, she almost leaped out of her chair.

It was Robert, and she had been too engrossed in her work to hear him come in. 'No need to rush for the tram,' he said, smiling as he came towards her. 'I'd consider it a pleasure to take you home.' In fact, he had just taken delivery of a new Vauxhall Velox, and would welcome the opportunity to show it off.

'Mr Fellows!' Rosie gasped with relief. 'You gave me a fright.'

'Well now, I certainly wouldn't want to do that.' Seating himself on the edge of her desk, he asked with genuine concern, 'What are you doing still here at this time of night?'

'As I won't be in tomorrow, I wanted to get the stock-sheets done.' She thought he looked incredibly handsome. She had only ever seen him in his office suit, with a sober tie done up at the neck and his fair hair slicked back. This evening, though, he was dressed in brown cord trousers and a grey cotton roll-top jumper. His thick fair hair was tumbling loose about his ears, and he had a sense of devil-may-care about him. For some reason, his closeness was making her nervous. 'I'm finished now, so I'll be on my way. Thank you for the offer of a lift, but the tram-stop is only a few minutes' walk. It drops me off right outside my street, you see.' Fumbling for her bag, she leaned forward. It was then she smelled the drink on him. She hadn't noticed it before, but now she could see he'd had one over the eight. 'Goodnight, Mr Fellows,' she said, quickly turning away.

'Please.' Putting his hand on her arm, he said softly, 'Let me take you home. Besides, I've been waiting for the chance to get to know you better.' Drawing her to him, he smiled into her eyes. 'You're very lovely. As soon as I saw you, I knew you would brighten up this dreary office.'

Rosie was affronted by this remark. 'Oh? And is that why you gave me the job?' she asked angrily. She made an effort to release herself from his grip, but his fingers were like iron bands round her arms.

'At first, maybe. But in those first few days when you showed yourself to be remarkably able, I realised I'd found the best of both worlds . . . a good-looker who could actually *work*!' When he realised she was not favourably impressed with his flippant remarks, he apologised in a sincere voice. 'Please, Rosie, don't be offended. I do mean it as a compliment.'

'I'm sure you do.' She struggled against him. 'But I really don't wish to discuss it. Right now I have a son waiting for me, and I mean to catch the seven-fifteen tram.'

With one mighty twist of her arms, she managed to free herself. Leaving her cardigan draped over the back of the chair, she grabbed her bag and made for the door. But he was right behind her. Before she could open the door, he stretched out his arms and pressed her to the wall. 'So you won't let me take you home?' he murmured brushing his face against her neck. 'If that's the way you want it, fine. But surely you won't deny me one little kiss?' Swinging her round, he brought his mouth down on hers. The kiss was long and passionate, with Rosie struggling beneath him and his arms wound tightly about her.

Just once he loosed his hold on her, and that was when the kiss was over. 'I think I love . . .'

Rosie didn't give him time to finish his sentence. Taking the opportunity, she lashed out with her foot and caught him on the shins. When he reeled back, she was out of the door and down the stairs. Even before he recovered from the vicious kick, she was running down the street. The tram was just drawing out. Quickening her steps, she reached it before it got up full speed. With one mighty leap she fell on to the platform and straight into the conductor's arms. 'A threepenny ticket, please,' she gasped breathlessly, then fell into the nearest seat and closed her eyes.

When she opened them again, she peeped out of the window to see how far the tram had got. 'This isn't the way to Castle Street,' she told the conductor.

'I should hope not!' he replied, his eyes twinkling. 'This tram goes to Whalley End.'

It was ten minutes to the next stop, quarter of an hour before the right tram came along, and gone eight by the time Rosie knocked on Peggy's door. Danny came running down the passage to meet her, and Peggy announced, 'About time too. We thought you'd decided to stay the night.' Rosie was tempted to explain there and then, but decided against it. Instead, she made her apologies all round and went home with Danny. Once there, she sat him on her knee, and he told her about everything he'd done that day.

Normally, Rosie was all attention when Danny described his little escapades. Tonight, though, she found it hard to concentrate, because something else was cluttering up her mind. It was Robert Fellows, and that long passionate kiss. It was the realisation that he was a very handsome man. It was the way his eyes made love to her. And, much to Rosie's astonishment, she was recalling it all with a great deal of pleasure. 'Watch yourself, Rosie, gal!' she muttered beneath her breath. 'He's probably had more fools like you than you've had threepenny tram rides.'

The court was assembled. The public galleries were full to bursting. 'Answer the questions truthfully, and explain it exactly the way it happened,' the lawyer told Rosie. She was fine until Doug was brought into the court flanked by two burly officers. Their eyes met and he was still staring at her when she looked away. If she had entertained any hope that he regretted all those terrible things he had said to her, she saw her mistake then. Hatred for her shone out of his eyes and smothered her.

Court was quickly in session. The jurors' heads followed the prosecutor like spectators at a tennis match, first this way then that. The pathologist gave his evidence. 'Killed by a single stab wound to the neck,' he said. When the clear plastic bag containing the knife was held up for the jury to see, there was an audible gasp from the galleries. Rosie hung her head. In her mind she was reliving every detail of that night, and she felt sick to her stomach.

The day wore on. Rosie was called to the stand, and in as clear a voice as she could, gave her version of what took place on that awful night. 'Martha had a knife to my son's throat,' she said, her voice falling to a whisper as she looked on the long sharp blade.

'Is this the knife in question?' she was asked. The bag was thrust under her nose. She was allowed to handle it, but the touch of the bag made her flesh creep.

'As far as I can tell,' she answered, quickly returning it. The knife had a white bone handle which was secured to the blade by the means of round flat rivets. It had been Rosie's meat knife, which had gone missing some time back. It made her shiver to think how many times she had used it for mundane tasks in the kitchen. She wondered again how Martha had laid hands on it. Perhaps it had been in an upstairs drawer all along.

'Describe the incident in question, exactly as you remember it,' she was urged. And a great hush fell over the court.

Rosie took her time. Doug's life was at stake and she did not want to get anything wrong. She explained how she and Doug were in bed when they heard the scream. She went on to describe how she was the first to enter her son's room, and was horrified to see that Martha had him and was threatening to kill him. 'She looked completely mad. Danny was crying,' Rosie recalled. And the memory was overwhelming.

'Please speak up.' The voice was not unsympathetic.

Clearing her throat, Rosie went on, 'I knew if I made even the smallest move, she would kill him.'

'Please tell the court what happened then?'

'Doug . . . my husband, he came into the room and tried to reason with her. But she wouldn't listen. She . . .' It was on the tip of her tongue to say how Martha claimed that Danny was not

Doug's but Adam's. The mere thought of revealing such a thing made her hot with shame because, even though there wasn't a vestige of truth in it, she had often wished that it was so.

'Yes? You were about to say?'

'She was insane.'

'That was what you assumed?'

'Yes, sir.'

'Can you think of any reason why your mother-in-law should want to attack your son?'

'She had always been very fond of him.' Rosie silently prayed he would not press the point.

'Had you yourself rowed with her on that day?'

'Martha was not the easiest woman in the world to get on with.'

'I asked . . . did you row with her on that day?' Pausing on his way to the jurors' bench, he swung round and stared at her from beneath long bushy brows.

'Not a row exactly.'

'What then?'

'Martha liked to make things difficult for everyone she came in contact with.' Glancing at the day nurses who had already given evidence as to Martha's unpredictable character, she wondered why they had to keep asking the same questions. It was almost as though *she* was on trial.

'Apart from the deceased . . . and your son, whose evidence has already been read out, the only other witnesses to what actually happened were yourself and your husband?'

'Yes, sir.' My God! She *was* on trial! Suddenly she was even more aware of the many accusing eyes all focused on her. In that split second her gaze fell on Doug's face. His smile was sinister, and she wondered whether he wouldn't mind being hanged, as long as she was hanged with him. There was a moment of silence when she felt as though the whole world had her in its sights.

There were more questions. 'Was there bad feeling between the accused and the deceased?' 'What exactly happened in that moment before the accused lunged forward?' 'Describe it to the court.' 'What happened immediately afterwards?' The interrogation was relentless. Then, just when Rosie had reached screaming point, the examination was over and she breathed a sigh of relief. 'Thank you. You may now step down.' Her legs felt like jelly as she made her way back to her seat.

After Doug's evidence was heard, and was seen to be compatible with her own, the jury retired to consider their verdict.

When an hour passed, and then another, many people left the court to gather in small chattering groups in the outer hall. Rosie remained in her seat. Almost alone and feeling totally exhausted, she stared up at the huge domed ceiling; carved with crowns and eagles, it was a spectacular feat, and even in her dilemma she couldn't help but admire it. In these awe-inspiring surroundings, she felt like an insignificant little speck. What would it matter if they *did* take her away and hang her? At once she thought of Danny, and was horrified by her own thoughts. 'God forgive you, Rosie,' she whispered, and her voice came back like an echo.

Unbeknown to her, when she had suffered all manner of fears in that confined witness box, Adam had lived the moments with her. From the back of the courtroom, he had willed her to be brave and not be afraid. He had listened to her version of what happened and had seen how distraught she was at the memory. And he had loved her with all his heart. Yet, when the jury was sent out, he made no attempt to let Rosie know he was there. He was so afraid she would turn him away. He needed to think, to decide whether he should approach her. He vividly recalled her reply to his letter, when she had made it clear he was not welcome in her life. It was true that she was married and he accepted that. Even so, if she would only have him, he would spend the rest of his life taking care of her and Danny. As the years passed, he found it increasingly harder to accept that Rosie was not his, and neither was Danny. What made it worse was that they *might* have been his, if only he hadn't been so blinded by jealousy on that day she told him the truth about her and Doug.

Now, after all that had happened, the last thing he wanted was to alienate Rosie even more, and so, with this in mind, he went away to think. His heart told him to go to her. But his instincts warned him otherwise. After all, Doug had made no secret of his loathing for Adam, and he was still Rosie's husband. As far as Adam could tell, she must be suffering agonies for him. If either of them saw him there, it was bound to make matters worse. The best thing you can do is stay out of sight, he decided, cursing himself for having made the journey here. But his love for Rosie would not let him stay away.

As the crowd surged out, he went with them. In the grimy little café across the road, he ordered a strong black coffee. After paying, he took the coffee and himself to the farthest corner where he sat alone and friendless, his heart and mind with Rosie. And his thoughts in chaos as he wondered whether or not to return home without making his presence known to her.

It was mid-afternoon when the jury returned, and all this time Rosie had not moved from her seat, except to pace up and down when her legs grew stiff and sore. Deeply agitated, she wondered how Doug was bearing up. Her mind went from him to Danny, and then she was filled with fear for all their futures.

Suddenly the crowds were pouring back and the court was in session again. The jurors filed into their seats and, when requested by the judge, the foreman stood up to give the verdict. As he read it out, Rosie's heart almost stopped. Doug had been cleared of murder, but convicted of manslaughter. The judge's voice rang out in sentencing him. Doug stood in the dock, pale and nervous, his hands gripping the rail as though he desperately needed that support.

Rosie leaned forward as the sentence was given. 'Five years' imprisonment.' The words echoed over and over in her mind. Doug was to be put away for five years.

It was finished. She felt empty, shocked, but relieved that Doug had been cleared of murder. As he was being led away, he called her name. She looked up to see him struggling with his captors. His head was turned towards her, his face twisted into a grotesque mask. 'Five years, then I'll be back,' he yelled, that same sinister smile on his face. 'Mind you wait, my lovely!'

Long after he had gone from her sight, Rosie could see that devilish smile. She could hear his words, and knew they were a warning. Doug blamed her for what had happened, and would make her pay. *That* was the veiled warning he meant to convey. And, because of it, he had committed her to the same sentence he himself had received, just as surely as if the judge had put them away side by side.

From his place at the back of the court, Adam also heard Doug's message. But, unlike Rosie, he had not seen the wickedness on Doug's face. He wasn't aware of the awful rift between these two. Nor was he aware that Martha, and now Doug, had come to believe that he and not Doug had fathered the boy. Adam knew nothing of all this. So, when the court was almost emptied, he remained, waiting for Rosie to pass by, and marking the moment when he could talk to her. She needed a friend. He could be that much at least, he thought.

Rosie took a moment to recover from the ordeal, though she would remember every minute for as long as she lived. Now, collecting her bag and fastening the buttons on her jacket, she turned – and almost fell into the arms of Robert Fellows. 'I've come to take you home,' he said. He studied her lovely face, and was touched by the sadness there. 'I behaved like a fool last night,' he murmured regretfully. 'Can you forgive me?'

'You have no business here, Mr Fellows,' she said sharply.

Seeing him was quite a shock. 'As for last night, it was plain to me that you'd been drinking. I've seen that kind of behaviour before and it's never very pleasant.' She had seen it all too often, she thought bitterly. 'Now, if you'll excuse me, I have to go . . . that is, if you think I should be allowed to live a life outside office hours?' Her voice was deliberately sarcastic. The truth was, she felt he had a bloody cheek coming here. Not only had it angered her, she felt mortified with shame.

'I deserve that,' he admitted. 'But I promise you, Rosie, it won't happen again.' He looked like a small boy caught out in mischief. 'Won't you give me a chance to make amends? After what's happened here, won't you at least let me see you safely home?'

Rosie was about to give him a piece of her mind when something happened that took her completely aback. The moment she raised her eyes, she saw Adam coming down the steps towards her. He was smiling. Then he was saying, 'Can we talk, Rosie?' And her heart was leaping out of control. With Robert Fellows on one side, and Adam on the other, she felt trapped. Which way should she turn? For the briefest moment she was tempted to go with Adam. But then she remembered. If only he hadn't turned from her years ago, they might have been together now. Yet it was she who had gone astray, and not him; she must not forget that. Still, hadn't he conned Ned out of his business? Wasn't he also married? And wasn't she? On top of all that, her husband had just been jailed for five years, and here Adam was, asking if they could talk. What in God's name was he thinking of? Surely he must know his presence was like a red rag to a bull!

Her steady gaze belied the turmoil inside her as she told him in a cool calm voice, 'I really don't think we have anything to talk about.'

Acutely aware of the other man standing nearby, Adam murmured his reply. 'I wouldn't agree, Rosie. But if that's the way you feel?' His broad shoulders stiffened and his dark haunted eyes set her alight.

'I do.' Her voice was crisp and hostile. 'Besides, I have a business matter to attend to.' She bestowed a smile on the bemused Robert Fellows. 'I think we should leave now.' He nodded and gestured her to lead on.

All the way up the aisle she could feel Adam's eyes on her. When she thought about it later, she didn't know how she stopped herself from running back to fling herself into his arms. Leaving him there was the most painful experience of her life.

'Handsome bloke.' Robert Fellows was faintly jealous. 'Married, I hope?'

Rosie turned the question. 'Are *you?*'

'What?'

'Married.'

Momentarily astonished, he stared at her then grinned, showing a good set of teeth. Except for one which jutted out at an odd angle to touch his lower lip – though it took nothing away from his good looks. 'You know very well I'm not married.'

'Makes no difference to me whether you are or you're not.' Come to think of it, she didn't even know what she was doing giving him the time of day.

'That bloke . . . he seemed to care a great deal for you.' His gaze dwelt on her face. 'Who was he?'

'No one you know,' she said curtly.

'In other words, mind my own business?' He smiled, amused but curious. Back there he had sensed hidden emotions.

'If you say so.'

Afraid that Adam might be watching, Rosie allowed herself to be shepherded into the big black car. Soon they were driving away from the court and towards the narrower streets of Blackburn town. 'Castle Street, isn't it?' He gave her a sideways grin. 'You'll have to direct me.'

Too engrossed in her own thoughts, she made no answer. But when they neared the area, she indicated which way he should turn. Outside the house, she quickly disembarked, having spoken no more than two words the entire time. 'Are you all right?' he asked, walking with her to the front door. 'I can stay a few minutes if you like?' He *wanted* to stay. He wanted to take her to bed, but he knew he had to be very careful or he would lose her altogether.

'Thank you for the lift,' she said, deliberately putting herself between the door and him. She wasn't ungrateful. In fact, she had taken a liking to him.

'See you tomorrow then?' His brow furrowed. 'Only if you feel able, of course?'

'I'll be in tomorrow, Mr Fellows. You can rely on it.' There was no point in sitting at home moping. For the time being, work was her salvation.

He nodded and smiled. Then he climbed into his grand car and drove away. She didn't watch him go. She didn't turn around when he had to slam on his brakes because he was staring at her and didn't see the lorry almost on top of him. Instead she quickly unlocked the front door and hurried inside where she fell against the wall and sobbed her heart out. 'You fool, Rosie!' she sobbed. 'Adam was there, and you let him go!' So much had happened that day, and all of it bad. All of it, that was, except for seeing Adam. In her mind's eye she recalled the desperate longing in his beautiful dark eyes. It was the same as her own. And it was wrong. That was what she must keep telling herself. The love she felt for Adam was wrong. And, however much it hurt, she must harden herself against it.

'I've got to know, Adam, how did he seem when they led him away? And what about Rosie . . . did she look well? Was she taking it all right? And what about the boy? Did you get news of him?' Ned Selby had been a haunted man when he first came to Adam some weeks back. He was still troubled, and it showed in his haggard face as he leaned over Adam's desk, pleading for news of his family.

'Sit down, Ned.' He waited until the older man was seated, then stared at him, shaking his head in frustration. 'For God's sake, man, you look dreadful,' he chided. Ned was unshaven, his hair was now streaked iron grey, and his face that of a man at war with himself. 'Where the hell have you been? By all accounts you never turned up for work yesterday, and here it is, eight o'clock, and I'm just about to finish for the day.'

'I'm sorry. I couldn't face work. I wandered about . . . just walked and walked. It were late when I got to bed, and late when I woke up. I've come straight here.' His large work-worn fists plucked at the baggy material of his trousers. 'I ain't been drinking. You know I don't touch the stuff.' His bloodshot eyes closed, he groaned and asked again. 'What happened? I need to know.'

'I don't expect you've had anything to eat?'

'*Couldn't* eat.'

Closing the ledger before him, Adam got out of his chair. 'Come on. I dare say Mrs Jessup has left more than enough for one.' He intervened when he saw how Ned was preparing to speak again. 'We can talk later. You look as if you're ready to drop. Come on.' He rounded the desk and heaved the big man out of his chair. Ned felt lifeless and heavy in his grip. 'Let's get you washed and shaved, then I'll tell you all you want to know while we eat. A deal?' He looked Ned in the eyes, his warm smile encouraging the other man.

'All right . . . a deal.' Ned actually returned the smile. It was a rare occurrence these days.

While he used the upstairs bathroom, Adam waited in the living room. Mrs Jessup had left a note on the mantelpiece.

'Lit the fire in case there's a nip in the air. The dining table's set, and your meal's all ready on the table. Though why I couldn't have got you a roast of sorts, I do not know!' Adam chuckled. She was a real old tartar, but worth her weight in gold was Mrs Jessup.

Ned came down looking a changed man. He had combed his hair and shaved the grey stubble from his chin, his shirt-collar was done up, and as he came into the room, he told Adam 'You're right, son. I thought I weren't hungry, but now I'm bloody famished!' He rubbed his great fists together and stood awkwardly at the door.

Instantly putting him at his ease, Adam strode across the room and grabbed him by the shoulders. 'Here's another one who's famished,' he laughed. 'So we'd best go and see what the wonderful Mrs Jessup has to offer.' He led the way into the kitchen, and there, spread out on the table, was a feast; there were numerous dishes, all covered with pretty little cloths hung with beads; one contained a huge slice of salmon, another was full to the brim with tiny potatoes cooked and cooled in their skins, there were peas and carrots, and plump green beans, and right at the back on a long-stemmed earthenware dish stood a thick round apple pie and beside it a jug of pouring cream. 'By! It's enough to feed an army,' Ned declared, his eyes popping out of his head and his stomach playing an audible tune.

'Mrs Jessup has turned out to be a real gem,' Adam readily admitted. 'She comes in every day from nine to five and I never have to worry about clean shirts, unmade beds or dirty dishes in the sink. Her only fault is trying to fill me with meat puddings and piping hot stews in the height of summer.'

Ned laughed at that. 'She wouldn't be looking for a husband, would she?' he teased. Then he remembered Martha, and the smile fell from his face.

Adam was quick to notice how Ned's mood had changed.

'You take these two dishes,' he pointed to the peas and green beans, 'and I'll take the rest.'

In the dining-room, the table was set for Adam. It took only a minute to lay another place opposite. When Ned was seated, Adam brought the jug of ice-cold water from the fridge. Placing another tumbler on the table, he said, 'If water isn't to your taste, there's beer . . . or I could make you some strong black coffee?'

Ned waved away his suggestion. 'Water's fine, son. Anything else would only spoil Mrs Jessup's beautiful food.'

Aware that Ned was hungry, not just for food but for news of the trial, Adam told him. 'The verdict was manslaughter. Doug was sentenced to five years.' He spread the napkin across his knee and sat, still and upright, looking at Ned and feeling great sympathy for this man who sadly appeared to have lost his way in life.

Sighing, Ned closed his eyes, slowly shook his head and spread his hands over his face. For what seemed an age he remained like that, with his head drooped on his chest and his thick fingers hiding his eyes. Then he raised his face and his hands fell away to his knees. 'For what he did, five years ain't so bad.' He smiled faintly. 'And how did he take it?'

'He appeared to take it very well. Certainly he seemed in high spirits when they led him away.' He was remembering how Doug had called out Rosie's name, and how he had asked her to: 'Wait for me, my lovely.' The words were imprinted on his brain. 'He and Rosie appear to have been happy together, Ned,' he said now. 'Being separated this way will be hard for them both.'

For a moment Ned was tempted to tell Adam everything, to reveal how there was very little love between Doug and Rosie, and that for some long time she had led a bitter life with him. But, even now, he felt it was not for him to expose these things. He reasoned that if Rosie wanted Adam to know, she would tell him. 'And how was Rosie?' If he was mortally ashamed, it was because he had abandoned her and the boy, not because he had any lingering feelings for either Martha or Doug. They were two of a kind, and had made their own beds.

'Rosie's made of strong stuff,' Adam replied softly. Almost to himself, he added, 'I don't think I've ever seen her looking more beautiful.'

'Did you speak to her?'

Adam frowned as he recalled the man who had left with Rosie. 'I spoke to her only briefly. But she was fine, don't worry.'

'And the boy . . . my grandson. Did you get to see him?'

'No, I'm sorry.'

'Still, I know he's all right. Rosie would never let any harm come to Danny.' He swallowed hard. 'Was it all as they said in the papers? Martha threatened to kill the boy? She really did that?' At times he'd wondered whether there was any end to that woman's wickedness. But it was ended now, wasn't it? And who could have imagined it would take Doug to put an end to it? Yet, in spite of that, he couldn't feel any compassion for his son, no forgiveness or affection, no sympathy or sense of family feeling. Instead, he felt only the repugnance that Doug had felt for him.

'Everything was exactly as the papers reported it,' Adam confirmed. 'It's done now, Ned, and there's nothing you can do to turn the tide.' He had never seen the big man so devastated, and it touched him deeply. 'Why don't you eat?' he asked. 'Happen later, in a few days or weeks when the dust settles, you can visit Doug . . . go and see Rosie and Danny. Heal the rift, Ned. You can do that.' He would have given anything to enjoy that same freedom. But, for reasons known only to herself, Rosie had shut him out.

Seeming to consider what Adam had said, Ned heaped the vegetables on to his plate and cut himself a slice of that succulent salmon. He took a bite and moaned with satisfaction, then put down his fork and told Adam in a thoughtful voice, 'It's too late for that. What I did was unforgivable, and I can't ever go back.'

Adam didn't argue. A man had to come to terms with his own failings; just as he himself was trying to do.

At half-past nine, after the meal was ended and the two men had relaxed awhile in the big armchairs, Ned stretched his legs and stood up. 'I'd best be off,' he said, looking down on Adam. 'Or I'll be shut out of me lodgings.'

'You could always stay here, Ned. You know that.' Adam stood before him, and his words were sincere.

'Naw.' Ned shook his head. 'It wouldn't work, and you know it.'

'Happen you're right,' Adam conceded. 'But while I've a roof over my head, so have you. Remember that.'

'I will,' Ned promised. 'But you've done enough, son. No man could do more for a friend. You've given me a job, so I can hold my head up among my own kind, and you pay me more than I deserve . . . especially when I left you in the lurch after you were good enough to buy me out. If it hadn't been for you, I'd have slid deeper in debt and happen be in prison myself now.' When he'd turned up some weeks back, ill from sleeping rough and full of remorse at having left Martha, Adam had taken him under his wing and made him whole again.

'I thought we'd agreed never to talk about that matter again. Besides, there was nothing lost. It's now a flourishing business and, like I've told you, Ned, you can be part of it any time you want. To my mind, you're still the best coal-merchant there ever was. It isn't your fault you came on hard times.'

Ned put his great hand on Adam's shoulder. 'Happen not,' he said gratefully. 'But I've done my share of worrying about contracts and coal-rounds, and how to balance the books. Shovelling coal and doing odd-jobs suits me just fine. Besides, there are far sharper men than me out there now, son, and you know it.' He grinned. 'Look at yourself,' he pointed out. 'Young and ambitious enough to make it all come right. What's more, the buggers don't come much sharper than you, and that's a fact.'

'I've had some lucky breaks, that's all.'

'And you've made the most of 'em, son. That's what sorts the men from the boys.' He reached out to shake Adam by the hand. 'Goodnight, son, and thanks again. I'm a different man from the one you saw a few hours back. And you needn't worry, I'll be in the yard sharp on seven tomorrow morning.' He looked embarrassed. 'I don't know what got into me yesterday. I'm not sorry I stayed away from the trial. It's just that, well, everything got on top of me, and I couldn't think straight.'

'Enough said, eh? Get off home to your bed.' Ned was special to him, a lovely man Adam was always delighted to help.

He watched Ned amble down the street, and was glad to have been there for him. As Ned rounded the corner and Adam turned to go back inside, his attention was caught by two more figures hurrying towards the house; one was a man, the other a small girl. She was crying bitterly. The man was dragging her along, viciously tugging at her arm when she resisted. Adam recognised them at once. They were Connie's husband and daughter April. 'What the devil do you think you're doing?' he demanded, running down the street towards them. By this time the girl was in a dreadful state and the man was red-faced with fury. 'What kind of man are you?' Adam snapped, straddling his legs and blocking the path so there was no way past. 'You'll break her arm, pulling her along like that.' It was all he could do not to lash out with his fist. But the child was upset enough, and he thought the best thing now was to contain the situation.

'She's gone.' The little fellow spoke in a sob, snatching at his face with the tips of his fingers as though some insect was plaguing him. Adam recalled how Connie laughed when she told him: 'Sometimes I upset him just to watch how he grabs at his face until it's red raw.'

'She's gone, I tell you!'

'Who's gone? *Connie*?' The child had stopped crying and was staring up at Adam with red eyes. He wanted to snatch her up, but he hadn't the right.

'Who else?' the other man snapped. Suddenly he produced a note from his pocket. 'Read this, you bastard!' he snarled, thrusting the note into Adam's hand. When the child whimpered, he tugged at her again. But he stopped when Adam glared a warning at him.

In the lamplight, Adam read the note. It was short and cruel:

I've stuck it as long as I can. Don't look for me this time, because I'm never coming back.

I've taken only what's mine, apart from the girl. But you don't need to be lumbered with her, because she was never yours. She belongs to Adam.

Goodbye and good riddance,
Connie

Adam was shocked to the core. 'Good God above!' He put out a hand and leaned his whole weight against the wall. Could it be true? In his frantic mind he tried to calculate when it was he had made love to Connie. The child had passed her third birthday some months back, so when was it he and Connie made love? When? For God's sake, he couldn't even think straight. No! The girl couldn't be his. But could she? Happen it wasn't altogether out of the question.

Before Adam could answer, the other man thrust the child at him. 'Take the brat! And to hell with the lot of you! I must have been mad to get mixed up with the slut in the first place.'

With that he swung away and almost ran down the street, leaving the sobbing child clinging to Adam's trouser leg, and looking up at him with big sad eyes that tore him in two.

'Well now. It looks like you'll be staying with your Uncle Adam for a while.' The child smiled through her tears when he told her, 'I've got apple pie and cream. Want some, do you?'

Blinking away the tears, she nodded eagerly.

'But you needn't think you're getting it *all*, gutsy.' She giggled at that, and he hoisted her on to his shoulders. As they went down the street, he muttered through his teeth, 'You bugger, Connie. You've really dropped me in it this time!' What the authorities would say about it all, he really didn't know. 'And whatever will Mrs Jessup have to say when she finds out?' That made him laugh. And the sound of her Uncle Adam laughing aloud was such a tonic that the child began laughing too.

'Laugh today, tears tomorrow!' Adam muttered. He couldn't get it out of his mind that Connie had said he was the girl's father. What he felt was hard to describe. But it was a mingling of sheer frustration, dark anger at Connie for having done such a cowardly thing as this, and a sense of bewildered pride that such a beautiful and lovely-natured girl as April might really belong to him.

Chapter Sixteen

'You surely can't be so heartless as to turn me away on Christmas Day?' Robert Fellows stood at Rosie's front door, a great bunch of flowers in one hand, and under his arm a pile of boxes all wrapped in pretty festive paper. 'Ask me in, and I promise you won't be sorry,' he pleaded in his most charming manner.

It was obvious he had made an extra effort on Rosie's behalf. He looked attractive in a long dark overcoat and white scarf. His shoes were highly polished as usual, and his hair carefully smoothed down from a side parting, making him look older. Snow was just beginning to fall. It settled on his shoulders like a sprinkling of flour, and the breeze which had chilled the air all morning gathered momentum. He visibly shivered, asking through numbed lips, 'Or would you rather I froze to death on your doorstep?'

'Whatever are you doing here?' she asked incredulously, her brown eyes widening with astonishment. 'It's Christmas Day, for goodness' sake. Have you no home to go to?' When the knock came on the door, Rosie was just taking the mince pies out of the oven. After that, she and Danny would be ready to take the presents along to Peggy's house; there was a new scarf for Peggy's mam, a pair of pearl-drop earrings for Peggy, and a selection of inexpensive games and trinkets for the younger ones.

Convinced the visitor must be Peggy, she was taken aback when she opened the door to Robert Fellows.

'No home, no woman, and no one to share the festivities with,' he replied. He looked like a lost soul, and Rosie couldn't help but smile.

'In that case, you'd better come in.' Stepping aside, she waited for him to pass her, then shut the door on the weather and shuddered. 'Brr! You've brought the cold in with you. Give me your coat. I don't want snow all over my new front room carpet.' It wasn't entirely new; in fact it was showroom soiled, but she had got it for two-thirds of its value. Best quality, with a dark red background and big cream roses all over, it gave the room a cosy feeling. Next, Rosie wanted two new fireside chairs and perhaps a dining table . . . a round oak one, and four tall-backed chairs with pretty seat cushions. But money was still short and her savings didn't mount up as fast as she would have liked, so a new table and chairs would have to wait. Meanwhile, she enjoyed window shopping in the big stores in Manchester and Blackburn. On top of that she comforted herself with the knowledge that she was keeping up with the rent and when it was cold outside, there was always a cheery fire in the grate, Danny had a new coat, and the larder was full to bursting. Life was ticking along without too much upset, and that was enough to be thankful for.

These days, since Martha and Doug were gone from it, the house had taken on a new lease of life. Thinking of her husband made her blood run cold. Two days ago she had received a letter from him. It was the letter of a madman.

'You really don't mind my calling round like this, then?' Robert's voice shook her out of her reverie.

'You're here now,' she said absently, her thoughts lingering on Doug and the letter. As for Robert Fellows, she *did* resent his arriving unannounced, even if it was only because this was hers and Danny's day. Coming up to Christmas, the store was busier than usual and everyone, including Rosie, had been called on to work extra hours. Though she loved the job and knew that Danny was content with Peggy's mam, Rosie had been eager for Christmas Day when she and her son could make up for lost time. For that very reason, she had even turned down Peggy's invitation for her and Danny to spend all Christmas Day at their house. Now, Robert Fellows' arrival was an intrusion, and though Rosie hated herself for thinking of it in that way, she still didn't know whether to be angry or pleased that he was here.

He seemed to know what she was thinking. 'I wouldn't have intruded like this, Rosie,' he claimed. 'Only, it is Christmas, and there I was, all alone in that miserable flat, and I couldn't stop thinking of you.'

She didn't answer straightaway. Instead, she shook the snowflakes from his coat and hung it on a peg, and placed the scarf over it. Now she was regarding him with friendly brown eyes that sent a thrill through him. 'I suppose it must be lonely all on your own. And after all, it *is* Christmas . . . goodwill to men and all that.' Even when he smiled, or perhaps *only* when he smiled, there was something about him that disturbed her. Yet, at the same time, she was grateful for the friendship that had developed between them these last few weeks. Certainly he had helped her get over the trauma of the trial, and how could she deny that his interest in her as a woman was very flattering?

He seemed peeved. 'I hope it isn't only because it's Christmas that you've asked me in?' he said softly. 'I'd much rather it was because you want me with you?'

'Look, Robert, I really am sorry to sound inhospitable.' It was strange how these days his first name sprang easily to her lips. In the office it was always 'Mr Fellows', but outside working hours they had seen more and more of each other. So much, in fact, that Rosie believed it was time for her to keep her distance. 'It was just that I didn't expect you to turn up here today,' she told him. 'Still, now you're here, you're very welcome.' A genuine smile appeared despite herself. 'Go on through. I know Danny will be pleased to see you.'

Regarding her with flat hard eyes, he said softly, '*Danny* might be pleased to see me, but you're not, are you, Rosie?' It was more of a statement than a question.

'If you must know, Robert, I'm thinking of the neighbours. I'm also thinking how I've been seeing a lot of you lately, and I think we're getting too involved . . . taking Danny to the Saturday afternoon matinée . . . walking arm in arm through Corporation Park . . . eating hot chestnuts from the barrow in the boulevard. The three of us acting like a family, when we're no such thing. It's wrong, that's all I'm saying. And it's not fair on Danny.'

'How can it be unfair on Danny?' he demanded. 'We take him everywhere we go, except for that one time when I finally managed to have you to myself. And don't say you didn't enjoy it, because I know you did . . . a day in London, dinner and dancing at the most expensive night club.' His meaningful smile spoke volumes. 'It was only spoiled when you refused to come back home with me.'

'I'm not denying I enjoyed it,' Rosie assured him. In fact, it was one of the most memorable events of her entire life. 'It's just that I can't afford to make mistakes. Whether I like it or not, I do have a husband. I also have a son I dearly love, and people's tongues can be wicked.'

'What are you saying, Rosie?' He reached out, the tips of his fingers stroking her face. Her skin felt soft as velvet beneath his touch. Her obvious reluctance to accept the growing affection between them only made him more determined to have her. 'Have I offended you? Are you saying you don't ever want to see me again?'

Rosie sighed. The last thing she wanted was to hurt him. In fact she had a very soft spot for Robert. 'All I'm saying is this . . . if the circumstances were different, I'd be delighted to go on seeing you. I like you, you must know that.' But she didn't *love* him. She loved Adam and always would. 'But we can't forget I'm a married woman. Even more important, I have Danny to consider. Tongues are already wagging. It's got out that we're seeing each other, and now here you are, turning up at the door, laden with presents. You've been seen, you can rely on that. And your visit here will be common knowledge all over Blackburn before the week is out.' Anger rose in her, and her brown eyes darkened. 'I'm not blaming you, but that's the way it is.'

'Do you want me to go?' Whatever her answer, he had no intention of leaving.

'I didn't say that.' All the same, she would have felt better if he'd stayed away. Some neighbours would understand, and others would make a meal of it. Malicious gossip could lead to all kinds of trouble.

'Say you're pleased to see me then?'

'All right. I'm pleased to see you.' Oddly enough, she was regretting having been too honest just now. Robert had been good company. He'd taken her out when she was at a low ebb, and restored her faith in herself as a woman. It wouldn't do any harm to make him feel welcome today. Besides, what woman wouldn't enjoy a good-looking man wanting to spend some time with her? Just as long it stayed within certain limits.

She ushered him through to the living room. 'Of course I'm glad you're here. What's more, if you have nothing else to do, you're welcome to stay all day.' God! What was she saying? When would she learn not to let her tongue run away with her like that?

He stared about the room. It was warm and cosy, and the small Christmas tree for which Rosie had paid half-a-crown at the market stood bright and sparkling in the corner. He wrinkled his nose. 'Something smells delicious.'

'It's a turkey I bought for me and Danny. I left it cooking all night on a low light, and at six o'clock it was done to a turn.' The air was warmed by all manner of aromas; the newly baked mince pies, the simmering brandy pudding, and the bacon rolls lying crispy and hot atop the turkey. 'I hate leaving everything 'til the last minute,' Rosie explained. It had been hard work to get everything done, but it had been a labour of love.

'You're a real little homemaker,' he declared, seeing the blazing fire in the grate.

Excited, Danny leaped up from the rug where he'd been sitting cross-legged with his new jigsaw. 'It's *you*!' he cried, flinging himself into Robert's arms. In a minute he was being swung into the air as Robert sat him on his shoulders, nearly knocking the ceiling light down in the process. 'Your mam says I can stay all day if I like,' he told the excited boy. 'What do you think, Danny, shall I accept?'

'Yes, yes!' the boy cried, and the argument was won.

'In a little while, Danny and I have to play Father Christmas to the Lewis family,' Rosie explained, 'so you'll either have to amuse yourself here while we're gone, or you can come with us. Which is it to be?'

'I'll come with you, of course.' He thought it might be a good time to let the neighbours know he had staked a claim on Rosie.

Peggy was delighted when she saw Rosie at the door, but her smile fell away when she saw who was with her. 'You know Robert Fellows?' Rosie said as they all entered the hallway. Danny ran ahead, but Rosie stayed with Robert. She sensed Peggy's hostility and felt the need to protect him.

'Rosie kindly invited me to share Christmas Day with her,' he said in his most endearing manner. 'I hope you don't mind my coming along?'

Peggy merely nodded, her face stiff. Turning her back on him, she led the way to the living room. Behind her, Robert glanced at Rosie, and she returned a reassuring smile. Unbeknown to him, Rosie had already suffered a warning from Peggy where he was concerned. 'He'll bring you nothing but trouble, gal!' she'd said. But Rosie paid little mind. Instead, because she suspected Peggy's warning was not without a touch of envy, she explained how there was nothing serious between her and Robert. In fact, they were more good friends than lovers.

Peggy's mam was up to her elbows in baking. 'It's like feeding a bloody army!' she chuckled. 'I've been at it since yesterday morning and there's still the chicken to gut and stuff.'

'Away with you, our mam,' Peggy chided. 'You know very well you love it.' Turning to Rosie, she added, 'Honest, she's like a great kid at Christmas. I've told her I'll do the chicken and veg, but do you think she'll let me, eh?'

''Cause you've done your share, that's why,' her mam argued. 'If it weren't for your wages, happen we'd be having sparrer instead of a fat juicy chicken. So you look after your friends and leave me to do woman's work.' With that, she pushed the rolling pin over the pastry and began singing.

'There'll be no talking to her for hours yet,' Peggy laughed. 'What with her singing and that lot creating bedlam in the front room, I don't know whether I'm on my head or my feet.' It sounded like all hell was let loose in the front room. 'They opened their presents at four o'clock this morning,' Peggy groaned. 'You should see it in there. Honest to God, Rosie, it'll take a week to clean up the mess.'

She handed over her parcels. 'The more the merrier,' she said. 'But you can always hide them 'til next year.'

'What! That would be more than my life's worth.' Taking the presents, Peggy put them under the tree, all except her own. When she opened it and saw the pretty pearl-drop earrings there, she hugged Rosie hard. 'They're lovely,' she said. In fact, they were the very earrings she had admired in Slater's shop window when she and Rosie had taken a walk during one lunch break. 'You never forget a thing, do you, you bugger!' she said, eyes shining with affection.

Rosie's presents were from the whole Lewis family; a bottle of perfume and a pair of sheer stockings. She was horrified at what they must have cost. 'Oh, Peggy! How lovely. But I dread to think how much they were. I'd have been delighted with just *one*.'

'I know that!' Peggy exclaimed. 'And what they cost don't matter.' She shook her head and grinned. 'Anyway, it's me own fault for having a friend with expensive tastes, ain't it, eh?' Suddenly her mood was serious. Gazing fondly at Rosie, she said softly, 'You're the best friend in the whole world, Rosie gal, and after all you've been through, I wanted to get you something really special.'

Rosie was speechless. Her brown eyes softened with tears as she looked on Peggy's dear face. Choking back her emotion, she flung her arms round her friend and hugged her hard. 'I love you, you bugger,' she whispered. When Peggy suggested they should get a drink from her mam's secret hoard of gin, tears turned to laughter.

Robert gave a slight embarrassed cough, and Rosie was mortally ashamed. 'We're neglecting our guest,' she told Peggy.

'He ain't *my* guest,' Peggy said stiffly. But when Rosie gave her a pleading glance, she relented. In a warm voice which hid her true feelings, she told him, 'But you're welcome to a drop o' the old stuff, if you don't mind drinking out of a cup. You see, we don't drink in this house as a rule, and we only ever had two glasses. Our kid broke them when he was searching for his presents, so I'm afraid it's cups for now.'

Sensing her hostility, he decided that if he wasn't going to alienate Rosie, he had better play along. 'Thank you, a cup will be just fine.' His smile was devastating.

When the bottle of gin appeared, so did Peggy's mam. 'You little sod, our Peggy!' she exploded. 'I thought I'd hid that good and proper.'

'Do you want a drop or not?' Peggy asked her, slyly winking at Rosie.

Before you could say Jack Robinson she'd scurried into the kitchen and fetched out a mug. 'And don't be mingy with the measure!' she warned, holding it out. When Peggy was too cautious with her pouring, her mam tipped the bottle in her own favour. 'That should warm the cockles of me old heart,' she chuckled, returning to the kitchen with her good measure of gin. In no time at all she was singing louder than ever. 'Canny as a barrow-load o' monkeys, is our mam,' Peggy said. And Rosie was glad to have them for her friends.

Half an hour later, Peggy showed her visitors out. 'Don't forget we're going to the sales in the morning, kid,' she reminded Rosie. 'There are only one or two shops open on Boxing Day, so we'd best be away by eight if we're going to snap up the goodies.' Then she shot a last speculative glance at Robert and closed the door.

'I don't think she cares much for me,' he said as they walked back to Rosie's little house. What Peggy Lewis thought didn't worry him the slightest, but he didn't want that silly little cow setting Rosie against him.

'It isn't you personally,' Rosie explained. 'It's what I was saying before. The neighbours have started to gossip, and Peggy's worried it might backfire on me and Danny.'

'I can see she's a good friend.' There was a bad taste in his mouth when he uttered these words. All the same, he knew them to be true.

'The best.'

'I care for you too, Rosie, and I wouldn't do anything to harm you or Danny. You must know that?'

Rosie didn't want to be drawn deep into conversation just now. So she was immensely grateful when Danny commandeered Robert to 'Play with my new jigsaw', leaving her to bustle about preparing the lunch.

Everywhere she moved his eyes followed, unsettling her, making her wish she hadn't opened the door to him. Yet, for all that, she found a certain comfort in the idea that, on this special day, Danny had a father figure in the house. The two of them made a heartwarming sight, sitting on the rug together, finishing the jigsaw, with Robert looking like any loving father with his son.

In one quiet moment Rosie paused by the kitchen door, observing them together. The jigsaw depicted a giant and a boy, and Robert was telling Danny the story of David and Goliath. She wondered whether she had been too hard on Robert. She couldn't know that even at that moment he was play-acting, aware that she was watching, and hoping to get to her through her son.

'Up to the table, you two.' Lunch was ready. Decorated with parsley and wearing white frills, the turkey was laid on a large flowered plate in the centre of the table. Round the rim of the plate the bacon rolls made a colourful contrast. There were numerous deep dishes, one with crispy baked potatoes, another containing small round Brussels sprouts, and a third filled to the brim with fluffy mashed potatoes. Alongside stood a small shallower dish holding six tiny Yorkshire puddings, and nearby a pretty floral-patterned jug filled with rich brown gravy. The delicious aroma permeated the air. 'I'm starving!' Danny exclaimed. Robert said it was no wonder when they were faced with such a wonderful spread. And Rosie took all the compliments like any woman would, with a knowing smile and a large pinch of salt.

During the meal, she relaxed her rule of no talking at the table, and the excitement of Christmas spilled over. Danny laughed and giggled, he chatted and threw his arms in the air when relating to Rosie the tale Robert had told him of David and Goliath. Robert was his usual good company. When, after picking at his food as he always did, Danny declared he didn't want any more, Robert persuaded him he should eat up all his greens and grow as big as the giant. Danny's eyes grew wide at the thought, and Rosie couldn't help but laugh.

When the meal was over and the table cleared, she realised that she had thoroughly enjoyed herself. In fact, she felt more relaxed than she had for a very long time. 'You don't have to do this,' she told Robert when he picked up a tea-towel and began drying dishes.

'And you didn't have to invite me in,' he said fondly.

As the day wore on, Rosie came to believe that she had done the right thing. Certainly Danny loved Robert, and he appeared to feel the same affection for the boy. She was torn two ways. When the time came to shut Robert out of their lives completely, it was bound to be a real jolt for Danny. Conversely, how could she deny him the relationship that was already growing between these two?

The afternoon went quickly, and soon it was evening. Everyone was still too full up to want any tea, so while Danny insisted that Robert should finish the jigsaw with him, Rosie listened to a Sherlock Holmes mystery on the radio. Now and then she glanced at the two on the rug, and a warm feeling came over her. A little wry smile covered her face as she wondered whether it was the gin she'd downed at Peggy's house.

'I'm tired, Mammy.' At half-past nine, Danny rubbed his bleary eyes and fell into her lap.

'I should think so!' Rosie declared. 'It's way past your bedtime, young man.' Taking him into the kitchen, she undressed him and washed him all over. Normally she would have had a fire burning in the tiny grate, but what with all the baking and the oven remaining hot for some time yet, it wasn't needed.

'Can I help?' Robert got up from his chair when he saw Rosie carrying the sleeping child.

'He just keeled over,' she replied, her smile soft and loving as she gazed on the boy. 'But he does weigh a ton, so yes, I'd be grateful if you could carry him up for me.' Carefully, she delivered her son into his arms, and the three of them went out of the room and on up the stairs.

As she led the way, Rosie wished it had been like this with Doug. Even more so, she wished she had not lost Adam. Suddenly she brought herself up sharp. Who was she fooling? She *had* lost Adam. And even by the longest stretch of imagination it had *never* been like this with Doug.

To her surprise, she found herself wondering whether it would be so bad if she was to continue seeing Robert. Defiance grew in her. After all, she had no intention of ever living with Doug again. And if the neighbours gossiped, so what? It wasn't them who had to live her life. It was her. She was responsible for her own actions, and she was responsible for Danny. She had asked nothing from nobody, and while she had a strong back and two strong hands, she never would.

But when she looked at Danny, lying there in his bed, all her doubts came back. It did matter what the neighbours said, because gossip had a way of reaching the school playground and there was no one more wicked than children if they had a mind to bully. With Danny starting school after the holidays, she didn't want anything to go wrong. Then again it was common knowledge how his grandma had been stabbed to death, and that his daddy was in prison for it. So he already had his cross to bear.

'Penny for them.' Robert had laid the child in his bed before turning to see Rosie deep in thought.

She gave no answer, merely smiled, took him by the hand and

led him out of the room. Once outside she closed the door and whispered, 'Thank you.'

He was pleasantly surprised. 'For what?'

'For making this Christmas Day so special for Danny.'

'And have I made it special for you?' His voice was soft, sensuously persuasive.

She thought a moment and then answered truthfully, 'Yes, I think so.' He was looking at her in that certain way again, and it made her tremble inside. In the half-light, his eyes seemed darker. The very nearness of him was intoxicating.

'I love you, Rosie.' Reaching out he put his hands around her face and kissed her on the mouth.

'No!' Her voice was strong, but inside she was weakening. It was so long since she had been with a man in that way, and like any woman she was hungry for love. The feel of his mouth over hers had awakened something in her, something she couldn't deny any longer. More than that it brought back tender memories of Adam, and with the memories came a kind of rage. The rage became passion, and passion blinded her to reason.

'Don't push me away, Rosie.' He kissed her again, and this time she responded. Encouraged, he murmured sweet endearments, tickling the inside of her ear with the tip of his tongue to set her pulses racing.

The need in her was as great as his own. 'Not here,' she said, glancing worriedly at Danny's door. Curling her fingers into his, she led him down the landing to her own bedroom. The room had been hers and Doug's. Now it was newly decorated, with a brand new bed and two pretty rugs that were soft underfoot. It was as though Doug had never been there. But none of that mattered now. He was out of her life and she was her own mistress.

Inside the room, she half drew the curtains, some deep instinct in her making her ashamed. Slowly, she undressed. He watched her; first the straight blue skirt that showed off the shapeliness of her ankles, then the cream blouse with its deep revers and pearly buttons. Then her full-length slip with the lacy hem. Now the see-through brassière and flimsy knickers.

While she took them off one by one, he watched lasciviously, appreciating the slim and lovely form that was being temptingly revealed to him. At last she stood there in all her naked glory, and he gasped aloud. He had never seen such beauty. He knew he never would again.

Quickly now, all reserve gone, he threw off his clothes and took her in his arms. The small taut breasts touched the hardness of his chest, making his skin stand up in goose-pimples. 'You're magnificent,' he breathed. She didn't answer. She wanted him, and was not ashamed. He swept her into his arms and carried her to the bed. There he laid her down. All tenderness was gone now. Like a wild animal he cried aloud, gathering her to him and driving deep inside her. Hard and penetrating, he took her to himself in a frenzy, frantic she would escape him. And she returned his passion with the same ferocity.

Afterwards they lay, side by side, bathed in sweat and clinging to each other. 'I knew you would be wonderful,' he murmured. In bed, in the throes of lovemaking, she'd been as wild as he.

Rosie climbed out of bed. She dressed with haste, a sense of guilt overwhelming. Before he could realise her intention, she went from the room and made her way downstairs. The guilt went with her, the awful shame of what she had done.

He followed. When he came into the living room, she was sitting in the fireside chair, her shoulders hunched forward and her troubled brown eyes staring into the dying embers of the fire. 'I want you to go now,' she said. Her voice was firm. It startled him.

Sensing her mood, he thought it best not to provoke her. Some women were like the spider, so filled with malevolence after mating that they devoured their mate. 'If that's what you want,

Rosie.' She didn't answer. He felt uncomfortable. Glancing at the clock, he saw that it was gone ten. 'It might be just as well,' he conceded. 'But I will see you tomorrow, won't I?'

'Maybe.' It wasn't him she hated. It was herself.

He came to her then. 'Rosie, we made love just now. Doesn't that mean anything to you?' He actually believed it had given him a claim on her for all time.

The desperation in his voice made her look up. 'Of course it did,' she told him kindly. 'But it's been a long tiring day, and it's getting late.'

'But we *will* see each other again?'

'Why not?' She wasn't certain, but she could think about that later.

'Tomorrow?'

'No.'

'When then?'

'After I'm back at work.' She needed to spend the rest of the holiday with Danny. Just the two of them. Somehow, she felt as though she'd betrayed him.

'Whatever you say, Rosie. Just as long as I haven't done anything to turn you against me.' As far as he was concerned, the fun was only just beginning and if it was to be ended, it would be him and not her who did the ending.

'No. You've done nothing,' she promised him. Standing up, she kissed him lightly on the cheek. 'I'll see you out.'

They didn't exchange words at the door. He whispered goodnight, and she nodded. Then she closed the door and shot the bolt. A few moments later, she had a strip-wash after which she kissed Danny goodnight and went to her room, where she sat before the mirror brushing her thick brown tresses. 'You've done it now, Rosie gal,' she told herself in the mirror. 'The bugger won't leave you alone now.' She smiled, her mouth wide and beautiful in the mirror. 'Maybe that won't be so bad,' she murmured. 'Happen when you've got Doug out of your life forever, there'll be a better future with Robert Fellows. Danny won't mind, that's for sure.' Before she could stop herself she was saying what was on her mind. 'And what about Adam? What would he think of your behaviour tonight?' Instantly her mood changed, and the pain was unbearable.

When she climbed into bed, she was still thinking of Adam. And when she slept, she dreamed of him.

'ROSIE!' Peggy's voice sailed up from the street. 'You lazy little sod, get up and let me in.'

Half asleep, Rosie hoisted herself up on to her elbows. It was a minute before she realised it was daylight. One glance at the bedside clock told her it was already eight o'clock. 'Gawd! Half the day's gone!' With one bound she was out of bed. As she reached the window, a stone clattered against it and Peggy's voice yelled, 'ARE YOU BLOODY DEAD IN THERE?'

Raising the sash window, Rosie leaned out. 'It wouldn't matter if we were, gal,' she shouted back. 'Because you're enough to *wake* the dead. And stop throwing stones! If you break this window, it'll cost you.'

Peggy laughed. 'Oh? And who's got up in a crotchety mood this morning, eh?' Kicking the door with the tip of her shoe, she moaned, 'Get a move on, gal. It's bloody freezing out here.' The milkman hurried by, his arms laden with bottles.

'I'll warm you up if you like,' he promised.

'Huh!' she retorted. 'It'll take more of a man than you, Ben Slater. Anyway, you've been holding them bottles and your hands must be like ice, so you can bugger off.' He went on his way chuckling to himself.

Rosie inched open the door. 'Get in here, you,' she ordered. 'Before the whole street's up.' As Peggy rushed in, the cold came with her and Rosie's teeth started chattering.

'The whole street *is* up, gal.' Marching into the living room, Peggy went straight to the window and threw back the curtains. The daylight flooded in. 'It's a bloody good job we managed to get this holiday off, 'cause I don't reckon you'd have made it to work today anyroad.' She regarded Rosie with suspicious eyes. 'It ain't like you to oversleep, gal,' she teased. 'Ain't you well?'

'I'm fine.' Rosie went into the kitchen and filled the kettle. While she was lighting the gas ring, Peggy came in. She didn't say anything, but stood there, her eyes following Rosie's every move.

Rosie put the kettle on the ring and scooped up a bundle of kindling wood from the pile in the corner. Taking it into the living room, she proceeded to light the fire. She knew Peggy was waiting for an explanation, and was unsure how to start. Little by little the events of last night were coming to mind, and were very disturbing to her.

'You slept with him, didn't you, gal?' Peggy knew Rosie like the back of her hand. 'You *did*, didn't you?' Coming into the living room, she sat in the fireside chair. Rosie was still on her knees, blowing into the grate, trying to fan the flames through the kindling wood.

When it got hold, she leaned back on her haunches and looked up at her friend. 'Can't hide anything from you, can I?'

Peggy stared at her. 'You bloody little fool!'

Rosie shrugged her shoulders. 'Happen I am.' Clambering up, she rubbed her knees. 'I'll just go up and see if Danny's all right.' With that, she hurried from the room, leaving Peggy exasperated.

When Rosie returned, her friend was just pouring the tea. 'Is he awake?' she asked. She was quieter now, more understanding.

Rosie shook her head. 'He's still fast and hard asleep.' Now that she had her dressing-gown on, she was more comfortable, but still shivered when her bottom touched the cold wood of the dining chair. 'I'm sorry,' she said when Peggy sat down beside her. 'I know I promised I'd be ready by eight, but we can still make the ten o'clock tram if you like.'

'Don't fret, gal,' Peggy answered. She slurped her tea and stared at the tablecloth. 'Last night . . . do you want to talk about it?'

Rosie peeped at her from the corner of her eyes. She did want to talk, yet she didn't. In the end she decided to stall. 'I had a letter from Doug the other day.'

'Oh?'

'I think he's gone off his head.'

'If you ask me, he was *always* off his head.' Her mind was still on Robert Fellows, and she was just the tiniest bit jealous.

Rosie got the letter from the drawer. 'I'm afraid for Danny,' she whispered, handing it to her. 'Read it, and you'll see what I mean.'

Sensing the fear in Rosie, Peggy unfolded the letter and read:

> My darling wife,
>
> I expect you're wondering why I haven't written to you, especially when you've so often taken the trouble to write to me?
>
> I've been thinking of you a lot lately, and it's time, my love. Time to lay down some rules and regulations. You see, I have to abide by them, and it's only right that you should do the same.
>
> How is the boy? Are you looking after him? I want you to keep him well for me. I wouldn't like it if you let him forget me. It was a shock to discover that he wasn't mine, but soon as ever I get out of here, I plan to deal with that little matter.
>
> I'll be home sooner than you think, my love. Meantime, don't do anything that might anger me. I think you know by now that I'm not a very forgiving man.

I'm being made to pay the price for what I did. I think you should be punished too, you and the boy.

I know you must be lonely for me, but it won't be too long now.

Your loving husband,

Doug

Peggy dropped the letter on to her knee. 'I see what you mean,' she said, looking up at Rosie with shocked eyes. 'It ain't what he says . . . it's what he *don't* say that's so frightening.'

'Do you get the feeling that he means to hurt Danny?' Rosie spoke in a whisper in case the boy should come creeping down the stairs.

Instead of answering, Peggy put her own question. 'I didn't know you'd written to him several times?'

'I haven't,' Rosie confessed. 'I wrote to him just the once, soon after he was locked away. He never answered, so I didn't write again.'

'After he threatened you in court like that, you shouldn't have written at all.'

'I thought I should. He was under stress that day, and though I know it's over between us, I couldn't altogether abandon him.' Rosie was frantic. 'This letter . . . tell me what you really think?' Taking the letter from Peggy, she absent-mindedly folded it, over and over, until it was small enough to hide in the palm of her hand. The very sight of it sent shivers down her spine.

'You're not to worry about it,' Peggy entreated. 'It's plain he doesn't know what he's talking about. I mean, fancy thinking Danny ain't his!' She shook her head in disbelief.

'It was Martha who put the idea into his head, and where his mother was concerned, Doug could never think for himself.' Every word she spoke brought back the horror of that night. 'He means to hurt Danny, I just know it.'

Peggy forced a smile. 'Give over, gal. How can he hurt anybody when he's locked away in jail?'

Now for the suspicion that had haunted Rosie since she'd received the letter. 'I'm sure he plans to escape.'

Peggy was adamant. 'Never!' She came to Rosie and put her arm round her. 'You're letting him get to you, kid, and that's exactly what he wants. Doug is a bad lot but he's a coward. Mark my words, gal, while he's in there, he'll toe the line. He'll do his time, and when he comes out, you and Danny need have no fear of him.'

'I wish I could believe that.' Rosie had tried hard to put the letter out of her mind, but it was always there, festering away in her mind. Suddenly she leaped up and threw it into the flames. It curled in the heat and then was gone, eaten up, like Doug was eaten up with jealousy and madness.

'That's the best place for it,' Peggy told her. She had returned to her chair and now was looking up at Rosie. 'Get on with your life, gal,' she said. 'Doug had his chance. Now it's yours.'

'What if I took up with Robert Fellows?'

'I reckon you'd be jumping out of the frying pan and into the fire.'

'Why?'

'Because, in a different way, he's as bad as Doug.' She was on her feet now, showing her anger. 'Robert Fellows has played around with everybody. He'll use you just like he used them. Once he's got what he wants, he'll be gone, looking round for another plaything.'

The only young woman he hadn't played around with, was Peggy herself. She bitterly resented that.

'He doesn't seem that kind of man to me.'

'Well, you can take my word for it. You'd do well to steer clear.' She didn't wait for Rosie's response. Instead she asked quietly, 'What happened here last night?'

'We had a wonderful day, the three of us. Last night after Danny was asleep in bed, we just . . . sort of fell into each other's arms.' The memory brought mingled pleasure and regret. She recalled the wild and wanton way she had behaved last night. That wasn't love. It was a raging desire for sex, and now she questioned herself as to why it had happened. It seemed like another person had been in his arms, not her. Just thinking about it sent a pink flush over her face.

'I've got to be going.' Peggy suddenly made for the door. 'I expect I'll see you later, gal.'

Rosie ran down the passage after her. 'Wait a minute, Peggy, I thought you wanted to go into town?'

'Changed me mind.' The door slammed and woke Danny up. After that, Rosie had little time to think about Peggy's abrupt departure.

An hour later, when breakfast was over and the two of them were getting ready for the ten o'clock tram, Rosie was fastening Danny's coat up. She couldn't think why Peggy had behaved in such a strange manner. It was when she began going over what they'd discussed that it suddenly dawned on her. When she'd first started at Woolworths, Peggy had mentioned that she liked Robert Fellows. But Rosie had taken that to be a bit of fun, something and nothing that she'd taken little notice of. 'Gawd! I must be blind,' she chided herself. 'Hurry up, sweetheart,' she told Danny, who had run back into the living room for his lead soldier. 'I want to call on Auntie Peggy.' If she didn't put things right now, she would never forgive herself.

As Rosie closed her front door, Peggy came out into the street. For one uncomfortable minute the two of them stared at each other. Then Peggy laughed. And Danny laughed. And Rosie shook her head, a smile on her face and a lilt to her heart as Peggy came towards her. 'What must you think of me?' she asked.

'I've already told you,' Peggy replied, 'I reckon you're a bloody fool.'

Rosie laughed then. 'So do I. What's more, I'm not even sure he's worth it.'

'But you can have a bloody good time finding out, eh?'

'Friends then?'

'What else?'

'A long walk into town if we don't catch that tram.' With that, they went at a smart pace along the street and down towards the tram stop. Danny skipped all the way, and Rosie felt that everything would come right, as long as Peggy was beside her.

Chapter Seventeen

Ned was all done up in his Sunday best. He knocked on the door and stood back, his shoulders against the wind. In no time the door was opened and Adam was heartened to see him there. 'By! Here it is, February, and there's still no sign o' this shocking weather easing up,' Ned complained. As Adam opened the door to admit him, he took off his hat and shook the snowflakes on to the front doorstep.

'It's good of you to come round on a weekend.' Adam quickly let him in. As they went across the spacious hallway, Ned was surprised to see that he was being led towards the library. Still, he said nothing. However close he and Adam were, and however much Adam would have argued, he was still only a guest in this house. All the same, usually when he paid a visit, he was always made welcome in the grand living room. There must be a reason for Adam receiving him in the library, he thought, but it wasn't for him to question why.

The reason was soon made clear. 'Sit yourself down, Ned,' Adam invited. Taking the other man's coat, he flung it over the back of a chair, oblivious to the little pool that was formed on the carpet as the heat of the room melted the snowflakes. He poured Ned a stiff whisky. 'That'll get the blood moving again,' he chuckled. Raising his own glass, he took a great swig.

Ned was shocked to see him drinking like that. As a rule, Adam rarely drank anything stronger than a pint of best or a glass of red wine with his meat on a Sunday.

'Mrs Jessup's in the other room with April.' Adam smiled and it was a smile filled with love. 'The little beggar won't sleep, and she's running rings round that poor woman. Still, since the dear old soul was widowed and came to live here, she's been a real godsend.' He strode to the window and stared out. 'Anyway, I don't want April hearing what I have to say, so I thought it best if we talked in here.'

'What's on your mind, son?' Still suffering the effects of the bitter wind outside, Ned sipped eagerly at his drink, shivering when it fired his veins.

Silence greeted him. He looked up to see Adam staring out of the window, his head bent and his dark eyes pained, and knew straightaway what was on his mind: the same thing that had been on his mind these past weeks; the same thing that drove him half-crazy when another day passed and still she wasn't home. 'You'll have to face it, Adam,' he quietly pointed out, 'Connie's not coming back.'

Deep in thought, Adam appeared not to have heard the older man's statement. Now, he swung round to face him. 'For God's sake, Ned, how could Connie just walk out and leave her child?' Slamming his fist on the window frame, he strode to the desk and sat down heavily in the chair. Picking up a pencil, he turned it over and over against the desk top. 'If she wants to end the marriage that's fine. It was always rotten anyway, and it's got nothing to do with me or anyone else. But the girl's a little innocent.' April was a warm and delightful little creature and he couldn't understand how Connie could have left her.

'It's no use. You'll have to go to the authorities,' Ned told him. 'Happen they'll find Connie.'

'Oh, aye! And happen they'll put April in some bloody awful institution.' The very idea was loathsome to him.

'Look, Adam. You've done all any man could be asked to do for a friend. But Connie's clearly gone forever, and you can't hold on to that child indefinitely . . .' He paused, making his next words convey a particular meaning. 'Unless, of course, she really *is* yours?'

Adam leaned back in his chair. 'I don't know, Ned, he answered truthfully. 'I can't say she is, and I can't say she isn't. All I know is this . . . until Connie tells me otherwise, I've got to behave as though she is . . . and that means taking care of her when there's no one else.'

'And how long is that?'

'As long as it takes.'

'It's been almost six months since she's been gone, and there's been no word whatsoever. Why don't you have another go at her old man?'

'Because he's about as bloody useful as an empty paper bag! I've lost count of the times I've tried to reason with him.' Adam had come close to thumping Connie's husband in the mouth on more than one occasion. But violence never solved anything, and it certainly wouldn't do the child any good. 'He swears April is mine, and so does Connie . . . the letter's in the cupboard there, you've seen it yourself. Anyway, it doesn't matter now whether she's mine or whether she isn't. The lass is with me, and she's staying put. And even if Connie's old man was to go down on bended knee, neither hell nor high water would make me hand her back to that bloody little creep. Not when he's thrown her out and turned his back on her, like she was so much muck out of the midden.'

'Well, he's not likely to want her back, is he?' Ned snorted. 'Or he wouldn't have disowned her in the first place.'

'To tell you the truth, Ned, I don't know who's worse, him or

Connie. I just thank the good Lord the child is too young to know what's happening.'

'Does she still ask questions . . . about her mam and dad, I mean?'

'Not any more. I don't have to tell you how distressed she was at first. But, thanks to Mrs Jessup, she's happy as Larry now.'

'Is there no news from that private detective?'

Adam sighed. 'No, not yet. But he's only been on her trail for a fortnight. There's time enough yet.' Groaning, he leaned forward to push his long fingers through his mop of hair, his whole expression one of misery. 'Dear God above! How can any mother leave her own flesh and blood like that?' He had come to love the child as his own, and now wanted only to keep her. Looking up with tortured eyes, he said in a gruff voice, 'The trouble is, Ned, even if Connie does come back, I won't want her to take April away.'

'I told you to watch out for that.' Time and again, Ned had warned Adam he was getting too close to the child, and that it would only end in heartache; not just for Adam but for April too. 'When the time comes for you to give her up, will you cope?'

Adam gave a wry little smile. 'I don't intend giving her up,' he confessed.

'What in heaven's name are you talking about?' Ned was horrified. 'If Connie turned up tomorrow and demanded the child back, there wouldn't be a single thing you could do about it.'

'There is just one. I'm not searching for Connie so she can take April away. When I find her, I mean to ask her to marry me.'

Ned couldn't find words to speak. Instead he stared in disbelief. Presently he warned, 'You'd only be making real trouble for yourself, son. Connie's already brought you enough grief. And besides, she's already married, or have you conveniently forgotten?'

Adam shook his head. 'No, I haven't forgotten. But for the

legalities, that marriage is already over. It's April we have to think of now.'

'You don't love Connie, do you?'

'Not in that sense.' How could he love her? How could he love anyone when he only had thoughts for Rosie? But she had thrown him aside, just like he had thrown her aside all those years ago, just like Connie had thrown her daughter aside now. Thinking of Rosie made him sad. But then a little glow came into his heart. The child was the best thing that had happened to him since Rosie. Though she may not be his own, April loved him as though she was. She had even begun to call him Daddy. And why not? Certainly she had no one else but him. And he had no one else but her. Nothing in the world would be allowed to spoil the loveliness that had grown between them.

'Adam, think what you're saying. If you don't love Connie in that way, then how can you even think of marrying her?'

'If it means keeping April, I'm prepared to do almost anything.' He got out of the chair and came round the desk. Perching on the edge of it, he regarded Ned with honest eyes. 'You're the only one I can talk to, Ned. I need to know what you think. Sometimes it takes a different point of view to spot the pitfalls. What do you think? I mean, *really* think?'

Ned thought long and hard. He knew Adam had come to adore the child, and he knew that he was not prepared to give her up without a struggle. A fight for custody would harm everyone involved, particularly the child. Connie had claimed the girl was Adam's. She could have lied just to spite her husband. Equally, she could lie again, in court, on oath. Connie was the kind of woman who would break all the rules to get what she wanted. And even now, nobody knew what it was she really wanted! Moreover, a court case like that would cost Adam a small fortune. At the end of it all, he still might not have the child. 'As you've asked me, I'll tell you exactly what I think . . .' he said now.

'So, to my mind,' he concluded, 'marrying Connie to keep the child might be the lesser of two evils.'

Adam sighed with relief. 'Everything you've just said only echoes my thoughts. I've agonised for weeks on this, Ned. At first, I wanted Connie to come home and take charge of her daughter. But gradually I began to think it could be the very worst thing that could happen to April. I've always known that Connie didn't care one way or the other about the girl; she saw her as a nuisance, someone who got in the way of what she wanted to do with her life. She even blamed April for ruining her marriage. Now she's just up and left, leaving a note claiming I'm the father. God Almighty, Ned! He might have done the child harm. He was certainly in a rage when he turned up here with her, and that's a fact.'

'So your mind's made up?'

'It is. And I'm not likely to change it.'

'Then there's nothing else to be said. But what if you don't find her?'

'I'll give it a few weeks, then I'll have to talk to a solicitor.' His face stiffened. 'But I won't let them take April away. I'm a wealthy man now. I can give her the best education that money can buy, and I'll see to it she never wants for anything. I've got the letter, signed by Connie, saying I'm the father.' His dark eyes glittered with defiance. 'Let anyone try and deny that, and they'll wish they'd never been born!'

Some time later, when Ned left, Adam returned to the living-room. Mrs Jessup was just coming back from the child's bedroom. 'She's wide awake,' she said with a patient smile, 'and she'll not sleep 'til you've been up and told her a story.' Shaking her head she began mumbling about how, 'Auntie Jessup ain't good enough to tell her a story! Auntie Jessup don't do it properly . . . not like Daddy does!' She wagged her finger at him and chortled, then shuffled off to the dining-room where she would lay the table ready for breakfast. After that, she would wash and make her way to her own room at the back of the house. There she would fall on her knees and say her prayers before gratefully falling into her bed. 'That little rascal would wear an elephant out!' she called after Adam as he went up the stairs two at a time.

He opened the door cautiously, in case April had gone to sleep. But no. As soon as he poked his head round the door, she was squealing with delight: 'Daddy! Daddy! April wants a story.'

'You should be hard and fast asleep, my girl,' Adam lovingly chided. No sooner was he seated on the edge of the bed than two thin little arms wound round his neck and his face was wet where she'd planted a sloppy kiss. 'Daddy tell April a story?' Her whole face lit up with joy on seeing him. It was the tiniest heart-shaped face, with a small upturned nose and the prettiest mouth; her fair hair curled about her neck and ears, and her huge brown eyes put him in mind of Rosie.

Suddenly the sadness had returned, and his mood was changed; though he was careful not to let the child sense it. 'Shall I tell you about someone I once knew?' he asked softly. 'A lovely creature by the name of Rosie.'

'Rosie.' The child mimicked the way he spoke her name and it was beautiful to his ears. He began. First he told her about the prince who used to be a soldier. 'The prince had fallen in love with a beautiful princess,' he went on. 'All his life he'd loved her, but while he was making up his mind to go home to her, someone else came and took the princess away.'

'Did the prince cry, Daddy?'

Not wanting to convey his own sadness to the child, he changed the story, gave it a happier ending. And soon the brown eyes closed and she was sound asleep. But as he turned away, there were tears in his own eyes. 'You were all kinds of fool,

Roach,' he told himself. 'If you'd only been half the man you are now, you might never have lost her.'

He sat in the library until the small hours. The clock struck midnight, then it was two o'clock, and now the daylight was beginning to peep over the horizon. Tired and weary, but with the tiniest hope in his heart, he took up the pen and began to write:

Dearest Rosie,

Won't you see me? There are so many things I need to say to you. So many times I've started out with the intention of coming to you. But then I've realised you would only turn me away.

With Doug imprisoned, I wonder how you're coping? Is there any way I can help? All you have to do is ask, you know that.

The man who escorted you from the courtrooms, he was a stranger to me. Is he Doug's solicitor? Was he a friend? Does he have your interests at heart? Oh, Rosie. How can I say it without it sounding wrong? I love you. As long as I live, I will always regret losing you . . .

He stared at the partly written letter, and his heart was broken. 'You bloody fool! What makes you think she'll even open it?' Torn in so many directions, he knew he could never send that letter. Now, when he voiced his thoughts aloud, he realised he had no claim on Rosie, and never would. What right have you to say such things to her, with Doug in prison and Rosie trying to make her way without him? She loves him . . . not you! You lost the right to Rosie years ago, and now it's too late. He crumpled the letter in his fist. Then, like all the letters before, when he'd poured out his heart and seen the futility of it all, he flung it in the bin. Besides, you have to think about April now, and Connie.

And how, if your plans work out, you'll soon be a married man yourself.

Later, when he lay in bed, in the quiet, he couldn't shut Rosie out of his thoughts. When he slept she was there; when he woke, and all day as he worked, she was with him, breathing every breath he took, like a tangible presence that wouldn't leave him. And though he was prepared to move heaven and earth for that dear rejected child he adored, nothing in life could compensate for having lost Rosie. And just as surely, he believed, nothing would ever bring her back to him. As he surveyed the years ahead, with or without Connie, all he could see was a great empty void that not even the child could fill. And he was desolate.

Part Two

1955

WHEN WE LOVE

Chapter Eighteen

'Let me look at you, sweetheart.' Rosie gazed down on her son, and her pride was so strong it was like a physical lump in her breast. 'My! You look so grown up,' she said, her smile enveloping him, 'It's hard to believe you've been at school for a whole year.'

During this past year he had taken on the appearance of a real little gentleman. Dressed in short grey trousers with knee-length socks, a smart dark blazer and a little cap adorned with the school badge, he was different somehow. Already she could see the man in him, and the realisation brought its own kind of regret. Somehow, Rosie couldn't help but feel that in her son's transition from bairn to boy she had lost something very precious to her, something that was gone forever and could never be recaptured.

'Oh, Mam!' Danny had acquired a habit of biting his bottom lip when he was worried. He did that now as he glanced at the mantelpiece clock and it told him they had only five minutes to get to the tram-stop. 'Miss Jackson will only shout if I'm late again,' he groaned.

Rosie feigned a look of horror, 'And we mustn't let *that* happen, must we, eh?' In fact, Miss Jackson was a kindly soul who had brought Danny's learning on in leaps and bounds, and Rosie viewed her with great respect, 'Get your overcoat on,' she told him, 'it's still snowing outside.' The snow had come with the beginning of January, bursting from the skies with a vengeance. The next day it fell steadily, and now, two days later, had lessened to a slight trickle. But the wind had grown in strength, and Rosie was wakened that morning when the windows began rattling in their frames.

Danny put on his coat. 'I don't want my scarf on,' he grumbled. 'It tickles my neck.'

'Sorry, love, but your mam wants you to wear it.' Rosie wrapped the scarf round his coat collar and tied it securely at the front. 'It's freezing out there.'

'Are *you* wearing a scarf?' He fidgeted, tugging at the scarf and grimacing.

'I'm not going out there without one, that's for sure.' Taking her long brown coat from the back of the door where she'd hung it the night before, she threw it on and quickly buttoned it up. Fishing a soft blue headsquare from the pocket, she wrapped it round her head, tying the knot tightly and tucking the ends beneath her coat collar. Next came woollen gloves. Now she felt ready to brave the elements.

Collecting a smaller pair of mittens from the sideboard drawer, she handed them to Danny. 'Here you are, young man. 'You'll need these.'

She watched him pull the mittens over his fat little hands. Satisfied, she collected her handbag from the chair, glanced round to make sure everything was ship-shape, and, propelling the boy before her, went along the passage and out into a cold wild day. 'We'd have done better to stay in bed,' she said through chattering teeth. Danny would have gladly gone off snowballing, but she dragged him back. 'There's no time for that,' she reminded him. 'We've a tram to catch.'

Peggy's voice sailed along the street. 'Hey, you bugger! Wait for me.'

Rosie was astonished. Not wanting to stand in the howling

wind, she slowed her pace until Peggy caught up. 'I thought it was your day off?'

'It was. Until your fancy man asked me to come in.' Bending her head against the wind, she shivered and moaned, 'If I'd realised how bloody cold it were, I'd have stayed where I was . . . nicely tucked up in a warm bed.'

'Robert Fellows isn't my fancy man,' Rosie reproved. 'Anyway, I didn't know he'd asked you to come in.'

'Well, you would have if only you hadn't buggered off at half-past three of an afternoon, when the rest of us were still working,' Peggy complained indignantly. 'You don't expect to know what's going on if you ain't there, do you now?'

'Aw, give over, Peggy.' Rosie said light-heartedly, 'I *start* an hour earlier, so I'm entitled to leave an hour earlier.' Lately, Peggy seemed to go out of her way to antagonise.

'Oh, I'm sorry, gal,' Peggy apologised. 'Take no notice of me. I reckon I've just got out the wrong side of the bed. Besides, if I had a lad to take care of, I expect I'd rearrange my hours an' all.' Glancing sideways at Rosie, she explained, 'There ain't no real mystery about why I'm trudging in this morning when I should be abed. All of a sudden we're one short at work, so I were asked to substitute.'

'One short. How come?'

'You know that silly little sod from stationery . . . Meg Withering, as big as a bloody ship an' ready to drop any minute?'

''Course she's not!' Rosie argued. 'She's only five months gone . . . still got two weeks before she finishes at work.'

'Aye, well, that's what she wanted everybody to think, so she could earn a few more wages. Crafty sod.' Shivering aloud, Peggy pulled her coat collar up. 'The bugger's *eight* months gone, and if your fancy man hadn't rushed her to the Infirmary in his car, happen she'd have given birth there and then, on the floor behind her counter, in full view of everybody.'

'Why didn't you tell me this last night?' Clutching Danny's hand, Rosie quickened her steps. Peggy had made them lose a few minutes and if they missed the tram they'd have to stand in the freezing cold waiting for the next one.

'I was about to. In fact, I were halfway down the street when it struck me that *he* would probably turn up any minute. I reckoned three would be a crowd, that's all.' There was just the slightest hint of envy in her voice.

Rosie still wasn't certain whether Peggy had forgiven her for spending more and more time with Robert. 'That's nonsense, and you know it,' she said sharply. 'You're always welcome in my house, whether there's anyone else there or not. And anyway, he didn't turn up, so I knew nothing about Meg Withering and her little drama.' She chuckled. 'Was it panic stations?'

Peggy giggled. 'You *could* say that. Meg were just serving this big fat fella when she grabbed at her stomach and screamed out that the baby were coming. Honest to God, you should have seen his face! He went bright red, then he went a dirty grey colour and looked like he were about to throw up. Then he turned and ran. Well, he waddled at a fast pace anyway . . . his huge arse knocking all the displays over as he went. Cor! You should have been there, talk about a mess! Still, it ain't surprising when he were as far round as the bloody gas works, and his belly hung over his shoes.' She laughed aloud, then clamped her lips shut when the cold made her catch her breath. 'Bleedin' weather!' she said through stiff lips. 'I should'a stayed in me bed.'

She lapsed into a sullen silence, but Rosie chuckled all the way to the tram-stop. There was little said until the tram pulled up outside the school where Rosie saw Danny safely off. As he went through the gates with all the other children, she called out, 'I'll see you this afternoon. Wait inside the classroom now.' He waved and nodded, and in a minute was lost in the playground amongst the other children. The teacher blew the whistle and the children quickly formed straggly lines outside the door. The tram trundled away and Danny was lost to sight. 'It doesn't seem possible he's been at school for a whole year,' Rosie said, shaking her head and thinking it seemed like only yesterday that he was a newborn in her arms.

'A year, eh?' Peggy nodded her head, blue eyes surveying Rosie with curiosity. 'That's how long you've been seeing your fancy man.' When Rosie seemed preoccupied with her own thoughts, she went on, 'I expect you'll be announcing your engagement soon, eh? Then it'll be off with the jailbird, on with the new, wedding bells and happy ever after.'

Turning in her seat, Rosie looked her in the eye, 'What's bothering you, Peggy?'

She blinked with embarrassment. 'What d'yer mean?'

'You still don't like me going out with Robert, do you?'

'It ain't up to me.'

Rosie sensed the undercurrents and didn't like what was happening. 'Look, Peggy, you and me have always been able to talk things through. Why can't you say what's really on your mind?' When Peggy remained sullen, she murmured, 'Please. You've always been like a sister to me. Don't let anybody spoil that. Not Robert, not anyone.'

Peggy looked into those troubled brown eyes and felt ashamed. 'I'm sorry, gal,' she said sincerely, 'I don't want to mar any happiness you might have found, because God only knows you deserve it. But, well, to be honest, I just don't trust the bugger.'

'It's got nothing to do with you wanting him then?' Rosie knew if she was to protect her close friendship with Peggy, it was cards on the table time. This wasn't the first occasion they'd discussed Robert Fellows, but Rosie always felt that they had only ever skirted the real issue.

Taking a deep breath, Peggy sighed. 'All right. Happen I do

still fancy him,' she admitted. 'But he ain't got the time of day for me. He never has had. So even if you were to finish with him tomorrow, it wouldn't make no difference as far as I'm concerned.'

Rosie looked away. 'I honestly don't know what to do,' she said softly, looking out of the window and watching the thickening snowflakes splash against the pavement. 'I hate it being this way between you and me.'

'Do you love him?'

'I like him a lot.' She met Peggy's gaze honestly. 'I haven't really thought too much about it.' Rosie had grown closer to Robert without even realising it. 'But he's good and kind, and Danny has really taken to him.'

'I know all that. But you're not answering my question. What I said was, do you love him?'

Rosie smiled, but it was a sad smile. 'Happen I could learn to love him, but no, I don't feel that way now.'

'Still Adam, eh?'

This time Rosie smiled widely, but said nothing.

Peggy was relentless. 'Would you wed Robert Fellows if he asked you?'

'I'm married, Peggy. Don't forget that.'

Something in Rosie's voice made Peggy regard her more closely. 'My God! He's already asked you, ain't he?'

Rosie turned away, her attention caught by a group of youths throwing snowballs at the tram. The day was grey and bleak, just like her heart. 'He asked me a week ago, when we went to the pictures,' she admitted softly, thinking it was a good job the tram was nearly empty. These days more people went on the buses. Soon the trams would all be gone, and that would be a terrible shame, she thought sadly.

'Well, you little sod!' Peggy cried in a hoarse whisper. 'And you never even said.'

'There was no point.' The reason she hadn't said anything was because she didn't really know how Peggy would react. The last thing she wanted was to hurt her friend's feelings, and anyway things were already delicate between her and Peggy. The thought of losing what she and Peggy had was a source of great pain to Rosie.

'And what did you tell him?' Peggy's voice betrayed her disappointment.

'I told him I already had a husband.'

'And what did he say?'

Rosie was reluctant to answer, because if she did she would have to tell the truth. 'Divorce him then,' Robert had said. 'I'm prepared to wait for as long as it takes.'

Peggy had guessed. 'Don't tell me. He wants you to get a divorce from Doug?'

'Something like that.'

'And will you?' Her voice was low and cynical. 'After all, it's over between you and Doug, ain't it? I mean, he's threatened to hurt you, and you ain't got no feeling left for him anyway. So you might as well put an end to it, ain't that right?'

Wisely, Rosie turned the tables. 'What would *you* do, Peggy? I mean, if you were in my shoes.'

Peggy was taken aback for a second, then she laughed. 'You know bloody well what I would do,' she confessed. 'I'd drop Doug like a hot cake, then I'd set myself up with Robert and look forward to a cushy life. *That*'s what I'd do. But then you ain't me, are you? You've got values and a high-minded sense of right and wrong. I mean, look how you took care of that bloody old battle-axe Martha Selby, even after she made your life a misery. Me? I'd have laced her fried eggs with poison and danced on her bloody grave!'

'No, you wouldn't.'

'Hmh! You've got a better opinion of me than I have of

meself, gal.' She sniffed. There was an awkward silence between them, before Peggy cuttingly remarked, 'So? I expect you'll be dumping Doug for Robert, eh?'

Before Rosie could answer the tram pulled in to the kerb. In a minute the two of them were tumbling off and rushing through the cold towards Woolworths' main doors. The warmth inside the building did little to melt Peggy's hostility. 'Well?' she asked as they wended their way between the counters, Peggy to the cloakroom and Rosie to the bottom of the stairs which would take her up to the offices. 'Do you mean to wed him?' Her blue eyes were cold as the day.

'I don't know,' Rosie answered truthfully. She had seriously toyed with the idea, but it was a complex issue, and always at the back of her mind was the fear that everything could go wrong.

'You'll be sorry if you do.' Peggy whipped her coat off. Normally she would leave Rosie with a smile on her face, but not today. Today she was unhappy. 'Like I said, I don't trust the bastard.'

'What do you mean, Peggy? *Why* don't you trust him?' Strangely enough, there were times when Rosie herself had her doubts, though she couldn't say why.

'Just a feeling, that's all. Happen it's 'cause I'm just a jealous bugger who wants him for herself, eh?' With that she swung open the doors to the cloakroom and left Rosie feeling dejected. For a minute she was tempted to follow, but then decided against it. This was neither the time nor the place for a heart to heart with Peggy. Tonight, though, after work, it would be a different matter.

Rosie was the first to arrive in the office. She hadn't been at her desk for more than five minutes when Robert came in. Striding across the office, he went straight to her and kissed her on the mouth. 'How about a meal and a show tonight?' he asked. 'Afterwards, maybe we could go back to your house.'

He sat on the edge of her desk, looking splendid in his well-tailored suit and with his fair hair neatly parted. His wide smile as always was a sight to see and his eyes sparkled. Rosie couldn't help but think about Peggy's words just now. 'I don't trust the bastard,' she had said. Now Rosie felt uneasy. 'Not tonight,' she replied.

'You still haven't given me an answer to my other question.' His smile was gone and in its place was a look of expectation. 'You promised to put me out of my misery in a week. Time's up, my lovely.' Leaning forward, he breathed in her ear, 'When can we be married?'

'There's so much to think about. It won't be easy. There's Doug and everything.' Rosie was shocked to hear herself using him as an excuse.

'You're not leading me on, are you?' Robert was smiling again.

'I wouldn't do that,' Rosie answered truthfully.

'Good. Because I wouldn't like it if you did.' He took her in his arms, and she couldn't help feeling it was good to be wanted.

The outer door swung to and in came Meg Benton, puffing and panting from the long walk up the stairs. 'By! It's cold out there,' she complained. Having taken off her coat in the cloakroom, she was still wrapped up like an eskimo, with a high-necked blouse beneath a thick woolly jumper haphazardly tucked into the waist of her long tweed skirt. She was wearing ankle boots and blowing into her frozen fingers. 'I'm getting too old to come out in this kind of weather.' Seating herself at her desk, she put on her tiny rimless spectacles and stared at Robert Fellows, who was still perched on the edge of Rosie's desk. 'Good morning, Mr Fellows,' she said in a loud bold voice. Judging by the look on her face, she obviously disapproved of the boss fraternising with the workers.

'Good morning to you, Mrs Benton,' he returned, at once clambering from the desk and straightening his tie.

The two men came in together. Mr Mortimer's eyes were watering from the cold and he coughed all the way to his desk. Horace Sykes took a minute to rub the warmth back into his balding head, then glanced at Rosie, shifted his gaze to Robert and remarked rather loudly to Mr Mortimer, 'Some of us are born to work, and some of us would rather play!' With that, he went to the filing cabinet and slammed the drawers about.

Putting his two hands on Rosie's desk, Robert Fellows leaned towards her. 'I'll pop round to your house this evening,' he told her softly. 'I promise you, my lovely, I won't take no for an answer.' He winked and hurried away, and she was left in a turmoil.

'You want to be careful,' Meg Benton warned quietly. 'Men like that can get you in trouble.'

Rosie smiled and bent her head to her work. Strange, she thought, because Meg's warning was the second of its kind today. She was beginning to wonder whether others knew more about Robert than she did.

As always when Rosie buried herself in her work, the morning was gone before she knew it. The telephone started ringing at nine o'clock, and it was still intermittently ringing at five minutes to twelve, when she thankfully made her way down to the canteen.

Halfway down the stairs she looked out of the window. The snow had stopped falling, and the watery sun was already breaking through. 'Thank God for that!' she exclaimed, running down the stairs. She was in a hurry to see Peggy. They had parted on bad terms, and it had worried Rosie all morning.

The canteen was always busy at this time of day, and there was already a long queue for the tea counter. Searching it for Peggy and realising she was nowhere to be seen, Rosie tapped one of Peggy's work colleagues on the shoulder – a big girl with huge bosoms, and peroxide hair piled high on her head. 'Have you seen Peggy?' Rosie asked. The girl shook her head. But from further along the queue came the reply, 'She's up with Mr Fellows. Been up there over an hour now she has. And I'm bloody well fed up, because I'm having to cover her counter as well as my own. "Where the bleedin' hell is she?" you ask. And that's what I'd like to know an' all!'

Rosie was astonished. What on earth was Peggy doing with Robert for over an hour? Surely to God she wasn't in trouble? How could he reprimand her for anything when she had turned out 'specially today to cover for an absent colleague? On top of that Peggy was a loyal and conscientious worker.

As she neared Robert's office, Rosie forced herself to be calm. It wasn't unusual for one of the floor staff to be called into the office; often it was merely a matter of quality assessment, or something to do with holiday periods, and sometimes it was the member of staff who called the interview. But an hour! Rosie felt instinctively there was something very wrong here.

At the same moment as she reached the top of the stairs, Robert came out of his office. 'Rosie!' He came towards her, eyes glowing with pleasure. 'Were you coming to see me? Have you decided to make an honest man of me then?' He would have kissed her but she drew away.

Glancing through the open office door, Rosie was surprised to see that except for his secretary, who was preparing to leave for her lunch, the room was empty. 'Where's Peggy?' she asked, turning to Robert with a puzzled expression.

He smiled, then gently ran his fingers down her face. Now he was drawing her towards the office. 'She's gone.'

'Gone?' Rosie was vaguely aware of the secretary passing them on her way out. 'Gone where? Isn't she well? Is she in some kind of trouble?' She and Robert were facing each other and he appeared to be concerned by her distress.

'No, my lovely,' he said. 'She is not in trouble, and as far as

I know she's quite well. Or at least she was when she left me.'

'If she isn't in trouble and she's not ill, where is she?' Rosie was growing impatient, sure in her mind that whatever was wrong with Peggy, it must have something to do with the conversation they'd had that morning. Certainly Peggy had not been in her usual bright mood when they parted. In fact, now that she thought more deeply on it, Peggy hadn't been happy for some time. A sense of guilt spiralled up in Rosie. Maybe she should have been more tactful about her relationship with Robert? Happen it would have been better if she had tried to find another job? Whatever the reason for Peggy's problems, Rosie somehow felt it was all her fault.

'Sit down, Rosie.' Robert Fellows stood over her while she sank into the chair then sat on the desk before her, his legs stretched out and his face concerned. 'There's nothing at all wrong with your friend,' he assured her. 'Peggy came to see me about a certain professional matter.' He sighed. 'All right, my lovely, in the circumstances I'm sure she wouldn't mind my confiding in you. Peggy Lewis is a bright young woman who wants to better herself. Apparently she's been toying with the idea of applying for a training post in London.' He saw the light dawning in Rosie's eyes and quickly prompted, 'You know the one . . . a year's intensive training in one of our bigger stores, with a view to management?'

Rosie nodded. 'I pinned the details on the notice board myself,' she recalled. 'And you say Peggy's applied for it? Funny, she never mentioned it.' Something occurred to her then. 'You're not telling me she's gone straightaway? I mean, how could she?'

'She *wanted* to leave right away. I rang head office, told them she was the perfect candidate, and of course there was no objection. So, yes, she's probably on her way home to pack. After that no doubt she'll be travelling to London before the evening. As I say, it's all been arranged, right down to her accommodation.'

He grinned handsomely. 'If it's handled right, these things can be done very quickly.'

Rosie was stunned. 'Was it you? Did you encourage her?' Suspicions were forming in her mind. He appeared too smug about the whole thing, too full of his own importance. Too pleased at the outcome.

'Shame on you, Rosie!' His eyes grew round with horror. 'What are you saying?' He came to her and placed his hands either side of her face. Expecting her to raise her face to his, he was shocked when she tugged away. Standing to confront him, she said angrily, 'There's something about you that seems too good to be true. I couldn't see it before because I was too blind and too hungry for affection. But now I'm beginning to wonder. Peggy's warned me about you all along. You can't deny it would be better for you if she was a long way away from here, far enough away so she can't come between us.'

Taken aback, he confessed, 'No, I won't deny that. It's also no secret she's made eyes at me in the past and I've made it clear I'm not interested. She's never forgiven me for that, and you know it.' His voice softened. 'You can't hold me to blame for whatever decisions she makes. And, as God's my judge, all I care about is you and me, and our future together.'

'I wish I could believe that.' Rosie wasn't altogether convinced.

Groaning, he declared, 'Believe me, Rosie, I had nothing whatsoever to do with it. I was just as surprised as you are. Peggy asked to see me, and I honestly didn't have a clue what it was all about until she requested to be transferred to London at the earliest opportunity. I did what she asked, and that was all there was to it, I swear.' He sounded desolate.

'I'd best get back to my work.'

'Oh, look, Rosie, have you had your lunch? We could go out somewhere. What do you say?'

'I'm not hungry. Besides, there's a lot to do before I collect

Danny.' And a lot to do before she knew what was behind Peggy's disappearance, she thought worriedly.

'All right, my lovely. Have it your way.' Putting his arms round her, he drew her from the chair. 'I do love you, you know.' His mouth was close to her face, and he stole a kiss. Though he regretted it when Rosie shrank away. 'It's clear you're not in the mood for company,' he said, releasing her. 'But I will see you tonight, won't I? You haven't forgotten I'm still waiting for an answer?'

She looked at him then, at his forlorn face and bright eager eyes, and her heart melted a little. Perhaps she was being unjustly hard on him? After all, it wasn't his fault if Peggy had decided to up and off. What was more, she must have sneaked out through the tradesman's entrance or Rosie would have seen her leaving. 'I haven't forgotten,' she said softly. 'Make it around eight o'clock. I know Danny will want to see you before he goes to bed.' She laughed, and he thought she was never more lovely. 'You'll be taken through every lesson he's had today,' she warned.

'I'll look forward to that,' he promised. And she believed him. She wasn't to know that on the stroke of three that afternoon, something would happen to betray to her the kind of man he really was.

Meg Benton bustled out of the office with a fistful of papers. Two minutes later she bustled back in again. 'Honestly!' Slamming the papers down on her desk, she groaned, 'It's no wonder the work never gets done around here. I've got a whole pile of queries which I want Mr Fellows to check, and there's no sign of him.'

Mr Mortimer coughed and said, 'That's because he's in consultation with the floor manager downstairs.' Smiling irritatingly, he reminded her, 'It's almost three o'clock, my dear. Have you forgotten they meet every week at this time?'

'Bloody management!' muttered Horace Sykes, scratching his near-bald head. 'I wouldn't give a shilling for any of 'em.'

'What about his secretary then?' demanded Meg Benton. 'She's nowhere to be seen either.' She glanced at Rosie, but looked away when the girl appeared too busy to hear.

'You know what they say?' interrupted Mr Mortimer sulkily. 'While the cat's away, the mice will play.'

Resuming her seat, Meg Benton put the papers aside. When the telephone began ringing, she warned, 'If that's a call that should be going through to *his* office, I'll scream down the line!' It was. And she didn't. Instead, she spoke in a very refined and polite manner that made the other three chuckle. Though when she put the phone down, she had plenty to say.

For the next ten minutes, the phone constantly rang, and each time the call was for Mr Fellows. 'That's it!' Flushed with anger, Meg Benton pushed her chair back and stood up. 'I haven't even had time to pick up a pen, and my work is mounting by the minute.' Striding to the door, she declared, 'I intend to find that secretary and give her a piece of my mind.' With that she was soon gone and the others, including Rosie, couldn't help but laugh.

Rosie was eager to be done and get home. She hoped Peggy hadn't yet gone because there was a great deal she had to say to her. Feverishly she tore into the last pile of stock-sheets, moaning beneath her breath when the jangling ring of the phone interrupted her line of thought. 'Good afternoon. May I help you?' Pressing the phone to her ear, she tried to write with her other hand. It was impossible so she paid attention to the voice at the other end. It was a woman's voice, soft and pleasant. 'I'd like to speak to Mr Fellows, please?' she said.

'I'm sorry, but Mr Fellows is in a meeting right now.'

'Oh!' There was a pause. Then, 'Who am I talking to?'

'This is Rosie Selby. Would you like to leave a message for

him? I'll make certain he gets it the minute he returns to his office.'

'Could you please put me through to his secretary?'

Rosie sighed. 'I'm sorry, but she's out of the office right now. She should be back any minute. Perhaps if you called again later?'

There was a sigh followed by a request that shocked Rosie to the core. 'I have to go out in a minute so I'd better leave a message. Would you please tell him his wife phoned? Has he managed to acquire a house for us yet? Ask him to ring me this evening, would you? Oh, and tell him his daughter Sadie sends her love. Thank you so much.'

'Good Lord, you've gone a pale shade of grey!' Mr Mortimer peeped at Rosie from beneath his reading glasses. 'An irate customer, was it?'

Even Horace Sykes was made to look up, mouth open to deliver some scathing comment. The fact that Rosie was sitting bolt upright, phone in hand and all the colour drained from her face, struck him dumb. Without a word he bent his head and resumed his work.

Just then Meg returned. 'Would you believe she was downstairs chatting to the floor supervisor?' Falling heavily into her chair, she explained, 'Apparently, Mr Fellows has put his foot in it by allowing someone to leave at short notice, at a time when we're desperate for floor staff.' When nobody commented, she grunted, scraped forward her papers, and began scribbling. 'Anyway, she's back at her desk now, so we shouldn't be bothered with any more of her calls, thank goodness!'

Rosie's mind was preoccupied by the woman's words . . . 'Tell him his wife phoned . . . His daughter Sadie sends her love.' She couldn't think straight. It was impossible to settle her thoughts enough to continue with her work. When she glanced up at the clock, she was greatly relieved to see that it was almost three-thirty. 'I'll be away now,' she said, collecting her belongings together.

'What? There's still a few minutes to go yet.' Horace Sykes had found his tongue, and it was as sharp as ever.

'You get off, my dear,' Meg Benton said. 'If the truth be told, you do more work than the three of us put together.' Glaring at the little man, she silently dared him to say another word.

When Rosie was out of the door, however, a little argument ensued. It took only a few chosen words to silence the two men, and for the remainder of the afternoon the atmosphere was so thick it could have been cut with a knife.

All the way home, Rosie tried to reason with herself. Was it a mistake? Had the woman somehow got the wrong number? Did she really say 'Mr Fellows', and did she mean Robert? 'You're a fool, Rosie gal,' she muttered as she looked out of the tram window. 'Peggy was right about him, and you've fallen for the worst trick of all.'

Aware that she was talking aloud she glanced nervously about. With the exception of an old man who was buried in his racing paper, the tram was empty. Just as well, she thought, or they'll have me locked away for being out of my mind. She chuckled to herself. She *was* out of her mind, or she'd have seen him for what he was months ago!

The bad feelings began to subside, and in their place came a calm and rational mood. He didn't know she had spoken to his wife. So, as far as he was concerned, nothing had changed, and he was coming round to see her tonight. Want an answer to your 'proposal', do you? she thought bitterly. Stepping off the tram and on to the pavement, she went straight to the school gates. As she scoured the yard for a sight of her son, she forced all thoughts of Robert Fellows out of her mind.

The children were pouring out of the school doorway. Danny

saw her and ran forward. 'Mam, look what I've done today!' Wide-eyed and excited, he raised a huge square of paper for her to see. It was a colourful drawing of nothing she could identify. 'Why! That's lovely!' she exclaimed, her face wreathed in a smile. Taking the paper between her hands she turned it this way then that, and still she couldn't understand what the coloured blobs were meant to signify.

'It's *you*!' he told her, eyes shining.

'Well, of course it is,' she returned, giving him a hug, 'I knew that all along.'

There wasn't another tram for fifteen minutes, but the bus was waiting as they ran up the street. 'I'm hungry,' Danny moaned, clambering into the seat beside her. When Rosie produced a digestive biscuit wrapped in foil from her handbag, he sat back in the seat and contentedly nibbled at its edges all the way home. When they got off the bus at the end of Castle Street, he popped the last bit in his mouth and grinned up at her. 'I love you,' he said.

'Only because I gave you a biscuit,' she teased. Then she grabbed his hand tightly and hurried him away. The wind was as keen as ever, and the thought of a cosy fire grew more and more welcome the nearer they got to home.

Rosie's first stop was Peggy's house. 'I need to talk with her,' she told Peggy's mam, who quickly ushered her and the boy in out of the cold. She would have taken them into the parlour, but Rosie graciously refused. Her instinct told her that Peggy was not here.

'I'm sorry, luv, but she's gone . . . been gone this past hour.' The older woman chuckled. 'By! That were a turn up for the books, eh? Our Peggy's gone on a training course to London. The next thing you know she'll be after the manager's job.' Her eyes grew round as two silver shillings. 'She's done her old mam proud, that she has.'

Rosie was disappointed to have missed her. 'Did she say where she'll be staying?'

'Nope!' She shook her head, frowning hard. 'But I expect I'll know soon enough. She's promised that soon as ever she's settled, she'll write, and if our Peggy says she'll write, then she will.' Suddenly she was going into the parlour at a run. 'I nearly forgot. She's left a note for you.'

She disappeared into the far room. For the next few seconds Danny hid behind Rosie's skirt when Peggy's Mam could be heard shouting and bawling at one of the children, 'Clean up this bloody mess, unless you want yer arse belted!'

It wasn't long before she came rushing out again. Handing a long white envelope to Rosie, she explained, 'Peggy said I was to give you this the minute you came round.' She peered at Rosie through curious eyes. 'You two fallen out, have yer?'

'We had a few words,' Rosie admitted. Waving the letter in the air, she added hopefully, 'Happen this will put it right.'

'Aye, happen. But I wouldn't count on it, lass. I'll not ask what's come atween yer, but I know this much . . . our Peggy can be a stubborn little sod when she's put out.' She shook her head and saw Rosie to the pavement. 'Get away in, luv. It's enough to freeze the balls off a pawnshop sign.' Without further ado she slammed the door shut and, even as Rosie and her son walked away, the dear soul could be heard threatening blue murder at one of her hapless brood.

Rosie would have opened the letter straight away, but Danny was shivering and hungry, and so was she. 'Come on, sweetheart,' she told him, reluctantly placing the letter in a drawer. 'You lay the table while I light the fire.'

As always Rosie had already laid the paper and kindling wood before she went to work that morning, so the fire was quickly alight. Danny slowly but happily set about laying the table although he had the knives and forks round the wrong way, and brought out pudding dishes for dinner plates. But Rosie was grateful, and told him so. Besides, it took only a minute for him to rectify his mistakes.

Soon the living room was warm as toast, and not long after the smell of meat pie and vegetables cooking in the kitchen permeated the air. 'I'm hungry!' Danny wailed, again sniffing the air.

'Do you know, so am I!' Rosie was surprised that she could even think about food after the shocks of the day. But she was even more surprised to discover she was oddly relieved that Robert was already married. This way she was off the hook. She even chuckled as she went about her work. Wait until she told Peggy! No doubt her reaction would be: 'Told you so.' But Rosie wouldn't mind a bit. In fact, she felt she deserved it.

Within an hour of arriving home, the meal was set before them, and they ate heartily. 'What else did you do at school?' Rosie asked with interest.

'I spilled paint all over Bobby Dixon,' he announced proudly. Seeing the horror on Rosie's face, he giggled. 'We all painted his picture, and Susie Lock got jealous and knocked my paint tray over, and it went all across my drawing.' He pulled a face. 'I don't like her any more.'

'Oh, Danny, I'm sure it was an accident.'

'No, it weren't. She did it because I wouldn't kiss her in the playground.' Picking up a piece of pastry he pushed it into his mouth and would have gone on muttering, but Rosie told him to finish his dinner and they could talk afterwards. Unable to speak, he nodded his head and forked another piece of pie into his mouth. When his cheeks bulged out and his eyes began to pop, Rosie warned him not to take such big bites or he might choke. He heeded her warning, and the meal was finished in silence.

Insisting he should help, Danny carried his own plate to the kitchen where Rosie was already running the hot water into the bowl ready for washing up. 'After everything's put away, you can tell me what else you did at school,' she invited.

'Will you read me a story?'

'If you like.'

'Will you read me Auntie Peggy's note?'

'I don't think so, sweetheart,' she said solemnly.

'Why did you and Auntie Peggy fall out?'

'Who said we have?'

'Her mam.'

She nodded. 'Oh, so you heard that, did you?' Dropping the dishcloth into the water, she wiped her hands and put them on his shoulders. 'You know how you fell out with Susie Lock at school today?'

'I hate her!'

Rosie smiled. 'Do you *really* hate her? Do you think she *meant* to spill that paint over your drawing?'

He shrugged his shoulders. 'I 'spect not.'

'So she's forgiven, eh?'

'I 'spect so.'

'Why?'

He looked astonished that she should even ask such a thing. ''Cause she's my friend!'

'That's right, Danny. And Peggy's *my* best friend. We did have a falling out, but I hope it won't spoil our friendship either.' She went to the sideboard. With trembling fingers, she took out the envelope and opened it. The note inside was short and to the point:

Dear Rosie,

You may think I had no right to say the things I said. And you may think I never stood a chance with Robert Fellows. All I know is he had started noticing me. Then you came along, and I had no chance at all. By the time you read this I'll be on my way to London. No doubt you already know all about it, seeing how close you are to *him*.

Don't try and contact me, because I've got a lot of thinking to do.

Peggy.

'Oh, Peggy!' Rosie was desolate. It was so ironic, especially when Robert was already married and had no right to promise either of them anything.

'Is she still friends, Mam?' Danny came in, covered in suds and the front of his jumper soaking wet. 'Has she gone away for ever and ever?'

'We'll see.' Rosie's bright voice belied her true feelings. Taking off his jumper and draping it over the chair in front of the fire, she told him softly, 'Good friends don't ever say goodbye, do they?' She hoped not. Oh, she really hoped not.

At half-past eight, Danny was ready for bed. Rosie read him a story about a little boy who went on a great adventure, and before she reached the last page he was fast asleep. 'Goodnight, son,' she murmured, tucking the blanket about his shoulders.

She then dimmed the light and went on tiptoe into the bathroom. Here she bathed and put on her dressing-gown. She too was ready for an early night, and it was obvious Robert had changed his mind about calling. 'More's the pity,' she said, glancing out of the window and down the street. 'I was looking forward to passing on your wife's message!'

Downstairs, she tucked herself into the big old armchair and settled down to read the book which she had bought a few days before. It was a romance, and somehow it only reminded her of Adam and what she herself had lost. Disillusioned, she dropped it in the drawer and re-read Peggy's letter. 'All I can do is wait for you to come to me,' she said. After that, she sat in the chair, raised her legs beneath her chin, criss-crossed her arms round them and stared forlornly into the fire, watching the flames leaping and dancing, and wondering how poor folk ever managed to keep warm on a night such as this.

With the warmth fanning her face into a rosy pink glow, making her deliciously sleepy, and her far-off thoughts carrying her first to Peggy then to Adam, she didn't hear the knock at the door. When it sounded again, this time with more determination, she sat up, startled. A glance at the clock told her that it was almost ten-fifteen. 'Good God above, whoever's that at this time of night?' Springing from her chair, she drew her dressing-gown closer about her and went along the passage to the front door. 'Who's there?' If Peggy had been home, she would have assumed it was her. Certainly it was too late for Robert Fellows to come calling.

'It's me . . . Robert.' At once she recognised his voice. 'I'm sorry it's so late,' he apologised in lower tones. 'Let me in, my lovely. It's freezing out here.'

The tiniest smile crept over her face as she opened the door, but when he looked at her the smile was radiant. 'Robert! It doesn't matter whether it's late or not,' she cooed coyly, 'I'm just so pleased to see you.' He would have taken her in his arms but she quickly closed the door and went before him down the passage. 'I was just thinking about you,' she lied, coming into the room and watching him take off his coat. 'I've got the answer you've been waiting for.' Now she let him take her in his arms and kiss her. She returned his kiss passionately and was secretly delighted when she felt him harden against her.

'You've decided to marry me?' he declared eagerly, gazing down on her with the look of a cat who's got the cream.

'How could any woman resist?' she purred, and he kissed her again.

'Why don't we celebrate . . . let me spend the night?' His

hands were probing beneath her dressing-gown, exciting and repulsing her all at once.

'Why not?' she murmured. 'Especially now that we're to be wed.' She opened her gown and he was shocked by her beauty; the taut pert breasts and the long shapely legs, the tiny waist and that dark enticing area between her thighs. Groaning, he gathered her to him. 'I've been thinking about you all day,' he whispered in her ear. 'Wanting you until I'd go half-crazy.' Quickly, he began to undress. He didn't see her smiling to herself.

When the two of them were naked, she held him off a moment longer. 'I'm so looking forward to being your wife,' she said softly. 'Mrs Fellows . . . it has a nice ring to it, don't you think?'

'Must you drive me mad?' He was kissing her hair, her eyes and ears, murmuring words of endearment, while she was pushing at his chest with the flat of her hands, and rolling her lovely brown eyes with childish excitement. 'I think I'll have my dress hand-made . . . you can afford that, can't you, Robert?' When he groaned and nodded, she went on, still resisting when he would have pushed her to the floor. 'And where shall we live? I'd like a big house in the country. Can you afford that too, Robert?' He nodded again, this time succeeding in laying her beneath him. He was about to push into her when she said in a low trembling voice, 'Of course, your wife won't like it. I mean . . . hasn't she been waiting for you to find a house for her . . . and your daughter Sadie?' Her eyes darkened with anger as they looked up, meeting his horrified gaze calmly.

His face was stark white in the firelight. 'How did you find out?' His voice was harsh and broken as he shivered with fright.

Lowering her gaze, Rosie saw that his member, which had been large and erect, was now shrivelled. It gave her a curious sense of satisfaction. 'I'm sorry if I spoiled your enjoyment,' she said cuttingly, getting up to replace her gown, 'I think you'd better go.' Fastening the belt around her waist, she gazed down at him with contempt.

'Bitch!'

'Don't come to my house ever again,' she warned.

He quickly dressed. When he was ready to leave he boldly suggested, 'Tomorrow, when we've both calmed down, perhaps we can talk this through? I could take you to lunch. I know a nice little place on the Preston New Road . . .'

While he was talking, Rosie was thinking ahead. It was obvious he'd had a great shock. It was also obvious that he would still pursue her for his own ends. Men like him never gave up their quarry. 'I won't be in tomorrow,' she said. 'Nor any other day. In fact, you can send me my cards and money owing.'

'You'll regret this, I promise you.'

'I'm already regretting it.' With that she opened the front door and pointed to the cold black night. 'Like I said . . . don't ever come round here again.'

As he brushed past her, he murmured, 'You're a fool, Rosie!'

'No,' she corrected him, 'I've *been* a fool. Not any more though.' That said, she physically pushed him out of the door and closed it against him.

While Rosie returned to her cosy parlour, Robert climbed into his car, his face like thunder and his heart as black as night. 'You'll be sorry, Rosie.' He smiled, his white teeth shining in the moonlight. 'You *will* be sorry!' He started the engine, and was still smiling wickedly as he turned out of the street.

Rosie had made a bad enemy. The consequences of this night would turn her world upside down.

Chapter Nineteen

Adam had interviewed at least twelve suitable men since Monday. It was now six o'clock on Friday evening and he was facing the final candidate. The man seated before him was in his early-thirties, broad of back and experienced in the coal-business. 'You'll have no cause to complain about me,' he promised now. 'Like I said, Mr Roach, I can lift a full sack of coal better than any man. I use a shovel like it were part of my own arm, and I'm trustworthy as they come.'

'Do you have a family?' Almost the minute this man had walked through the door, Adam had taken to him. Over the years he had learned to trust his instincts. He trusted them now, believing Roger Leyton to be the kind of fellow he was looking for. Built like a bull elephant, he was also likeable and intelligent.

A flicker of doubt crossed the man's face. 'I have a woman,' he said. 'Hopefully, the family will come later.'

'I see.' Adam had sensed the man's change of mood, and realised there was something painful there. Never one to pry where he wasn't wanted, he stood up to shake the man's hand. 'I'm glad you responded to the advert,' he said.

The man looked disappointed. 'Will I hear from you?'

Adam walked him to the door. As the man passed to leave, he

told him, 'Report to me at six o'clock four weeks from Monday. The job's yours if you want it.'

Relief appeared on the man's face. 'How can I thank you?'

'By proving I've done the right thing in taking you on.'

'I'll do that right enough, don't you worry,' he said. Then he crossed the yard at a run and went down the street whistling a merry tune.

Ned looked up as Adam approached. 'By the look of it, you've given him the job.'

'He were the best man for it, that's why.' Slapping Ned on the back, Adam invited him inside. The yard was empty now. As usual, Ned was the last to leave.

Dropping his shovel into the bay, he shook the coal-dust from his clothes and followed Adam through to the office. 'Now then, happen you'll tell me what you're up to?' he suggested, pointing his thumb to the outer yard. 'There's no vacancy out there, yet you've taken on four new men to start in a month's time. There's summat up, ain't there, you artful bugger?'

While Ned talked, Adam brewed a strong pot of coffee. He poured the dark liquid into the mugs, adding milk and sugar as he pondered on Ned's words. 'You're right,' he began. 'There *is* summat up, as you put it.' Handing Ned one of the mugs, he took his own and sat on the edge of the desk. 'I'm not telling you anything you don't already know when I remind you how a man by the name of Len Sutcliffe has carved quite a business for himself. To tell you the truth, Ned, if I hadn't nipped in there when I did, he'd have snapped up many of the big contracts.'

'Len Sutcliffe?' Ned's expression hardened. 'By! He spreads his wings, don't he, eh? That bugger has a habit o' moving in on the lame, and sucking at their blood, and I should know. Thanks to you, though, he got his nose pushed well out of joint, I'm happy to say.'

Adam took a long warming gulp of his coffee, his dark eyes

regarding Ned over the brim of his mug. Presently, he put the mug on the table before saying, 'Well now, you might be happy to know that he's got his own come-uppance, because I've just bought him out, lock, stock and barrel.' He grinned widely, cocking his head at Ned, and taking delight in the look that came over the other man's face.

Ned was on his feet in an instant. 'You sly bugger, and you never said a word!' he cried jubilantly. Wrapping his two huge hands over Adam's, he shook it up and down. 'By! But you're a canny businessman, Adam Roach, that you are!'

'There's still a lot to sort out. And I'm keeping the name Sutcliffe's,' Adam informed him. 'At least until I've got it running on the straight and narrow. It's a well-respected name, and there are still those who are fiercely protective of Sutcliffe himself. There are debts to settle and bridges to cross before I'll risk putting my own name on the trucks and letter-heads.'

Ned was back in his seat now, his brow furrowed as he listened to Adam's plans. 'I think you're right,' he agreed. 'Sutcliffe is a powerful name in coal-merchanting, and there are still those who haven't forgiven you for snatching my contracts from under his nose.' Leaning forward, he asked in a low voice, 'But what of Sutcliffe himself? You must know he's the kind of man who wouldn't hesitate to spread the poison about. It wouldn't matter a jot to him that you'd saved his bacon. He's a spiteful nasty bugger when all's said and done.'

'You've no need to worry on that score,' Adam told him confidentially. 'I'm one step ahead of him there. It's all written into the contract of sale. One false move from him, one malicious word in the wrong quarter, and it'll cost him every penny he's got.' Adam levelled his gaze at the other man. There was something more important he had to say. 'As far as I understand, Sutcliffe intends to move right away. However, we do have another problem, and I'm hoping you can help me there, Ned.'

Since the deal was done, Adam had agonised over a particular quandary. To his mind, there was only one man besides himself who could turn Sutcliffe's business around. That man was Ned. But, for various reasons, Adam was reluctant to broach the subject. But broach it he must, so taking a deep breath, he declared confidently, 'I want you to run the Sutcliffe contracts.'

Ned was shocked silent. He stared at Adam with quizzical eyes, then dropped his gaze to the floor. 'I can't do it,' he said.

Adam couldn't hide his disappointment. 'I understand,' he replied. 'I had to ask though, but I don't want you to fret on it.'

Ned shook his head. 'I'd *like* to help you out, son,' he said sorrowfully, 'because God knows you've done enough for me. But it's memories, you see? I honestly don't think I could go back.'

'Then it's enough said, and I'm sorry I asked you. It was wrong of me to put you in that position.' Secretly, Adam still hoped Ned would reconsider. He felt it would be good for him to face the things that haunted him still, and he could only do that if he went back to where it had all taken place. Besides, with Doug in prison, it would be comforting for Rosie to have Ned close at hand.

Still, he respected and loved the older man, and right now, he half regretted ever raising the subject. 'Tell you what,' he said, his mind racing ahead with an idea. 'why don't you and I meet in the pub later, have a pint or two, and you can give me the benefit of your experience? After all, I've a mountain of decisions to make in the next month.'

Ned shook his head. 'I've already decided to have a night in,' he apologised. 'But I'm here now, so if you've any other ideas to bounce off me, I'm in no hurry.'

Adam laid out his plans then for how he meant to build up Sutcliffe's round and eventually merge it with his own. He told Ned he intended to send four of his most trusted and able men to get it off the ground. 'I've yet to approach them about it, but none of them has a family, and as far as I can tell, they'd have no objection to a spell away. The four new recruits will come here in their place.'

'And who will you send to manage?' In spite of himself, Ned was curious. Not realising that Adam had counted on that, he fell headfirst into the trap.

'If you didn't want it, I thought maybe Jack Rutherford. He's been with me from the start, and he knows the business inside out. He's good with figures, and seems to get on with everybody.'

'That's just it, son.' Ned shook his head.

'You're saying you've got reservations about him?'

'Like you say, he's a good man. But I work with him on the ground, and I reckon he falls short of what makes a good manager.'

'Oh?' In fact, Adam already knew what Ned was getting at. Though Jack was an excellent man in many ways, he was not managerial material. Suggesting him for the job was Adam's way of drawing Ned out. 'I reckon he'd be ideal.'

Ned shook his head again. 'You're wrong, son,' he insisted, standing up to make the point. 'He's *too* pally. A manager has to raise himself above that, while at the same time being accessible to the workers. It's all a matter of balance . . . discipline with respect.' He groaned. 'I'm sure I don't have to tell *you* that?'

'I'm sorry, Ned, I don't agree,' Adam fibbed. 'As far as I'm concerned, Jack's the only other man for the job. I intend to put it to him at the first opportunity.' Walking to the door, he thanked Ned. 'I hear what you say, but this time we'll have to agree to differ,' he remarked craftily. He then repeated his invitation for Ned to join him in the pub later.

'No. Like I said, I'm in for an early night.' Ned's voice was sharp and he didn't look up when he spoke.

Adam saw that as a good sign. 'Goodnight then. See you Monday,' he said. When Ned had gone, he closed the office and went through to the living room where April was waiting for him.

'Daddy kiss,' she said, wrapping her arms round his neck when he picked her up.

'There's a man waiting to see you,' Mrs Jessup told him as she lifted the child from his arms. 'I've put him in the library.'

The man was the private detective hired by Adam to trace Connie. 'I've found her,' he said, 'but it's not good news, I'm afraid.'

'You mean she won't co-operate?' Adam was at the end of his patience where Connie was concerned.

'I mean she *can't* co-operate.' He explained, 'She's in a bad way. According to the doctors, it's only a matter of days, hours even.'

Adam was frantic. 'Why in God's name didn't you phone me?'

'Because I thought it more appropriate to bring that kind of news personally. Besides, there's no time wasted. I only just found out myself, and I've come straight here.'

'Which hospital?' Reaching for the telephone, Adam began dialling. 'How long has she been there? Dear God! What happened?'

'She's in the Liverpool General . . . been there about three days, according to the pub landlord.' He could have told Adam that Connie had been earning a living as a prostitute, but in the circumstances he thought better of it. 'Run over she was, that's all I could find out.'

Just as suddenly as Adam had snatched the phone up, he slammed it down again. 'No answer!' He groaned. 'Look, get yourself off to this address.' Feverishly scribbling into a notepad, he read out the name and address of Connie's husband. 'Give him this note.' Handing the scrap of paper to the little man, he ordered, 'Be as quick as you can.'

Even before the other man was out of the door, Adam had informed Mrs Jessup that he didn't know when he would be back. In another minute he was in his car and heading towards Liverpool General. Being Friday night, the workers were pouring out of the factories and many of the roads out of town were busy with traffic. The journey seemed neverending, and he knew he would not forget it for as long as he lived. He had sent for Connie's husband, but he wasn't too hopeful that the man would have either the decency or the inclination to come. There was too much hatred there, too much water had flowed under the bridge.

He prayed all the way there, and when he was taken to see the doctor in charge, felt physically sick when told, 'I'm sorry, Mr Roach, but there is nothing else we can do.' As he walked towards the side ward, the doctor's words rang in his mind . . . Nothing else we can do . . . nothing else we can do. Try as he might, he couldn't believe that Connie was on her deathbed. Connie, that wild vibrant creature who could always laugh in the face of adversity; Connie, unfettered and free, madly infuriating, the waif who could never cope with responsibility; alive and laughing, forever young and devil-may-care. 'Dying?' The word fell from his lips. 'No!' His protest was lost in the clatter all about him. Nurses going about their daily work, doctors rushing back and forth, the lady down the corridor pushing a tea-trolley and humming a merry melody. And Adam, striding towards the room where Connie was, afraid and angry all at the same time. It wasn't true. It couldn't be!

Everything the doctor had said played over and over in his mind. According to their information, Connie had been drunk and dazed when she wandered into the road. 'There are several witnesses who all say that she didn't even look where she was going . . . could hardly stand up, said one.' The doctor went on to explain how, when the lorry hit her, Connie's internal organs were crushed beyond repair, 'I'm so sorry,' he finished. And the sorrow showed in his face.

Coming into the side ward, Adam was taken aback by the sight that met his eyes. A frail bruised figure lay buried beneath swathes of bandages. 'Gently does it,' warned the nurse. 'We've given her the strongest painkillers, but I'm afraid she's still in great discomfort.'

While the nurses discreetly withdrew, Adam came closer. There were tears in his eyes as he gazed down on what had been the prettiest face, now swollen almost beyond recognition. 'Oh, Connie . . . CONNIE!' Raising his face to the ceiling, he swallowed the choking tears. Inside he was all churned up. All this time he had been trying to find her, to lay all manner of guilt and shame at her door. Well, now it was *he* who felt guilty. *He* who was ashamed.

Desolate, he sat in the chair beside her, and held her hand. Somehow the warmth of his touch alerted her, and she opened sad eyes to look at him. 'Adam.' The voice was soft and loving, the very same, it had not changed. 'I knew you'd come to me.' Squeezing his fingers with surprising strength, she gave the merest glimmer of a smile. It cut him in two.

Returning her smile, he wanted to speak but the words wouldn't come. His eyes burned with threatened tears. But he knew he must not show them. It was when she said, 'I don't mind if you cry,' that they trickled down his face. 'What am I going to do with you, eh?' he asked softly.

'Hold me,' she said. And he did, ever so gently.

Taking her in his arms was like gathering a fragment of the past to himself. Like the past she felt brittle and delicate, yet she clung to him ferociously, flesh and blood, memories and regrets, touching his heart and breaking it.

For what seemed a lifetime he held her there, his free hand tenderly stroking her hair and his face close to hers. Suddenly she shivered in his arms and softly laughed. 'Some women always find the rotters, don't they?'

'Don't think about that now,' he begged.

Closing her eyes, she smiled. In the smallest whisper she pleaded, 'Look after her for me.' Then, before he could answer, she gave a shuddering sigh. When he looked into her quiet contented face, he knew Connie's suffering was ended for all time. 'I'll look after her,' he promised. And it was a promise from the heart.

'She left this for you.' The nurse gave him a note which Connie had dictated. In it she gave Adam all legal rights over her daughter April. 'Who else could be her father but you?' she wrote ambiguously. It was plain that she was taking the truth with her to the grave. But, whatever the truth, Connie had secured the child's future. It was her legacy to Adam, a great big thank you for all he had been to her. More than that, she knew the girl would be safe with this gentle giant, the kindest, strongest man she had ever known. She would rest now. And he would never forget her.

During the following week, Adam took it on himself to arrange the finest funeral for her. His own work took second place, and everything he had planned was postponed. 'It can wait,' he told Ned. 'Some things are more important than work.' The hardest thing was how to tell April about her mother.

'The truth, son,' Ned advised. 'You must tell the truth.' And that was what he did. Two days after Connie died, Adam broke the news to the child, telling her that her mother had been a warm and lovely creature who had placed her only child in his care before going to stay in heaven. But the child was too young to understand the full impact of what he was saying. She thought on his words, and looked at him with worried eyes, then she threw her arms round his neck and asked in a tearful voice, 'You're still my daddy, aren't you?'

His answer was to hold her close and reassure her, 'I'll always be your daddy.' A moment later she was laughing, and it was as though he had said nothing of Connie to her. But that was the best way, he decided. In the future, he would only talk about Connie if the girl asked. In his heart he was content, and so was she.

It was a bright cold day when Connie was laid to her rest. The mourners numbered two: Ned and Adam. Connie's husband never came to the hospital. Nor did he turn up for the funeral. And, as far as Adam was concerned, it was just as well. In his heart he knew Connie would not have wanted him there.

Afterwards, when it was all over, Ned told Adam he had made up his mind. 'Whenever you're ready,' he agreed. 'I feel a need to be near Rosie and the young 'un.' Something about the events of the past week had raised a great longing in him.

Adam was both delighted and sad. 'It would help us both to lose ourselves in our work,' he said. But now he regretted ever asking Ned to take on the new acquisition. For the moment he had a temporary manager running the new contracts, so he would have Ned with him for at least another month. All the same, the thought of losing his friend brought on a great feeling of loneliness. More than that, the idea that Ned would be so near to Rosie, and he so far away, was almost unbearable.

Chapter Twenty

The clerk smiled frostily. 'I'm sorry, Mrs Selby. You left work of your own accord. I'm afraid it will be weeks before we can help you.'

'But I've got a child to take care of. What are we supposed to live on in the meantime?' Rosie was desperate. It had taken a great deal of courage for her to call on the Welfare, and now here she was, being told by a scrap of a girl that she couldn't be helped. It was humiliating. 'It's not as though I haven't *tried* to find work,' she exclaimed. 'I've applied for that many jobs my fingers are worn ragged, and I must have trudged miles these past weeks.' For some reason she couldn't fathom, no one was prepared to take her on.

The clerk picked up her pen. 'I really am sorry,' she said, writing furiously on a piece of paper which she then passed to Rosie. 'I've made an appointment for a month's time. We can review the situation then.' She was already turning her gaze to the next candidate when Rosie crumpled the paper into her pocket and walked away.

'Thanks for nothing,' she muttered defiantly. But there were tears in her eyes as she emerged into the unusually warm sunshine of a February day.

Dejected, she thrust her hands into the pockets of her overcoat and made her way to the railway station. Here, she went to the café where she had parted from Adam. These days, it was the only place she could find sanctuary. There were memories here, both good and bad. Here in this cosy welcoming place she confessed her betrayal to her first and only real love. Here she had talked with him, longed for him to forgive her, and lost him because of her own foolishness. In this place she and Peggy had spent many a busy hour, gossiping and making silly plans for the future. 'What's the future now?' she asked herself. 'With Adam gone . . . Peggy gone, and now my work, the only thing that made me feel useful. What is there for me to look forward to?'

With the realisation that she was fast falling into debt and could see no way out of it, her spirits fell like a lead weight inside her. Taking off her coat, she hung it over the back of the chair. Thoughts of Danny flooded her heart, bringing a smile to her face. Suddenly the day seemed so much brighter. 'We'll manage,' she promised herself. 'Somehow we'll manage.'

'Mornin', luv. What can I get yer?' Mrs Brown was the owner of these premises, and never a day went by when she didn't have a broad smile on her face.

'A cup of tea and . . .' Rosie pressed her face to the glass cabinet. Inside was the most delicious display of fresh cakes and buns '. . . one of your Eccles cakes,' Rosie decided, and when she smiled at the round rosy face before her, her own smile was dazzling.

'Still ain't got a job then?' Mrs Brown always showed an interest in her regular customers.

Rosie shook her head. ''Fraid not,' she replied. 'But it isn't for want of trying.' In fact, today was the only day she hadn't done her usual rounds . . . all the big stores, the smaller shops, and even the factories hereabouts. 'It seems nobody's setting on.'

'Hmph! It's their loss I'd say.' Mrs Brown carefully placed Rosie's order on to the tray and slid it across the counter. 'There y'are, luv. That'll be one and ninepence.' While she got Rosie's change from half a crown, she chatted on. 'I can't understand it,' she said thoughtfully. 'You know you told me last week you'd been to that big store on the corner and they turned you down?'

'Taylor's store, you mean?' Rosie recalled it very well. In fact she had seen the advert on Monday, applied the very next day, sending her references and everything, and on Thursday she was called for interview. However, when she got there she was told there had been a mistake and that the post had already been filled. It puzzled her then, and it had puzzled her ever since.

'You went for an interview, didn't you . . . on the Thursday if I recall correctly?'

'That's right. I was told there had been a mix-up and that the job had already been given.'

Mrs Brown leaned close, as though about to impart a confidence. 'Then how come Judy Craig from Harper Street got set on, for the very same job you applied for . . . on the *Friday*?'

Rosie was astounded. 'Are you sure?'

'Sure as eggs is eggs!' She put the change into Rosie's outstretched hand and left her to think about it.

For a full hour Rosie sat at the table, her gaze following the passersby outside the window. Her thoughts however followed Mrs Brown's remarks. It seemed inconceivable to Rosie that the office manager of a large store should deliberately lie to her. Yet what else was she to think? Certainly there were any number of possibilities as to what had happened. Maybe the girl who was promised the job had failed to turn up, and they merely called the next person on the list? On top of that, maybe this Judy Craig was better qualified than she? Either way, Rosie told herself, it was no use crying over spilt milk. Maybe she'd be luckier the next time?

Yet the more she thought on it, the more she felt there was something not quite right. Why had she been turned down for so many jobs? Work of a kind that was exactly what she had been doing for Robert Fellows, and doing very well? Why was it that the employers always seemed keen until she sent in her references? And of course she was obliged to offer her previous employer as reference.

Slowly but surely, the merest glimmer of suspicion crept into her mind. The idea was so shocking that she startled the couple at the next table when she cried out, 'Surely to God, it *can't* be!'

Mrs Brown however, was not startled. She knew the reason why Rosie had given up her job, and though she suspected there was a smear campaign being mounted against her, was not one to get drawn in. Now though, hearing Rosie's exclamation, she was satisfied that she'd got the message across without actually having to spell it out.

Rosie glanced up to see the kindly soul looking at her, and her doubts vanished. Rising from her chair, she put on her coat and took the tray back to the counter. 'You knew, didn't you?' she said softly.

Mrs Brown still wouldn't be drawn. 'Mum's the word,' she replied, pressing a chubby finger to her lips. Then she took the tray and attended to the next customer.

Robert Fellows was not surprised to see Rosie. In fact he was delighted. Dismissing his secretary, he closed the door. Turning to Rosie, he said charmingly, 'I wondered how long it would be before you paid me a visit.'

Looking at him now, she was amazed that she could ever have been fooled by him. 'You've blackened my name, haven't you?' There was no use beating about the bush. She had never been surer of herself, so the best thing was to come right out and say it. 'You're giving me bad references, and don't deny it!'

'My, my! Are you telling me you can't get a job?'

He sat on the edge of his desk in that arrogant fashion she had foolishly mistaken for elegance. In that moment Rosie had to fight down an urge to knock him sideways. 'I'm warning you here and now, I intend to report you to a higher authority. If it was known what you're doing, you'd be shown the door pretty damn quick.' Inside, she was boiling with rage. Outside, she kept a cool head. It shook him just a little.

'I hope you can prove everything you're saying, my dear?' he was the cool one now. 'Wait just a minute.' He strode out of the office and returned a moment later with the entire office staff.

Lining them up, he explained in a bold voice, 'Mrs Selby has made a very serious allegation against me.' He gave a small laugh, effectively ridiculing her. 'Now then, if any of you are aware, or indeed suspect, that I am returning bad references on her behalf, or casting the slightest doubt on her ability, I want you to speak up.' The charm was gone as he glared from one to the other. Finally fixing his gaze on Rosie, he snapped, 'Apparently this vindictive young woman intends to complain to the highest authority. If that be the case, then each of you will be called on either to substantiate her story . . . or uphold my own blameless character.' With his hands behind his back, he walked down the line, smiling at each one in turn. 'Mrs Benton, what have you to say?'

Meg Benton's face grew scarlet and she could not bring herself to look at Rosie. 'I would rather not be involved, if you don't mind,' she muttered. When he stared at her, she quickly added, 'Not for one minute could I say you would do such a thing.' With every word her face grew hotter, until she was visibly uncomfortable.

Mr Mortimer shuffled his feet. 'I would have to agree with Mrs Benton,' he offered. Then he had a coughing fit and Mrs Benton had to fetch him a glass of water.

Horace Sykes grunted and complained that, 'If you'll excuse me, sir, I have better things to do with my time than to stand here and listen to spiteful accusations. As far as I can see, a respected member of this establishment is being wrongly accused, and I would have no hesitation in saying so, if called upon!' Having said his piece, he curled his bottom lip over his top one, and stood smartly to attention.

The secretary swore she had seen every reference sent out on Rosie's behalf. 'As far as I'm concerned, they gave an excellent report of your work here,' she lied brazenly.

Robert Fellows was pleased. He knew every one of his staff and how to play on their weaknesses. When all was said and done, nobody wanted to lose their livelihood. 'Thank you. That will be all,' he said, sending them all out.

'You should be ashamed.' Rosie knew she was on to a losing battle. 'Somehow you've got them all to lie for you.'

He laughed aloud. 'You really are the limit!' he told her. 'First you accuse *me*, and now you're accusing the entire office staff.' Perching himself on the edge of the desk, he wagged a finger at her. 'I think I warned you that you'd be sorry,' he murmured.

Rosie was incensed. Realising she could do nothing without involving those people outside, she decided to settle her account another way. 'I could tell your wife how you proposed to me,' she said sternly. 'But that would hurt her, and to be honest, I don't know if I could bring myself to do it.'

Relieved, Robert chuckled and her temper broke. 'You bastard!' With one great swing of her arm, she caught him sideways. He lost his balance and fell to the floor. 'I don't need your references anyway,' she said, looking down at him. 'I'm only sorry I couldn't see what a pathetic trickster you were. But they do say sometimes you can't see the wood for the trees.'

Shocked, he made no attempt to get up. Instead he asked in a small voice, 'You didn't mean it did you? About telling the wife?'

She gave him a withering look. 'I haven't decided yet,' she

declared, then straightened her shoulders and walked sedately to the door. 'Goodbye, Mr Fellows. Oh, and by the way, don't kid yourself that you're good in bed . . . more passable I'd say.'

With that scathing remark she swept out. It was only when she got to the street door that she began chuckling. She felt elated, wonderfully satisfied. Robert Fellows would never know whether she meant to contact his wife or not, and that was the way she wanted it left. 'Let the bugger suffer!' she told Mrs Brown later. 'It's what he deserves.'

For the rest of that week, Rosie lowered her sights, going round the coal-yards and into the marketplace, searching high and low for any kind of work. Unfortunately, though Robert Fellows' influence hadn't reached this far, there was no work. 'If you were a fella with arms like Popeye, I'd set yer on straightaway,' the fishmonger said. 'Them crates have to be packed, lifted, weighed and loaded on to yon lorry. It needs a man. Sorry, luv.' The message was the same wherever she went. 'Not strong enough' . . . 'Need a bloke with a broad back' . . . 'You can make the tea but these fellas swear like bloody troopers and, besides, I can't pay above four pounds a day.'

It was Friday night. Weary but not beaten, Rosie had just put Danny to bed and was sitting by the fire wondering what to do when a knock came on the door. It was Peggy's mam. 'Saw you come home earlier,' she said. 'You looked fair worn out, so I thought I'd come and keep you company for a while. What's more, I've some news that might cheer you up.'

Rosie went into the kitchen and made them each a brew of tea. 'I need cheering up,' she confirmed. 'Look at them.' Pointing to a pair of battered shoes, she explained, 'They were hardly worn when I left Woolworths, and now I can feel the pavement through the soles.'

'By!' The older woman slowly moved her head from side to

side, loudly tutting and looking sorrowful as she gazed at the shoes. 'You poor little sod, I'd no idea.'

'Oh, don't worry,' Rosie told her. 'I ain't given up yet.' It was funny, she thought, how she had reverted to saying 'ain't' when all the time she was working, she would say 'isn't'. Laying a comforting hand on the older woman's arm, she urged, 'What's this news you've got that might cheer me up then?'

'I had a letter from our Peggy . . .'

Before she could finish, Rosie's brown eyes were shining with excitement. 'Did she mention me? Is she getting on all right? Coming home for a weekend, is she? Oh, I'll be that glad to see her.' One of her greatest regrets was the rift that had developed between her and Peggy.

'No, lass, I'm sorry.' Unable to look Rosie in the eye, she lowered her gaze to the crumpled letter clutched in her hand. 'She never mentioned you at all.'

Rosie looked away. 'That's a real shame,' she said with heart-felt disappointment. 'Still, we mustn't blame her, eh? Happen she's too busy to think about me.' What she said was one thing. What she thought was another. Now, when she glanced up at the other woman, her smile was painted back on. But it didn't fool Peggy's mam.

Her eyes sparkled with anger. 'She wants a bloody good shaking if you ask me. An' I've told her that! Every time I write, I'm full of what you've been doing . . . how you've packed up your job, and now you can't seem to find another. I've told her how things is getting really difficult for you, and that you miss her.' She tutted loudly again. 'And still she makes no mention! By! I shall give her a piece of my mind when I write back, an' that's a fact.'

'No. Please don't do that.' Rosie didn't want to be the cause of bad blood between Peggy and her mam. 'If our friendship is worth anything, she'll mend it in her own good time.' Hesitating,

Rosie added softly, 'Or not at all.' The very thought of never again having Peggy for her friend was overwhelmingly sad. So she chose not to dwell on it. 'How's she doing anyway?'

'Well, that's what I came to tell you,' came the proud answer. 'She's going through the course with flying colours. According to this 'ere letter, the bosses are really pleased with her.'

Rosie nodded approvingly. 'That's the way,' she said, 'I'm glad it's turning out right for her.'

Stuffing the letter into her pinnie pocket, the older woman regarded Rosie with admiring eyes. 'You're a grand little thing,' she said. 'And I'm a silly old bugger.'

'Whatever do you mean?'

'Well! I mean fancy me boasting about how well our Peggy's doing, when here's you with two mouths to feed . . . out of work, let down by the Welfare, and not knowing where the next shilling's coming from. By! I must have me brains in me arse.'

That remark was so characteristic of Peggy that Rosie laughed out loud. 'You're a tonic, that's what you are,' she chuckled. And Peggy's mam giggled like a schoolgirl.

'Children abed, are they?' Rosie asked brightly.

'Aye. I've put 'em abed early, 'cause bed's the warmest place. Especially when that silly bloody coalman ain't brought me weekly ration. Honest to God, Rosie gal, I've a mind to change to Sutcliffe's.'

'I should think twice about *that*!' Rosie urged. 'From what I've heard, folks are leaving him in droves. What with late deliveries and high prices, it's a wonder Sutcliffe's are still in business at all.'

'According to her from the draper's, there's a new manager, and things is a lot better now. Happen I'll give him a try.' Stretching out her hands to warm them, she was mesmerised by the leaping flames and the hazy glowing coals beneath. 'That's some good coal, lass. Where'd you get it? Not from *my* coalman, I'll be bound.'

Rosie smiled wryly as she explained, 'I can't afford a full sack at a time, and the coalman won't deliver less, so I get it by the shovelful from the corner shop.'

'Cost you more in the long run, though. Surely the coalman will let you have a full sack if you pay half one week and half the next?'

'I've already tried that, but he won't do it. Not since I've lost my job, he won't.' Rosie laughed. 'Miserable old bugger! Happen I should teach him a lesson . . . get myself a truck and set up against him.'

'Aye, an' I'll bet you could show him a thing or two.' Peggy's mam saw it for the light-hearted suggestion it was. 'I mean, you had a good teacher in Ned Selby, ain't that a fact?' Unaware that Rosie had lapsed deep into thought, she yawned and stretched her fat little figure, then said, 'Right. I'd best be off, else Lord knows what that lot'll be getting up to.'

'Wait a minute,' Rosie told her. Quickly now, she tipped a small pile of coal out of the scuttle and into a cardboard box. 'Take this with you,' she offered, pushing the box into the other woman's arms. 'There's nothing worse of a morning than getting up to a cold house.'

Dumbstruck by such kindness, Peggy's mam could only stare. When she caught her breath, she gasped, 'God love and bless yer.' Tucking the box under her arm, she made her way to the front door, where she promised to return the favour the following week.

Rosie threw the bolt home and went back to the living room. Here she stood before the fireplace, her eyes searching her own features in the mirror. Something Peggy's mam said had set her thinking.

It wasn't quite thought through yet but the germ of an idea

was planted in her mind, and now it was slowly beginning to blossom. Suddenly, Rosie's face broke into a smile. 'That's it, Rosie gal!' she cried, thumping her fist against the mantelpiece. 'Buy the coal from the sidings and build up a little round of your own, why don't you?'

Staggered by the measure of her ambitions, she fell into the chair and for a long time gazed into the red raw heat of the fire. Excited and daunted all at the same time, she made herself be calm. 'Think it through,' she murmured. 'There must be dozens of folk like you . . . folk who can't afford a full bag of coal, and who have to cart the smaller bags on their back from the corner shops. On top of that they're made to pay the earth for it.' Now the idea was really beginning to take shape. 'The regular merchants won't split a bag in two. Nor are they too willing to take half payment one week, and the rest the next.' She was on her feet now, eyes glowing as bright as the coals and her heart going ten to the dozen. 'Do it, Rosie!' she whispered harshly. 'Get together every penny you can, and give it a go. You've got nothing to lose.' She chuckled. 'Well, happen the few pounds I put by for a rainy day. But the rainy day is here now. The Welfare won't help, so the money will be gone soon enough. Why not put it where it might reap rewards?'

Thrilled, she even did a little jig on the spot. After that she went to the sideboard and took out an old tea-caddy. Taking off the lid, she tipped it upside down on the table. A small bundle of notes fell out, together with some loose coins. 'How much have you got then, Rosie, gal?' she asked herself. A quick count produced twelve pounds and eighteen shillings. 'Will it be enough to carry us over?' she wondered. Only time would tell.

Carefully, she replaced the tin and went upstairs. Danny was fast and hard asleep. 'We're going into business, sunshine,' she told the sleeping form. 'What do you think to that, eh? Rosie and son . . . coal-merchants.' She smiled a soft and secret smile.

'Sounds good, don't it, eh?' she murmured. At the door she turned. 'You and me, we're off to see the man at the sidings tomorrow.' It was something to look forward to. At long last she had a real reason for rising from her bed. It was a good feeling.

Excited by her new enterprise, Rosie hardly slept a wink. Consequently, when she sat opposite Danny at the breakfast table the next morning, her head was thumping like an old steam engine and she had no appetite. 'If you don't want your cornflakes, I don't want mine either,' Danny declared. And because she wanted him to set out with a full belly that morning, she forced every mouthful down her throat.

First stop was the rag and bone man, 'A pram, you say?' he repeated, rubbing the stubble on his face. 'There's a couple down the yard, I reckon, but one's got a wheel missing, and the other ain't got no bottom to it. You can have the pair on 'em for half a crown.' He blew his nose through his fingers and regarded her with amusement. 'It's Doug Selby's missus, ain't it?' he asked meaningfully. 'Well now, I thought your old man were in prison? Been naughty, have you, eh?' He winked at her and she was nauseated.

'What I want the pram for is none of your concern,' she said, putting him smartly in his place. 'I'll give you one and six for the both.'

'There must be summat wrong with your ears. I said half a crown.'

'If you know so much about me, you must also know there's no money coming into my house.' Meeting his leer with defiance, she said, 'Two shillings. That's my best offer. Take it or leave it.'

Spitting on his hand, he held it out. 'Let's shake on it.'

'I don't think so,' she replied, grimacing.

Roaring with laughter, he took her money and pointed the way to the corner where the prams were stacked. There was a black tatty one, and a navy blue thing with a great hole in the bottom. 'We can't get no coal in there,' Danny said, getting down on his knees and peeping up at her through the pram bottom. 'And that one's only got three wheels.'

'Then we'll take a wheel off the one with no bottom, and put it on the other,' Rosie declared. She lifted the prams one at a time and examined them. The one with only three wheels had a sound base, strong enough for her purpose, at least until she could buy a hand cart. But she was thinking ahead of herself. 'One step at a time, Rosie gal,' she cautioned.

'Can you change the wheel, Mam?' Mimicking her actions, Danny was pretending to examine the articles.

'It's not a big job.' She tousled his hair. 'But we'll need a spanner.'

No sooner had she said it than he was running down the yard. A minute later he came back with the man in tow. 'The hire of a spanner will cost you sixpence,' he told her, handing it down.

'Fair enough,' she said, 'I'll give you sixpence, and you can give me a shilling.'

'How do you make that out?'

'Because I paid for two prams and I'm only taking the one.'

He coughed and stared and coughed again. 'All right,' he grumbled. 'Take the bloody spanner and we'll call it quits.'

'And I'll need that hand-shovel.' She pointed to a small black scoop lying on top of a scrap heap.

'Take the bloody thing!' he snarled. He stalked off, leaving Rosie very pleased with herself. 'This spanner will come in handy,' she told Danny. And he was never more proud of her.

The foreman at the sidings was astonished. 'What! You're telling me you mean to take that monstrosity round the streets and sell coal from it?' He walked round and round the pram, grinning from ear to ear. 'I'd rather you than me,' he declared.

'Nobody's asking you to do it,' Rosie reminded him. 'All I

want from you is a load of coal, enough to fill the pram to the very top.'

'You've got some balls, I'll give you that.' He was standing before her, hands in his pockets and a look of admiration on his face as he glanced from her to the pram and back again.

'I don't know whether to take that as an insult or a compliment,' Rosie returned. Impatient to be gone, she enquired, 'How much will it cost me . . . to fill the pram right up to the brim?'

'All depends what grade coal you're after.'

'I want the best.' Just in case he had it in mind to cheat her, Rosie reminded him, 'And don't forget I knew Ned Selby for a while, so I do know muck from gold.'

He laughed at that. 'I'm sure you do,' he confessed, 'I'm sure you do.'

Satisfied that Rosie and the boy were following, he strode to the far end of the yard. 'You'll not get better than that,' he pointed out, indicating the pile of shiny black nuggets piled high in the bay. He watched her go over and take a piece in her hand. He saw her expression fall, and knew she wasn't fooled. 'Is there a problem?' He winked at Danny, who gave him a withering look.

'I said I wanted the "best",' she retaliated angrily. 'This is too scaly. It'll spit and fizz and be gone in minutes.'

'Well now, you *do* know your coal, don't you?' he said with renewed interest. 'I'm impressed, lady.'

'I don't want you impressed. I want my pram filled. How much will it cost me?'

'Let's see now.' He scrutinised the pram, weighing up the contents in his mind. 'Three shilling . . . happen a bit more.'

Rosie stared at him in disbelief. 'Try again.'

He knew he'd met his match, 'All right, pay what you can afford. Wheel the thing over here. I'm a busy man with a yard to run, so the quicker we get it done the better.' He had enjoyed his fun. Now it was a nuisance. 'We don't normally trade this way, with folk just coming in off the streets,' he advised her. 'What's more, the merchants wouldn't like it.' He again winked at Danny, who surprised and amused him by winking back.

He stood at the door to his office as Rosie and the boy trundled off with the coal-laden pram. 'Good luck to you,' he muttered under his breath. 'You're a trier, I'll give you that. I'm buggered if you don't deserve to do all right.'

As he went back into the warmth of his office, he wondered whether he'd see her again. In fact, so successful did she become that Rosie was destined to return to his yard again and again.

First stop was Albert Street. Mrs Lewis couldn't believe her eyes. 'You're a godsend,' she declared; a wizened little thing with poor eyesight, she was virtually housebound. 'Our Katie in Bolton, well now, *she* has a lovely coal-merchant by the name of Anstee. It's a pity the ones round here aren't like him. The one I've got is such a surly devil. He'll not split a bag, you see, and he won't give credit. Being on a small income, I find it very hard to pay the price of a full bag all at once.'

'You can have as much or as little as you like from me,' Rosie explained. 'And I'm not against giving credit if needed.' Realising she had to earn this week to pay for her next load, she warned, 'I'm only just starting up, so I can't carry debt beyond a week.'

'Oh, I can pay for what I have,' came the answer. 'I don't burn much more than a couple of shovelfuls a week . . . have to ration myself, do you see?' Peering into the pram, she asked, 'Good stuff, is it? Long-burning?' Rosie reassured her and so her next question was, 'How much a shovelful . . . heaped up, mind?'

Rosie had already calculated she would need to charge two shillings a shovelful if she was to make a profit. 'Can't really do it for less,' she apologised. After all, she had to find food and pay the rent the same as anyone else.

Mrs Lewis was delighted. 'If I were you, I'd call on Mr

Runcorn at number four. He and the coalman had one blister of a row last week. Since then he's been without coal.'

Mr Runcorn had three shovelfuls. The next-door neighbour had two. And by the time Rosie got to the end of the street she was sold out. 'I can't believe it!' she laughed, hugging Danny, the two of them covered in coal-dust. 'We've sold out! Do you know what that means?'

'Are we rich?' Danny's big eyes shone like candles out of his smutty face.

Rosie was choked. She looked into that small dirty face, and her heart was full to bursting. 'What say we sit right here on the kerbside and count our earnings, eh?'

And that was just what they did. Spreading the shiny coins over Danny's grubby little palms, Rosie reckoned they had got their money back, plus a small profit. Taking the shillings which she had paid for the coal, she dropped it into her purse. 'See that, son?' she said, pointing to the remaining coins. 'That's our reward for working hard.'

His reply was to lift her own small hand and touch the blisters there. 'Your hands are bleeding, Mam,' he murmured, 'I don't like that.'

She looked at him as though seeing him for the first time, and her love for that little man almost broke her heart. Wrapping her arms around him, she tugged him into an embrace. 'If we want to be rewarded in life, we *must* work hard,' she whispered. 'We haven't made a fortune today, but it's a start. That's all we need. The rest is up to us.' As she held him close, Rosie was unaware that the tears were running down her face to create tiny rivulets through the coal-dust. 'There's no shame in hard work, son. Always remember that.'

'Yes, Mam.'

'Hungry?'

'Yes, Mam.'

Rosie smiled. 'Do you reckon we've earned a treat from the fish and chip shop?'

Danny leaped high in the air. 'I want a great big fish with a tail that hangs right out of the newspapers!'

'So do I!' she announced. And it was quick march to the fish and chip shop. 'Good Lord above! Have you been up the chimney?' asked fat Mrs Heeney as they went in.

'We've been working hard,' Danny told her proudly. 'And we've earned our reward.' At that everyone laughed, and he got an extra big fish, with an extra long tail.

'That'll put hairs on your chest,' said the man at the end of the queue. Danny told him he didn't want hairs on his chest. When he and Rosie left, the laughter followed them all the way down the street.

'Do you know what, Mam?' Danny asked, stuffing a coal-smeared chip into his mouth.

'No, but you can tell me.'

'If we had *two* prams, we'd have been twice as rich.'

The very same idea had crossed Rosie's mind. 'Or if we had a hand cart, son. Now, *that* would take three times as much coal as this old pram. What's more we only went down *one* street. There are hundreds of others yet.'

'Thousands!' He dropped a chip on the pavement and would have picked it up if Rosie hadn't stopped him.

By the time they got home, both she and her son were bone-tired. Their clothes were stripped off and put into soak. Danny was bathed and put to bed; no sooner had his head touched the pillow than he was fast asleep. A few moments later, Rosie too bathed then fell thankfully in between the clean white sheets.

But she couldn't sleep. 'Today is just the beginning,' she told herself. 'Before the month's out, I mean to have a hand cart, and a sign written on it with the name ROSIE AND SON.' The idea grew and grew, until she realised that nothing less would do.

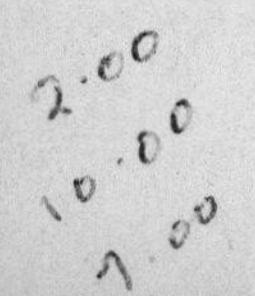

'Carting coal is what I know best,' she whispered into the darkened room.

She wondered what Adam would think of her enterprise, and smiled. Then she thought of Doug, and the smile slid away. 'Oh, Adam, if only we could turn the clock back,' she sighed. But the years had ticked away. There was no going back. Only forward. That was her path now, and she must travel it; however daunting it might be.

Doug watched the warder out of the corner of his shifty eye. He was nervous, anxious that all would not work to plan. But he wasn't reckless. Oh no! He had waited for this moment a long time. He could wait just another few minutes, long enough to make certain that everything was in place.

The big man with the rough face moved nearer. It was unbearably hot in the kitchens. The sweat ran down his face, glistening on his chin stubble and meandering along his neck in slow-moving, jerky rivulets. 'Now, Doug?' he grinned childishly, displaying an uneven row of yellow teeth. His great fists gripped the handles of the cauldron; it was a huge iron thing, blackened by use and weighing upwards of twenty pounds. 'Look!' He inclined his head towards the warder. There was another man with him now, distracting his attention, 'Taylor's there. I'll do it now.' He grew excited, edging towards Doug, the sweat pouring down his face as he begged, 'Please, Doug. Let me do it now!'

Glancing up, Doug satisfied himself that the warder's attention was taken by the third man, a slim figure, a 'trustee' lately in Doug's pay. 'I knew we could count on Taylor,' he muttered. He grinned as the big man moved in.

In that moment, Doug Selby showed the madness that had overwhelmed him. Suddenly, his broad grin became an expression of fear as the big man raised the cauldron. A moment's hesitation, then: 'For Christ's sake, get on with it!' Out of his mind with hatred and the thought of revenge, he could see nothing beyond that. Nothing else mattered.

When the cauldron came smashing down to slice off his toes, his cry of agony echoed across the kitchens and beyond, bouncing off the prison walls. Then he slithered to the floor, and all hell was let loose. 'He needs surgery of a kind we can't do here,' the doctor said. 'He'll have to be taken to an outside hospital.'

Drifting between sense and unconsciousness, he heard every word. It was exactly what he'd wanted to hear. Everything was going to plan. They gave him an injection to put him to sleep, and out of his misery. But he couldn't rest. For the umpteenth time he dreamed of his mother, of the hatred she had always felt for Rosie. He remembered how she had wanted to kill the boy. It wakened a thirst in him. She was right. She had *always* been right. And he had not seen it until it was almost too late. Oh, but it wasn't too late yet. Not yet. Not until Rosie and the boy had been punished.

Only then could he rest. When he had carried out his mother's wishes, like the good son he was.

Chapter Twenty-one

On Friday 2 March, Rosie collected Danny from school. All the way home he chatted about how he had: 'Got two stars for helping to put the ink-pots away.' He related how he and Bob Marcus had made friends again, after having several tiffs over the last few days, and Rosie told him how pleased she was at his good news.

She, however, had some good news of her own, and found it really hard to keep the secret. When they got off the bus, she almost ran him all the way home. 'How much coal did you sell today, Mam?' he asked, puffing and panting as they went at a fast pace up the street.

'More than yesterday,' she answered, with a twinkle in her brown eyes. 'And a lot more than the day before.' She too was puffing and panting. After having been at work all day, and now with a surprisingly warm sun beating down on her back, she suddenly felt exhausted. At the same time she was exhilarated by what had taken place only two hours earlier.

As they neared the house, Rosie slowed the pace. Glancing down, she watched the boy's expression turn from astonishment to curiosity. 'Look, Mam!' he cried. 'Somebody's left a hand-cart outside our house.' Breaking free from her, he ran towards it. The cart was quite small, not much longer than a pram in fact. But it was deep and cavernous, with sturdy wooden sides and huge spoked wheels. Painted white, with blue along the carved rim, it was a thing of joy. The shaft was not too long, but, being sturdy and wide, was big enough to house a small horse or donkey. But the most exciting thing of all was the name emblazoned on the side in large gold lettering . . . 'ROSIE AND SON' it read 'COAL MERCHANTS'.

'It's ours, sweetheart,' Rosie murmured, watching her son's eyes widen with disbelief as he carefully read the letters out loud.

'*Ours*?' Swinging round, he stared at her, his whole face open with surprise. 'Where'd you get it, Mam?'

'Well, you know the wheel on the pram was beginning to wobble?' He nodded so she went on, 'I took it down to the rag and bone man, to see if I could buy some other wheels.' She pointed to the handcart. 'I saw this and fell in love with it.'

'Did it cost *all* the money we've earned?'

'Not quite. It's made a great hole in it, but we're still in profit, and we're getting more customers every day. *And* I got half back on the pram what I'd paid for it.' She chuckled. 'That's not bad, especially when we've had the best out of it.'

'Can I play with the cart?' His chubby hand roved lovingly over the wheels which were taller even than he was.

'It's not a plaything.'

'Can I polish it then?'

'I don't see why not.' She had already washed and polished the cart, especially where the lettering showed. But she didn't want to dampen his enthusiasm, so told him it was a wonderful idea. 'Tea first though,' she declared. 'Then into your old togs.' Before she finished speaking, he was waiting at the door. When she turned the key in the lock he was gone, along the passage, up the stairs two steps at a time, and down a minute later, changed out of his school clothes and into his play things.

'Ready, Mam!' he called as he ran into the living room where she was waiting at table for him; the fish pie had been left gently baking while she went to the school, and now it was done to a turn.

'Wash your hands,' she told him, glancing at the dust he had gathered from the cart wheels.

Several times through the meal Rosie had to caution him. 'You'll choke yourself eating as quickly as that, my boy!' Danny sighed and took his time. But it was plain he couldn't wait to get out and into that cart. 'Go on then,' Rosie agreed. 'There's a tin of polish in the kitchen drawer, and a box of polishing rags under the sink.' Before she could draw breath he was out of the front door, with the articles held firmly in his arms. When she looked out of the front room window a minute later, he was proudly showing the cart to Peggy's younger brother and sister. 'That's me there,' he said, pointing to the word 'Son'. 'And that's my mam . . . "Rosie".'

The big lad shoved him playfully. 'We know that, you little squirt. Here, let me polish the wheels.' At first Danny resisted when the lad picked up a polishing cloth. But then the lad's pretty sister smiled at him, and he went all silly. 'Do *you* want a polishing rag?' he asked shyly. She shook her head and hurried away. 'Take no notice of her,' the lad said. 'She's a pain in the arse.'

An hour later, Danny came back in. He was covered in polishing wax and smelled like a perfume counter. 'Can *I* pull the cart tomorrow, Mam?' he asked, standing at the door with the polish in one hand and a clutch of rags in the other.

'I don't think so, sweetheart.' Taking the rags and polish from him, she drew him into the kitchen where she proceeded to take off his shirt. She had already run a bowl of hot soapy water for his wash.

'Why not? I nearly come up to your shoulder, don't I?'

'I'm afraid you'll need to grow just a bit more,' she explained. 'The cart is different from the pram, sweetheart. You see, it was much easier with the pram, because you *pushed* it along. But the cart has to be *pulled*, and besides, it will be carrying nearly three times as much coal.'

'I want to help though,' he insisted, a frown darkening his face.

'And you will, I promise. Anyway, I don't know if I could manage without you,' she said, humouring him.

'When I'm at school, you'll have to,' he solemnly reminded her.

'Well, then, I won't put so much coal in the cart, eh?' she fibbed. That seemed to satisfy him. 'Now then, get yourself washed and into your pyjamas, and we'll spend an hour on your jigsaw before bedtime.

They were halfway through the jigsaw when Danny suggested they should bring the cart into the house. 'In case somebody pinches it.'

'Now, who on earth would want to pinch our cart?' The idea was unthinkable.

'If I can't pull the cart, can I sit on it then? When it's not too heavy,' he quickly added.

''Course you can,' Rosie assured him.

'I love you, Mam,' he said, planting a sloppy kiss on her face. 'And I love our new cart.' A look of seriousness came over him. 'Are we rich yet?' he asked.

'Not yet,' she said, laughing. 'But we're doing all right.'

'When will we have enough money to buy a horse?'

'When we've sold a good few cartloads of coal, I should think.' With that they finished the jigsaw, each of them preoccupied with their own thoughts and growing more bone tired by the minute.

At half-past eight, Danny went to his bed. Rosie went to hers an hour later. 'It's up with the lark for us tomorrow,' she muttered, climbing into bed. But she wasn't daunted by the thought. In fact, she was happier than she had been in many years.

It was the dark hours when Rosie woke with a start. The circle of light travelled over the bedroom, sweeping from wall to wall and over the ceiling. At first she couldn't make out what the light was. Then she realised. It was a torch. Someone outside was shining a torch into the bedroom.

Scrambling out of bed, she turned on the overhead light and rushed across the room to open the window. Down below in the street, she could just make out the dark shapes of two men standing in front of the steps. There was another figure at the door, and a fourth one standing beside a car. It was a police car, and the men were uniformed. 'Sorry to wake you, Mrs Selby,' said the officer nearest the door. 'But we need to talk with you.'

Trembling in the cold air, Rosie put on her dressing-gown and went down to open the door. Afraid even to wonder why they were here, she merely stepped aside to let them in. The one who had first spoken to her removed his helmet and stepped inside; his colleague, a tall fellow with a round friendly face, accompanied him. The other two remained posted outside.

Once they were inside the living room, the round-faced officer addressed Rosie in quiet, considerate tones. 'Mrs Selby, isn't it? Husband by the name of Douglas Selby?'

'That's right.' Rosie trembled as she clutched her dressing-gown about her. Try as she might, she couldn't stop herself from shivering though the room was still quite warm, and the fire had not altogether died down in the grate. 'What's happened?' she asked nervously, looking from one to the other. Her stomach was churning over. She felt physically sick.

'Sit down, luv.' The round-faced officer gestured for her to sit in the armchair. 'It's not what you think.'

As Rosie sank into the chair, she wondered how he could possibly know what she was thinking. All sorts of terrible possibilities assailed her mind. Was it Ned . . . had something happened to him? *Or Adam*? Oh, dear God above! She couldn't bear to think on it. Suddenly, her instincts came into play, and every muscle in her body seemed to relax. 'It's Doug, isn't it?' Yes. She was sure now. But why were they here? Had he got into a fight and been killed? Her thoughts flew to Danny. He would suffer too. Not now, but later, when the truth came out about his daddy, he was bound to suffer.

'Yes, Mrs Selby. It is. I'm afraid your husband has escaped.' Unaware that she wasn't listening beyond those words, he went on to explain how, following an accident some weeks back, when Doug lost most of the toes on his right foot, he had been confined to hospital. 'Of course there were men posted outside, and he was regularly checked. But somehow he fooled the night duty constable, and managed to get out of the hospital unseen.'

Rosie had not heard a single word, other than that Doug was on the run. Would he try and get right away from this area? Or would he head for home? The idea that he should come here terrified her.

'Mrs Selby?' Seeing how the colour had drained from Rosie's face, the constable sat in the chair beside her, his quiet voice betraying his concern. 'Are you all right?'

Rosie mentally shook herself. 'I'm sorry, I didn't hear what you were saying?'

Patiently, he repeated everything he had told her. 'We found a trail of blood along the corridors,' he revealed. 'Your husband is obviously in urgent need of medical attention. According to the doctor, he's lost a great deal of blood, and can only get steadily weaker.'

'What do you want from me?'

'If he turns up here, or if you hear from him, we want to know. Will you do that?'

'Yes.'

'You haven't had news of him already, have you? I mean . . . he hasn't been in touch?'

'No.'

'Do you mind if we look around?'

'I don't know. My son's asleep upstairs. I don't want him frightened.'

'It's all right.' His face beamed. 'We may look like big hulking lumps, but you'd be surprised how quiet we can be.' He jerked a thumb at his colleague who went softly out of the room and up the stairs. A few minutes later he returned, went into the front room, and finally came back to report, 'Nothing, Sarge.'

'Right.' The senior officer nodded at Rosie. 'We'll leave you in peace then. Thank you for your time.' He turned to go, but looked round to instruct her. 'Lock the doors behind us, and be careful when you go about your business.'

'What do you mean?' Fear clutched at Rosie's heart.

'I don't want to worry you unduly. But, well, he did make a threat in court, didn't he?'

Rosie hadn't forgotten. 'Thank you, officer,' she said, following him to the door. 'If I hear anything . . . anything at all, I'll let you know. And don't worry, I'll be careful.' And she would. Normally she left the kitchen door unlocked of an evening. But from now on, when she and Danny were in the house alone, all the doors would be locked and bolted.

Rosie didn't go back to her bed. She wouldn't have been able to sleep anyway. So she made herself a cup of tea and piled a few more coals on the fire. 'You'll have to get past me to get to him,' she muttered. If it came to it, she would gladly lay her life on the line for that innocent little boy upstairs.

When the dawn broke through, Rosie was curled up in the

chair fast asleep. Tiredness had overtaken her. But when the sun came filtering into the room she opened her eyes. The events of the night came back to her, bringing a new and strange kind of fear.

Her waking instinct was to run upstairs to see if Danny was all right. He was stirring as she came into the room. 'All right, sweetheart?' Sitting on the edge of his bed, she stroked the tumble of hair from his forehead.

'I dreamed about our cart, Mam,' he yawned, rubbing the sleep from his eyes. 'Can we fill it right to the brim?'

'You see if we don't!' Rosie was thankful that his dreams had been much happier than her own.

Fed, washed and dressed for carting coal in worn old clothes that had seen better days, Rosie and her son emerged to a new morning. The mantelpiece clock struck seven as they went out the front door. Peggy's mam was just collecting her milk bottles from the step. 'Morning, dear,' she called. With thin straggly skeins of hair wrapped round numerous flat tin curlers, and her feet clad in enormous red slippers, she made a frightening sight. 'Saw your new cart last night. It'll do you a good turn, will that.'

Taking Danny with her, Rosie went to the other woman. 'Any news from Peggy?'

'Only the usual . . . telling me how she's going on.' She looked downcast. 'I'm sorry, lass, but there's no word for you.'

'Oh, it's not your fault,' Rosie comforted. 'Besides, that's not the only reason I came to see you.'

'Oh?'

'I wonder if you'd do something for me?'

'You've only to ask, you know that.'

'Did you hear anything untoward last night? In the early hours to be exact?'

She shook her head, sending a tin curler clattering to the

ground. Bending to retrieve it, she grunted, 'Can't say I did. But then, I've always slept like a log.' Hugging the milk bottles she asked, 'Why? Was there a disturbance?'

Rosie was glad she didn't need to go into any detail. 'I just thought I heard something,' she said. 'It's made me a bit nervous, leaving the house empty all day an' all. Could you maybe keep an eye on things?'

'Goes without saying, dear.'

Rosie put on her brightest smile. 'Right then, I'd better make tracks or the best coal will be all gone.' She hurried Danny away, sat him on the cart with his little legs dangling over the side, and trundled off down the street, dragging the cart behind her.

Peggy's mam watched until Rosie and son had turned the corner. Shaking her head, she muttered harshly, 'By! It's coming to summat when a lovely young woman like that has to fit 'atween the shafts of a cart, like a bloody donkey!' With that, she thanked her lucky stars, and went indoors to write Peggy a stinging letter.

If Peggy's mam had stayed on the doorstep a few minutes longer, she would have seen a crouched bedraggled figure sneak out of a doorway some short distance down the street. She would have seen him go, in a slow painful gait, after Rosie and the boy. And never in a million years would she have believed that Rosie's pursuer was none other than her own husband, now an escaped convict. His injuries had become badly re-infected and his blood was carrying the poison to his heart. He was dying. And he meant to take Rosie and the boy with him.

A short time after Rosie left Castle Street at one end, the dark saloon drew in from the other. Ned was in the passenger seat. Adam was driving. 'I'm not sure about this, Ned,' he protested. 'I'd much rather have gone straight to the hotel. You could have come back on your own once we'd made all our other calls.'

'That's an empty argument, and you know it,' Ned chastised. 'Castle Street is on our way in to town. It makes more sense to see her now. You said yourself we've enough appointments to keep us going 'til dark, and what with everything else, and the pair of us having to get back the day after tomorrow, it won't leave that much time for visiting.' Consulting the address on a slip of paper in his hand, he stretched forward to read the number on the door. 'This is it,' he said. 'Pull over.'

Edging the car into the kerbside outside Rosie's front door, Adam was thrilled yet nervous, his knuckles chalk white as he gripped the steering wheel. 'I shouldn't have let you talk me into this,' he groaned.

'Like I said, it makes sense to call in. We're practically passing the front door anyway.'

'I doubt if she's up at this hour of a morning.' Adam looked at his watch. 'Good God, man! It's not yet eight o'clock. *And* it's Saturday. If she's got any sense she'll still be abed.'

'It's no good you using that as an excuse to drive away. Rosie was never one for staying in bed of a morning, and I can't see why she'd change the habit of a lifetime now.' He glanced at Adam and was moved by his plight. There was no doubt that Adam adored Rosie. 'I wish you'd come in,' Ned pleaded.

Adam groaned. 'I can't, Ned. There's bad feeling between us, and if I barge in without being asked, it will only make matters worse. Her last letter made it very clear she wanted no contact with me whatsoever.' The memory of that cold short letter cut through him. 'I have to respect her wishes. You must know that.'

'I'm sorry, son.' Ned still made no move to get out of the car.

'If you're going, you'd best get a move on.' Leaning over, Adam unlocked the door and pushed it open. 'I know you mean well, Ned, but you're only prolonging the agony. You go. I'll wait here.' He thought it strange he could sound so calm when his insides were in turmoil. It was all he could do not to leap from the car and bang on that front door. To see Rosie again, to feel the warmth of her radiant smile, would be the most wonderful thing.

'All right. But I'd like to bet that once she knows you're here, she'll be straight out to see you.' He climbed out of the car and poked his head back in to say, 'Our Rosie was never one for bearing grudges.'

'It's not a matter of bearing grudges and you know it.' Slowly winding the window up, he urged, 'Go on, Ned. And look, it might be best if you don't let her know I'm here.'

'Whatever you say.'

Twice he knocked on the door, but there was no answer. Turning to look at Adam, who was peering from the car window, he stretched out his arms in a gesture of helplessness. 'Seems like there's nobody in,' he said, expression downcast.

Peggy's mam was just putting out the empties. 'It's no good you knocking on that door,' she told him sharply, 'because Mrs Selby ain't there.' Regarding Ned through suspicious eyes, she came a step closer. 'What's your business with her anyway?' She hadn't forgotten how Rosie had asked her to keep an eye on the house.

'I'm her father-in-law . . . Ned Selby.' As he came towards her his face was wreathed in a friendly smile. 'It's been a while since I've seen Rosie. We're in the area and, to be honest, I thought it was time I mended a few broken bridges between me and mine.'

'Hmh! Ned Selby, you say?' Retreating up the steps, she eyed him up and down. 'As far as I'm concerned, you could be Jack the bleedin' Ripper, 'cause I ain't never seen you in my life afore.' Oddly enough, though she knew of Ned Selby, and Peggy had mentioned him umpteen times, Peggy's mam had never clapped eyes on him.

Ned was faintly amused. Out of the corner of his eye he could see that Adam also appreciated the situation. 'I've never been accused of being Jack the Ripper before,' he told her. 'Honest, luv, I really *am* Ned Selby, and if our Rosie was here, she'd vouch for me right enough.'

'Well, she *ain't* here, is she? What's more, if she *was* here, you wouldn't need vouching for, would you?'

'You're right, I wouldn't.' Reaching into his waistcoat pocket, he withdrew a pen. Fishing out a scrap of paper from his jacket pocket, he asked, 'I don't suppose you'll tell me where I could find her.'

'Nope!'

'But you won't refuse to give her a message?'

'I suppose I could do that all right.'

Pressing the scrap of paper to the wall, he scribbled:

Rosie,

I'm sorry I missed you today, but I'll call round later tonight. Hope that's all right? I need to explain why I stayed away. I hadn't realised how much I'd miss you both. I'm here for only a couple of days, and there's so much to tell you. Look forward to seeing you and Danny.

Love,

Ned

He folded the note and gave it to Peggy's mam. 'It's important,' he said, and there was a strange kind of sadness in his voice. The exchange ended, he climbed back into the car. When he saw her crumple the note into her pinnie pocket, he muttered, 'I hope she remembers to give it to Rosie.' Pushing himself down into the seat, he wondered how his daughter-in-law might welcome him.

Adam gave no answer. He was engrossed in his own thoughts and, as always, Rosie was at the heart of them.

* * *

The guv'nor of the sidings had stopped being astonished at Rosie's fever for work. Every morning, six days a week, she would arrive at the yard at seven-thirty on the dot. There was always a smile and a cheery greeting as he came to help her fill her pram. This morning, however, even with her new cart and the prospect of earning more, there was no cheery greeting, and her face was serious as she paid over her money. 'I don't know what time I'll be back,' she said. 'There's enough in the cart to take me twice as far as usual on the first round.'

'If you had a horse to pull it, you could fill the cart right to the top,' he declared, trying to bring a smile to her face.

'Well, seeing as it's *me* that's doing the pulling, I'll settle for what's in it now.' While she and the guv'nor were talking, Danny had wandered away. Suddenly she caught sight of him and her heart froze inside her. 'DANNY, NO!' Her voice sailed across the yard as she took to her heels and headed towards the railway tracks; the coal-filled wagons were silently shunting towards the bays where they would off-shoot their loads. Danny was close to the tracks. Too close for safety.

'Jesus Christ!' The guv'nor saw Danny only seconds after Rosie spotted him, and now she was running like the wind, terror in her eyes as she realised that Danny was unaware of the wagons creeping up on him.

Rosie heard the guv'nor calling out way behind her, fearing that she too was in danger of slipping beneath the wagons. But there was no stopping her now. All she could see was Danny, and he was in terrible danger. 'DANNY, COME AWAY!' Her voice sounded like that of a stranger, and her chest was so tight she could hardly breathe.

Before the big man could catch up, she had grabbed Danny and swung him out of the way. Clutching him to her, she watched the big iron wheels trundle by, and gave up a prayer of thanks.

'Cut a man in two them wheels would.' The guv'nor leaned forward, hands on his knees, gasping for breath. His small eyes were fierce with anger. 'How many times have I told you to keep away from this part of the yard?' he croaked.

'I think he's learned his lesson,' Rosie replied protectively. She could feel the boy trembling in her arms.

Staring at her, the guv'nor snapped, 'I shouldn't really let you in here at all, bugger it!' He had been frightened out of his wits. His fear made him angry, and the fact that he hadn't been able to catch up with a slip of a woman like Rosie irked him down deep. 'It'd be my bloody job on the line if they knew I let you in here.' Having regained his breath enough to stand up, he breathed hard through his nose. The next rebuke came out on a rush of air. 'What have you got to say for yourself, young fella?' he demanded stonily.

'It won't happen again,' Rosie promised. Holding Danny away from her, she looked into his white face. 'Isn't that so?' Her voice was hard, chastising, and he knew she had been terrified. 'You will never come near this part of the yard again, will you?' He shook his head and she was satisfied.

'I don't know.' The guv'nor scratched his head and thought. He had a great sympathy for Rosie. She was a woman with a man's heart, a fighter he couldn't help but admire. Yet, when she looked at him now, it was through the soft, pleading eyes of a mother. He couldn't turn her away. 'All right,' he conceded. 'But he's not to leave your side.' Glaring at the boy, he asked, 'D'you understand?'

Danny nodded. 'I'm sorry.'

The guv'nor studied him awhile. He studied Rosie, and told them both, 'I must be stark staring mad!' Then he ushered them back to the far end of the yard, where the cart was ready for off.

Only when they had gone with Rosie between the shafts

and the boy pushing the cart from behind, did he go into his office.

Always too far behind to grab her, and wanting to be sure that the moment was right and she could not escape him, Doug Selby had followed Rosie to the yard. Exhausted and in crippling pain, he dropped behind one of the railway bays. His weakness and the altercation between Rosie and the guv'nor were enough to keep him there, with the intention of recouping his strength. 'So you're coming back, are you?' he sneered, settling deeper into the coal pile. 'Well, you can be sure I'll be waiting, Rosie, my lovely.' He laughed softly and it was a chilling sound. 'How could I think of leaving without you?'

He rolled his agonised eyes to the heavens, but it was hell he was contemplating.

The guv'nor put the kettle on. 'Need a brew to calm my nerves,' he muttered. Taking out a whisky bottle from the filing cabinet, he poured a measure of the golden liquid into a cup. 'And a bit of fire to drive away the cold,' he chuckled.

An hour later, he sat down to sort the mail. It was three days old, and he still hadn't got round to dealing with it. 'Best get this lot out of the way before the postman arrives with another bag full,' he grumbled, slitting open the envelopes one after the other. There were two bills, a catalogue for shovels and equipment, a reminder that the holiday periods had to be entered, and a letter. 'Hello, what's this then?' Normally there were no letters as such, only official documents and trade brochures.

The letter was from Adam Roach, advising the guv'nor that he would be calling in at the sidings Saturday at midday: 'to discuss business'. 'Bloody hell!' He glanced up at the clock in horror. 'That's *today*.'

The clerk, who up to now had made himself scarce in the back office, poked his head round the door. 'What's that, guv?'

A small thin man with a flat face and a great shock of black hair, he resembled a floor mop.

'You should have checked this mail, bugger you. Am I expected to do everything round here?' Like all men in high places, he knew how to delegate the blame.

'I've no idea what you're talking about.'

'I'm talking about this.' He threw the letter down. 'I've a meeting with Adam Roach, you daft sod, and thanks to you, I knew nothing at all about it.'

'I don't see how you can blame me.' Collecting the letter from the floor the clerk read it and replaced it on the desk. 'Especially when I'm not even allowed to open the mail.'

''Course it's your bloody fault! Keeping tabs on things like that is what you're paid for.'

'If he's not due 'til midday, there's plenty of time yet,' came the cheeky reply. 'I don't know why you're panicking.'

'He's one of the biggest coal-merchants in the North . . . he's built up Ned Selby's old round into a huge concern, and now he's looking to expand,' gabbled the guv'nor. 'Happen *that's* why I'm panicking.' Growing thoughtful, he rubbed the flat of his hand over the stubble on his chin. Eyeing the other fellow with a grim face, he murmured, 'The word is, Roach has bought Sutcliffe out. If that's the case, he'll be looking for a supplier. Happen he's coming here to talk terms.' The prospect brought a smile to his face.

'We could do with a few big contracts an' all.'

''Course we could. We've not yet found a market for all the tons we normally supply to Sutcliffe. You know yourself how that contract has been falling away these past months. Why do you think I'm letting such folk as Rosie Selby come in here with a bloody hand cart, eh? Because we need all the help we can get, that's why! What's more, Roach won't just be coming *here*, you can bet on that. There are other suppliers beside me, and with a man like that, you can depend on it he means to see every one of 'em.'

'Then we'd best get this pig-sty cleaned up, eh? First impressions count, or so they say.'

'Not so much of the we. *You* can get on and clean the place up while I attend to the more important part. He won't be looking for a tidy office. He'll be looking at the quality of what we can offer. And that's out there . . . in the yard.' That said, he grabbed a clipboard and pen, and stormed out. He wasn't seen again until gone ten-thirty.

In the time between, he calculated the amount of stock on the ground, and assessed the different grades of coal readily available. 'Anybody'd think it were royalty coming, instead of Adam Roach,' he declared sullenly, striding across the railway tracks to examine the stock on the other side. He muttered and moaned, and checked his watch every few minutes. At half-past ten he reminded himself, 'If the bugger's coming here at midday, that gives me just over an hour to work out my best figures. By! And they'd best be favourable, unless I want him to take his money elsewhere.' With a greater sense of urgency, he pushed the pen behind his ear and went at a smart pace back to the office which was now clean and tidy as a new pin.

Fearing every minute he might be discovered, the bedraggled creature pressed down into the dark coals; covered in a thick film of dust, he was barely detectable. 'Seems it's my lucky day,' he chuckled wickedly. 'Rosie and the boy, and now Roach . . . and all I have to do is be patient.' Taking the crudely made gun from his trouser belt, he stroked it lovingly as a man might stroke a woman. In prison he had made many friends, all of his own devious kind and all from different walks of life. The man who had made the gun was a blacksmith. The one who had smuggled it out was a trustee, working in the prison library. 'Nice to have friends in high places,' he laughed. It was good to laugh out loud, and know that for the moment he could not be heard. Soon though the laughter turned to whimpers of agony. One glance at his leg told him it was beyond redemption. 'Rotten,' he observed without regret. 'Like me.'

Hearing the rumble of trucks, rolling into the yard for their second load of the day, he slunk deeper, lying silent, hoping he would not be exposed to curious eyes. When the trucks went by, he breathed a sigh of relief. Already that morning the loaders had dipped into the bay where he was hiding. Now they were here to load only slack and top quality coal.

An hour later, when the trucks had left and all was quiet again in the yard, Rosie came through the gate. Danny was helping her to push the empty cart. He was also complaining that he was 'starving hungry'.

Rosie had heard it all before. 'You're *always* hungry. You had two helpings of porridge and both my sausages for breakfast,' she reminded him good-naturedly. 'I'm beginning to think you've got hollow legs.' She was not unaware how hard he had worked that morning, and thanked the Lord for such a plucky little chap. 'What about that apple Brenda Watson gave me? Will that keep you going for a while? On the way to Whalley Banks, I'll stop at the bakers on King Street, and you can get us each a meat and potato pie.' She now realised just how hungry she was too.

'All right, Mam.' He held out his hand for the apple, then groaned when Rosie produced a small damp towel from beneath the cart instead. 'Oh, Mam, you're always washing me.' He wrinkled his face while she rubbed it with the corner of the towel.

'Just because we sell coal don't mean to say we have to look like chimney-sweeps,' she scolded. She then wiped her own face and hands, and gave him the apple from her pocket, first taking a bite herself. 'That should keep you going,' she said. When he ate it in two great bites, she was afraid he might eat his arm into the bargain. 'Anybody would think you were starving,' she laughed. Pushing against the wagon, she started it moving forward. 'Come on. We'll pay for the next load and be off. We'll have to look sharp because we've still got four streets to do, and I don't want us making our way home in the dark.'

'Mam?'

'What now?' Every bone in her body ached and she could hardly put one foot before the other.

'Are we rich yet?'

Rosie laughed out loud. 'Not yet, but we're getting there.' She jangled the coins in her pocket. 'We've made more money this morning than we normally make in a full day.'

His face lit up. 'Can we do *six* streets before we go home?'

Rosie frowned at him. 'Are you trying to kill your poor mam off?'

Danny was horrified. 'I don't care if we're *never* rich!' he declared, and she hugged him until it hurt.

Rosie was halfway between the office and the gate when *he* saw her. His eyes lit up. 'At last,' he whispered. Edging himself out of the bay, he stalked her as far as the railway tracks. Summoning every ounce of strength left in him, he got in front of her to hide behind the tall shuttering. From here they could not be seen from the office. It was a perfect place for an ambush, he thought. He watched through an open knot in the planks, chuckling to himself as Rosie and the boy came nearer. He could hear them talking and laughing, and the hatred in him grew until he was out of his mind.

Rosie stopped to shake the dust from her skirt. 'It'll be nice to get a bath,' she said.

'When we're rich we can have a bathroom each, can't we, Mam?'

Rosie smiled her approval. 'And gold taps.'

'And big silky towels with swans on?'

'And a deep soft carpet that shows your footprints after you've walked on it.'

'I'd like that, Mam.'

'Oh, I expect by the time we're rich, you'll have a wife and a home of your own. And you can share all these things with her.'

'I won't.'

Rosie stopped the cart and looked at him. 'Oh, and why not?'

''Cause when I grow up, I'm going to marry *you*!'

There was no answer to that. Instead, Rosie started forward again.

She was humorously mulling over what Danny had said when a furtive movement in the bays made her swing round. Like a fiend from hell he was on her. In his blackened face his eyes were stark white, almost luminous. As the twining coiled round her neck, Rosie's first thought was for her son. In a strangled cry she told him. 'RUN, DANNY! FOR GOD'S SAKE, GET HELP. RUN! RUN!'

'That was a stupid thing to do, my lovely.' Doug's voice reached her through the fear. 'Be careful, this twining can cut through your throat like a wire through cheese.' But Rosie's fear was not for herself, because even while he was speaking another, even greater fear rippled through her. Her eyes were on Danny as he ran away, stumbling and crying. Rosie's prayers went with him. In his haste, Danny fell over again, and Rosie was frozen in horror as Doug tightened his hold on the twining, almost throttling her. He then raised his free arm and took aim, deliberately taking his time as Danny struggled to get himself upright.

In sheer desperation, and without a single thought for her own life, Rosie began violently struggling, desperately trying to knock Doug sideways. But the twining was embedded in her throat, stifling her breath and slowly killing her. Suddenly there was an explosion. Danny was lifted off his feet and hurled forward, lying where he fell, silent and twisted, his small white face turned towards Rosie. In that moment it was as though all the life drained out of her. She felt the heat of her tears as they flowed down her face. She heard Doug's sinister chuckle, but it held no fear for her. Not now. Not any more. All she wanted was to be with Danny.

The two men in the office ran to the window. 'That was a gunshot, I'm telling you!' The clerk pressed his nose to the pane, but he made no move to go outside.

'Gunshot!' the guv'nor scoffed. 'What in blazes would you know about a gunshot?'

'There!' The younger man pointed to the small twisted bundle lying halfway across yard. 'What's that?'

He came to the window, straining to see. 'God Almighty! It's Rosie's lad.' Running across the office, he flung open the door and raced down the steps. The clerk, a self-confessed coward, remained in the safety of the office. Watching from the window, he saw the other man run towards the boy. Before he could reach Danny, another shot rang out, forcing the older man to take cover. 'Come back, you bloody fool!' yelled the clerk.

But there was no way back without crossing the gunman's sights. 'Call the police . . . and an ambulance,' came the reply.

As the clerk grabbed the telephone receiver, Adam's car turned into the yard. The guv'nor saw him and ran round the back, approaching the car from another direction. 'Go back!' he cried, frantically waving his arms. 'GO BACK!'

'What the hell's the matter with him?' Ned was the first to see him. But Adam was quick to slam on the brakes.

'You'd best get out of here,' the guv'nor told them. 'There's a bloody maniac out there. He's got a gun, and he's already shot the lad . . .' His eyes grew wide with shock as he realised who he was talking to. 'Ned Selby!' He had expected Adam Roach, but not Rosie's father-in-law. There was talk that he'd either gone abroad or died long since.

'Anybody'd think you'd seen a ghost,' Ned exclaimed as he and Adam climbed out of the car.

Adam glanced about the yard. 'What's going on in there, you say?' he asked impatiently. 'Spit it out, man, spit it out.'

He hesitated. Sweat was pouring down his temples as he looked from Adam to Ned and back again. 'It ain't your problem. It'll be taken care of,' he promised. 'Police and ambulance are on their way.' How could he reveal that it was Ned's own grandson who was lying there shot, probably dead? His nerve failed him. 'Get back in your car and turn it round. Get out of here, I'm telling you.'

Adam placed his hand on the man's shoulder. 'Calm down. We might be able to help. Now then . . . tell us exactly what happened here?'

It took only a moment for him to spill out the details of how he and his clerk had heard what sounded like a gunshot. They had looked through the window and seen a child lying in the yard.

Sensing there was more to it than that, Adam insisted he should show them. 'And what was a child doing in the yard? You should have had more sense than to allow it.' He knew the rules, and he was angry.

Ned and Adam were taken to a safe spot from where they could see what had taken place. The man pointed to the bundle. He looked at Ned, saying in a small frightened voice, 'I don't know how to tell you this but . . . it's your grandson.'

Ned stared at him, a look of sheer horror crossing his features. It was Adam who spoke. 'What are you saying? The child out there is *Danny*?'

When he nodded, Ned would have charged out. It was only Adam's restraining hand that stopped him. 'Easy, Ned. If the boy's alive, we want him to stay that way.' Incredibly calm but thinking fast, he addressed the guv'nor in a solemn voice. 'You say the police and ambulance are on their way?'

'Yes, I've told you.'

'Who's out there?'

'I don't know.' With the flat of his hand he wiped the sweat from his face.

Now the question that Adam was afraid to ask. 'And Rosie? Where is Rosie?'

Again, the man shook his head. 'She and the lad came in for a load this morning, and I saw them leave the yard myself. I didn't see them come back, and I don't know what's happened here. All I know is what *you* know.'

'Came in for a load?' Adam couldn't believe his ears. 'I think you'd better explain,' he said in a hard voice.

The other man gave a sigh of relief when he heard the sound of sirens piercing the air. 'They're here,' he cried, racing to meet them. 'The police are here.'

'I'm going out there.' Adam moved forward. 'I've got to get the boy . . . got to know that Rosie's all right.' Before Ned could stop him, he was already walking out, arms in the air as he went towards Danny. 'I'M GETTING THE BOY,' he called. There was no answer, so he kept walking, nearer and nearer, until now he was standing over the child. 'All right, son,' he murmured as he took the limp figure into his arms. His heart lurched when the boy's head dropped. There seemed no life at all.

'STAY WHERE YOU ARE.' Doug's voice sailed across the yard. 'I'VE GOT ROSIE. IF YOU WANT HER, YOU'D BEST COME AND GET HER.' He laughed then, and it was the laugh of a maniac.

Adam was astounded to recognise the voice. 'DOUG!' He brought his arms up to give the boy more protection. All manner of emotions went through him. What was Doug doing here?

Shouldn't he be in prison? Why had he shot his own son? And why was he holding Rosie in terror? It was obvious he had lost his mind. 'WHY ARE YOU DOING THIS?'

Laughter again. Then: 'YOU SHOULD KNOW, YOU BASTARD.' His voice fell away. 'You and her . . . cheating on me behind my back. I'm glad the boy's dead. You're next. Then her.'

'You're so wrong, Doug. Rosie has always been faithful to you.' No answer. Adam prayed Rosie was all right. 'There's an ambulance here. Let me take the boy, and I swear I'll come back. It isn't Rosie you want. It's me. Don't hurt her, Doug. Rosie has always been faithful to you. Don't hurt her.' Still no answer. 'All right. I'm taking the boy now.'

'MOVE ONE INCH AND I'LL CUT YOU DOWN.' The shot rang out, hitting the ground before him. When Adam looked up, he was horrified to see Doug standing before him. Rosie was pressed to his side, with a length of twining round her throat, and a look of sheer terror in her brown eyes. Where the twining had cut deep, there was a smudged trail of blood. Weak now, she could hardly stand. She couldn't speak. She couldn't move. But through those lovely stricken eyes she told Adam everything he wanted to know. 'Let her go, Doug,' he pleaded softly. 'She's done you no harm. Neither has the boy. It's me you want. You have to let them go.' It broke his heart to see her like that. Now her eyes were on Danny, and she was softly crying.

'Oh, you'd like that, wouldn't you?' Doug sneered, tightening his hold on Rosie and making her wince. 'You think I'm mad, don't you?' He took a step forward and cried out with pain. Neglect and rough living had turned his leg gangrenous. He knew he had nothing to lose. 'I can't let her go. She has to die.' He aimed his gun at Adam's temple. 'But first she can see you and the bastard lying at my feet. It's only right.' His eyes narrowed as he prepared to pull the trigger.

Not far away, the police were closing in, ready to move. But the situation was fraught with danger, and one wrong move could end in tragedy. Adam saw them creeping forward. 'Think what you're doing, man,' he said sternly, 'Rosie and the boy, you have to let them go.' If it wasn't for them, Adam would have launched himself at Doug and taken his chances.

'Say your prayers,' Doug advised, grinning. 'Are you watching, Rosie?' Tugging on the twining, he made her cry out.

Incensed by her pain, Adam twisted sideways and kicked out with the intention of knocking Doug off balance. He caught Doug on the shin, causing him to double up in pain. Suddenly, out of nowhere, Ned's burly figure crunched against Doug, sending him back with such force that Rosie was thrown sideways. Everything happened at once.

Gently taking the twining from round her throat, Adam cradled Rosie in his arms. 'You're safe now,' he whispered. 'You're safe, sweetheart.' Her smile was full of pain.

'Danny?' she whispered hoarsely. When Adam told her that her son was in good hands, her eyes closed in relief.

Behind them was chaos. Police emerged from every direction. Ned's formidable weight had driven his son to the railway tracks, and now he was holding him down, pressing his back to the iron tracks.

Warnings were being shouted that the wagons were bearing down on top of them. He wasn't listening. Instead, he was cursing his son for being the despicable person he was. 'I can't altogether blame you for what you are,' he said finally, his voice and heart broken. 'Happen if I'd been more of a father to you, none of this would ever have happened.'

Crippled with pain, Doug told him wickedly, 'I never wanted you. It was my mother I loved, not you.'

Ned shook his head in despair. 'And I hated her,' he said simply. 'Like you, she was a wicked creature. Never happier than when she was hurting others.' The memory of all those wasted years with Martha was more than he could bear. Now the evil in her had been perpetuated in her son. Something inside him opened out to swallow him up. *And, at long last, he knew what he must do.*

The police were helpless. They saw Ned pin his son flat with the weight of his own body. As the laden wagons sliced through the two squirming figures, there was an odd murmuring sound, almost like a prayer, and then a shocking, deathly silence.

Adam was devastated and yet, in some strange way, he understood. Then he turned and went to Rosie. That was where his future lay. If only she would have him.

Chapter Twenty-two

On 20 July 1955, Rosie sat by the empty fire-grate inside her little house in Castle Street. As she looked around that familiar living-room, with its sturdy well-polished furniture, low ceilings and black-leaded range, she was filled with nostalgia. 'There are both good and bad memories here,' she told Peggy, who was seated opposite. 'I'll miss it.'

'No, you won't,' Peggy declared brightly. 'You've got too much to look forward to.' Lowering her gaze, she flushed with shame. 'I'm sorry if I made you unhappy,' she said softly. 'I didn't mean to.'

'Don't, Peggy, that's all in the past.' Reaching out to touch her hand, Rosie assured her, 'You're here now, and we're friends again. That's all that matters.'

Peggy groaned. 'God! I can't believe what a bitch I was to you. And all because of a swine like Robert Fellows.' She saw Rosie smiling and laughed out loud. 'Got what he deserved though, didn't he?' she chuckled.

'Honestly, Peggy, I think it was rotten of you to tell his wife he was carrying on with every female in the office.'

'Got him transferred though, didn't it? Pity it didn't get old Meg Benton and that measly pair thrown out too. Especially after the way they let you down.'

'All water under the bridge,' Rosie said. 'Best forgotten.'

'What time is he coming for you?'

Rosie glanced at the mantelpiece clock. 'Any minute now.' Her stomach fluttered as she realised the moment was almost here.

'Rosie?'

'Yes?' She knew what was coming, but she didn't know how to answer.

'Do you think you and Adam will get wed?'

'It's too early to say. So much has happened, Peggy. I have to be sure.' Adam had asked her to be his wife weeks ago, and still she hadn't given him an answer.

'Surely it wasn't all his fault? Think about it, Rosie. Take your mind back over the years. He came home, hoping to marry you, and you tell him you're expecting his best friend's child. Wouldn't *you* have walked out? And as for Ned's business, well, hasn't he explained all of that to you . . . about how it was Ned himself who asked him to take the responsibility off his shoulders? We all knew Ned was in debt . . . that Martha was dragging him under. You believe Adam's account, don't you?'

'Of course I do. Deep down, I expect I knew it all along.'

'And he wasn't married to that poor young woman who died?'

'I've told you.'

'He's handsome as ever, don't you think?'

Rosie blushed pink. 'As ever.'

'And Danny loves him, doesn't he?'

'I've never seen him so happy. Those two are so right together. When Danny was in hospital, Adam was always there for him . . . and me,' she added softly. 'Since Danny's been home, the same.'

'You've already admitted you love him.'

'Since the day I met him, I've never stopped loving him. All through the awful years with Doug, I kept on loving Adam. Even when he walked out on me, I couldn't help but love him still. And now, with everything that's happened, I love him more than ever.'

'Then why can't you tell him you'll marry him?' Given half the chance, Peggy would have jumped at the offer. But then she was one kind of creature, and Rosie was another. 'It's time you had some happiness,' she said. 'You and Danny. And Adam too.'

'I know.' Rosie gazed at her dear friend and all her emotions were laid bare. 'It's not Adam,' she murmured. 'It's *me*.'

'What do you mean?'

'It's the guilt *I* feel. The awful things *I've* done.' Sighing, she stood up and walked to the window. The July sun was blazing down. Outside it was warm. In her heart it was cold. 'Doug was cruel, I know. But I was worse.' Peggy would have spoken then, but Rosie put up her hand. 'No, Peggy, hear me out. In the beginning, Adam did what he thought was right, and he deeply regrets it. Doug did what he did because he was tortured by jealousy. But me . . . there is no excuse for what I did. Since Doug and I were married, every minute of every day I was with Adam, through every waking hour, in my heart and soul, I was committing adultery. How can I forgive myself for that?' She was crying now, the tears rolling down her face. 'Oh, Peggy, I feel as though I have no right to happiness now. If only I'd been a better wife to him. What happened to Doug and Ned, I feel it's my fault.' The sobs racked her body, and all the pent-up emotions flooded out. 'I'm a bad woman,' she said. 'Adam deserves better.'

Peggy went to her then. Taking her in her arms, she said softly, 'You mustn't punish yourself like that, Rosie. What happened was never your fault. If anyone was to blame for what happened to Ned and his son, it was Martha. The woman was evil through and through. She controlled Doug in a way that you and I could see, and Ned too . . . but Doug never realised. He was a victim of her tyranny, just as Ned was. You must see that?' She gently shook Rosie. 'What happened to them was not your fault, and you have a right to happiness. Take it, Rosie. For once in your life, put yourself first. Open your heart and go to him. Spend the rest of your life with the man you've always loved, and don't be ashamed or guilty. There's no need.'

Rosie looked into those sharp blue eyes and laughed through her tears. 'You're a bossy bugger, Peggy Lewis,' she said.

'So you'll do it?'

Taking a hankie from her skirt pocket, Rosie wiped her face and blew her nose. 'We'll see,' she said. Then brightly she declared, 'Oh, Peggy, I'm glad we're friends again. I honestly thought you'd turned your back on me for good.'

'Silly cow that I am!'

These two had cried together, and now they laughed together, and Rosie's heart was full. 'I'll be in touch.'

'You'd better.'

'And you'll take care of everything while I'm gone?'

'I said, didn't I?'

'Do I look all right?'

Taking a moment to study her, Peggy thought Rosie had never looked more beautiful. She was dressed in a soft blue blouse with a sweetheart neckline, and a straight knee-length skirt which showed off her shapely legs. Her rich brown hair, which had grown longer, was tied with a pretty blue ribbon and draped over one shoulder; tiny wispy curls framed her lovely face, and her brown eyes still sparkled with tears. 'When were you ever anything but all right?' Peggy said, with only the tiniest hint of envy.

Collecting her coat, Rosie draped it over her arm. Then she picked up her suitcase and went with Peggy to the door. Danny was sitting on the step, watching the corner of the road. 'He ain't here yet, Mam,' he said mournfully.

'Anybody would think you hadn't seen him for months,' she said. 'It's only been a week since Adam was here.'

'He would have stayed if you hadn't sent him away.'

'We're not the only ones he loves, you know,' Rosie reminded him. 'He has a little girl waiting at the other end, don't forget.'

'Are we staying long with him?'

'We'll see.'

Peggy's voice whispered in her ear. 'I hope you don't come back at all.' When Rosie stared at her, she went on, 'I hope I get a letter from you . . . telling me to sell everything, and send you the money. I hope the letter says you're to be married, and I'm to be maid of honour. And I hope the letter isn't long in coming.'

Rosie might have answered, but Danny's whoop of joy deafened them both. Adam's car turned into the street and Danny was limping along the pavement, waving his arms and yelling for Adam to hurry up. 'The little bugger might have been close to death's door a few months back,' Peggy recalled. 'But it ain't hurt his lungs, that's for sure.'

Rosie's face clouded over as she remembered how Danny had been shot through the thigh. He had lost a great deal of blood, and for a time it was touch and go. But then he rallied round, and now even the limp was less pronounced. 'Take care of yourself,' she told Peggy, hugging her close.

Adam ushered Danny into the car before coming to put his arm round Rosie. 'Hello, sweetheart,' he said, sweeping her into his arms and kissing her shamelessly. 'You look good enough to eat.'

'Not in front of the neighbours if you please,' Peggy protested good-naturedly. 'We're not used to such goings on down our street.'

'You're a good friend to Rosie,' Adam said, 'I won't forget that.' He kissed her lightly on the cheek. Taking the case from Rosie, he told her, 'Danny and I will wait for you in the car.'

'You've got a good man there, Rosie gal,' said Peggy. 'Don't let him go a second time.'

Rosie hugged her again. 'Take care of yourself,' she said. In a minute she was hurrying after Adam.

'And don't forget that letter,' Peggy called as the car drew away. 'I'll be watching for it.'

'What letter's that, sweetheart?' Adam asked, steering the car with one hand while with the other he took hold of Rosie's.

'Oh, just something Peggy and I were talking about.' As she glanced at him, she wondered whether she would ever send that letter to Peggy. For now, she felt safe, content to be with him, and deeply in love as always. But the guilt and the doubts still lingered. She wasn't sure if they would ever leave her.

Chapter Twenty-three

'They get on so well, and to think I was worried.' Adam beckoned Rosie to the window. 'Look there,' he said, sliding his arm round her waist. Outside, sitting on the step, Danny and April were laughing together.

Rosie laughed. 'She knows how to flutter her eyelids.'

'She's making a lovely person,' he agreed, 'both in appearance and personality.'

While he lovingly gazed at the children, Rosie lovingly gazed at him. Though they were both seven years older now, and so much had happened during those long years when they had been apart, there was still something uniquely wonderful between them. Physically, Adam had not changed all that much. He was just as strong in physique, and his dark eyes were still filled with the same vibrant passion whenever he looked at her. But now there was something else. Something even more precious. There was complete trust, a warm and glorious contentment she thought could never happen. And, even as she was thinking it, he turned to her, gazing at her through dark love-filled eyes. 'I love you, Rosie,' he murmured.

'And I love you,' she said.

'We could be married next month,' he said, half-afraid. 'You would make a wonderful August bride.'

Rosie was glad when a small voice piped up, 'April wants to be bridesmaid.' It was Danny. He had a protective arm round the little girl. 'And I want to live here forever,' he told Rosie.

Sensing her dilemma, Adam reminded them, 'You two, go and ask Mrs Jessup to wash your hands and face. We're going out. Or have you forgotten I have something to show you?' When they raced off, screeching with excitement, Rosie asked, 'Where are you taking us?'

'You're worse than the children,' he teased, kissing her on the mouth, delighting her when he pressed her close to him. 'Don't you know you should never tell secrets?'

Within minutes the four of them were in the car and heading towards the outskirts of town. 'Where are we going?' asked the children excitedly. And Rosie did the same.

'Wait and see,' they were told.

Half an hour later Adam steered the car into a country lane. At the bottom stood a thatched cottage, with wild brambles and honeysuckle climbing all over the walls. The windows were criss-crossed with leaded lights, and the beautiful gardens seemed to go on for miles. 'It's yours if you want it,' Adam said, turning to Rosie, his eyes alight with hope.

'We want it, don't we?' Danny asked April, and she screamed with delight. Adam opened the door and, after issuing the warning, 'Stay where we can see you,' he let them loose.

'So this is your surprise?' Rosie whispered, looking up at him with soft brown eyes.

'Do you like it?'

'I love it,' she said. 'It will make a wonderful home for a growing family.'

'So, you'll stay?'

'You think I'll stay because of the cottage?' She was offended. 'You know better than that.'

She fell into his arms and they kissed long and passionately.

'Are two children enough for you?' she asked.

'Not really.' His eyes twinkled mischievously.

'I've always thought the more the merrier.'

'My own sentiments exactly,' Adam murmured, kissing her again. 'Shall we go and see what the little monsters are up to?'

When they were out of the car, she led him in another direction. 'Now it's my turn to ask where we're going?' he declared curiously.

Linking her arm with his, she explained, 'I saw a post-box as we came in just now.' Taking the stamped letter from her pocket, she said, 'I wrote this last night. I intended posting it first thing this morning, but you whisked me off to see your surprise instead.'

'Sounds like it's urgent,' he remarked, squeezing her tight. 'Who's it for?'

'It's for Peggy,' Rosie told him, popping it in the post-box. 'This is a very special letter. She'll be waiting for it, I know.' Then, her brown eyes twinkling, she turned him back towards where the children were playing. 'Now then, about this cottage.'

'You don't like it after all?' His spirits fell to his boots.

'Whatever gave you that idea?' As she urged him on, his hopes soared. 'I think we should go and see if it's big enough for *four* children?'

Now it was Adam's turn to whoop for joy. Lifting her from her feet he carried her through the front door. 'This is our new home,' he told the children.

'Are we rich now, Mam?' Danny asked excitedly.

Rosie's brown eyes brightly twinkled, and there wasn't a single shadow of doubt there. 'What we have, sweetheart,' she told him, 'is much more than riches.'

On the last day of August 1955, Adam and Rosie were married in a simple ceremony at the town register office. Peggy was maid of honour. It was a happy affair, attended by Peggy's family and many of Adam's friends and colleagues. Mrs Jessup was there too. The cottage was being extended to make three extra bedrooms, and she was to move in with them. Rosie chose to go to Weymouth for her honeymoon, and the children went too.

Fifteen years later, on a beautiful day in June 1970, Danny and April made their vows. This time, the ceremony was in the church of All Saints. April looked exquisite in her ivory gown and satin slippers. The two younger children, Susan and Martin, aged eleven and nine, attended the happy couple. The honeymoon was to be in Cyprus.

'It's times like this when you realise your age,' Rosie sighed, walking through the church, her arm linked with Adam's.

Drawing her to a halt, he regarded her through a lover's eyes. She was now turned forty, but ever slim and lovely, and her brown eyes still sparkled in that magic way he had loved from the very first. 'We'll never grow old,' he said. 'We're too much in love.' And they were.

JOSEPHINE COX

The Gilded Cage

Powerful, hard-hearted Leonard Mears is a man with a dark secret; an illegitimate daughter that he forced his sister to bring up. The girl is now a young woman who, unbeknown to him, is determined to find the father that abandoned her.

James Peterson, a gifted young man, runs Mears' factory with more success than Leonard's own sons. He lives for the day he can have his own business and make his fortune. Only then will he be able to declare his love for beautiful Isabel Mears who he means to release from the gilded cage her father has created.

But when the lonely, lovely Sally comes in to his life, his heart and dreams are turned upside down.

JOSEPHINE COX

Tomorrow the World

Bridget Mulligan loves her husband. He is caring, loyal and dependable – everything a woman could ask for. But she can't quite forget Harry – the one that got away – and when a snowstorm drives her into his arms, she cannot deny her feelings.

Overcome with remorse, Bridget is determined that her husband should know the truth, but her confession can lead only to heartbreak. Although he allows his wife and her child to continue living in his home, Tom Mulligan makes it clear that their marriage is over. Lonely and afraid, Bridget finds comfort in the friendship of Fanny, a feisty young mother who knows what it is to be alone.

But Bridget's life can never be complete until she has the love of the only man she ever really wanted . . .

JOSEPHINE
COX
Rainbow Days

'You're everything to me. I'd have to lose my life before I'd lose you.'

This is the vow Silas makes to Cathleen on the day he asks her to marry him. Throughout their childhood their love has grown stronger and now, in 1900, they start to plan a life together. But a jealous woman is determined to ruin their happiness and uses Silas's father – a good and honest man – to do so, forcing him to make an impossible sacrifice. As a dutiful son, Silas has no choice but to obey his father, and Cathleen must pay the bitter price. Separated, each is swept along to a place where there is no love or peace and no way back . . .